THE LAST DAYS
VOLUME 2

Pioneer One

DISCARDED

CONCORD PUBLIC LIBRARY
45 GREEN STREET
CONCORD, NH 03301

Books by Kenneth Tarr

The Last Days Series
Gathering Storm
Pioneer One
Promised Land

THE LAST DAYS
VOLUME 2

Pioneer One

Kenneth R. Tarr

This is a work of fiction, and the views expressed herein are the sole responsibility of the author. Likewise, certain characters, places, and incidents are the product of the author's imagination, and any resemblance to actual persons, living or dead, or actual events or locales, is entirely coincidental.

Pioneer One (Last Days Series #2)

Published by Truebekon Books

Copyright © 2013 by Kenneth R. Tarr
Man photo copyright © Katrina Brown | Dreamstime.com
Road photo copyright © Zoran Simin | Dreamstime.com
Cover design and typeset copyright ©2013 by ePubMasters

All rights reserved. No part of this book may be scanned, uploaded, reproduced, distributed, or transmitted in any form or by any means whatsoever without written permission from the author, except in the case of brief quotations embodied in critical articles and reviews. Thank you for supporting the author's rights.

ISBN: 978-1494227746

Printed in the United States of America
Year of first printing: 2013

To my family, who persuaded me to write this novel, and to the many readers who enjoyed *Volume One*, *Gathering Storm*, and who encouraged me to continue the series.

Prologue

After the year 2000, Babylon and its wickedness reigned supreme on the earth. Man worshiped wealth, power, and pleasure rather than God. A great secret combination sought to destroy the freedom of all nations. Because of man's sins, God's anger was poured out without measure upon the disobedient inhabitants of the world.

The structure of world society was shaken to its foundation, but still managed to maintain a semblance of order. The greatest disintegration occurred in North America, where the land was filled with scenes of brutality, devastation, and anarchy. This was the home of those who had been most favored of the Lord, but who had rejected him in favor of the excesses of Babylon.

The only place in North America where decent people could find a refuge from the storm was in the Rocky Mountains. Here society was held together by the influence of God's Church and the faith of the saints. Yet even in this place, civilization was hurled into primitive conditions. Supplies of power, fuel, and consumer goods quickly dried up. Mobs stormed stores and fought violently over anything they could find. Within weeks markets were empty. Since many of the saints had not stored food as their leaders had taught, there was widespread starvation and misery.

The people with health problems agonized the most. Because medical equipment became useless, and the supply of medicines quickly disappeared, medical professionals were helpless, and those with serious illnesses found themselves in peril. Some perished swiftly. Others had the choice of adjusting or suffering needlessly. Most adapted by finding natural remedies. Eventually the decent people who survived, especially those living in the Rocky Mountains, learned to work together to solve their problems. Within six months after the great Collapse, they had begun to establish thousands of home-based businesses, which supplied the basic needs of the people. Since the banking system had also fallen, they used barter instead.

Then the prophet, a seer like Moses of old, announced that now—even in this period of extreme hardship—was the time for the saints to begin the monumental work of establishing New Zion. This meant that those who were called would be asked to travel a thousand miles across forbidding lands to Jackson County, Missouri. Since they would be forced to make the journey without the conveniences of modern society, it would be a difficult trail, fraught with perils of all kinds.

And when they arrived in the Promised Land, the Lord would require further sacrifices at their hands. Their great task would be to build an ideal society—the opposite of Babylon. The first wagon train, called Pioneer One, was soon to leave, and the man called to lead it was Steven Christopher, who had been selected by the Lord himself. The saints who were chosen to go, the new pioneers, were eager to start the journey and prayed they were equal to the task. It wouldn't be easy, for the Lord had declared that Zion, which was destined to fill the American continent, could only be built upon the principles of righteousness. None but the faithful and the pure in heart could flourish there, and the citizens of that sacred land must be of one mind and one heart.

Chapter 1

W hen Pioneer One left Provo at eight in the morning on Friday, April 14, heading for the Promised Land, the modern pioneers were full of energy and enthusiasm. As they hurried along Interstate 15 toward Salt Lake City, they chattered, laughed, danced, and sang, enjoying themselves to the utmost. After all, they faced, as they saw it, an unbelievably exciting and fulfilling journey ahead of them, traveling in the name of God. But to many of the thousands who watched them embark on that dangerous trek, it was a shocking sight to see the strange assortment of vehicles the travelers had chosen and the unusual clothes they wore.

The spectators stared in amazement at the strange assortment of old-fashioned wagons and handcarts, modern cars, vans, pickups, trailers, and a swarm of two- and three-wheeled bicycles. Those who rode bicycles pulled children or provisions in bike trailers. One brother had even converted a small bus for the occasion. The onlookers might have thought they were seeing the strangest Fourth of July parade ever.

Since there was no oil or fuel to be found anywhere, the pilgrims couldn't simply drive to Missouri. But when some travelers saw how difficult it would be to build new "authentic" covered wagons, they decided to use the "modern" vehicles rusting away in their driveways or in wrecking yards, or they accepted more functional ones from friends. They stripped the metal carriages of every unnecessary part, such as the engine, and then packed the empty spaces with food, bedding, and other necessities. Their greatest challenge was to figure out how to attach tongues and hitches from the frames of the vehicles to the poor animals destined to pull the weird contraptions.

As for those who had built—or had someone else build—covered wagons, or "prairie schooners," they gazed at those transformed modern vehicles with amusement or disdain, depending on the bent of their minds. The wagoners were extremely proud of their wooden works of art, which they had furnished with every kind of "modern" convenience. There were spring seats—some with shades—fancy braking systems, exterior tool boxes, double board boxes, full suspension springs, and even steel covered wheels with spokes. They tried to hide the fact that many of their authentic covered wagons had wheels and rubber tires taken from modern vehicles.

Some of the builders and the converters made bets as to which type of vehicle would best survive the arduous journey. But, of course, there was no money involved in those bets. As time passed, the two groups adopted names to describe themselves and their rivals. The wagon builders used the terms "Creators" vs "Converters," while those who drove gutted vehicles preferred "Ancients" vs "Moderns." It was never hard to understand what they referred to, if you knew who was doing the talking, and you had any sensitivity at all to vocal tone.

All those conveyances, except the bicycles, were pulled by mules, work horses, or oxen. And in order to spare the draft animals, which had to pull wagons heavy with supplies, most of the travelers walked or tried to walk—at least at first. But reasonably good drivers were always needed for any type of vehicle that was drawn by mules or horses. As for conveyances pulled by oxen, someone had to walk beside the leading team and control the animals with whip or goad.

Steven Christopher, the leader of Pioneer One, rode up and down the caravan on his sturdy mustang to check the progress of the company, amazed at the surprisingly brisk pace of the people. He decided to let them go, figuring there was no way to hold them back. After all, they were the courageous ones who would make history by being the first to reach Missouri and by building New Zion. And yet he felt a certain trepidation, seeing all that exuberance and overwhelming self-confidence. He noticed many were not wearing proper clothing, in spite of the guidelines he and his assistants had given them. Most had bare heads and arms, and wore shoes that would be more appropriate at a dance than on a 1,100-mile trek under the most trying circumstances.

Steven was especially surprised to see many teenagers—and adults too!—wearing T-shirts and shorts. Some of the beautiful daughters of Zion pranced along merrily, although awkwardly, on platform shoes. It was as if they were going to some exciting outing at a nearby shaded campground. Steven wondered if they had remembered to bring their homemade sunblock and mosquito repellent.

"They don't look too prepared, do they?" Steven's brother, John, called as he rode up on his rugged horse. "You know, the way some are dressed."

"I'm afraid not. I guess a lot of them didn't take our guidelines seriously."

"Well, it won't be long before reality hits them," John declared with a grin. "They'll get more blisters and sunburns and whatnot than they ever dreamed possible . . . But there are other things that worry me more than clothes."

"Like what?"

John struggled to control his frisky horse. "Some of these people don't look too fit. We warned them to take long hikes and trim up as much as possible, but it doesn't seem as though they paid much attention."

"Don't worry. The trail and the sparse diet will shape them up in no time." Steven guiltily touched his own stomach. He certainly wasn't as trim as he could be.

"I guess you're right. I only hope they don't suffer too much before that happens. And I suppose it's only a matter of a few miles before they get the idea to maintain a slow, steady pace."

"Yes, I know what you mean. Some of them act as if they're frantically trying to get to a special sale before everybody else does." Steven gazed at one chubby guy chugging along as fast as he could go.

"Well, I'd better get back to my post at the rear." John turned his horse and trotted down the caravan.

A mile farther along the freeway, Steven noticed many of the pilgrims eyeing their wagons with longing. Soon, along the entire length of the caravan, they began to hop onto wagons, desperately seeking rest. A rest which would last a long, long time. The draft animals slowed their pace with the extra weight. A mile later, nearly every pioneer was hitching a ride, and the wagons slowed even more. At first Steven was irritated to see such laziness, but then a pang of guilt hit him. He had to admit that he was no paragon of physical fitness, and he started to worry about whether or not he'd make it through the day without embarrassment. After all, he was supposed to be a good example. Thank heavens he had to ride around on his horse for a while—to check on the welfare of his people, of course. He wondered how long he'd get away with that excuse.

On that first day of the journey, Steven asked himself if he'd already made a mistake. He had planned to increase travel time by one hour a day every two weeks: first ten hours, then eleven, and finally twelve. In that way, he had hoped to break the pioneers in gradually, to make the transition from unfitness to fitness less painful. But from the looks of the saints, maybe he should have asked them to walk no more than three or four hours a day at the beginning, and increase the time gradually. He might have to make a quick change of plans.

⌘

Four days later, as Pioneer One struggled up the six-percent grade on I-80, three miles from Parley's Summit, Steven knew for sure he had made a mistake in expecting the pioneers to maintain such a grueling early schedule. He was grateful that he and the other leaders had decided to call a halt for a day and a half after they reached the summit, and then proceed at an easier pace. But they still had to traverse the next three horrible miles. He continued on slowly, walking beside his wagon, his legs and feet hurting terribly. Mary, Steven's bride of six days, drove their wagon and glanced at him often with sympathy. He couldn't imagine a worse way to spend a honeymoon. It was only eleven thirty, and already the temperature was ninety degrees. And since there was no breeze and the skies were cloudless, the heat was sizzling on the hot freeway surface. John had informed him that the temperatures of the last few days were twelve degrees higher than normal for this time of year. Steven wasn't surprised, because the weather had been erratic and extreme around the world for a long time. The peaks to the south were covered with snow, but that seemed to have no effect in moderating the temperature.

"Do you want to take the reins for a while, sweetheart?" Mary said, looking down at him. "You need rest."

"No, I'm okay. Maybe later." Steven agonized over what the other pioneers must be going through. At least he was wearing sneakers which gave his feet good support. They were two sizes too large so he could fill the bottom with foam pads to absorb as much shock as possible. He had wrapped his lower legs with Ace bandages just tight enough to give his muscles a measure of support. He wore a long-sleeved shirt and a wide-brimmed hat. Yet, in spite of this preparation, he had shin splints, aching muscles, blisters, dry skin, red eyes, and chapped lips.

He knew others must be suffering even more than he, because some were older and less fit. Many had not made careful preparations nor worn the right clothes. Already most of the company was smitten by sunburn, blisters, pulled muscles, fatigue, dry skin, and a multitude of other ailments. Steven and his brothers had instructed the pioneers from the beginning to take regular doses of water, but many had not done so and were suffering from heat exhaustion and dehydration.

Steven knew that even the early Mormon pioneers, who were used to hard labor and physical exertion, had endured great physical exhaustion and pain as they made the journey to Utah. But most of the new pioneers had led lives of ease and inactivity. After only four days, several families had already given up and returned to the city, protesting that nothing was worth the agony they were going through. A few had no choice: they had developed such severe symptoms that the caravan doctor, Quentin Price, had warned they might die if they didn't return to civilization.

Steven was proud of those who persisted despite great distress. He felt especially sorry for the ones who were overweight. Their initial brisk pace had soon turned into painful trudging. Their agony was so great that they moaned from pain during the night instead of getting the sleep they needed so badly. Many saints still found it necessary to hop into wagons or mount horses to continue the journey. This added to the burden of the animals that had to pull overloaded wagons. Steven wondered how many more saints would have to go back to Salt Lake City, and how many draft animals would perish from exhaustion.

He was surprised to see that the people driving converted vehicles did not seem to have more difficulties than those using wagons. But the bicyclers had given up trying to climb the steep road, and had fastened the bikes to hooks on their wagons. The people pulling handcarts had the most trouble, and it took every member of the family to keep the carts moving. Steven knew their struggle would ease as soon as the highway leveled out.

The Prophet Josiah Smith had warned Steven that not all the pioneers would have the strength of character to endure the trials the Lord would send them on the road to Missouri. Some would abandon the wagon train, and others would become traitors before the trip was over. One of the purposes of the difficult journey was to prepare a sanctified people worthy of establishing New Zion and the holy city. He told Steven that he must use his own judgment in solving problems, after seeking the counsel of his assistants and the wisdom of the Lord, but he advised him to maintain reasonable company rules and to travel as fast as the saints could bear.

The previous evening, on Monday, Steven had called a meeting with the caravan leaders, his brothers—John and Paul—and four colonels. They had decided to allow the company to go somewhat slower for a while and have a rest day after they reached Parley's Summit, which would occur around noon on Tuesday. So on Tuesday morning before the pioneers had hit the trail, Steven announced that after reaching the summit, which was only a few hours away, the entire company would stop shortly thereafter to rest for the reminder of the day and the next day too. When they began the journey again on Thursday, they would travel no more than five hours a day for about a week. At that welcome announcement the entire company cheered and rejoiced.

"Steven, please take these reins," Mary called down. "You've been walking almost three hours now. I can see your legs are hurting you."

"Don't worry. I'll be fine. It isn't far to the resting place." Steven saw a sign on the right indicating that Parley's Summit was only a mile ahead. He knew they could rest shortly after reaching that point. Then the road would descend and the going would be much easier. He looked at his three children and felt a wave of pride as he saw them maintaining the pace without complaint. Only Andrew, who was nine, found it necessary to jump into the wagon at times. Jennifer, his eleven-year-old daughter, doggedly kept up with William, who at thirteen was proud of being a teenager.

He looked back and saw his non-Mormon friend, Douglas Cartwright, plodding wearily beside his wagon, his eyes staring at the road in front of him. Apparently this march was taking its toll, even on a man as strong as Douglas. Steven gritted his teeth and steeled his mind to the idea that he was going to set a good example for his children and the others in the company, no matter what the cost. His legs had always been one of his weak spots, his Achilles tendon. In past years they had prevented him, during workouts, from running too fast or jogging more than three or four miles.

He looked at Mary again and called out, "We can stop in about two hours. In about three miles we come to a wide valley, where there will be plenty of room to place the wagons into circles. It's near Jeremy Ranch." Mary nodded and threw him a kiss.

The next few miles seemed endless, but finally the road began to level out and turn downward. Steven felt a huge relief. He looked to the right and saw a community of cabins and other buildings on the side of the mountain, not far from the freeway. He was astonished to see that all of them were demolished, and there was no sign of life. It reminded him of the housing developments he had seen on the bench east of I-215 on the third day of their journey just before the wagon train turned northeast into the canyon. They too had been flattened by some gigantic force. At the time Steven had wondered if the devastation had been caused by the great earthquake that had struck the Cottonwood Fault nearly a year ago in May. Or was it the result of the massive mud slides which had occurred this year after three weeks of ceaseless rain? Perhaps both disasters had taken their toll.

In the case of this mountain community, marauders may have been involved also because many of the cabins looked as if they had been burned out. A sudden chill went up his spine. He remembered the words of the prophet, who had warned him several weeks ago that Pioneer One would face dangers from wicked men that would be almost insurmountable.

After the wagon train had traveled another mile, Steven's thoughts were abruptly interrupted.

"We can camp over there," a voice said. It was Paul, who appeared beside him as if from nowhere. Steven looked in the direction indicated by his brother and saw a wide-open space on the left, large enough for hundreds of wagons. It was about a mile south of Jeremy Ranch. Since the ditch on the side of the freeway was shallow, Steven knew they would have no trouble crossing it to reach the site.

"Looks good, Paul," Steven said, climbing into his wagon.

Paul waved and disappeared. As Mary slid to the right on the seat to make room for her husband, she handed him the reins. He drove the mules toward the field and turned his wagon into a wide circle. If the other drivers followed him, as they knew they should, they could form a ring of about a hundred wagons. As soon as he finished the first circle, he jumped from the wagon and, with the help of Paul and Douglas, guided the second line of wagons into another circle.

They repeated the procedure until the final section of wagons formed the last circle. The result was three complete rings, one inside the other, of about a hundred wagons each, with openings at opposite sides. Seeing this company all together in one spot for the first time, Steven was amazed at how huge it really was. The prophet had told Steven that the brethren realized that such a large body of travelers would be extremely difficult to oversee and to lead. But they had purposely planned it to be large to provide the pioneers with a vital measure of safety on such a dangerous journey.

The handcart pioneers parked their carts in the center of the circles. Most of the livestock was herded to forage on the north side of the camp, where Paul posted several bachelors as guards. John put sentries around the entire encampment.

It was the first time Steven had tried to form the wagons into such large circles. When they had stopped for the night on the first few days, they simply had stopped where they were on the freeway because there wasn't enough room to form protective circles. But today the pioneers spent a half hour to complete the three circles. This time-consuming task was frustrating to the leaders, but they knew the circles would provide them with greater protection.

It was two thirty in the afternoon when the saints finished the work of organizing the encampment. Most of the travelers found a shady spot and fell asleep immediately. But many found it necessary to nurse their aching bodies before they were comfortable enough to rest. Only a few showed any interest in visiting neighbors, telling stories, or playing games, as they had that first night on Interstate 15.

Paul, John, and Douglas gathered at Steven's wagon as soon as their chores were completed. They hugged Mary and Steven's children. A few minutes later, Jarrad Babcock and Leonard Reece, Paul's traveling companions, turned up. Like Paul, they were not married.

"I suggest we mount up and check the region east of here," John said. "There are several communities farther along the freeway. Or at least there used to be."

"I agree. We need to check it out," Paul said.

Steven saw anxiety in the eyes of the other five men. He guessed that they too had seen the destruction at the entrance to the valley. "All right. Let's go." He turned to Mary and said, "We won't be long."

"Please be careful, Steve," she said.

"We will." He gave her a kiss.

Mary said no more but Steven saw the worried look on her face. He knew she feared for their safety but realized, at the same time, that it was something they had to do.

"Can I go, Dad?" William said.

"Not this time, son, I'm depending on you to stay here to help protect the camp." Steven was afraid for the boy's life if they ran into trouble. William frowned, but didn't protest. Steven knew his son was secretly pleased that he had expressed confidence in him.

The six men mounted their horses and trotted east on the freeway. Each carried a rifle. With great caution they spent two hours exploring the area several miles from the encampment. Desolation was everywhere, evidence that some great natural disaster had struck the region. Nearly every building was smashed and covered with a thick layer of hardened mud. Yet the searchers found something even more sinister.

Some of the buildings had been consumed by fire, and there were many dead bodies everywhere, including women and children. It was clear they had been shot or stabbed to death. Whoever had committed these heinous crimes had also poured out their rage upon pets and farm animals. The situation became even more frightening when they realized that the tragedy had taken place only a few days earlier. Finding no life and sickened by what he saw, Steven called off the search, and the men headed back to camp.

Before they reached the camp, they agreed to report the destruction in general terms, but to avoid revealing the violence committed against human beings. Steven did not want to provoke terror in the hearts of the pioneers. As they reached the outskirts of the camp, they were met by two colonels and seven captains. The colonels were in charge of fifty families, and the captains oversaw ten families. Steven told them what they had found and asked them to be cautious as to what they told the families in their charge. He also asked John to make sure he doubled the guard. The leaders left immediately to do what he requested.

After saying goodbye to Douglas and the others, Steven joined his little family, who had gathered around a campfire not far from their wagon. It was nearly six in the late afternoon, and Mary was preparing supper. Steven sat beside his wife on a log and kissed her gently on the neck. The children snickered at his display of affection. As he sat there looking into the fire, the feeling suddenly came to him that he wouldn't want to live another minute if his wife and children ever suffered the kind of violence he had just witnessed not far away.

Even though Mary was his second wife and not the mother of his children, Steven knew that she already loved them almost as much as he did. She had no children of her own because her first husband hated children and eventually abandoned her for another woman.

Mary stopped her work and insisted that Steven take off his shoes and roll up the legs of his pants. The children giggled at his white legs, but Steven didn't care, because Mary knelt in front of him and began to rub his legs with pain-relieving ointment.

"Why don't we invite the Cartwrights and the three bachelors for supper?" Mary asked as she worked on him, her facing glowing like that of a typical newlywed.

"Good idea," Steven replied. The Cartwrights and the three bachelors sometimes ate meals with them, and Steven was especially anxious to have their company tonight.

"I'll go get them," Andrew yelled enthusiastically, not waiting for his father's approval.

Andrew had become the unofficial family courier, and Steven didn't mind as long as the boy didn't stray too far. He watched as his son ran the forty feet to where Douglas was doing some chore. Hearing Andrew's message, Douglas smiled and waved his acceptance to Steven. The boy ran to another wagon and spoke to Paul. Paul said something to Andrew and the child quickly sped away toward the center of the camp. Steven figured he was hurrying to find Leonard and Jarrad. No doubt the two bachelors were hanging around the best-looking young ladies of the camp, hoping to score points. Steven was sure that Anastasia Borisovich would be one of them.

Mary had just finished working on his legs, when Paul and the Cartwrights arrived and sat around the fire. Elizabeth Cartwright, Doug's wife, had brought a huge bowl of potato salad with her. She and Doug had five lively children. Like her husband, Elizabeth was not a member of the church.

Steven was growing concerned that Andrew had not yet returned, and he was relieved when he finally saw the boy hurrying toward them, pulling on the Leonard and Jarrad's arms. "What took you so long, Andrew?" Steven asked.

"Well, Dad, to make a long story short," he said with disgust, "I couldn't get these two lover boys away from the chicks."

"Hey, what's the problem, Andy boy?" Jarrad said with a twinkle in his eye. "We were merely having a profound religious conversation with two serious young women."

"Yeah, right," Andrew said, smirking. "You looked pretty googly-eyed to me."

Everyone laughed at Andrew's choice of words. Steven was astonished to hear his son use terms like "lover boys," "chicks," and "googly-eyed."

By that time Mary had finished preparing fried chicken with pork and beans. Doug offered a prayer. Steven looked at all the food and wondered how long they'd be able to enjoy such feasts. He felt guilty that he hadn't done a good job of encouraging everyone, even his own wife, to ration food. Obviously, other people were ignoring the guidelines also. Maybe he'd have to do what John said—put the food in special wagons and give every person a specific allotment every day. Another thing to bring up in the leadership council.

As they ate, the friends discussed the difficult trip up the mountain, the ailments of the pioneers, and especially the terrible destruction around them. At ten o'clock Mary put Andrew and Jennifer to bed, but William begged to stay up until midnight. As a teenager, he felt he had the right to listen to the adults talk. Steven agreed in spite of the frown he saw on Mary's face. At that moment John and Tania Christopher joined the group and were greeted warmly by everyone.

When everyone had settled down, Paul said in a mysterious voice, "I wanted to tell you all that I think something very strange is going on."

Steven looked at him in surprise. "Like what?"

Paul gazed around the campfire as if to make sure he could speak freely in this group. Seeing William, he declared, "William, what I'm about to say is a secret. It's important that you don't repeat it to anyone, no matter what."

Normally, Steven would have considered Paul's attitude to be no more than one of his usual jokes. But after the terrible things they had seen that day, he sensed that Paul was serious. He noticed that no one in the group was smiling.

"Don't worry, Uncle Paul," William said, "I'm an expert at keeping secrets."

"I'm sure you are . . . Okay, as everyone here knows, Leonard and Jarrad have spent a lot of time in the last few days visiting the available females in the caravan."

"Hey, we were only doing a little quality home teaching," Jarrad protested.

Paul smiled. "That's understood. Anyhow, Jarrad and Leonard tell me that some of these young ladies couldn't resist pouring out their tender hearts to them. To make a long story short, these young ladies inadvertently revealed that they've heard a lot of murmuring."

Douglas Cartwright said, "Murmuring? What kind of murmuring?"

Paul leaned forward and placed another branch on the fire. "Well, it seems someone is spreading rumors about us, the leaders of Pioneer One. According to the gossip, we are dangerously incompetent. The brunt of the attack seems to fall on Steven."

"You're joking!" Douglas said angrily.

"No, I'm serious."

Steven felt the heat of shame flow from his neck to his face. The idea of incompetence was particularly embarrassing, since he had always believed that someone else, almost anyone else, would be better qualified than he to lead Pioneer One. "Incompetent in what way?" he asked nervously.

Jarrad answered for Paul. "In lots of ways. Not establishing rules that are strict enough. Neglecting to enforce the rules we have. Supporting the weaker saints, who are slowing us down. Refusing to make the people ration their food more carefully. Not posting enough guards at night. Choosing a poor route . . . And believe me, that's only the beginning. Those sisters just couldn't stop talking."

"The attitude seems to be," Leonard added, "that you—all of you—are endangering the lives of everyone in the company by not doing your jobs properly."

"But it was the prophet who chose this route for us, not Steven," Elizabeth objected.

In spite of his humiliation, Steven was pleased to hear Elizabeth, who was not a member of the church, refer to Josiah Smith as "the prophet."

Mary was visibly upset. "Paul, do you think these criticisms represent a general opinion, or is it just gossip spread by a few individuals?"

Before Paul could respond, John said, "It's obviously a conspiracy. I've talked to a lot of the pioneers. Most of them like Steven and have complimented us on the way we're handling the trip. I believe someone is trying to corrupt the others and undermine our authority by circulating lies."

"But why?" Douglas said. "What do they hope to gain?"

"That's what we need to find out," Paul said. "Also, we may have another problem. Several people have told me that someone is stealing supplies."

"I've heard the same thing," John observed.

Steven was stunned. "Stealing? Are you sure?"

Paul replied, "Yes. Two wagoners told me this morning that someone stole tools and ammunition from their wagons. They've no idea when it happened, but both are fit to be tied."

"And what did you hear, John?"

"What I heard came from Byron Mills."

"Oh, yes. I remember him," Steven said. Byron had been an elder in the Grandview Second ward. He was thirty-eight years old and considered himself a scriptorian.

"Well, Byron said he had a sack of wheat and a rifle stolen. He doesn't know when it happened either."

"Do you think these people simply made a mistake? Maybe they forgot to bring the items they believe were stolen."

Both Paul and John shook their heads. The group discussed the matter another half hour without coming to any firm conclusions.

Finally, Steven said, "Listen, everyone, we're not going to find the truth without more information. I want you to keep your eyes and ears open. I suggest you enlist the aid of as many people as possible, if you know you can trust them. I especially want Paul, Leonard, and Jarrad to use their special talents and connections to uncover some solid evidence. We need to resolve these problems quickly."

After the guests left, Steven and Paul walked around the camps to check the guards, who reported that they hadn't seen or heard anything unusual.

"You sure are lucky," Paul said as they trudged back to their wagons.

"Lucky? What do you mean?"

"You get to go home to a beautiful, tender wife, while I have to put up with two dirty bachelors who burp constantly and think it's funny to let smells."

"You poor boy. Look, I happen to know that your companions are pretty high up on the cleanliness chain, so don't give me a line of bull."

When they reached the wagons, Paul sighed, "what a life without a wife. How can I bear it?"

Steven laughed. "Good night, Paul."

"Good night, you lucky devil."

Later, as he snuggled close to Mary, Steven couldn't sleep. He struggled to think of something pleasant but failed. He was tormented by the problems of the wagon train and the murdered people he had seen in the nearby communities.

"You can't sleep, sweetheart?" Mary whispered. "You're tossing and turning constantly."

"Sorry to keep you awake."

"Listen. There's no problem we can't solve with the Lord's help. Maybe we should ask him."

"Yes, of course." Steven was grateful for the suggestion because he had forgotten to have prayer that evening except over the supper. Another thing to feel guilty about. They kneeled, and Steven asked God for protection and help in solving the troubles of Pioneer One.

After putting more balm on his legs, Mary said, "Now, roll onto your stomach, so I can rub your back."

The gentle touch of his wife and the warm ointment made him feel better immediately. He remembered how Selena, his ex-wife, had rubbed his back sometimes when they were first married. Strange how it was that you never seemed to forget completely a woman you once loved. And yet, because of Mary, he could think of Selena now without the terrible pain he had felt before. What would his life be like today if Selena had not abandoned him and the children three years ago to join a polygamous cult? Would it be her rubbing the pain out of his legs instead of Mary?

At last the great fatigue of the day gradually overtook him and he began to relax and feel sleepy. He hoped that he and the other company leaders would be equal to the task of solving their current problems and perhaps even greater ones as they continued their trek eastward.

Chapter 2

Gerald Galloway sat back in a luxurious couch at his country mansion in Hampshire, England. As he sipped a glass of 1903 Chardonnay and contentedly smoked a Gauloise, he thought about the recent renovations to his estate. They had cost a fortune, but as the supreme leader of the new world government—UGOT—he could afford it. Fortunately, the final changes had been completed three days ago, in plenty of time for the meeting later today with his associates. He knew his confederates would be elated because of the stunning success of their plans for world domination. Especially significant was the fact that it had taken less than two years to undermine and destroy the European Union.

Yes, it had been necessary to assassinate a lot of people and bribe others. But their most effective tool had been to accuse—through his European network of propagandists—some member nations of abusing the terms of their agreements. He had undermined political harmony in those countries by placing operatives in important positions, so they could plant false evidence against national leaders. He had hired a secret society of professional killers to destroy factories and poison harvests. All of it had required a great deal of planning and money . . . Gerald chuckled at memory of the turmoil he had caused by promoting Alwin Zimmermann as prime minister of Germany, and then leaking to the press that Zimmermann had a secret affiliation with neo-Nazi organizations.

His success in gaining control of the United Nations had been equally as spectacular. Because of the fall of the American government, the natural catastrophes on a global scale, and the collapse of the international banking system, the UN had been in chaos. Thirty nations had declared war on one another and had begun immediate hostilities to settle old scores. Pakistan had made the mistake of attacking India with nuclear weapons, and the Indian retaliation had been dreadful. India had struck the largest Pakistani cities with four one-megaton hydrogen bombs, and then had invaded with an army of a million soldiers. The war had lasted only five weeks, with violent repercussions in surrounding nations.

There was a grave shortage of grain and foodstuffs throughout the Middle East and the Russian Federation. Millions of starving people had fled poor countries and illegally entered rich nations: from Africa, Afghanistan, Eastern Europe, Vietnam, Cambodia, and North Korea they had escaped to Western Europe, New Zealand, Chile, Taiwan, South Korea, and Japan. War, mob violence, natural disasters, devastating diseases, drought, and famine had been everywhere. The complete disintegration of world civilization seemed imminent.

Therefore, when Gerald Galloway had come to the UN and offered the help of his wealthy megacorporation, a desperate world accepted his leadership gratefully. His plan was tough and radical, but he convinced the UN that it was essential. A council of twelve people would govern the United Nations, with Gerald Galloway as chairman. This inner circle would be called the Supreme Council of the Twelve. Their power would be absolute. The member nations would continue to send delegates, but they could no longer vote. They would function only as representatives to inform the Council of the needs of their homeland.

Every country must show implicit trust in the wisdom and goodness of the Council to handle their needs in the best ways possible. Their governments could stay in power if they strictly followed the will of the Twelve. Gerald promised the people of the world that the new regime would be just, effective, efficient, absolute, and righteous. The first step that the nations must take to show their good faith was to replace many of their current administrators and officials with the new leaders whom the Council would send.

Gerald vividly recalled his moving speech to the assembled representatives, and he had to admit that he had been brilliant. He had always had a special talent for oratory. They had bought his provisions almost without question. And what was the name of the new world government? The Universal Government of the Twelve, or UGOT.

Yet his joy and satisfaction were not perfect. Thirty-one nations had not sent representatives to the assembly where he had taken control. Some of these nations, such as China and Japan, were very important. Without them, he knew it would be difficult, perhaps impossible, to make his rule universal and to reach his ultimate goal of destroying Israel. That was why he had called today's meeting with his associates. Together they would have to create a master plan to capture the allegiance of the uncooperative countries. Gerald was confident that they would succeed, eventually, in making the disobedient fall into line. He also looked forward to the meetings because he knew that they would give him an excuse to spend time with Lucienne Delisle, his lover, who planned to attend.

A few minutes later, at five o'clock, the inner circle began to arrive. As usual, the associates greeted one another with the secret words and gestures. The first person to appear was Dominic O'Brien, whom Gerald had appointed three months earlier as the twelfth associate. He was in charge of South Africa. Lucienne was the last to arrive. These were the chosen ones who made up the Supreme Council of the Twelve. Other trusted people had been selected to replace them temporarily in the areas of the world where they had functioned as Gerald's powerful associates.

After they had taken seats in his vast study, Gerald said, "I'm glad you all arrived in time for supper. My cook is a master chef, and I'm sure you'll be delighted with his creations."

"I know we will, Mr. Galloway," said Randolph Benson, Gerald's associate in the Middle East. "You always do things in style."

"No, not Mr. Galloway. I want each of you to call me Gerald from now on. After all, we're trusted friends, aren't we?"

"Yes, of course, Gerald," Lucienne said. "We can always trust you to give us the best you have."

"Thank you, Lucienne," Gerald said with a straight smile.

After a half hour of small talk, they moved into the dining hall where domestics served them a six-course meal. Later the associates returned to Gerald's study, where they enjoyed bottles of dry sherry and more friendly banter.

At eight o'clock Gerald asked them to pull their chairs into a circle. "I think it's time we got down to business. First, let me compliment you. As members of the Council, you've done a remarkable job. You've given me excellent advice and handled your individual areas of responsibility with amazing competence. I called you here today because I know you get tired of communicating by phone. I feel the same way. Here we can be more intimate, let ourselves go, and say what we really think."

On hearing those words, the visitors stiffened. They admired Galloway and were in awe at his many talents, but they also knew that their power and destiny depended completely on his wishes. So, they did little without his approval. The very idea of offering alternative suggestions or objecting to

Gerald's views could be dangerous. Their situation resembled that of Adolph Hitler and his henchmen. Most of the associates feared this arrogant master, and a few of them secretly conspired to bring him down. Only his mistress Lucienne dared to challenge Gerald's ideas openly, and she did so often, but always with charm and skill.

"Yes, it's nice to be able to say what we really think," Lucienne said with subtle irony.

Gerald smiled and took a sip of sherry. "Let me say that as masters of the world, we have accomplished a great deal." Several associates nodded. "But there are still important things we need to do."

"You are referring to Israel, of course," said Francis Bonnard, UGOT's associate for North Africa.

"In part, yes. As you know, last year Israel defeated the invading forces of five Arab nations. It took them only eight days. Israel is still strong and independent and refuses to acknowledge the authority of our new government. We must bring her into line." Everyone knew Gerald meant that Israel must be annihilated. "However, Israel is not the only government we must reach. Thirty other nations remain that have ignored our invitations to become part of the new world government. They neglect to send delegates to our general assemblies, and have refused—no, not refused, but declined—to participate in our economic, political, and military operations."

"Still, most of those countries are fairly small," Alexi Glinka observed. "Do we really need them?"

"You're forgetting China, Alexi," said Janet Griffin, the associate for East Asia. "It has the bomb, a skyrocketing gross national product, and a population of almost 1.7 billion people."

"Oh yes, of course," Alexi mumbled.

"What about the United States?" Randy Benson asked.

Gerald replied, "The United States is a wasteland full of anarchy and pollution. There's no civil authority whatsoever. We, of course, played a role in that. At this time it is in a world apart, and we don't have to worry about it. The same is essentially true of Mexico and Canada. Central America and South America, however, are a different matter. If any of you want details concerning the United States, talk to Lucienne before you leave in a few days." Lucienne was Gerald's chief operative in North America.

Lucienne said, "I'd be happy to answer their questions. But what do you want to do with the recalcitrant nations, Gerald?"

"I'm open to suggestions."

"I think we should send delegations to them," Janet Griffin said.

"To do what?" Gerald replied.

"Well, to encourage them to join us. We could offer them incentives."

"What kind of incentives?" Lucienne asked.

"Well, mostly economic. Send them money to develop their infrastructure. Things like that."

"And if that doesn't work," Benson said, "we could make it clear that we would see their refusal as a sign that they don't care about their neighbors and don't want to participate in solving the world's predicaments. Problems like global warming, depleting the earth's resources, and overpopulation. We could let them know that solving these problems is so vital that we are ready to use military force to ensure that every nation cooperates. But if they join us they would, in the long run, reap great financial benefits. "

Gerald was surprised at Benson's answer. "Excellent, Randy. I like the way you think. The end justifies the means. We want a peaceful, happy world, and we may have to break some traditional rules to get it. First we exploit altruism, then greed, and finally fear. Now, what else, people?"

Lucienne knew perfectly well where Gerald was leading. She had spent many hours beside him at night, listening to his biases and hatreds. "Well, I like the idea of exploiting all three of those motives at the same time. We explain our concerns about Zionism. We convince them that the Jews are wealthy because they've exploited the people of the world through their multinational corporations and their international banks. We might even blame genetic engineering on Jewish greed. We try to persuade them that we truly need their help in ridding the world of the Zionist plague. We maintain that without their help, it may take decades for us to accomplish it. At the same time, we promise them a significant portion of Israeli wealth." The other associates nodded their heads in appreciation at Lucienne's rhetoric.

"Good, Lucienne," Gerald agreed. "I want you people to think about all these ideas. Remember that we are responsible for converting the thirty-one resistant nations. Since I believe in giving you great independence in your areas of responsibility, I leave the details up to you. I'm only concerned that you bring me results. Of course, I will assign some of you to visit the defiant nations in person to obtain their compliance. All except Israel, of course. The people I choose will have a special emissary at their disposal. Most of you already know him—Colton Aldridge, the American prophet recruited by Lucienne. I've seen him do miracles with my own eyes, and I know you can use him to convince credulous leaders of the justice and righteousness of our cause."

After the twelve associates discussed the goals of UGOT until midnight, they retired to comfortable beds. Gerald and Lucienne were proud of themselves. The meeting had been a great success. For an hour longer they planned how they would use Colton Aldridge and their other holy men to consolidate their power.

Pierre Laborde entered the foyer of the three-story building and pressed the button to his friend's apartment. The building was located in Rueil-Malmaison, a suburb of Paris.

"Yes?" a voice said through the speaker directly above the row of buttons.

"It's Pierre."

"Okay."

After waiting to hear the hum which indicated that André had released the lock on the inner door, Pierre pushed it open and hurried to the elevator, the only access to the upstairs apartments. André Renan had given him an urgent call forty minutes earlier, asking him to rush over as quickly as possible, but refusing to give details on the telephone. Pierre was intrigued and a little nervous. These were dangerous times, and André wasn't the kind of person to play silly games. Pierre was glad that his friend had been able to find his excellent apartment. André and his wife Mireille were the kind of LDS members who opened their home and hearts to any members in need.

There were almost eighty thousand saints in France, and when the prophet had made his call last July, most had sought safety in the main centers of the church in Paris, Marseille, and Lyon. But often it was difficult for them to find work and accommodations. Most of those who had gathered to the Paris area had to live in the nearby countryside with friends or church members. Others had no choice but to live in abandoned farm buildings or other structures. Pierre had been a civil engineer in Vendôme, a city seventy-five miles southwest of Paris. But now he and his wife Diane, and their two young children, lived in church facilities in Paris. Since Pierre had appeared on television a number of times in opposition to UGOT, landlords were afraid to rent to him.

When the elevator reached the correct floor, the door slid open, and Pierre rushed out, turned right, and knocked on the first door he came to. Almost immediately, André unlocked the door and let him in.

"Have you heard the news yet?" André said after closing the door.

"What news?"

"Come in and sit down."

Pierre entered the living room and was surprised to see that two other families were visiting André and Mireille. He recognized them as members of the church. He was surprised at the terror he saw in their eyes. As Mireille turned off the television, the others made room for him on the couch.

"What's going on?" he asked.

André said, "Pierre, an hour ago we heard a news report which said that French authorities are requiring all Mormons to register with the government within three weeks."

Pierre was shocked. "Only Mormons? But why?"

"No one knows for sure. They want us to bring our official papers: birth certificates, mortgages, a list of assets, bank accounts. We'll also have to answer personal and family questions."

Pierre was furious. "The despicable tyrants!"

One of the visitors, Carl Mauriac, said, "I got a call this morning from a friend who is visiting relatives in Rome. He told me that the same thing has been going on for weeks in Italy."

"It's restricted to members of the church?" Pierre asked.

"Yes, only Mormons. My friend said he heard that UGOT is disenfranchising Mormons in many countries, confiscating their property, and forcing them to live in special camps."

"Sounds like the Nazis all over again to me!" Mireille exclaimed.

"Yes, it does, but I wonder how accurate those reports really are," André said.

"We may not find out until it's too late," Pierre said.

"We should get counsel from our local church leaders as soon as possible," Carl's wife declared.

Mireille added, "And do a lot of praying."

André said, "Yes, of course. Most of all, we need to find out for sure what UGOT is doing to the saints in other countries. I don't intend to report to the government unless I get the facts."

"Well, I'm not putting my family into their hands—no matter what," Pierre replied.

Chapter 3

The bugle which normally announced the beginning of the day for Pioneer One did not sound. Since it was a day of rest and recovery, the pioneers wouldn't have to arise early. Steven, however, awoke at six and couldn't go back to sleep. Afraid his tossing and turning would awaken his family, he decided to get up.

"Can't sleep?" Mary asked.

"Oh, you're awake . . . No, too much on my mind."

"I'm sorry. What's bothering you?"

"Everything, I guess."

Mary gave him a hug. "Can I help?"

"You always help. But there are some things I must handle myself."

"How do your legs feel?"

"Much better, thanks to you. As I said, you always help." He pulled his boots on without bandaging his legs. "I have to go a short distance from camp. To be alone. Please don't worry, okay?"

"I'll try not to. Will you be gone long?" Mary suspected what her husband was going to do, and decided to respect his privacy.

"No, not long." Grabbing his rifle, he slipped out the back of the wagon and lowered himself to the ground. As he walked away from the wagon train, he waved to a guard posted nearby. I should have taken my turn as guard last night, he thought. I didn't sleep very well anyway. John had the important responsibility of arranging the hours and rotation of camp guards and was doing a good job of it. Steven walked another five minutes and found a secluded spot partly surrounded by trees. After looking around to see that he was alone, he placed his rifle against the trunk of a tree and knelt down to pray. He spent the next ten minutes telling God how inadequate he felt and asking him to give him the strength and wisdom to lead Pioneer One the right way.

By the time he had finished, he felt a little better and was no longer sleepy. He arose and descended a gentle slope toward the encampment until he could see the entire camp clearly. From that vantage point, he sat on a huge boulder and stared at the immensity of his responsibility. No wonder some of the people were starting to complain. Their lives were in the hands of an idiot who had no experience whatsoever at leading other people. It certainly wasn't a job he had asked for. His eyes full of tears, he thought about Jesus asking the Father to remove the bitter cup from him. Of course, his pain and responsibility didn't begin to compare with Christ's, but still his turmoil and fear were real. As he watched the first few people slowly exit their wagons and tents below, he thought he heard a voice close by. He looked around, but saw no one. He listened carefully and heard the voice again. It was louder now, and he discerned a few words.

"Who is there?" Steven said cautiously.

"It is I," the voice said clearly. It seemed to come from inside him and yet from the outside at the same time.

Steven remembered something he had read in the scriptures and replied, "I'm here, Lord."

"Fear not, my son," the gentle voice said, "for it is I who have chosen you."

Steven was so astonished that he couldn't say a word. The powerful words came as in a whisper, but they penetrated deep into his heart.

"Pray to me always and I will guide you and go before you. Your enemies are now combined, but they shall not prosper."

As he listened, Steven's heart burned with healing fire and his mind was filled with unspeakable joy. It was the strongest and most thrilling experience he had ever had.

Steven asked the invisible being other questions which were bothering him, and received satisfying answers. At last, the soothing voice faded away slowly, and Steven realized that his visitor was no longer there. He sat there another ten minutes, pondering the experience. Now, instead of fear, he felt happiness and self-confidence. Before long, he set out for the encampment.

As he approached camp, he saw the Cartwrights emerging from their large tent. Since Douglas and Elizabeth had five children, they usually slept in the tent instead of their wagon. Then he caught sight of Mary waiting for him just outside the ring of wagons. He saw her troubled face brighten suddenly when she saw him from a distance. Apparently the children were still asleep.

"Steven, you were gone so long," she said. "In another minute I would have sent Paul and his friends to search for you."

Steven looked at his watch and was surprised to see that his interview with the invisible being had taken almost two hours. He took Mary into his arms and kissed her tenderly. He told her that he had heard the voice of a messenger from God and had received the help and inspiration he so desperately needed.

Mary burst into tears and embraced him earnestly. "I'm so happy," she declared.

Steven kissed her cheeks and dried her tears. They walked a short distance from camp and sat on some boulders at the edge of a gully. Mary couldn't control her curiosity. "Who spoke to you, Steve? Was it the Lord?"

"I feel that it was him, but I'm not sure. He called me 'son.' I know that in the scriptures Jesus sometimes speaks as though he is the Father, and angels sometimes refer to themselves as the Son. Of course, they're actually speaking as agents for those higher in authority. I believe it's called the Doctrine of Agency."

"Is that why the angel in the first part of the Book of Revelation says that he is Alpha and Omega?"

"I believe so. The angel simply quotes what the Son said." Steven stopped and faced Mary. "I suppose it really doesn't matter who spoke to me. Still, I'm convinced that it was the Lord himself."

"Why?"

"Because I don't believe that any personage other the Lord or the Father could tell me so many intimate, personal things about myself or communicate such an intense feeling of love to my heart. No, I know it was him."

They heard a voice calling from camp and saw Paul waving them in.

"I guess it's time for breakfast," Mary said.

While they walked back to the wagon, Steven's three children ran to meet them.

"Uncle Paul is making pancakes," Jennifer yelled as she rushed up and seized her father's arm. "The Cartwrights are coming for breakfast too."

"Yeah." Andrew added enthusiastically. "Big fat pancakes, covered with butter and maple syrup."

"Wow!" Steven shouted gleefully, trying to match their enthusiasm. He got the impression that his children were still treating this long trek through what might be some of the most dangerous places in America as a camping trip to Vivian Park in Provo Canyon.

"The trouble is, he wants us to drink milk with the pancakes," William said.

"I hate that milk." William had refused to drink the cow's raw milk ever since they had acquired her a week before leaving Provo.

Mary laughed. "Well, we have Stockings now and she gives us milk twice a day. So we have to drink it." William scowled, not in the least convinced.

"Besides, it's delicious," Steven said. "I'm sure you'd get used to it if you just tried it."

"Yuck!" William stuck out his tongue.

"You guys should see Jarrad trying to milk our cow," Andrew yelled, chucking. Jennifer began to laugh, and William rolled to the ground giggling and holding his belly, paying no attention to the dirt sticking to his clothes. "Sometimes . . . the stuff doesn't . . . doesn't even come out," Andrew went on, laughing so hard he could hardly talk. "And . . . and sometimes it sp—spurts and hits him smack . . . smack in the face."

"That's right," Jennifer hollered. "But all Jarrad does is make that silly little grin of his and keep right on squeezing those long things. I think he enjoys it." She laughed even louder.

As soon as they reached camp, they said a prayer, and Paul served pancakes. While they were cleaning up, John appeared and sat next to Mary. "Mary, I need your help," he said. "One of the brothers broke his ankle a little while ago. You're the only registered nurse in camp."

"But Quentin Price—"

"The good doctor's nowhere in sight. I suppose he's off fixing someone else. Will you come?"

"Certainly." Mary ran to the wagon and retrieved her medical kit. When she returned, she said to Steven, "Can you help?"

"I'd love to."

The children begged to accompany them. Steven looked at Mary, who nodded her approval. "Okay," she said to the children. "It'll be a good experience for you. But I don't want you to get in the way. Come on. Let's go!"

They followed John a quarter of a mile from camp to a small stream, where they came upon a middle-aged man lying on the ground moaning in great pain, a few yards from the water. Mary was relieved to see that the victim was conscious and that a second man was kneeling nearby, talking to him and holding a cloth against the wound. A crowd had gathered, but had shown enough sense to stand back so the victim could get air. Mary knelt beside the injured man and removed the cloth. A bone protruded through the skin near his ankle and the wound began to bleed. Immediately she reapplied the cloth. She noticed the shocked expression on the children's faces. It does look kind of scary, she thought.

"What's your name?" Mary asked the victim.

"Name's Judd Hawks."

"Are you married?"

"Nope," Judd's friend, Wesley Duke, said. "He's an old bachelor. I've been trying for years to get him to repent and accept one of those beautiful ladies who are always trying to wrap him up in the joyous bonds of matrimony—just like I am—but he doesn't seem to care if he goes to hell or not."

Mary smiled at Wesley's comment and the irritated look Judd threw him. "Wesley, why don't you hold this cloth against the wound again. You did a good job of slowing the bleeding before." Wesley did as he was asked.

"Judd, do you have any chest pains?" He shook his head, still scowling at Wesley. "Do you feel dizzy?" Another head shake. Mary checked his pulse as she watched his breathing, pleased that he didn't show signs of shock.

Mary turned to Steven and said, "Will you help?" As Steven moved into position beside the patient, she took a clean bandage from her kit. She handed it to her husband and said, "We need to apply direct pressure to stop the bleeding. Are your hands clean?"

Steven checked. "No."

She handed him a bar of soap and nodded toward the stream. "You can wash them over there."

Steven ran to the water and washed. He returned quickly, and Mary poured rubbing alcohol on his hands. She handed him the bandage and said, "Take it from the wrapper."

Wesley spoke up, "We was climbing around on those rocks over there when Judd slipped and fell." He pointed to a line of rocks which extended several hundred feet along the side of the stream. "I guess they was just too slippery."

"Evidently," Mary said. "Did he hit his head?"

"I don't think so."

"We can be grateful for that." She looked at Steven. "Ready?" Steven nodded. After removing the cloth, she poured alcohol on the wound. "Okay. Now hold the bandage against the wound."

While her husband held it, Mary checked the victim's airway, his breathing, and his pulse once more. Next she examined him for other injuries. When she had finished these important checks, she examined the wound. It began to ooze blood again, so she reapplied the cloth with her right hand and pressed the fingers of her left hand into the victim's groin, about one-third of the way across. She felt the underlying pulsation of the femoral artery—the arterial pressure point—and pushed against it firmly.

She called for the people standing nearby to bring blankets. Within minutes a woman brought several blankets, and Mary asked her to cover the top of the injured man's body with one of them. While Mary worked, she explained to Judd what she was doing and assured him that she expected Dr. Price to be there soon. Although he was still in pain, her kind words seemed to quiet him.

Six minutes later she asked Steven to hold the cloth against the wound because her right hand had started to ache. As she continued to apply pressure to the artery, she checked her patient again for any of the signs and symptoms of shock. She continued to apply pressure to the artery another five minutes and then checked the wound again. She smiled when she saw that the bleeding had almost stopped.

"Things are looking really good, Judd," Mary said. "All we have to do now is dress the wound and splint your leg. That should help with the pain."

After wrapping the wound with clean gauze, she checked the leg to see if it still had sensation and a normal pulse. Next she rolled up one of blankets tightly and gently placed it between his legs. It extended from his feet to several inches above his knees. After that, she tied the legs together with four lengths of cloth to stabilize the injured ankle. Steven was amazed at the speed and skill with which his wife worked.

"I think you can make a stretcher now to carry him back to his wagon. Please make sure you don't move the ankle, if possible."

"Thank you, sister. You're an angel of mercy," Judd declared gratefully.

Mary smiled as she patted him on the hand. She gave Wesley some final instructions on how to care for the patient and turned to her husband. "That's all I can do for him. The doctor will have to repair the injury when he shows up. We can go now. Can you come and visit for a while, John?"

John looked at his watch. "I suppose so, but Tania will be expecting me for lunch."

On the way back to their wagon, Steven put his arm around his wife and said, "He's right. You are an angel of mercy."

"Gee! That was awesome," William exclaimed. "For a moment I thought that old guy was going to bleed to death."

"Not with Mary around," Jennifer stated.

Steven detected a hint of pride in Jennifer's voice, and he was glad. His daughter was still jealous of the attention he showed Mary, but she seemed to be changing slowly. As for the boys, William remained reserved, while Andrew was already calling Mary "Mom." Steven noticed that Mary had a pleased look on her face.

As they approached the wagon, he caught sight of a second crowd. He sighed, figuring it must be another problem. Oh well, after the marvelous thing that happened to him that morning, he felt strong enough to face any challenge.

Forty people had gathered around a large old man resting on a stump. Most of the listeners were sitting on the ground, but some had plopped onto boulders or logs. A few lucky ones used folding chairs. Steven noticed that Paul, Jarrad, Leonard, and the Cartwrights had found places close to the visitor. Everyone seemed transfixed by the newcomer, who appeared to be a mountain man. His clothes resembled something from an old western film, except that they were incredibly worn and filthy. His ravaged hat was turned sideways after the manner of George "Gabby" Hayes, the old-time movie sidekick of Roy Rogers, and his gray beard flowed halfway down his chest. When he talked or grinned, which he did constantly, you could see that six front teeth were missing. In his left hand he grasped the barrel of a long-range Sharps buffalo rifle. Steven estimated that he was about fifty-eight years old. In spite of his age, his demeanor and rugged appearance suggested strength and vitality.

Paul and the other bachelors squatted close to the formidable old-timer. Seeing Steven and the others arrive, Paul said to the mountain man, "This is my brother Steven Christopher, the leader of the wagon train, and his wife Mary." He nodded toward John. "And this is my other brother, John. He's second in charge. The kids belong to Steven and Mary."

The visitor pulled himself off the stump and said, "Nice ta meet yuh. I'm Rutherford Johnston, Ruther for short." After shaking hands with Steven and John, he rotated toward Mary, took her hand daintily, leaned over gracefully, and kissed the back of her hand gently with puckered lips. Steven heard a light smack as the man's toothless mouth encountered her hand. "And good morning to you, Ma'am. Now that I sees yuh, I know why this day is gittin' so bright and sunshiny."

Steven and Mary looked at each other and grinned. Several of the people who sat nearby vacated their seats so Steven, Mary, and John could sit close to the guest.

After they talked about the weather and other polite things for a while, the old man said, "So is it true that every last one of yuh is Mormons?"

"Most of us, yes," Steven answered cautiously. He motioned to the Cartwrights. "However, Doug and Elizabeth here are Methodists."

Ruther shot the Cartwrights a toothless grin. "That's real nice. I like the Methodists. But don't that beat all! So many Mormons traveling all together up the highway, purdy as yuh please." Steven decided the man either had watched them arrive the day before or had examined their tracks to see which way they were going.

"Well, Ruther, you're more or less in Mormon country here. You know, the state of Utah. And Salt Lake City is only fourteen or fifteen miles west of here."

The old man replied, "Yep, I knows that. Even though I been livin' a long time in the mountains a hundred miles east of here, I still know this here's Mormon country. But the reason I was so surprised is that there's a heap of danger in the wilderness these days, and it seems strange to see all you folks campin' up here and traipsin' around without a care in the world. Where are yuh going? Don't yuh know it gets worse and worse as yuh go east?"

"What do you mean?" Steven asked.

"I mean, there ain't much food and water out there. This big highway is broke up—you know, big gaps and sinkholes and sech—in a thousand places. So they tell me. But that ain't the worst, not by a long shot."

"It isn't?"

"Heck no. There's savages out yonder. Both men and women."

"You mean, American Indians?"

The visitor guffawed. "Shucks. The Indians is downright genteel in comparison to the savages I'm talkin' about. They's nothing but wild brutes, without a humane conscience. Didn't yuh see what they done to the people in this valley, both Mormons and non-Mormons?"

Steven wanted to avoid this subject, but knew it was already too late. Douglas seemed to realize it also and said, "Yesterday we searched the communities east of here and found a lot of bodies. Mr. Johnston, were those people killed by the men you're talking about?"

"Well, first there was some bad floods which destroyed all kinds of property and a heap of people. I seen the floods coming, so I headed this way ta see if I could help. But then I seen those creatures from a distance. I used my binoculars and I could see 'em a comin' down from the mountains north of here. Musta been at least two hundred of 'em. I got out while the gittin' was good. Because of the disasters, the nice people livin' here wasn't prepared and didn't have a chance."

No one said a word for moment. Steven looked around. The fear of the crowd was evident. If only the old man had spoken to him about the massacre in private instead of making it public. Would the old-timer's report undermine the morale of the caravan? Or would it make the pioneers stop straying off into the countryside against the rules?

"Do you know who those people are?" John asked.

"The killers?"

"Yes."

"Yer durn tootin'. From what I see'd myself, and from what the mountain boys say, I've a purdy good idea. Some of 'em used ta be respectable people who lived in these parts. But most of 'em came from the cities west of here. Then, when all heck blew loose, and there was no control from the authorities, the people I'm a talkin' about just went crazy. Like everybody else, they ran into every kind of trial and privation and they couldn't handle 'em. When the goin' got tough, and there was fewer restraints, their baser instincts took over. That's the way I figure it."

"Do you know where they are now?" Steven asked.

"Don't rightly know fer sure, but I heard they set up their main camp near a mountain called Windy Knoll. That's about twenty-three miles northeast of here as the crow flies. But that's only one of their camps. It appears they move all over this region so they can plunder, murder, and rape every chance they git. I understand they have some trail bikes so the leaders can move around real fast when they need to. I broke bread with an old-timer last week who swore he saw a storage tank in one of their camps. It looked ta him like they was drawin' gas from it for their bikes. He was too afraid of them devils ta git close enough ta make sure."

"Doesn't our road lead us close to the area of Windy Knoll, Steve?" Mary asked.

"I think so, but I'm not sure."

Ruther said, "Are yuh stickin' to I-80?"

"Yes, for nearly nine hundred miles, if we can," Steven replied.

"Yuh don't say! I'll be a long-tailed bobcat. That brings me ta my first question. Where are yuh all going to?"

Steven asked himself whether he had blundered by revealing so much about their travel plans. "Maybe we can talk about that some other time if we get the chance. What about Mary's question? Do we go near the headquarters of the gang?"

"Purdy close. When yuh goes through Echo Canyon on I-80, you'll be about four miles from their main camp . . . Come ta think of it, it might be smart for yuh ta contemplate taking another route ta git ta wherever you're going if you kin find one."

All eyes turned to Steven.

After hesitating, he said, "We'll consider your suggestion tonight when the leaders of the wagon train meet."

Ruther reached into his pocket for a chew of tobacco, but changed his mind and withdrew an empty hand. "Yuh know, the idea keeps a comin' to me that I ain't got nothin' special ta do in the next little while, so if you folks would like a bit of company, I might travel with yuh for a spell. You know, ta show yuh some trails and maybe make a few wilderness-type suggestions."

Steven wasn't fooled. He looked into the man's eyes and saw his worried look. You never knew what form human goodness might take. "I'm sure I speak for everybody when I say you are most welcome," he said. "However, what if we run into the gangs? Aren't you afraid of what might happen?"

"Yes siree! I'm scared plumb out of my wits, after seeing what they done." Then, with a twinkle in his eye, he added, "But sometimes a man has got ta take his fear into hand. Besides, I'm a hopin' ta get more of that female cookin'."

Everyone laughed.

"But thar's somethin' else I was wonderin' about." Ruther's face took on a subtle grin.

"What's that?" Paul asked.

"Well, when I first got here, I saw a shockin' sight."

"A shocking sight?" Steven said.

"I don't know if yuh noticed it, Mr. Christopher, but you've got a lot of people here who look like they've spent a lot of time livin' high on the hog. Those folks are sportin' on their very person enough vittles ta last them for the next three months. They shouldn't have ta eat a durn thing for the rest of your trip. The only trouble is, I wonder what will happen when they hit some really rough country or have ta run fer their lives."

"This isn't rough country?" John asked.

"Shucks, young feller. It ain't nothin' here like it is up the road a piece."

Steven laughed. "Mr. Johnston, I have confidence in our people. They'll become fit as they travel and—"

"And the greenhorns," Ruther went on as if he hadn't heard. "So many people wearin' the wrong clothes, and—"

"Maybe you can help us with those things," Douglas said.

Steven looked at his watch. "Listen. It's almost noon. Can you eat lunch with us, Mr. Johnston?"

"I'd be much obliged. But call me Ruther, young feller."

During lunch everyone delighted in the company of the mountain man, and it was clear that he enjoyed entrancing his listeners with his anecdotes about his experiences in the mountains. Mary left for fifteen minutes and returned to tell Steven that Dr. Price had reset the ankle of Judd Hawks, and the man was doing well. The only problem was that the resetting had been extremely painful because there were no anesthetics, and the small supply of pain killers had been exhausted during the first three days of travel.

The rest of the day, the new pioneers relaxed and nursed their aching bodies. Although the children had shown signs of distress the previous day, it took only one night of sleep to renew their spirits and bodies. After they completed their assigned chores, they flew into action, organizing races and games like "steal the bacon" and "capture the flag." Steven was careful to make sure that John had posted a double guard to protect the camp.

Since Steven was concerned about the dangers ahead on I-80, he visited John's wagon in the afternoon to use the only transceiver radio in the camp. He played with the frequencies for a few minutes, and finally reached Salt Lake City. He waited until they brought the prophet, Josiah Smith, to the set at the other end. Then he told the church leader his concerns. Josiah counseled him to go to God in prayer because he had the right to obtain revelation for his stewardship, which at this time was Pioneer One. The prophet suggested that he not change the preestablished route of the wagon train, but that he should get the final answer on that matter from the Lord himself.

Because of his conversation with the prophet, Steven told Mary that he had decided to return to the secluded spot he had visited early that morning. She was deeply concerned for his safety, but said nothing. Steven became excited as he hurried to the place which was sacred to him now. He hoped that perhaps he might feel at least a small measure of the ecstasy he had experienced before. And he wasn't disappointed. After praying for some time, he arose and returned to the camp. He knew that he had received the answer he needed.

Chapter 4

Doctor Sarad Jalil, head of the Jalil Medical Clinic in Calcutta, India, sat at his desk trying to wake up after a sleepless night. He had already consumed two cups of coffee, but his mind was still muddled. He poured himself another cup and drank it rapidly. Maybe a third shot of caffeine would do the trick. It was eight in the morning and he needed to find the strength to face the nightmare once again. Many lives were depending on him. He heard the door to his tiny office open, and he looked up to see his secretary.

"Doctor?" the secretary said in Hindi. Even though she lived in a great city, the secretary wore the traditional sari, which was a straight piece of colored cloth draped around her body as a long dress.

"Yes, Bansuri," he replied in the same language.

"It's time for your rounds."

"I know, I know," Sarad said wearily.

"Didn't you get any sleep last night?"

"I was in bed five hours, but I doubt that I got more than two hours of good sleep."

At two in the morning Bansuri herself had insisted that Sarad leave the wards for some rest. She caught sight of the blanket and pillow on his couch. "But you didn't go home. How many times have I told you that you can't sleep properly on that tiny couch? And I see you've been drinking coffee again. As a doctor, you should know coffee will kill you."

"I know, I know. I've heard this a thousand times before. You talk like my mother."

"Well, somebody has to watch out for you. You won't do it yourself."

"Are there many new patients?"

"Yes, doctor. Dozens and dozens. And more coming in all the time."

Sarad sighed deeply. "How many deaths from last night?"

"The nurses report that twenty patients died after you left."

"How many does that make since the beginning of the plague?"

Bansuri consulted a notebook she carried with her everywhere and made some quick calculations. "Twelve hundred and ninety-six."

Sarad couldn't believe it. Twelve hundred and ninety-six deaths in one small hospital in less than three months, and the incidence of infection was increasing every day. He wondered how many people had died in the entire city of Calcutta, with a population of fifteen million people.

"Remember that the news people will be here at nine."

"News people?"

"Yes, yes. I told you about them last night when I made you stop working."

Sarad remembered she had told him something unusual last night, but he still couldn't get his mind to work right. "Uh, yes, that's right . . . Why don't you go over it again? I was pretty beat last night."

"Like I already said, the government gave the BBC permission to send a news team here to cover the plague first hand."

"Why on earth did they pick my clinic?" Sarad groaned. "We're nothing but a tiny facility in the suburbs."

"Well, who else are they going to choose? Most of the big hospitals in the city still haven't recovered from that sneak air raid from Bangladesh last month. You know that."

Every time Sarad thought about the air raid, he seethed inside. "Fifty thousand people slaughtered and billions in property damage! Those ungrateful Muslims. We helped them gain independence from their Pakistani brothers in 1971, and that's how they repay us." Sarad hesitated as horrible scenes from the past raced through his mind . . . "Still, I'm sure some of the big hospitals are back in service by this time. The reporters should go there."

"Frankly, sir, I don't know why they're coming here . . . Are you ready, doctor?"

Sarad supposed that the caffeine in his system had finally reached sufficient levels, because his mind was clearing and he was starting to feel better. "What is my staff for today?"

"Two RNs, four LPNs, and six volunteers. That's all I could round up."

Twelve people to help treat fifty or sixty very sick patients. "All right. I'm ready, I guess."

Sarad hurried to the first ward. Thirty patients were lying in four rows, taking up all the available space. Some occupied cots, but most had been laid on floor mats. The aisles which permitted access to each patient were no more than three feet wide. The noise and the stench were terrible! Sarad knew that by eleven the heat would reach more than a hundred degrees in the room, and the situation would become almost unbearable. Even now the temperature was eighty-five. There were only two small fans, one at each end of the ward, and their effect was scarcely noticeable. Already six of his assistants were busy laboring over six victims. They looked up when he entered the room, and one motioned to him. He rushed to her side, put on protective gloves, and began to work.

An hour later he had just finished clearing a patient's lungs of vomit when he heard a sudden commotion at the entrance to the ward. A tall man with red hair and a short mustache bore down upon him, followed by a woman in Levis and a white blouse and a long-haired hippy carrying a camera. So this is the crack news team from the BBC? Sarad thought.

"Dr. Sarad Jalil?" the tall man said in English.

"Yes."

"I'm Edward Courtland. The reporter from the BBC." He held out his hand. Sarad removed his right glove, and the reporter shook it warmly. As Sarad put his glove back on, he noticed that Courtland didn't bother introducing his assistants. The hippy lifted the camera to his shoulder, put his eye to the viewfinder, and started to pan the ward.

"Nice to meet you," Sarad replied, struggling to be friendly. He gestured toward a young RN standing nearby. She wore a white uniform and had short black hair. "This is Amy Jacobs, one of my nurses. She's an American."

Courtland glanced at the nurse and said to her, "Ah, yes. My condolences. No way to get home these days, is there? Not that it would be wise to go there." Without waiting for a reply, he looked around the ward and said, "So these people are victims of the dreaded cholera."

"Yes, they are," Sarad said irritably.

"Doctor, I understand that in the last five months cholera has been spreading throughout Southern Asia. Is that right?"

"Yes. And there are signs it is moving north and east."

"So I suppose we could call it a pandemic."

"Yes, of course."

"Well, doctor, do you mind if we do an interview at this time?"

Sarad thought that the interview had already begun two minutes ago. One of the patients nearby began to retch violently.

Courtland nodded toward the sufferer and said, "Dr. Jalil, why don't you tell us what is going on here?"

Sarad moved to the noisy, suffering victim. "Well—"

"Are you ready, Patrick?" Courtland said to the cameraman, who ceased panning and pointed the camera at Courtland. "Good. This is Edward Courtland of the BBC, reporting from a small hospital in a suburb of Calcutta, India. Dr. Sarad Jalil and his small staff run this facility with almost no modern equipment or the medicines and supplies that we Europeans consider so essential for good medical care. Every day Dr. Jalil and his staff are faced with almost insurmountable problems as they struggle to snatch hundreds of unfortunate human beings from the clutches of one of the most dreaded diseases in the history of mankind—cholera. And they perform this labor of love at the risk of their own lives. Dr. Jalil is a modest man, but in my estimation he's one of the true heroes of our times."

Sarad was angry and wanted to tell these invaders that his facilities were not all that inadequate, that their lives were probably not at risk, and that he was certainly no hero. Then he stopped himself. It suddenly occurred to him that through this interview he might be able to inspire people from the West to supply him with the intravenous equipment he needed to treat his patients properly.

"Doctor, will you please tell our viewers what is going on here with this patient?" Courtland moved aside so the camera could get a good shot of a middle-aged man lying on the floor, who was struggling to vomit, but couldn't. The American nurse had pushed him upright and was trying to make him swallow a clear liquid from a bottle.

Sarad said, "Well, this is one of the symptoms of cholera. The victim vomits or retches continually. Very often nothing comes out of his mouth."

"Why don't you start at the beginning, doctor? Tell our viewers what causes this illness."

"It is caused by a comma-shaped bacterium called Vibrio cholerae which is ingested by the victim in food or water."

"But how does the germ get into the water or food?" Courtland asked.

"Usually the water supply is contaminated in some way by human feces. In our area the sewer system was damaged in the recent war with Pakistan, and waste materials seeped into our wells and tap water. The hundreds of bombs and mortars have completely disrupted our essential services. You realize, of course, that a short time ago India and Pakistan attacked each other. Four nuclear bombs were—"

"Yes, of course," Courtland interrupted flippantly.

"That's why cholera is widespread in both countries."

The man on the mat behind them pushed the bottle away from his mouth and vomited a stream of liquid over the lower part of his body.

Visibly shocked and disgusted by this scene, Courtland's eyes bulged, and he struck his mouth with the microphone as he jerked it toward himself to speak. "No doubt. But, doctor, tell us what this deadly germ does in the body."

"If it's able to survive the natural acids of the stomach, which it often is, it produces toxins which cause the intestine to secrete huge amounts of water and salt. The result is dizziness, sweating, severe diarrhea, vomiting, loss of body salts, and dehydration. The onset of the disease is very rapid. Because of the loss of body fluids, the victim loses weight and his skin hangs on his body as if he had aged fifty years in a matter of an hour or two. His body goes into spasms and he has severe pain in his limbs. The patient becomes desperately thirsty. But the retching and vomiting make it extremely difficult for him to drink. Eventually, many areas of his body turn blue, and then almost black. If he does not receive proper treatment, he will go into a coma and die. The entire process normally takes about twenty-four hours."

The nurse behind them was trying to get more fluid into the victim, but he retched so uncontrollably that she couldn't get the water to stay down.

Sarad noticed that Courtland looked ill, and the two assistants behind him were also very pale. "But there . . . there is a treatment?" Courtland stammered. "You can cure this disease?"

"Yes, in many instances. There has been a vaccine for cholera since 1893, but it isn't effective against the mutated strain we face today."

"Mutated strain?"

"Yes. The bacterium Vibrio cholerae has mutated several times since it first came out of the Ganges River not far from here in 1817. The current strain is much more virulent."

Sarad saw that Courtland was less cocky and more nervous than he had been at first. "So how do you treat the disease?" He said uneasily.

"In the time-honored way, for the most part. If we can. We dissolve a mixture of salt and sugar into a liter of pure water, and try to get the victim to ingest it. The government supplies us with hundreds of small plastic bags with the right mixture of ingredients. Sometimes we have to mix the basic ingredients ourselves. It is one teaspoon of salt to four teaspoons of sugar. The sugar is needed mostly to make the salts acceptable to the gut. We should give the patient roughly the same amount of liquid as he loses in diarrhea, but that's difficult for us to keep track of when we have so many patients. The problem is, the current strain of cholera causes so much retching and vomiting that we find it very difficult to give the patient sufficient liquids by mouth."

"But aren't there better ways to treat them? It seems terribly ineffective to try to force liquids down their throats."

"Yes, there are better ways," Sarad said. Seeing the Englishman's ignorance, Sarad wondered if it would do any good to say that India needed hundreds of millions of dollars for intravenous equipment, new vaccines, and premixed solutions, without which 900,000 victims were in grave danger of losing their lives. He pointed to one side of the room where several patients were attached to tubes. "We could be more effective in saving these wretched souls, if we had the intravenous equipment we so desperately need."

"Well," Courtland said, partly recovered from his shock. "I'm sure that thousands of our viewers will respond to your terrible predicament, now that you've uttered such a passionate plea on international television . . . But, doctor, I see you're wearing gloves. Is that your only protection from the bacterium while you are treating your patients?"

"Yes, we always use plastic gloves. Also, we boil the water we use and we cook our food thoroughly. You see, our patients constantly pass stools which look like rice water, but it does not smell. That's one of the sure signs that the disease is cholera. The problem is, when the stool dries on the bedding and the patient's clothes, it becomes practically invisible. So it's easy for us to soil our hands without realizing it and ingest the dangerous contagion with our food. We have to be very, very careful."

"I can see the problem." After pausing a moment, the reporter continued, "Dr. Jalil, did you say that this plague was caused by damaged sewers leaking polluted water into the culinary water system?"

"No one knows for sure, but that's our best guess."

"Is it possible that there could be some other cause?"

"I suppose it is possible, but—"

"Yes, doctor, it is possible. And we have it from other sources—sources which have proven their reliability in the past—that it is not unlikely that this terrible plague was planted in the water systems of many Indian cities by entities that have declared themselves to be enemies of India." Courtland looked directly into the camera, "Now we hear from an expert in this field, Dr. Sarad Jalil, who confirms that such suspicions are possible, even probable."

Sarad was startled. "But I—"

"Thank you, doctor, for that remarkable revelation. Now we return you to the offices of BBC news. This is Edward Courtland reporting from Calcutta on the deadly—and suspicious—spread of cholera in India." Courtland smiled with satisfaction as he handed the mike back to his female assistant. "Okay, people, that's a wrap." Without another glance at Dr. Jalil and the patients suffering around them, the crack news team rushed from the hospital ward.

Sarad watched them go. Once again, his belief was confirmed. The leftist-liberal news media were nothing but corrupt social and political activists. Nevertheless, he prayed that someone out there cared enough to help the real people suffering from cholera.

Cholera was now the second of two major pandemics wreaking havoc on the earth. The avian flu, called the H6N1 virus, had begun nine months earlier in San Diego, and had already killed an estimated 125 million people. It was reported that deaths from cholera, which appeared only five months ago, would soon reach 95 million. So far, there was no end in sight.

It was dark and silent in Kansas City. Even in daylight it was dangerous to venture forth, but at night only the most foolish or the hungriest dared to risk it. And the gang was very hungry. Led by Silas Kitch, nine shadows slipped noiselessly down Sixth Street, looking anxiously for prey. Because of a full moon they could see where they were going, but with some difficulty. From time to time, Silas saw a dim light high up in some apartment. No use messing with that kind of stuff. The occupants had probably installed bars on the windows and had barricaded the door. Their kids would be lying around on the floors wrapped in dirty blankets, and the adults would be playing cards or reading some religious junk to give themselves a glimmer of hope for the future. And they always had plenty of weapons around to bolster that hope.

That was pretty much the way it had been every time he and the boys had blasted their way into those minifortresses and satisfied their hunger. But recently, it had cost them a lot of blood and two lives. No, what they needed was easier targets. Like those two fools they had beaten up about a year ago in Provo behind that market. Silas figured he should have killed those dudes, instead of just taking their wallets and their car. But these days nobody got off so easily, because the gang had much greater needs. He looked over the city and saw small fires burning everywhere, and he realized that his fellow anarchists would soon burn everything. In a week or so the gang would have to leave Kansas City and seek better pickings elsewhere.

"Silas, where's that mark you was talkin' about?" one of his boys whined. "I'm dying for a smoke, and if I don't get something to eat soon, I'm going to fall on my face."

"Shut up, Fats. It's not far now. You can eat when we get back." The gang called him Fats, an ironic nickname, because he was six feet two and weighed only a hundred and thirty pounds.

The going was rough. They had to fight their way through debris, scramble in and out of craters in the street, and crawl over smoldering vehicles and piles of twisted metal. Kansas City sure ain't as pretty as it used to be, Silas thought with amusement. Now and then they came across a body and stepped over it without even checking to see if the person was still alive. It was dangerous to check rotting corpses. Anyway it was probably just another casualty of the war for survival where friends and family members murdered one another for a can of cat food. Or maybe the plague got him.

They walked another ten minutes until they came to a four-story apartment building, which was partly demolished.

"This is it," Silas said softly. "Marny says the guy comes out of that building at 9:30 nearly every night. The girl's always with him."

After waiting fifteen minutes, Silas saw two figures at the entrance to the building. They stood in the doorway for a while, then moved around to the side of the building. They stopped at a Dumpster in the alley, and the girl climbed in. A short time later, she crawled out, and the two walked past the front of the building and down the dark street. Silas supposed they had checked the Dumpster for food and, finding nothing, intended to keep on searching. Silas waved his gang forward, and within a minute they had swooped down upon their victims.

"Hold it, buddy," Silas snarled at the man, who whirled to face the sudden threat. The little bald man, who seemed about fifty and was putting on weight, trembled with fear. The girl moved close to him for protection. Silas guessed that she was fourteen or fifteen years old. The man put his arm around his daughter and said, "What do you want? I have nothing of value."

Silas said, "Of course you do, old man. You've got the girl."

"No, please!"

"Look, we know you lend her out just about every night to any guy who can give yuh a bit of grub."

"No. I'd never do such a thing."

"Don't lie to me, man. I hate it when people lie to me. One of my boys seen yuh do it." The little man acted as though someone had hit him with a two-by-four, and the girl began to weep. "Take it easy, both of yuh," Silas snarled. "We ain't going to hurt nobody. We want to make yuh the same deal. The girl for food. She's not for all of us, I promise. I'm the only one who'll touch her."

"No, no, I beg you. This isn't right!" It was clear that the father didn't believe Silas for a moment.

Several of the gang members pulled out knives and guns to intimidate their victims. Fats seized him by the collar, and screamed, "You ain't got no choice, punk. We're taking her."

Silas handed the man a sack of food and pulled his daughter from his grasp. "Don't worry, old man, I'll return her when I'm done."

Silas dragged the girl down the street, and his boys swaggered after him, whooping with delight. They knew all of them would have their chance with her. They had done the same many times before, and when they became tired of their victims, they murdered them without mercy. The father cried out pitifully and tried to follow them, but Fats knocked him out with a blow to the side of the head. He picked up the small sack of food and stuck it in his backpack without the others noticing it.

"Why did yuh give him the groceries, Silas?" one of the hoods said to the leader, as they headed for their hideout on the outskirts of town.

"Hey, man, I got my integrity to think about. A deal is a deal. Maybe I'll even return this little girl after a few days, if I can keep you slobs from killing her. Marny says he's got another daughter and a wife who ain't all that bad."

❦

Because Kansas City had become such a dangerous place, three decent families desperately hoped to reach Wyandotte County Park, seven miles west of the city, before daylight. They knew it would not be easy to escape without risking their lives.

By Wednesday morning, April 19, the families had decided to leave the city together, to find food and a refuge from the violence. Since the six adults and eight children lived in the same apartment building, they had come to know and trust one another. During the day on Wednesday, they had pooled their supplies and weapons, determined to leave as soon as night fell upon the city.

Noel Luce was excited and relieved that they were finally doing something. At nineteen he was a young man of action, and he hated to sit around and do nothing but—as he saw it—whine about their situation. And he certainly wasn't afraid. After all, he was six feet tall, weighed a hundred eighty pounds, and had a black belt in wado-ryu karate.

The families waited until ten in the evening and then slipped out of their building. Noel acted as the lookout for the fugitives and was sure that no one had seen them leave. He felt marvelous to be outside at last after being holed up so many months in the tiny apartment, sneaking out occasionally with one or two of the men, at great risk, to seek the essentials of life. Lugging heavy bundles, the fourteen people headed immediately for the outskirts of the city.

They stopped and hid when Noel informed them that danger was near, and they started off again when he said it was safe to move on.

This worked well enough until a pack of animals wearing leather jackets and baggy, faded Levis surged around a building not far from them. Noel urged his charges to move back behind a nearby fence, but it was too late. With a shout of triumph, the hoodlums rushed forward and surrounded them, brandishing knives and guns. The fathers quickly trained three rifles on the intruders to keep them at bay.

"Well, well, what do we have here?" one of the savages said, as he waved a twelve-inch hunting knife back and forth. He was tall and skinny and the only thug wearing a black T-shirt instead of a leather jacket. His long unkempt hair, dirty teeth, and bushy face made a disgusting sight. Noel was amazed to see that his skinny arms were covered with tattoos of snakes and naked women. Then another thug, the leader of the band, waltzed through the ring of marauders, pulling behind him on a tether a fragile, tear-stained girl.

Silas Kitch eyed the weapons in the hands of his would-be victims and said, "I see you've found some new friends, Fats."

Noel's father, Anthony Luce, pointed his rifle at Silas. "Back off now, and no one will get hurt."

Silas raised his left hand in the air as a gesture of peace. "Hey, man, we don't want no trouble. Give us food and a few packs of cigarettes, and we'll move on. To show our good will, and to make sure there ain't no accidents, we'll throw our weapons on the ground. Right, boys?" The gang members grunted their agreement. "And then you do the same. You look like good Christian people to me, and I'm sure you don't want to see your fellow man starve." The girl standing next to Silas said nothing, but her eyes revealed her terror.

"Don't trust him, Dad," Noel cried.

"Hey! What's this world coming to when people can't trust each other?" Silas said fawningly. "We're victims of the circumstances too. Look, man, if you don't help us, we ain't got no choice. We'll do what we must to survive. Even if it means a little violence. You know how it is." While Silas was talking, one of his cronies moved behind the family group, who focused their attention on the leader. A father stood facing toward the rear to watch their back, but from time to time he turned his head to the front, straining to hear Silas.

After consulting in whispers with the other parents, Anthony said, "We can give you a small amount of food and four packs of cigarettes, but that's all. But we intend to hold on to our weapons."

"Dad, don't listen to him," Noel said. "Don't give them anything." He couldn't believe his father was so gullible.

His face devoid of emotion, Silas stared into Anthony's eyes as he took a pistol from his belt with his left hand and laid it on the street. His friends did the same at once. Each had several weapons, and in seconds the street surrounding the families was littered with rifles, knives, pistols, two numbchucks, and one Uzi. Seeing this apparent display of sincerity, Mr. Luce cautiously collected the packs of cigarettes and several small bags of food. Next he stepped forward to place them in front of Silas, lowering slightly the muzzle of his rifle.

At that moment, the gang member who had moved up behind the families leaped forward and slammed into two fathers standing close together. Instantly three other thugs pounced on the men, and Silas sprang toward Anthony, reaching him before he could raise his weapon. He forced the rifle barrel downward and punched his knee into the father's groin. Anthony dropped to the ground like a stone, groaning in agony. Gloating merrily, the thugs scooped up their weapons and trained them on their helpless victims. During the melee, the kidnapped girl bolted, but one of the thugs grabbed her.

Silas glared at his prisoners with hatred. "Now you'll all pay."

"Please let us go," one of the fathers said. "We'll give you everything we have."

"Listen, man, all we have to do is kill you and take what we want. Nobody stands up to me and gets away with it." He looked at Noel's thirteen-year-old sister and grinned wickedly. "Maybe if you people beg, we'll take that sweet young thing with us instead of killing her." Then he noticed Noel staring at him. Slithering up to him, Silas leaned into his face. "And you, pretty boy, I'm going to cut you up into little pieces."

With surprising calm, Noel said, "You're just a little punk coward."

For a moment Silas was stunned at those bold words. Then with eyes blazing he said, "What did you call me, buddy?"

"Little punk coward. You wouldn't dare face me one on one."

"Why you!" Silas dropped his knife, leaped forward, and swung his right fist at Noel's jaw.

Faster than the eye can see, Noel blocked the blow. Then he reached out with both arms, grabbed the thug by the head and neck, spun him around, and applied pressure to his Adam's apple. It was a killing hold that Noel had learned in karate, and applied even partially, it dealt excruciating pain to the victim. Since Noel was extremely strong, Silas was helpless in his arms. The gang leader's stifled groans and ghastly appearance showed everyone that his life was in serious danger.

"Come one step closer, and he dies," Noel said to the gang. None of them budged. Next Noel spoke to Silas. "In a second I'm going to release my grip a bit on your throat, and you're going to tell these creeps to leave. If you don't, I'll kill you. Since you were going to kill us anyway, I have no choice."

When Noel relaxed his grip a little, Silas began to struggle and croak. Instantly, Noel tightened his hold, and his captive uttered a muffled screech, squirming like a fish out of water. "You can't escape, tough guy. You'd better believe that I can kill you with one motion if I want to. So let's try it again. And you'd better do it right this time. Here's the rules: your boys leave now, without weapons, hostages, or food." He shouted this for all the gang to hear. Noel's family and friends were too stunned and afraid to help him.

Noel loosened his hold. Silas choked for a moment, but at last rasped, "Okay, boys . . . do like . . . like he says. Go—quick."

After briefly gawking at each other in confusion, the thugs slipped away. When they had disappeared, Noel released Silas, who fell to the street, moaning, choking, and struggling for breath. Walking up to him calmly, Noel knocked him out with a single blow to the chin. Immediately Noel's family and friends surrounded him and expressed their happiness and gratitude. Then they collected the gang's weapons, stashed them in a nearby ruin, and hurried away, fearing the gang might return. One of the mothers put her arm around the rescued girl and led her toward their place of safety.

Chapter 5

After dinner, Steven and Mary read scriptures with the children. At eight Steven met with the other caravan leaders. They held this meeting several times a week in order to resolve problems in the wagon train. Tonight, however, Steven also invited Dr. Quentin Price, Ruther Johnston, and the three bachelors. He hoped the mountain man might be able to give them valuable insights on the trail ahead. After they had discussed routine matters, Steven brought up a problem which concerned him greatly.

"I'm worried about the health of our people," he said. "Many have several ailments and are in poor physical condition. Mr. Johnston here said something today which made me realize how serious the problem is. At the time we were planning this trek, the prophet warned me to tell the people of Pioneer One to prepare themselves spiritually and physically. That's why the leaders, with the help of Dr. Price, gave them general ideas on how to improve their health and fitness. We left it up to them to decide exactly how they should do this. Now I'm afraid we made a mistake in not giving them more detailed advice."

Quentin said, "I think the counsel we gave was good. The people knew what to do, but many didn't do it. Now the only thing we can do is repeat the advice we already gave. They should eat nutritious food and avoid junk food and treats. Even though these things are hard to find these days, I saw many people in Provo eating homemade food which got awfully close to refined, manufactured foods. The second thing they can do is to cut down the amount of food they consume. That will improve their health and also ration our supplies. My last suggestion is to exercise. Of course, they'll get that automatically on this trip."

Steven replied, "Okay, I'll remind the pioneers of your advice again. As soon as possible." He hesitated. "You mentioned rationing. The problem of our general food supply has worried me as much as health and fitness. It would be a disaster if we ran out of provisions before we reach Missouri. But when I travel through our camps, I see people eating a lot more than they probably should. If this continues, we may have to institute rationing." Steven felt a twinge of embarrassment. "But I have to admit that I'm not a very good example. This morning I had pancakes smothered in butter and maple syrup."

"That was my fault," Paul admitted.

Mary put in, "What about our nursing mothers? I don't see how they can go on a starvation diet."

Quentin replied, "I didn't say people should starve themselves. Just reduce their calories by eating less. Nursing mothers, of course, need special consideration."

Jasper Potter, one of the colonels, said, "We may have to gather the food supplies into specific wagons and ration it like the early pioneers did."

Steven placed another log on the fire. "Well, you may remember that we leaders discussed that idea a month before we left Provo and decided that our caravan was so large that such a procedure would be impractical."

John said, "Still, it may become necessary to implement some form of rationing soon if our people don't take themselves into hand. As you remember, Steve, I was in favor of rationing from the beginning."

"Yes, I remember, and you may be right. I suppose I turned the idea down not only because of the size of Pioneer One, but also because it sounded too much like controlling the lives of other people. That's completely against my nature."

"Colonel Potter said, "You're probably right in theory, Steve. But in the real world you sometimes need to take firm measures when things get desperate."

Steven looked at the mountain man. "What do you think we should do, Mr. Johnston?"

"Like I said, call me Ruther . . . Well, let me see now. I really ain't got no say in this here group, but if I was in charge, I'd probably tell them what's what, and if they wasn't smart enough ta watch out for theirselves, they'd just have ta kick the ole bucket and leave fer the great beyond. I would have done my job . . . But I suspect yuh cain't look at it that way, Steve, so you'll have ta do the obvious."

Steven felt a sudden liking for the rough old hillbilly. "Which is?"

"Firstly, read 'em the gospel of vittles. Threaten a tad. Secondly, watch 'em fer a few days. Thirdly, start rationin' if they don't shape up."

Everyone laughed, and Steven said, "That seems like a wise course, Mr. Johnston—I mean Ruther. Do the rest of you agree?"

"Yes," came a chorus of voices.

"Okay, is there anything else we need to take up?" Steven asked.

"Yes," John said. "What about Ruther's suggestion this morning about taking another route to Missouri? You know, to avoid the gangs in the mountains?"

They discussed different routes for a while, but there were important reservations concerning them all. Still, several brothers maintained the position that it was vital to take almost any available route to avoid the animals who would callously murder their fellow human beings, as the gangs had done to the citizens of this mountain valley.

Finally, Steven said, "I appreciate your ideas. But it seems to me that the alternate routes which have been suggested are either impassable or would involve days or weeks of delay. So I've decided to continue on I-80. I want you to know that I've prayed a great deal about this and also talked with the Brethren in Salt Lake. Any questions? No? Okay, I guess that's it for tonight. Please circulate the message that the morning bugle will sound at six thirty, and that at eight I would like everyone to gather at the center of the encampment for announcements."

The meeting concluded after a prayer. Steven, Mary, Ruther, Paul, and the two bachelors remained at the fire to talk. Before long, Douglas and Elizabeth Cartwright joined them.

"Can I ask you folks a question?" Ruther said, after a moment of silence. Several nodded their approval. "Let me see now. How can I put this delicate like? Yuh sees, I'm an old-time Baptist. Of course, I ain't been ta church in years, unless yuh consider these mountains ta be a kinda church. But every time I run into other Baptists in these parts, they somehow end up talking about the Mormons, and it ain't always what you'd call flatterin'." He paused, evidently not knowing how to proceed.

"Go on, Ruther," Steven said.

"Well, what those Baptists always seem ta say is that Mormons really ain't Christians."

"You mean they think Mormons aren't good Christians?" Elizabeth asked.

"No! They say Mormons ain't Christians at all, not one little bit."

Several of the others shrugged but said nothing. Steven saw that Ruther's face took on a mischievous look, and he wondered how much this man really accepted the Baptists' point of view.

"What I want ta know is what I should tell my fellow Baptists when they talk like that."

No one seemed willing to get into such a discussion. Steven smiled and looked around. "Well, folks, what should he tell them?"

After a moment of silence, John said, "Ruther, I've always liked the Baptists because I think they're good people, and most appear to love the Lord. But I have to point out that churches and individuals have been saying all kinds of things about our religion from the very beginning, and most of those things have been misrepresentations. Yet nothing they've said has ever stopped our church from growing and accomplishing its mission. So please don't think me rude when I ask you why we should care what the Baptists think."

"I understand what you're saying, young feller, and yuh make a good point. But fer my benefit, what should I tell my fellow Baptists?"

Steven answered, "Before these guys answer your question, Ruther, I'd like to ask you a question."

"You betcha."

"Why is it that some Baptist writers profess to expose the errors of Catholics, Jews, Jehovah's Witnesses, and Mormons out of Christian love, but at the same time they develop their ideas in such an unkind spirit?"

Ruther squirmed. "I see what you're gittin' at." Steven guessed that Ruther had noticed the same weakness in Baptist books. "Believe you me, I'm plannin' on makin' yer point ta my friends the moment I sees 'em. I sure do expect they'll squirm some. Listen, yuh don't have ta answer my question if yuh don't want ta. I understand completely."

"No, we want to answer," Steven said. "I just hope I haven't offended you."

"Land sakes! No. Takes more than a little kick in the pants ta make me run."

When the laughter died, Paul said, "Let me say that the Baptists are right. Mormons are not Christians."

Everyone was startled, and most of all Ruther. "What! You say they're not?"

"No, we're not Christians according to the way the Baptists define the word 'Christian.' But we are Christians according to how we define the term."

"Okay . . ." Ruther said, looking a bit confused.

Paul continued. "So what is your definition of a Christian?" Steven was amused at how Paul was leading Ruther on.

"Well, let me see now. A Christian is somebody who believes in Christ."

"Okay, we do that."

"And he tries ta follow Christ's way of life."

"Okay, we do that. So are we Christians yet?"

"No, yuh have ta believe in the true Christ. Yuh have ta understand his real nature." Ruther was getting warmed up now. "Yuh have ta believe he's an aspect or a manifestation of the one God. Yuh have ta believe men can only be saved by his divine grace, and not by works lest any man boast."

"I see. You mean we have to accept the doctrines of the Baptists in order to be Christians."

"Well . . . yes. How can yuh be a true Christian if yuh don't believe in the true Christ?"

"What would you say if I told I can prove that those doctrines are false? If I can prove the Baptist doctrines on the nature of Christ and on grace are not scriptural, will you let us be Christians then?"

"Well, uh, yes, I suppose. But that might be a real high mountain ta climb. Yuh might of grabbed a mountain lion by the tail."

Steven said, "That's one of the reasons we hope you stay with our wagon train as long as you can. We can have fun trying to change your beliefs."

The group roared. Even Ruther got a gleam in his eye. "Yes siree, it might be fun at that. Of course, there's always the danger I might convert you instead."

Steven broke into a grin. "You'll never know unless you stick around to find out. And, Ruther, even if we could prove to you beyond any doubt that the Baptist doctrines regarding the nature of Christ are wrong, we'd still accept you as a Christian, and you wouldn't even have to become a Mormon."

Ruther gave Steven a toothless grin. "Why that thar is downright neighborly of yuh, Steve. How is it that yuh kin do that?"

"Because our definition of the term 'Christian' is fairly general. We believe that anyone who sincerely believes in Jesus Christ is a Christian, no matter what church he belongs to."

Steven saw that Ruther became silent suddenly, and he wondered if he had touched the old man's heart.

After the friends talked another hour at the fireside, they got up and went to their own wagons. Paul had invited Ruther to sleep in the bachelors' wagon. At first Ruther refused outright, declaring that he'd prefer to sleep under God's stars. But when Paul had promised him some good religious debates, the old-timer chuckled and accepted immediately. When Mary and Steven climbed into their wagon, they saw that the children were still awake. It took another half hour to get them to sleep.

"We sure don't have much privacy in this wagon, do we?" Steven said with a touch of irritation. "Newlyweds deserve to have privacy."

"Sweetheart, do you want to sleep under the wagon tonight?"

"Yeah right. Hey, I have an idea. Why don't we put the kids under the wagon, and we stay in the wagon?"

Mary let out a muffled laugh at her husband's little joke. "I know. We could leave the kids here and set up the tent."

Steven searched madly for the tent. Fifteen minutes later they had erected the tent and snuggled together in privacy.

"This is great," Steven declared, sighing. "But I wonder how long it'll take for the kids to realize we're gone and storm our position."

"Not long, I'm sure." She pushed closer, and for a long time Steven forgot about the children completely.

Chapter 6

✑

The bugles sounded at six thirty in the morning. Even though the pioneers would only travel six hours a day for a week, Steven did not want to spoil them too much. He hoped that by the end of the week the people who had been having trouble with their legs and feet would be able to increase the hours of travel gradually until they could tolerate ten hours a day. Later he would extend the travel time to eleven, then twelve hours a day.

By eight o'clock the saints had gathered in the center of the first circle of wagons. There were one thousand and four people. After six days, Pioneer One had already lost twenty people who had returned to Salt Lake City. Because of the great multitude gathered in one spot, Steven had difficulty quieting them down. Before long he stepped onto a folding chair and raised both hands high in the air. The crowd gradually became silent. John, who seemed to think of everything, handed him a homemade megaphone.

"Thank you, brothers and sisters," he said into the megaphone. "I just want to make a few announcements. As you know, we will be on a reduced travel schedule for a few days to help us adjust. That means we will travel from nine to noon in the morning, and one thirty to four thirty in the afternoon." The crowd cheered and clapped. "Afterwards, we will gradually increase our travel time until we can walk twelve hours a day." Steven heard a few groans, but went on. "Twelve hours a day seems like a lot, but we will have to make up later for the time we lose now."

After answering a few questions about the hours of travel, Steven continued. "As you know, the leaders have asked you to manage your own food supplies. However, we have noticed that many are consuming more food than is necessary. This is extremely dangerous because we may run out of provisions before we reach our destination. For that reason, we urgently caution you to ration your food carefully. Choose nutritious food, and eat only enough to keep you strong and healthy. Above all, we must increase our use of the wild edible plants available around us. We ask you to do so gradually until they constitute the bulk of your diet. Be careful about what you pick, because some of the plants are poisonous. If you have any doubts concerning the safety of a plant, please consult the people who have been trained to identify the safe plants along our route. You will find a list of their names in the guidelines."

"But if we ration our food and eat that many wild plants, we'll die for sure anyhow," shouted one of the brothers who was standing close to the front. Many in the crowd showed they agreed.

Steven smiled and said, "I'm afraid we have no choice. In any case, please don't worry. Dr. Price assures me that the new diet will not harm you, as long as the plants are safe and you increase their use gradually. Of course, if you begin to feel sick, dizzy, weak, or have gastric disturbances, you need to see one of our medical people. Besides the doctor, we have a registered nurse, Mary Christopher, and two practical nurses, Gertrude Jones and Karla Millman. I would like to emphasize that if we cannot learn to ration our food, the leaders will have to take more stringent measures to insure the well-being of all the pioneers." Steven was surprised that no one seemed to object to that statement.

"The next point concerns our safety. We learned yesterday that we may face danger from certain gangs farther along this route. There is very little more I can tell you at this time, so it's useless to ask questions. We ask only that you use common sense and obey the guidelines we gave you before we left Provo. Be especially alert to any possible threat. We expect the men to keep their weapons loaded and close to hand at all times. And if any of you sisters have a weapon and can shoot, please do the same . . . Okay, that's all I wanted to say." Steven looked at John and Paul. "Is there anything you wish to add?" His brothers shook their heads. "Okay, let's move out now!"

The saints trudged back to their wagons, carts, and converted vehicles. Ten minutes later they moved slowly onto the highway in a double column. Steven watched them from his horse as they went by. They looked weary already, and some could hardly walk. He knew that many would have to ride before long, but at least now they were trying their best. He was proud of them and admitted to himself that they had courage. He suspected that in the months ahead they would need every ounce of courage they could find. Steven's feet and legs were swollen and gave him a lot of pain, in spite of Mary's treatments, but he knew that others were worse off than he.

After he had finished reading the report, the president of the church, Josiah Smith, sighed and looked up at his counselors. "Well, Brethren, what do you think? Is there any truth to this?"

Bennion Hicks, the first counselor, spoke first. "In my opinion, the report seems largely based on rumor, and is simply too crazy to believe. A Mexican renegade army preparing to travel on foot and horseback to invade Utah. It's ridiculous."

"How far away is this army supposed to be?" Josiah asked, searching through the report to find the information.

"About two thousand miles," Bennion offered. "It's really impossible."

Josiah smiled at his counselor's reactions. He felt it was always a mistake to dismiss something too rapidly just because it sounded fantastic. "What do you think, Samuel?"

"It certainly is hard to believe," President Law observed. "Why would these people risk their lives and property to make such a long trip? And why attack us?"

Josiah replied, "The report doesn't speculate on that, but it's obvious, isn't it? These wicked men, supported by criminal governments, desire everything we have—our land, our possessions, our wives, and our lives. My guess is that the bandits are the government."

"So you think the report is true?" Samuel asked.

"I don't know for sure, but we cannot afford to ignore the possibility. A few nights ago, when I thought I was asleep, I saw a vision in which a huge man in uniform stood over me with a sword raised above his head. Then the vision disappeared, and I found myself sitting up in my bed. I don't remember many details, except that my pajamas were soaked with sweat."

Samuel said, "So you believe this vision is a warning that we'll be invaded by some terrible enemy?"

"I learned long ago to trust the dreams and visions the Lord gives me." The prophet got up and stretched. His arthritis had been giving him trouble, and stretching helped ease the pain. "Therefore, Samuel, I want you to make sure the General Authorities know about these rumors. Next I want you to gather a group of men you can trust to investigate this report. The men you send should be Mexican saints, who can travel in Mexico with greater safety."

"What if it's necessary to send them as far as Mexico City, where the report says the army is gathering?"

"Then do it. And, Bennion, I want you to warn stake leaders to prepare for the possibility that we might be attacked. I don't want them to alert the people at this time, but simply to make plans on how the saints in their areas could defend themselves in case of attack. I would like copies of all those plans. If these reports are true, we may have to gather our own army. I know the Lord wants us to defend ourselves."

Bennion said, "It won't be easy, President. We have no telephone or cell phone service. And many stakes don't even have radio communication with us."

"Do the best you can. Send men on fast ponies if you have to. As soon as possible, bring me a list of the regions you were not able to reach."

"All right. I'll get on it today."

After his counselors left, Josiah got to his knees, determined to ask the Lord if the saints were truly in danger. He knew that if they were, he would have to take more drastic measures.

The two French families headed east on Boulevard Blanqui in Paris, moving slowly in the late afternoon traffic. Pierre Laborde was frustrated. The fuel pump on André Renan's Citroën Evasion minivan had stopped working, and the vehicle had been in a downtown repair shop until four o'clock. As a result, they had not been able to leave earlier. They had been forced to travel in the city at rush hour.

But Pierre felt grateful that his friend still had the van. He turned to see how the women were coping with the kids. The four children were obviously frightened by the sudden escape through the city, but they were holding up well under the stress. The two younger kids, a boy and a girl, belonged to him and Diane.

Yesterday evening Pierre and André had visited André's stake president to receive counsel on how to respond to the government's demand that all Mormons register with the authorities within three weeks. They had been stunned to see that the president and his family had already packed their car and planned to leave the city the next day. The leader had informed them that he had just received confirmed reports that UGOT was imprisoning Mormons in great concentration camps and confiscating their property. It was official government policy. There were even ugly rumors that some saints were being executed, but this could not be confirmed. As a result, church leaders in Europe were advising members to go into hiding in any way they could.

"Pierre, do you really think we will be safe with your friends?" André asked.

"I'm certain. They're not Mormons, but I've known them for years. They're good people. Their son fell into the Marne River one winter years ago, and I saved his life. They'd do anything for me."

"How far did you say it was to their farmhouse?" Mireille Renan asked.

"It's forty-five kilometers to the city of Meaux. At that point we turn off the main road and follow a country road for a mile. Their home is about half a kilometer south of the Marne."

As they approached the Place d'Italie, the vehicles ahead came to a complete stop. An ambulance flew by on the right with its siren sounding, but it was forced to halt two hundred feet ahead. Pierre figured that this was the biggest traffic jam he had ever seen in his life. The blocked ambulance continued to make its rapid up and down wail, as if it were mourning the passing of its patient.

None of the Parisians in the square paid the slightest attention. Pierre decided that the only way the ambulance was going to reach the hospital was for a giant helicopter to swoop down and hoist it up and out of this mess. However, if a helicopter did appear, it would no doubt be the military police of UGOT hunting for his family and friends. Instinctively, he checked the square and the side streets, looking for those ugly green uniforms, which in the last few months had replaced the familiar blue outfits of the Paris police.

It took them a full hour to move across the Place d'Italie, but finally they began to make progress. Before long, they left the city heading east on an excellent highway. They picked up speed as the traffic thinned out. Yet they were terrified that at any moment they would be stopped. Pierre got the impression that many of the other travelers stared at them in a strange way when they came abreast of their van. For a while, he wondered if there was a sign on the top of the van that read Mormons.

David Omert leaned back in his office chair. He and his best friend, Chaim Yehosua, were having lunch in David's office in the Knesset Building, home of Israel's parliament in Jerusalem. Both men were members of parliament.

"Chaim, I'm very concerned over how Israel will survive. What happened seven months ago in our eight-day war with the Arabs will be nothing in comparison to what we'll have to face someday."

Chaim frowned. "Do you really think we're in that much danger? I don't see any real proof that UGOT wants our blood. What I see is the same old thing from the Arabs: refusal to accept the Jewish state, guerilla warfare, manipulation of the world press, and threats of complete annihilation. It doesn't seem to matter how many times we defeat them in war, or how many pieces of land we concede later. They still won't give up. I'm afraid we'll have to continue warring with the Arabs until the end of time, or until your Messiah comes."

"It does seem that way, doesn't it? I seriously doubt there'll ever be a permanent resolution to the Arab-Israeli conflict, because the claims to the ownership of Palestine on both sides date from the time of Abraham. No, the hatreds are too deep. It will take more than diplomacy and treaties."

"I agree," Chaim said. "There are too many people on both sides whose reason for living is to hate their traditional enemies."

"Of course, not every Jew is like that."

"Oh, you must be thinking about that new group. The Coalition for—What is it?"

"The New Coalition for Reconciliation . . . But there are others too."

Chaim smiled broadly. "I know. Certain political leaders like David Omert."

"And Chaim Yehosua."

"Yeah, I suppose so. But I'm not as dedicated to love and brotherhood as you are."

David laughed. "You are too. You just hate to admit that you're one of the good guys. But we're not the only ones. There's a growing number of Christian Jews who want genuine reconciliation."

"Hah. Not here in Israel."

"Yes, here in Israel. Chaim, I've told you before that you need to pay more attention to what the independent media is saying. Also, what people are saying on the internet. Usually they give you news that is more honest and accurate than what you find on government channels."

Chaim groaned. "Yeah, yeah, I've heard it a million times. So the people you're talking about used to be faithful to Judaism, but have turned to Christianity."

"Some of them."

"Liberal or conservative Jews?"

"I don't know. Does it really matter? I do know that some of these Jews are descendants of the victims of the holocaust. Because of the horrible tales their parents and grandparents related, they became agnostics or atheists in their youth. But later they converted to Christianity. Now they proudly claim to be both Christians and Jews."

Chaim said, "Some Jews believe that the term Christian Jew is a contradiction in terms."

"I know. That's why they often reject the Christian Jews as traitors to their race."

"Have you ever had the chance to talk to any of these converts?"

David put his feet upon the desk. "Yes, a few times. I found them to be proud of their Jewish heritage and yet to possess a strong faith in Jesus Christ. They believe he is the promised Messiah who came to bring salvation to the world more than two thousand years ago, and that he'll return someday."

"Whew! I'll bet that goes over big with other Jews. What do they say about the fact that the ancient Jews—their ancestors—were responsible for crucifying their Messiah?"

David paused as if he were trying to remember actual conversations. "Well, they don't condemn their ancestors . . . They feel it was all part of God's plan."

"How do they explain the two thousand years of suffering, disenfranchisement, death, and exile that the Jewish race has gone through?"

"They blame it on Satan, who used the wicked nations of the earth to fight against the Jews because they're the race who gave the world salvation through the Son of God."

"So you think these Christian Jews are increasing in number?"

"From what I read, Jews are converting to Christianity by the thousands now, both in Israel and in other nations. But one point I've heard them stress is that the Jews as a nation will only turn to and accept Jesus Christ when he appears to them at Armageddon and shows the physical signs of his crucifixion. At that time, he will save the Jews from the mighty armies of Gog."

"Brother! I hope they're wrong. How crushing, how humiliating it would be to stand there on the Mount of Olives in front of the great Messiah, and suddenly realize that your ancestors had murdered him because of fear and jealousy."

David grinned. "I see you've been reading the New Testament."

Chaim looked at his friend sheepishly. "Oh, I check it out a little now and then. Nothing serious, you know. So what do you think about the claims of the Christian Jews?"

"I'm not sure what I think. Right now I'm carefully searching the Old Testament for every word which might pertain to the Messiah."

"So do the Christian Jews use other scriptures besides the New Testament to prove that the Messiah will appear on the Mount of Olives?"

"Yes. They often cite Zechariah 12-14."

"And you say this happens during the great war called Armageddon, where all the nations of the earth gather to wage war against Israel?"

"Not all nations. The wicked ones," David corrected. "Why?"

"Well, I was thinking about what you've said in the past about the dangers of UGOT. It has almost become a worldwide dictatorship."

"Yes, an oligarchy."

"So if UGOT is plotting against Israel, as you suspect—"

David interrupted, "It may be that the great power called Magog in the scriptures is none other than UGOT."

"I see. The wicked nations ruled by Gog, the great dictator."

David teased, "You're remarkable, Chaim. Yes, that's the idea I've been entertaining for months now."

Chaim scowled. "Hey, look. I didn't say I really believe all that stuff. I was simply exposing to the light of day the crazy things you've been imagining."

David laughed warmly, but quickly became serious. "This brings me back to my alarm concerning the future of Israel. If UGOT continues to undermine our reputation and security in what is left of the world community, as I believe it's doing, how can we possibly defend ourselves against such overwhelming forces? We'd be like a mouse crushed by an elephant."

"But soon we'll be better prepared to defend ourselves than ever before. Our army is much stronger than it was a year ago."

David shook his head sadly. "We're completely alone in the world. The United States can no longer help us, and no other nation seems to have the strength or the desire to do it."

"David, you're far too pessimistic. After all, we have the great Minister of Defense, Menachem Hazony. And soon we'll have a new prime minister. A forceful young man of exceptional talent and intelligence."

"Funny, Chaim."

"No, no, it's pretty certain that our party will gain the most seats in the election in May, and that it will choose you as prime minister. With you and Hazony, we have nothing to fear." David and Chaim were members of the Likud Party, which was an alliance of small parties. It believed in limited government control over the economy, a hard line against the Arab states, and retaining the territories captured from the Arabs in previous wars. Their chief rival was the liberal Labor Party, which believed in strict control of the economy and compromising with the Arabs over occupied lands, in hopes of finally obtaining a lasting peace.

"The chances are slim that they'll elect me. Frankly, if they did, I have no idea how to protect Israel."

"But you're forgetting your Messiah. The Jewish Messiah, that is. When the going gets tough, he'll descend from heaven and save our bacon."

In spite of Chaim's ironic statement, which revealed his lack of faith, those words had the remarkable effect of filling David's heart with peace. "You are forgetting something too, Chaim," David said calmly.

"Which is?"

"I told you last year that someday God would clear the Temple Mount of Islam's holy shrines, and you couldn't believe such a miracle was possible."

Chaim's face froze.

"And now we're rebuilding Jerusalem and have already set the foundations for the Third Temple."

"You've made your point, David. Please don't rub it in."

The president of the Republic, Alejandro Calvino, was adored by the people and had been elected to his office by a landslide vote. He turned from his map of Venezuela, which covered a third of the south wall of his office in Caracas in northern Venezuela, and sat on the front edge of his gleaming mahogany desk. His face was lined with worry and lack of sleep. He looked at the two men sitting on padded chairs in front of him. Ramón Sánchez was the president's top advisor and a longtime friend, but the second man was another matter. He considered Diego Ortiz, the new Minister of Defense, to be an evil little traitor who would sell his own mother for a profit. UGOT had forced the president to place the traitor in his high office three months ago for one purpose only: to make sure Venezuela's leaders did what they were told.

And since Diego had entered the administration, the government had been forced to do many things to curtail religious freedom in Venezuela. Now it was forbidden to display the cross or religious icons in public. One could no longer give public prayers to any deity, and religious holidays had been canceled. The normal use of cathedrals, churches, and temples was in grave danger. The president had even received reports that the green coats and the regular police, under the authority of the office of the Minister of Defense, had secretly invaded private homes to destroy religious images, Bibles, and other sacred writings.

The president was ashamed to think of what he had been compelled to do to the former minister of defense, another friend, in order to make room for UGOT's toady. Through his own office he had leaked false charges to the press accusing the previous minister of being involved in drug trafficking. The media had spent two weeks rehearsing every possible angle of the sordid story.

Secret agents from the new world government had already arranged some timely "accidents" for fifteen of the most prominent leaders in the National Congress, and had threatened to kill other national leaders, and perhaps Alejandro himself, if they did not fall into line and accept the ten new envoys sent by UGOT. As president, he could have ordered the military police to arrest the foreign agents, but most of them worked undercover like terrorists, and he had not been able to discover their identity.

And when he had first resisted orders to elevate Diego Ortiz, he had received another threat directly from UGOT headquarters in London: if he did not become more agreeable, UGOT would send an army to Venezuela to enforce compliance.

Alejandro had sought the aid of neighboring countries—Guyana, Colombia, Bolivia, Ecuador, Peru, Brazil, and Chile, but they had been too afraid to intervene. Peru, Chile, and Bolivia had already complied with the rules of the new world order, and the other four countries declined to interfere. Since UGOT had not yet disturbed them, they considered themselves safe.

"How can you expect me to do this terrible thing?" he said to Diego Ortiz in Spanish. "If I required the members of this church to register with the government, to the exclusion of other religions, it would cause a popular uproar. Especially since Venezuela has had a long tradition of giving religious freedom to all its citizens." Alejandro glanced at Ramón to see how his friend was reacting to the terrible news. Ramón showed no emotion whatsoever.

Diego smirked. "There'll be no uproar because you'll not make it public. The Mormons have a lay clergy which is highly organized. I understand that their church can get messages to its entire membership within hours if necessary. All you need to do is pass my instructions to their leaders, and the public will hear little of it. And if someone asks questions, we'll simply deny it. The main thing is, you must make them think this is just a routine census of religious groups in Venezuela, and that the government will require the other churches to register in succeeding months.

"You should also make it clear that it's the only way the Mormon church in Venezuela can maintain its tax-exempt status. If you do as I say, the Mormons will come running because they've a long history of obeying their government." Diego took hold of his briefcase and got up slowly from his chair. "I must go now, for I have other things to do. Mr. President, I want your message to reach Mormon leaders by Thursday, April 27, one week from now. Their members must comply by Friday, May 5. Are we agreed?"

"Yes."

"Don't be so glum, Mr. President," Diego said. "As I told you before, when we accomplish the great things I have planned, Venezuela and the world will be the better for it. You must have faith in that and in nothing else." He inclined his head. "Good-bye for now."

Alejandro and Ramón said at once, "Good day."

When the door closed behind Diego, the president turned to Ramón and cried, "The things he has planned for Venezuela! The arrogant little weasel. He's nothing but UGOT's dog. Ramón, my friend, you must go to your people and tell them to resist this registration at all costs."

"But why? Diego is just expressing his innate desire to lord it over others. I'm sure he simply wants to stick his nose into the church's business once again, or to make us Mormons pay higher taxes."

Alejandro shook his head urgently. "No, I have reason to believe it's much more serious than that. UGOT is far more interested in eliminating obstacles to its plans for total power than to increase its revenues."

Ramón was visibly shaken. "What makes you think that? What do they want with us?"

"This morning I received a report from people loyal to me in intelligence. They say that Diego and his henchmen have taken control of three of our major prisons in the last four days. I'm powerless to stop it. As Minister of Defense, he's head of the National Guard and has used this authority to replace the regular prison personnel with soldiers from the Guard. The report says that after he seized control, he released 50 percent of the condemned prisoners."

"Why? It's crazy."

"That's what I've been asking myself all day. But when Ortiz announced his plan a half hour ago to register the Mormons, it all fell into place."

"You don't think—"

"Yes, I do. He intends to throw your people into prison and confiscate their property. It explains the reports I've been getting some time now from abroad."

"What reports?"

"Reports that UGOT is incarcerating rebellious religious factions in many other countries. I didn't think much of it at first because I figured the new world government was using that tactic to insure order. You know, get control of the violent cults so it could promote its programs in peace. But later reports said UGOT started focusing on Mormons also."

"What do you think we should do, Alejandro?"

"Like I said, resist the registration at any cost."

"But will that be enough? I'm sure Ortiz has access to computer records and will come after us when we don't show up to register."

"Then you must go into hiding. Like the ancient Christians in the Roman catacombs. I believe it's a matter of life and death for your people to disappear as soon as possible. At least for now." Alejandro suddenly remembered that his office might be bugged. He walked to a radio sitting on a bookshelf and turned some music on high. Then he moved close to where Ramón was sitting and spoke very low. "I want you to know that I'm doing everything I can to regain control of this country. But it will take time."

Ramón also spoke in low tones. "When should we act?"

"Today."

"All right, I'll take your message to church leaders. I'm sure they'll follow your advice. And, Alejandro, Mormon leaders in Utah encouraged us two years ago to set up a special settlement about sixty-four miles southwest of Caracas, just south of Maracay Lake. We built thousands of homes, most of them underground, and gathered all types of supplies, including weapons and ammunition."

"Yes, I knew you were doing something unusual in that area. But why are you telling me this?"

"Because I trust you completely and I want you to know what some of your fellow countrymen are doing to preserve their freedom."

"Thank you, Ramón, you've always been a good friend."

"We also have six other isolated colonies in other parts of the country. We didn't fully understand why the leaders asked us to prepare like that, but we did it anyhow. Now I know the reason. The Venezuelan saints don't believe in violence, but we will defend the lives of our wives and children."

Alejandro touched Ramón's hand. "You may have to, my friend. You may have to."

Chapter 7

André Renan saw the patrol car behind them in the rearview mirror when they were half way to Meaux, France. It was nearly a mile back but overtaking them rapidly.

"The cops!" he shouted.

Pierre looked back and said, "They're gaining on us, but having trouble with the traffic."

"I didn't hear any siren," Mireille exclaimed.

"That is unusual," André said. "What do I do? Speed up, get off the freeway?"

"This van has a lot of power," Pierre said. "We might be able to outrun them."

"We don't even know they're after us!" Diane cried. "And they're the regular gendarmes, not the green coats."

"She's right," Mireille said earnestly.

"But you never know which of the regular police are taking orders from the green coats anymore!" Pierre stated with desperation.

André suddenly realized what he had to do. "Calm down, all of you. I'll handle this."

He maintained his speed and watched the approaching patrol car carefully. When it was two hundred feet behind, André heard the nerve-racking wail of their siren. He continued his pace until he saw his pursuers move up almost to his bumper and stay there. Then he gradually slowed down and pulled to the right side of the highway. The patrol car stopped ten feet behind, its siren silent, but its lights still flashing.

"I hope you know what you're doing," Pierre said, as they waited for the gendarme to walk up to the van. André rolled down his window.

"Get out of your vehicle," the officer growled. "All four adults. Not the children."

Mireille told the four children what the officer wanted and reassured them that there was nothing to worry about. As the adults exited the car, the second officer, who was standing behind the van on the passenger side, called out sharply, "Step to this side of the vehicle, away from traffic."

André was terrified, but tried not to show it. He noticed the same fear in the eyes of his companions. The policemen acted as if they were dealing with common criminals. After demanding their driver's permits, the first officer walked back to his vehicle.

While the patrolman checked their licenses on the government's central computer, André said to the other officer, "Did I break some law? What's going on?"

The gendarme rested his right hand on his gun holster, but did not draw the weapon. "You will not ask questions. You will wait."

After fifteen minutes, the dread in André's heart was so great that he could hardly breathe. Why was the first cop still sitting in the car? What were they waiting for? Then all at once the terrifying idea came to him that the man in the car must have radioed for the green coats to come. That had to be it. It was only a matter of time before a military truck arrived and carted them off to the concentration camp. André desperately wanted to warn his wife and friends, but was afraid to do it with the patrolman nearby.

While he was entertaining these gruesome thoughts, another patrol car appeared and stopped in front of his van. The officers in the second car did not get out. Now André was confused. Perhaps he was wrong. Maybe they had called for backup because somehow the computer messed up and listed them as dangerous criminals. He felt a little better now because the policemen he was dealing with were fellow countrymen, dressed in the normal uniforms of the French Highway Patrol. No doubt it would take only another minute or two for this matter to be straightened out.

"Why is this taking so long?" Pierre asked ten minutes later.

"As I said before, you will not ask questions," the officer replied.

André had begun to think about the green coats again when a third patrol car arrived on the westbound side of the freeway. It continued a few hundred yards past them, pulled to the left side of the freeway, and turned across the meridian. As it pulled up behind the first patrol car, the patrolman who made the radio call exited his vehicle and marched up to them.

"You're all under arrest," he announced.

"But why? What did we do?" Pierre cried. André wondered if they were under arrest because Pierre had opposed UGOT on television talk shows and documentaries.

The policeman turned a cold eye on Pierre. "We will not respond to your questions. They will be answered in due time by the proper authorities. You will get into your vehicle and follow the patrol car in front of you. The driver will turn across the meridian and return to Paris, and you will follow him very closely. If you try to escape, we will have to use deadly force to stop you. Do you understand?"

"Yes, sir," André said meekly.

André and Pierre hopped into the front seat of the van, and the two women got into the back with the children. They waited for the car in front to move. There was a great deal of traffic on the freeway, and it was more than five minutes before a gap came in the eastbound traffic. Finally, the patrol car in front took off abruptly, heading for the meridian. When André hesitated an instant, the driver behind leaned on his horn. André jerked the van into motion and slammed to a stop in the center of the meridian, behind the leading patrol car. He glanced through his rearview mirror and saw that the cars following him were lined up close behind on the meridian.

"So much for safety!" Pierre yelled. "We could have been killed pulling such a stunt!"

"Under the circumstances," Diane said, "it might have been much more dangerous if they had tried to stop the traffic."

"Yes, this traffic is brutal." Mireille observed.

Since the westbound traffic was also heavy, it took another four minutes of waiting before the four vehicles could move safely onto the freeway. The first car moved into the right lane and sped up to a hundred kilometers an hour. André followed about fifty feet behind, and the second car almost lay on his bumper. The third police car moved up on the left side and stayed there, blocking him in, but also forcing the freeway traffic to follow their convoy at the same speed. Obviously, the police had no intention of letting them escape.

"Talk about overkill," Pierre complained. "Three cop cars to escort one little minivan."

"André, we can't let them take us in," Mireille said tearfully. Her emotion caused the children to cry. Seeing what she had done, Mireille struggled for control and dried her tears on a sleeve. She and Diane shushed the children and encouraged them to be brave.

"She's right," Diane said. "They'll treat us like the Nazis did the Jews. I'm sure of it."

André himself was almost in tears. "But I don't know what to do. They have us boxed in."

"Think, everyone," Pierre exclaimed. "There has to be a way!"

"Dear Father in Heaven," Diane said in a clear, loud voice, "We, thy faithful children, ask for thy help in this desperate situation."

Everyone was surprised to hear Diane, Pierre's wife, openly appeal to God in such a simple, fervent way. The other adults and the children said "amen" almost instinctively. André's face burned and he suddenly felt a peace and confidence he had never known before. He constantly glanced into the rearview mirror as the miles passed, and soon a plan came to him. It was wild and dangerous, but it just might work. Since they were only seven or eight miles from the city, he had to act quickly.

"Listen, everyone," André said. "In a minute or so I'm going to do something shocking. You can prepare yourselves by making sure your seatbelts are tight, and by hanging on to something to steady yourselves."

"Tell us what you're going to do, please," Mireille pleaded.

"I'm sorry. There isn't time." André had decided not to scare them. He saw the turnoff two hundred yards ahead.

Pierre exclaimed, "But we may object to your plan."

"That's right!" At that instant, André jerked the wheel to the right and slammed on the brakes. The van skidded and nearly rolled over from the sudden turn, and everyone screamed. As André accelerated down the off-ramp, he stole a glance through the mirror, but could not see what had happened. His only impression was that the patrol car which had been following them had not made the turn after them. While the women and children continued to cry, Pierre strained to see the freeway. At the end of the off-ramp, André braked once more and made a sharp right turn without stopping. He gunned the powerful motor as he headed north. Checking the mirror again, he saw a pile of wrecked cars buried in fire and smoke.

"What happened?" André hollered.

Pierre let out a whoop. "They crashed into each other! The patrol cars." He looked at passengers in the rear and said firmly, "All right, everyone, quiet down. We're okay now."

A few minutes later, after the adults had succeeded in calming the children, André said, "I didn't see it, Pierre. What happened?"

"When you yanked the van off the freeway, the car in front slammed on his brakes. I guess he wasn't thinking about the results of such a reckless move. The car behind us didn't even seem to notice you had turned off and, still speeding merrily along, piled into the rear of the lead car. At the same time the character on the left must have figured that since you made the ramp, he could do it too, because he swerved violently to the right just after the second car passed by. But instead of making the off-ramp, his car slid sideways and collided with the second car just as it clobbered the lead car. The gas tanks in the front two cars exploded, and all three caught fire. The whole thing happened in two or three seconds."

"What a terrible way to die," Mireille moaned.

"Yes, it's horrible," Diane said. "I feel so sorry for those poor officers."

Pierre said, "Yes, but we have to remember that those 'poor officers' were taking us to imprisonment or death, and didn't seem especially unhappy about it."

"Do you think they knew what was going to happen?" Diane asked.

"I'm sure of it," Pierre said. He examined the road ahead. "Do you know where you're going, André?"

"Not really."

"Well, I know this area like the back of my hand. Turn right at the next road. I can take you there by the back roads. Unless you guys prefer not to go to our original destination." Everyone agreed that they should still seek refuge at the home of Pierre's friends.

After a minute of silence, Pierre looked at his friend and said, "André, what I'd like to know is what possessed you to do such a crazy thing back there? What made you think they wouldn't simply slow down, turn around, and come after us? What if the car behind us had been able to make the ramp like we did? What if the van had rolled over? There was so much risk. Frankly, I don't get it."

"Well, I noticed that the driver behind us was having trouble staying awake. He was following so close that I could see his face through the mirror. I figured that if I could make the ramp, he wouldn't even see it until too late. As for the lead driver, I didn't know for sure what he would do. But something told me there was a good chance he would panic and brake too hard."

"It turned out great, and I'm proud of you. But I still think you were possessed," Pierre said.

Diane replied, "He was possessed, all right. By the Holy Spirit."

Gerald Galloway admired the exquisite beauty of the sunset from the terrace of his manor house in Hampshire, England. He had spent many remarkable hours in this spot and others on his vast estate, expressing his soul through painting. And he was an expert at it too, for many of his master-pieces had sold for substantial sums on the world market. Recently, the critics had increased the crescendo of their adoration, and Gerald wondered if it was because of the improved merit of his work or because they feared his growing power.

"It's a splendid sight, isn't it, Gerald?" Lucienne said as she followed his gaze. "All the haze and dust from so many disasters in the world have only increased its beauty."

"Yes, what arises from pain and degradation is often more beautiful than anything man has seen before. They are the flowers of evil as Charles Baude-laire expressed it in the title for a collection of his best French poems."

"True, but people of superior genius must control the growth of the new beauty. Just as we have done in our meetings these last three days."

Gerald laughed. "Yes, but some of our associates are unable to rule them-selves, much less the world. One must always guide them and control them."

"I agree. The people of the world are primarily sheep, but we also have a few sheep among us. Maybe that's why the Bible calls the true believers 'sheep.' Like our stupid comrades, the believers have no intelligence of their own, but must be led like dumb beasts."

"That's why I asked you to come with me to share the sunset and a glass of sherry. I would like you to give me a personal report on your progress in controlling the world's religious communities." After the collapse of the United States, Lucienne had much less work to do as the associate for North America, and Gerald had made her the head of the Ministry of Religion and Spiritual Welfare.

"What exactly do you want to know?"

"Well, first I would like to know how you like your new assignment."

Lucienne frowned as she sipped her wine. "I admit that I definitely prefer my old job as associate for North America. It was much more challenging and rewarding trying to outwit political leaders whose primary goals were to enlarge their own power and fortunes. I understand such people. They're so much more intelligent than these gullible fanatics I have to deal with now." Lucienne pouted.

Gerald felt the urge to kiss her luscious red lips. He laughed and said, "Well, maybe someday we can return you the States, when the smoke clears away, and there is something for you to govern."

"You want me to govern the United States!"

"Why not? You could enjoy the intrigues and mind games as you did before, but this time as chief executive."

"Thank you, Gerald. You are definitely my favorite world dictator."

They laughed heartily at Lucienne's little joke.

A moment later, Gerald said, "But for now, you have this religious assignment. How is your project with the Mormons proceeding?"

"Very well. However, I must admit that it hasn't been easy. There are about thirteen million of them worldwide, excluding the United States, of course, and they're found in nearly every country in the world. Their population is especially dense in Central and South America."

"How is your registration going?"

"Fairly well. We've registered almost a million."

Gerald frowned. "One million out of thirteen. That's not many after all these months. What's the problem, Lucienne?"

"Well, they're an independent and rebellious people. Most have refused to register."

"Round them up and put them into concentration camps."

"It's not that easy. As soon as they hear about the registration, they go into hiding."

"But Colton Aldridge told me once that Mormons believed in—how did he put it?—oh yes, in obeying the law of the land."

Lucienne laughed. "Gerald, they believe in obeying what they call the constitutional law of the land, not in a dictatorship which seeks to control them, make them renounce their God, and—well—you know the rest."

"Yes. But how do they know we plan all that for them?"

"I've asked myself that many times. In spite of my excellent security, they just seem to know. Someone told me once that they claim to get personal messages from their God."

"All of them?" Gerald said, shocked.

"Yes, everyone who really wants it."

"Curious concept. But someday our laws will be the constitutional law of nations. I'm writing that constitution now. Will the Mormons obey the laws then?"

Lucienne yawned. "Somehow I doubt it."

Gerald got up and took another bottle of wine from a nearby cooler. "Then we'll ferret them out, and if they resist, we'll kill them . . . But now I want to hear about the other religions. You know, the Christians, Taoists, Buddhists, and so on."

"Generally speaking, they're not as hard to handle as the Mormons. We deal with them in many different ways, but we have only begun our work. If they prove to be rebellious, we'll round them up just like the Mormons. I have used

Colton Aldridge to advantage in some of my visits to governments which are greatly influenced by the biases of a dominant religion."

"Yes. That's what you said in some of your reports, but you didn't provide many details. Please explain."

"Well, for example, when we visited India, Colton went around for a few months doing miracles, and soon the news of the great new prophet spread like wildfire. The believers of Hinduism thought he was the incarnation of one of their many deities, and they were ready to listen to anything we had to say." Lucienne put her hand to her mouth to suppress a laugh. "They saw him as even more sacred than their cattle. So when we went to the government to encourage them to accept Colton's guidance—that is, UGOT's guidance— there were no serious objections. That's how we placed some good people next to the Prime Minister as his special advisors."

"I knew using Colton would get results. What kind of miracles did our favorite prophet do?"

"He healed the sick, blind, and lame in nearly every country we visited. He caused it to rain in India, brought down thunder and lightning in Korea, made statues bleed in Italy and Spain, and even led the police to a kidnapper in Taiwan. He has done so much that I can't remember it all. The truth is, he scares me sometimes. When he does a miracle, his body vibrates all over, and his eyes seem to turn into burning coals." Lucienne was mesmerized by the memory of Colton's incantations.

Gerald touched her shoulder and said, "Lucienne, Lucienne, are you all right?"

"Yes . . . I'm sorry. I got carried away."

"You must control yourself. After all, Colton is nothing but a tool."

"I know, but you should see him."

"He actually does the things you said?"

"Yes. I don't know where he gets his power, but I know it works . . . Listen, Gerald, you must be careful with Colton. He's very dangerous."

Gerald sat on a chair next to his mistress. "Don't worry. I know where he gets his power and I know how to control him."

"I hope so. I truly hope so."

"Maybe I'll just instruct my medical staff to put him to sleep someday and insert a biochip. Just to be safe."

"You mean, like the American Government did when they were having so much trouble with anarchists and paramilitary groups?"

"Exactly . . . Listen. I have a secret to tell you. I haven't announced it to the Committee yet, so you'll be the first to know. I've initiated a program to implant every person on the planet with a biochip. We've found ways to do it which are so subtle and quick that the subject doesn't even know he's been implanted."

"Everyone will get it? Does that include the Twelve?"

"Oh no. The Twelve and our close operatives are a secret society. They've made sacred vows and know that if they violate those vows, the penalty is death. Colton is not really a member of our inner circle. So I've decided to control him with the microchip."

"But I thought the chip was no more than a sophisticated identification card, which allows you to locate a person anywhere in the world and access his personal data. In other words, it only provides partial control of the carrier. Is that right?"

"Normally, that's the case. But the new chip is something special. It contains a tiny amount of a deadly compound which can kill the carrier within seconds. You can quickly locate a target carrier on a master computer and execute him or her with the touch of a key. The people who might be around him will have no idea why he suddenly collapsed. Obviously, we'll only use this special chip in people we consider a potential threat. We're also working on a chip which can explode the brain of the carrier."

"What wonderful idea. Gerald, you do think of everything. I hope you stick one of the new chips in Colton as soon as possible." She chuckled happily. "I also have good news. News from our trip to India."

"What?"

"Soon there will be millions of people who won't need a biochip."

"Meaning?"

"While Colton and I were in India, we learned that a new pandemic of cholera is sweeping the subcontinent. They expect it to spread throughout half the world within a year. A hundred million people will perish."

"Oh, yes. The BBC gave a minireport on it a few hours ago. You realize, of course, that this type of thing helps our cause. These plagues usually take their greatest toll on the poor and uneducated of mankind. Such creatures are a burden to the world community, and we'll find it easier to govern if they're eliminated. How can we ever have a perfect society if it's full of dross and refuse?"

Chapter 8

The wagon train moved slowly east along I-80, covering slightly more than one mile each hour. No breeze cooled their bodies. No clouds protected them from the scorching sun. The temperature climbed quickly to ninety-two degrees by noon, and every traveler was soaked in sweat. Steven felt that the heat was almost unbearable, and when they stopped for lunch at noon, he rolled under his wagon and lay on the hard freeway surface to rest. His legs throbbed, but he dared not look at them. He felt guilty for not having the strength to be a bold hero, like Moses. He should walk among the wagons when they stopped to encourage his people in their suffering. He knew that some must be worse off than he, but he feared what they might say when they saw him. He silently cursed himself for his laziness in leading such a sedentary life in the city.

"Steven, are you all right?" Mary called, squatting beside the wagon so she could see him.

William kneeled on the road beside her. "Hey, Dad, what are you doing? We need to make lunch."

"Okay, I'm coming."

He pulled himself from beneath the wagon and sat on the folding chair Mary handed him. He noticed that Jennifer and Andrew were exploring a ditch not far from the highway.

"How are your legs?" she asked.

"Painful, but I'll survive."

"I'll check them after we eat lunch. Then I'm going to make sure you ride for a while, either on your horse or in the wagon."

"But—"

"No buts, Mr. Hero. The other men are doing it, and you should too!"

Steven was about to protest when he saw two men and a woman heading toward them. The woman and one of the men were obviously married. He was not especially happy to see any of them because he supposed they were bringing complaints.

"I've got a problem I need to discuss with someone," one of the men said, looking at Mary.

"It's the same with us," the woman declared.

Steven replied, "I'm sorry. I can't remember your names. I guess it'll take me awhile to get to know everybody."

"I'm Joshua Hale," the first man said.

"And I'm Hannah Baldwin." She nodded toward the second man. "This is my husband, Victor. We're friends with the Hales, so we got Joshua to come with us."

Steven said, "Look, why don't you talk to your leaders and ask them to bring the problems to us at the review meeting tonight."

"I'm afraid it can't wait," Joshua said.

Hannah agreed, "I have a personal medical problem, Brother Christopher. I need to talk to your wife. I tried to see the doctor, but he's got a line of people at his wagon. Besides, I can't stand the arrogant—" She stopped short when she saw her husband's sharp look.

Mary said, "Steve, would you please make lunch so I can talk to these people?" She handed him the materials to make sandwiches. "Let's talk about things under the trees over there." Mary pointed to a few scraggly trees not far from the highway. "We'll take these folding chairs with us."

Steven began wearily to prepare lunch as he watched the visitors walk away with Mary. What was so important that they had to talk to Mary now? Why couldn't it wait until tonight? He shouted for the children to come and help. Twenty minutes later, he was pleased to see Mary returning so soon from the session with her patients.

"What was that all about?" he asked.

"Health problems. One has a caffeine addiction. He had a huge cache of caffeine pills, but ran out two days ago. I gave him advice on how to handle his withdrawal. The other person has ulcer pain, and I suggested she take natural remedies. I promised to help them look for burdock root and Brigham tea when we stop for the day."

"You're wonderful," Steven said.

She grinned and gave him a kiss. "I don't know about that, but I do know I'm hungry. Did you save me anything?"

"Yes, two sandwiches and a glass of milk."

While Mary was eating, Paul, Jarrad, and Leonard arrived with three young women. Paul was doing his best to escort all three women at once, as if they belonged to him. Andrea Warren, Anastasia Borisovich, and Rachel Crell, the third bachelorette, played along with Paul, laughing and joking in spite of their sweaty and bedraggled appearance.

Mary dropped the rest of her sandwich into her plate, sprang from her chair, and embraced her old friend, Andrea. "Where have you been? I went to your wagon ten times in the last few days, and you were always gone. Are you trying to avoid me?"

"Heck no. Whenever we stop, I wander around checking out the available men. I'm almost thirty-two now and I don't have time to waste. I'm tired of mothering these two female brats, and I want someone—a man—to take care of me for a change. Besides, I need to prove you wrong." The other young people enjoyed hearing Andrea's banter and gathered around her attentively.

"Prove me wrong? I don't know what you mean."

"Look, dear, you once told me that I gave a hard time to every male I met—available or not—and I'm determined to refute your faulty judgment during this trip."

Mary replied in the same tone, "Well, it's about time. You know the old Mormon belief: every woman needs a man to make her life complete."

"Yeah, right . . . No, Mary, the real reason you haven't seen me is because I saw you coming and I hid. I was afraid you might drag me to your wagon when Steven was there. And you know the danger of that. He might not be able to resist the temptation to run away with me. So I just couldn't risk ruining your marriage like that."

Mary laughed, but Anastasia only smiled faintly. "Heavens," Anastasia exclaimed. "Steven would never be interested in another woman when he has one as beautiful and intelligent as Mary."

Paul searched around a moment and said, "Hey, where's the grub? You didn't save anything for us?"

"Sorry, little brother," Steven said. "You need to feed yourself more often. Our supplies are limited, you know. And there's something else I need to chastise you for. Don't you think you should be a tad more circumspect? You're one of the leaders of the caravan, and this fooling around might give people a bad impression."

"Fooling around? I don't think I grasp your meaning, Brother Christopher."

"Going around the convoy and flirting with all the single women every chance you get."

Paul put on a face of terrible shock. "Shoot! Everyone understands how much I'm really suffering. They realize that my happy-go-lucky demeanor is just an act to cheer them up and give them courage."

"Oh, yes, I forgot." Steven wondered how it was that his brother could look so good and have so much energy, when he wanted to crawl into bed and sleep a week. He was only thirty-seven, but he felt like ninety!

Paul went on. "But, Steve, the real reason we brought the flowers of Pioneer One—the lovely ladies you see before you—to visit, is to let you hear them relate in person the rumors they've heard. Anastasia also overheard a new rumor this morning which I want you to hear."

Steven said, "Why don't we get off this freeway before we burn up?"

While Mary remained near the covered wagon with the children, the others headed for a cluster of trees which grew on the north side of the highway. Since many pioneers had the same idea, they had to walk a hundred yards before they found a band of shade. They sat in a circle, and the three young women related the rumors they had heard. Since Paul had already given him the same information two days ago, Steven was not surprised. He knew, however, that the three bachelorettes traveled in the same wagon and had plenty of time to discuss these intrigues. He wondered how much they had embellished the stories for effect.

"Okay, Anastasia, tell him the new gossip you heard," Jarrad said.

Anastasia smiled coyly and caressed Steven with her eyes. He wondered why it was that whenever she spoke to him, he always got the impression she was flirting. Maybe it was the way she acted toward all men, and she didn't mean anything by it.

"Well, this morning I visited my parents and overheard a man—I don't know his name—talking to my father. He said he was on guard yesterday and came across a group of men talking by a stream not far from the wagon train . . . I hesitate to repeat this because it's probably nothing except empty gossip."

"What did the guy say, Anastasia?" Paul said impatiently.

"He said that they said the leaders of Pioneer One have a hidden agenda . . ."

"And?" Paul prodded.

"They said Steven really wants to lead us to North Dakota—or was it Canada?—to set up his own kingdom and rule over us. I'm pretty sure that's what he said they said."

Steven couldn't believe his ears.

"It's the silliest thing I've heard in a long time," Jarrad said.

Paul added, "It's amazing how many nutty things people can imagine. I doubt any sensible person would believe it."

"But I sort of believed it—at first, that is," Anastasia admitted.

"Do you want us to chase it down, Steve?" Leonard asked.

"Oh, I don't know. Keep your ears open, but don't waste a lot of time investigating. You've got more important things to do." Steven glanced at his watch. "It's almost one thirty. We'd better get back to our wagons. By the way, Paul, where is Mr. Johnston? I haven't seen him since this morning."

"He took off on his big mule right after your talk this morning. Heading northwest. He told me he wanted to check out the road ahead, but should be back in time for supper."

Steven was disappointed. For some reason, he felt safer with the old Baptist hanging around.

The caravan couldn't start by one thirty. During the morning, several wheels on different wagons had begun to seize up, and the owners and wheelwrights were still busy repairing them. It seemed that whoever had made the wagons had forgotten to put grease in some of the hubs. The pioneers were learning that the wheel hubs were the weak spots in the construction of the wagons, in spite of the up-to-date grease and roller bearings that the builders had installed. The "Moderns" or "Converters" gloated. They had no problem at all with the wheels seizing up on their modern metal vehicles. They saw the wagon wheel repairs as proof that they had been right all along.

During the lunch period, the Moderns had spent most of their time promoting two basic ideas. First, they declared that Pioneer One should no longer be referred to as a "wagon train," because it was not comprised solely of "ancient" wagons. Instead, they suggested terms like "carriage cavalcade," "buggy column," or "conveyance convoy." This last term was their favorite. They claimed that all those designations could refer to any vehicle, old or new. Later they presented their suggestions at the regular meeting of the caravan leaders, who shook their heads sadly and said they'd take the proposal under advisement. For some strange reason, however, none of those terms ever really caught on, in spite of the campaigning of the Moderns.

On the other hand, their second idea became more and more accepted as Pioneer One continued its journey. This idea proposed that the pioneers should watch for wrecking yards along the highway. If they did, they'd eventually find a selection of salvage vehicles to gradually replace their broken-down wagons, which the Moderns contended they could convert in the blink of an eye.

Finally, at two thirty the caravan set out again in the terrible heat. At Mary's insistence, Steven drove their wagon for a while. Then he mounted his mustang and rode back down the road to check on his people. He was pleased and surprised when many pioneers waved at him. Several traveling on foot came up and declared how grateful they were for his concern for the hard time they had been having. By the time he returned to his wagon, he was elated. He climbed up next to Mary, threw both arms around her, and kissed her hard on the mouth.

"Yuck, Dad! That's gross!" Andrew cried.

Steven turned and grinned at his son. "Oh, I didn't see you, Andrew. I thought you were out walking with the other kids. Yes, it's gross, but it sure is fun."

Mary said, "Thank you for the kiss, dear husband. I'm sorry I didn't check your legs at lunchtime."

"You didn't have time. Besides, they feel better now. Pretty soon, I'll try to walk again—with your permission, of course."

An hour later, Steven hopped off the wagon and began to walk. The initial shock was bad, but soon the pain subsided and he could move more easily. The caravan continued laboriously along the highway until it came to the end of the valley. At that point the road narrowed to two lanes and turned to the northeast. There were many ups and downs in the freeway, but the overall upgrade was negligible. The mountains on both sides gradually moved closer until the road ran through a narrow gorge a few hundred yards wide.

The heat was still intense at four thirty when the pioneers pulled off the highway halfway between Exits 148 and 152. After they had formed the wagons into three circles, the pioneers found any shady spot they could to escape the heat. They lay around exhausted, too tired to do anything but doze and nurse their aching bodies. Only a few bothered to pitch tents this early. After checking that John had posted a double guard, Steven climbed under his wagon with his family and fell asleep immediately. A half hour later he was awakened by shouts.

"Brother Christopher, please wake up. I really need to talk to you. It's an emergency!"

Steven groaned as he rolled from under his wagon and looked around with sleepy eyes. He finally recognized one of his colonels.

"Who is it, Steve?" Mary called.

"It's Seth Crowell. He wants to talk to me. You can go back to sleep."

Steven staggered to his feet. "Can I help you, Seth?" He could see that his visitor was very agitated.

"You've got to do something about Brother Hamilton. He's driving me crazy."

"Frank Hamilton?" Frank was one of Seth's captains.

"Yes. He never cooperates. No matter what I ask my people to do, he invariably ignores me and does his own thing. It's hard enough to handle the things I have to do without having to put up with him. All I'm trying to do is follow the guidelines and do a good job."

Steven was astonished to see how angry the colonel was. "But why are you so mad, Seth?"

"You ask me why? Well, it's obvious, isn't it? That guy seems to do it on purpose. He enjoys torturing me. I've never seen such willful disobedience. The truth is, I think he refuses to cooperate because he doesn't respect me. Or maybe it's just a personal dislike. This afternoon I told him I was going straight to you about his behavior."

Steven was certainly awake now. He put his hand on Seth's shoulder and pointed to some boulders a short distance from the camp. "Why don't we go over there and discuss it?"

"Good. We need to solve this problem right now."

They walked to the boulders and found a seat. The area was not protected from the sun, and the late afternoon glare intensified Steven's headache.

"Why don't you tell me some of the things Brother Hamilton does that causes so much trouble?" Steven said.

"Hah. The list is endless. I have to remind him constantly when it's his turn for guard duty. Then he always insists on taking his wife with him, or he tries to exchange watches with someone else. He refuses to obey the rule about families quieting down at eight o'clock. When we're traveling, he sometimes moves his wagon alongside that of another young couple so they can joke around together. They make so much noise that an Indian war party could attack and they wouldn't even know it." Seth paused to catch his breath.

Steven pulled his hat down to cover his eyes better from the sun. "So you think what he's doing is dangerous?"

"It certainly is," Seth said angrily. "When he pulls that trick, he's traveling triple file instead of double file like the rules say. Also, I reminded him today that the men in our group were going to have a brief meeting tonight to report on their weekly visit to their assigned families. This will be our first meeting of the trip, and it's important that everyone be there. But Frank said he didn't feel well and wasn't coming. But I know for a fact that he's as strong and healthy as a bull. So it boils down to one thing. He's giving a terrible example to the other brethren."

"Is that all?" Steven said.

"Let's see. He doesn't keep his campsite clean and he—I don't know. The things I've already mentioned are probably the most important."

"That's a long list after only seven days. Let me ask you some questions, Seth. How well do you know Frank Hamilton?"

"All I know is, he's about twenty-four years old and got married two weeks before Pioneer One began this trip. It's difficult to get to know someone when you feel he doesn't like you."

"That's true. Yet the fact that he's so young and recently married might explain some of his behavior. It's understandable that a newlywed hates to be away from his wife even for a moment. I got married ten days ago, and it's very hard for me to leave Mary for one hour. Also, you said he constantly moves his wagon into triple file to talk to the other young couple?"

"Yes."

"Well, we probably should consider that behavior to be typical of young people who are full of excitement about life and want to share their feelings with people their age. The dirty campsite might also be explained by Brother Hamilton's youth."

"Being young is no excuse for being stupid." Seth exclaimed.

"But that's my point. Is his behavior really stupid?"

"I don't get your drift."

"Does Frank water his animals when and where you suggest?"

"Yes, he does."

"Does he do what you ask when you call on him to help members of your group repair wagons or do other important tasks?"

"I suppose so," Seth said reluctantly.

"Does he obey most of the guidelines such as keeping his weapon at hand, drinking plenty of water, staying close to his family, and rationing his food?"

"Yes, he obeys those rules, but he breaks others. What about him not quieting down at eight o'clock?"

"In what way does he not quiet down?"

"I hear him and his wife chattering until nine or ten. You can hear them a mile away."

Steven smiled a little. "And the other pioneers are completely quiet and trying to sleep?"

"Uh, well, no . . ."

"They're talking too?"

"Yes, I guess they are," Seth admitted.

"Well then, maybe we shouldn't blame Frank for doing what everyone else is doing . . . The reason I asked you about the good things Frank is doing is to point out that he seems to be obeying the guidelines which really count. For example, take the problem of him traveling triple file instead of double."

"Yes."

"The reason for traveling double file instead of single file is so the saints would be bunched closer together in case of attack. So if Frank travels triple file, isn't he really obeying the purpose of the guidelines?"

"Except you're forgetting that those two couples make a terrible racket traveling next to each other," Seth objected.

"I know, but most of the saints make too much noise as they go along. It's a problem everybody has. Hopefully, we'll solve that weakness in the next few days."

"Okay, okay, I understand. You want me to ease up on Frank a bit."

"A lot."

Seth picked up a boulder and heaved it in an arc, crushing a black beetle six feet away. "All right, a lot. But what about his refusal to come to the report meeting tonight?"

Steven was disturbed to see Seth's pleasure in killing the bug for no reason at all. "Yes, I wanted to ask you about that meeting. What do you intend to do there?"

"I'll go around the circle to check on whether or not they're doing their assigned visits. Then we'll discuss any serious problems their people might have. It's kind of like a meeting on home teaching."

"So you'll go around the circle and ask each man there to report on his activity in front of about forty other men?"

Seth replied, "Yes, it's a good way to get a report quickly without having to contact each man separately."

"Have you questioned Frank about his activity in front of people on other occasions?"

Seth paused. "Yes, but only in front of his wife and some of his friends. I had no intention of embarrassing him."

"I see. Well, I counsel you not to do it that way."

"But why? It's very effective."

Steven frowned. "Well, it may save you time, but you're using social pressure to get the men to do their duty. It's really a form of intimidation and manipulation, which are actually the same thing as compulsion. I prefer you don't use compulsion to influence the behavior of the brethren."

Seth raised his eyebrows as he declared positively, "But the brethren like that technique. I've used it many times in the past, and no one has ever objected. A lot of leaders do it that way."

"That's because they care mostly about what is convenient for themselves. Their main desire is to get that report, no matter what. Obviously, they're not sensitive to the men and women who might be exposed in public as negligent in their duties. And what is the result? The exposed individual is deeply humiliated and, since it's done out of convenience and not in the true spirit of love, he resents such treatment and may be tempted to rebel."

"No. I assure you that I do it in love."

"Maybe, but the method of public report is a terrible way to motivate anyone to do the Lord's work in the right spirit. The people who depend on it also tend to use excessive persistence, veiled threats, and even anger to intimidate the saints to perform. In my opinion, they've no idea what they're actually doing. They need to study and memorize the words of Doctrine and Covenants, section 121, especially verses thirty-six through forty-two."

Seth got a triumphant look in his eye. "Yes! But verse forty-three says, 'Reproving betimes with sharpness, when moved upon by the Holy Spirit.'"

"I'm afraid that's one of the most misunderstood verses in scripture," Steven said. "The sharp reproof it speaks of, which is inspired by the Spirit, cannot be anger as we know it, because the Holy Ghost never moves man to anger. There are other scriptures which say that anger is always evil. Also, the angry brothers who think they're using the Lord's 'sharp reproof' are usually too mad to remember the second part of the verse which declares that the reprover must quickly show an 'increase in love.' So if you're increasing your love, that means your reproof should have been done in love, not anger. I'm afraid no one can immediately show love after being angry."

"However, God sometimes uses 'righteous indignation' when he deals with man. I think that's an example for his children."

"I realize that, but we are not righteous like God, and our so-called indignation is quickly corrupted by negative anger. And that's not all. Irritation, impatience, and frustration are no more than veiled forms of anger. None of those emotions are righteous."

Seth arose and said, "Well, Brother Christopher, I see you have strong opinions on how to deal with people. Listen, I'll give your words some serious thought, but it's hard to stop doing things the time-honored way simply because one person thinks you should. I know the old methods get results. The work has to be done, and we need those reports."

"That's right, but at what cost? I suggest you forgive Frank Hamilton his weaknesses. Show him kindness, patience, and gentleness, instead of sternness and impatience. Show him you truly love him and care about him, and he'll come around eventually. Also, I believe that instead of focusing on getting work done, you might find out why he does what he does. After all, this is a gospel community of love, not a business or a job demanding performance."

"What do you mean by that?"

"Well, three months ago I interviewed Frank in connection with the journey to Zion. During our discussion I discovered that Frank's father had been an alcoholic. To make a long story short, the sick man brutalized his son. Instead of showing the boy love, he used threats, anger, and intimidation to control his behavior. So it may be that today Frank sees his father in you, at least to some degree."

Seth paused for a full half minute, staring at the ground, his face pale. Then he looked up and said, "We've all had problems in our lives, but that doesn't justify us being rebellious when we're adults. Every criminal has excuses for breaking the law and hurting other people. It doesn't mean we should let them get away with their crimes." Having said this, he turned abruptly and walked away.

Steven followed him with his eyes. He had seen this behavior before. There were some people who were so blind and stubborn that they were incapable of change, and all reason seemed beyond them. Somehow Seth had transformed Frank's innocuous behavior into real crimes.

Chapter 9

When Steven returned to camp, he saw William starting a fire for the evening meal. Mary was nowhere in sight. "William, where's Mary?"

"She went up the path a little way with some people. Toward the freeway. Doug and Liz and most of the kids went too."

Steven remembered that Mary had promised Joshua Hale and Hannah Baldwin that she would take them on an herb walk to find Brigham tea and burdock root. Steven walked a hundred yards up the path and finally caught sight of them not far away from the highway. Everybody had full baskets and seemed to be finding a lot of plants. Douglas was guarding them with a rifle in hand. Steven noticed that Hannah and Joshua had brought their spouses with them.

He walked back to his wagon, unwrapped his legs, and rubbed them with comfrey and cayenne ointment. He was pleased to see that the swelling had gone down. A few minutes later the plant pickers returned.

Mary laughed as she ran up and kissed her husband. "We found so many medicinal herbs! My patients have enough to last them over a week. I even remembered to tell them how to prepare and use them. Aren't you proud of me? And look at what else I found." Giggling louder than ever, Mary shoved a basket under his nose.

Steven gave it a sour look. "Yeah, nice. What are the weeds for?"

"For supper."

Steven swallowed hard and caught the other foragers laughing at him as they placed their baskets brimming with plants close together near the wagon.

He gazed at his wife in disbelief. "Tell me you're kidding."

Mary suddenly stopped giggling. "Not at all, young man, you told every person in Pioneer One that we had to live off the fat of the land, and that's what these weeds are."

"I told them that?"

"Yes, in your speech and your famous guidelines."

"Oh."

"Aren't they wonderful?"

"Yes, of course. So what's for supper?"

She smiled happily and her eyes shone. "A lovely salad of dandelion leaves and thistle stems, uncooked, of course. Also, we'll have bean soup seasoned with wild onions. It's all very healthy." Mary waved good-bye to the Hales and the Baldwins, who started to leave. They had been listening to Mary and Steven's conversation with amusement.

"Sounds delicious," Steven replied ironically. Although he wasn't looking forward to eating the new forage, he was very proud of her ingenuity. "I have a good idea, Mary."

"What's that, dear?"

"Tomorrow, instead of preparing a meal, why don't we just walk out into the fields and graze like the cattle?"

Instead of getting angry, Mary put her hands on her hips and thought hard. "Mmm, that might not be a bad idea. At least we'd be a lot healthier than we were when we bought our food at the grocery store in the city."

The women finished preparing supper at seven o'clock. The usual crowd was there: Steven and Mary's family, the Cartwrights, and the three bachelors. Ruther Johnston returned from his excursion in the mountains in time for the meal, which he ate with relish, as if it were the most normal food in the world. Steven loved the soup but hated the salad. From the look on their faces, he guessed that the other "civilized" people in the group shared his opinion. All except Mary, of course. After cleaning up, they sat around in a circle and stared at the fire without saying much.

The silence was broken by Ruther, who said with a twinkle in his eye, "Yuh know, folks, I kin understand why you Mormons is so sad and ain't got much ta say."

This remark stunned everyone, and every eye turned upon the mountain man. Steven smiled and said, "What makes you think we're sad, Mr. Johnston?"

"Like I said, call me Ruther. I hate that there formal stuff."

"Okay—Ruther. Why do you say we're sad?"

"Well, it's probably because yuh all suspect or feel somehow that you're goin' ta miss out on the real action. Because when the real stuff comes down, yuh won't be able ta do nothin' but set here chewin' yer cud, or doin' somethin' else inconsequential. Or yuh'll be out thar sweatin' blood and tears day after day on this here blazin' hot trail, strugglin' at all cost ta git ta yer chosen land, when the Christians—excuse me, the other Christians—are carried up ta bliss in the arms of Jesus in the glorious rapture. Now, I don't intend ta get yer dander up sayin' such a shockin' thing, because I'm really startin' ta like you folks. But the truth is the truth."

Steven suspected the old man was deliberately baiting them, purposely using the worst English he could to make them believe he was just a hick. But was the old coot as ignorant as he acted?

Steven took the bait. "I'm not sure what you're getting at, Ruther."

"Well, the scriptures teach that the true believers in Christ will suddenly disappear from the earth. Poof! Just like that. Millions of 'em gone. And the other folks who were talkin' to 'em will look around ta see where the heck they went, and they won't find a durn thing. The wunnerful thing is, those true believers will be taken up ta meet Jesus before the great triberlation hits the earth. Like I said, they calls it the rapture. Then, after the triberlation, Jesus'll come, full of wrath, and punish the wicked. Do yuh all 'member that scripture which talks about the two men in the field? One will be taken and the other left behind. That refers ta what I'm talkin' about."

"What about the other true believers?" Paul asked.

Ruther appeared confused. "What other true believers? There's only one church of true believers. They may belong ta different denomernations, but they're all a part of the one great church."

Paul kept going. "But some of those believers say the rapture comes after the tribulation, and others believe it comes during the tribulation. Even those who accept what you say, that it comes before the tribulation, are constantly fighting over the details of the sequence of events. Are the true believers who reject your point of view going to be raptured anyhow?"

"Oh, I suppose so. The believers disagree on details, but they'll still be raptured when the time comes."

"What about the Latter-day Saints?" Elizabeth asked.

Ruther replied cautiously, but with the same grin. "I wish I could say yes, but you folks don't believe in salvation by grace alone, and yuh don't believe there's only one God."

Steven wanted to challenge him on those two doctrines, but decided to wait until another time.

Paul said, "So you're saying the same thing you said before. Yesterday you said we aren't Christians because we don't believe the way you do, and today you say we can't be caught up to meet Christ for the same reason."

"Yep, that's purdy much it. But it's not really because yuh don't believe the way I do. It's because yuh don't accept what the Bible clearly says."

Jarrad Babcock said, "Ruther, we love the Bible, but it's not as clear as you say. That's why so many true believers—as you call them—can't agree on when your rapture is supposed to take place, and why there are so many different Christian churches."

Douglas added, "It seems to me history shows that those different sects often hated one another and fought to the death over their beliefs. Doesn't that seem strange to you when they based their beliefs on the same Bible?"

"Well, yuh got me there," Ruther said. "Let me think about it a few days before I answer that point."

"I have a question, Ruther," Mary said sweetly.

"Yes, Ma'am?"

"What happens to the people who aren't raptured?"

Ruther struggled to maintain his composure. "They goes through the triberlation."

"Does that mean they're damned?"

"Mmmm, uh, yeah, I suppose so."

"So what you're saying is that millions of believers are saved, but billions of unbelievers, like me perhaps, are damned forever."

"Well, uh— yuh know, I'm a thinkin' that if I was Jesus, which I ain't of course, I'd make an exception for a fine lady like you."

"Well, thank you Ruther. You're very thoughtful. But as for the people the Lord punishes, doesn't that include millions of good people who have never had the chance to hear about Jesus, and millions of babies who are too young to believe?"

"Well, I don't know about that. Yuh better give me a chance ta discuss that with some of my Baptist friends."

Steven said, "Ruther, you are a good man, and I'm sure you don't want anyone to suffer the tribulation. That's probably why you're trying to warn us. But I'd like to know where you find the idea of a rapture in the scriptures."

"Okay. I learnt where those scriptures are by heart." Ruther pulled out a tattered Bible from inside his coat, searched a little, and found a passage. "Here we goes. In First Thessalonians 4:16-17 it says Jesus will come from heaven, the holy dead will rise, the living believers will be caught up with the dead ta meet the Lord in the air, and all of them will live with him forever." He flipped a few pages. "And here in First Corinthians 15:51-52 it says we—meanin' us true believers, of course—will be changed in the twinkling of an eye at the last trump. So yuh see, the scriptures prove our belief in the rapture."

"But, Ruther," Leonard Reece said, "didn't you say at the beginning that Jesus will descend from heaven after the tribulation?"

"Yep, I did."

"I'm confused then. The verses you summarized in Thessalonians say that he will descend before the rapture. That means before the tribulation."

Ruther answered, "Well, actually Jesus comes from heaven more than once. He descends at the rapture, then later to punish the wicked."

Jarrad jumped in. "But isn't the rapture supposed to be a secret, quiet event that only the raptured recognize?"

"That's right."

Steven was concerned that the Mormon defenders were ganging up on the old man. Still, everyone continued to discuss the ideas with a good spirit, and Ruther seemed to love it, so he didn't come to Ruther's rescue.

Jarrad continued, "Then why does First Thessalonians say that the Lord shall descend with a shout and the trump of God? That doesn't sound very silent to me."

Ruther had an answer. "That there has a spiritual meaning. It isn't a physical event. Yuh got ta read all these here scriptures in context."

Jarrad smiled and let it drop. But Paul had something else to say. "Okay, let's put it into a context of other scriptures. Mark, chapter thirteen, and Matthew, chapter twenty-four, seem to put the three events we're discussing into the same order: first the tribulations, then the Second Coming, and finally the gathering of the elect from the four corners of the earth. Doesn't this contradict your idea of the rapture occurring before the tribulations?"

"Yes siree, Mr. Paul, I've read them scriptures and I cain't figure 'em out. So until I does, you'll have ta wait ta git my answer."

Steven was relieved to see John and the four colonels heading toward his wagon. "Well, the leaders are coming for our meeting. Thank you, everybody. It's been an interesting conversation." He looked at Ruther. "And thank you, Ruther. We certainly appreciate you keeping us on our toes."

"Glad ta be of help, Steve."

The meeting with the leaders of Pioneer One lasted a half hour. The item which caught their interest most was the report which Ruther gave at Steven's request. The mountain man explained that he had spent the day exploring the country ten miles up I-80 for signs of the gang which had terrorized the entire region. He discovered nothing except a few indications that members of the gang had passed over the area a week earlier. Steven told him he was grateful for his concern regarding their welfare.

After the leaders returned to their own wagons, Steven and Mary sat around the campfire discussing the events of the day with their friends. Later that night, Steven and Mary had their own conversation by the light of a lamp as they lay in their beds.

Mary asked, "So Anastasia said she overheard gossip that you're going to lead us to Canada so you can rule over us as king?"

"That's what she said."

"But it's so weird! How could anyone believe it?"

"I don't understand it. Still, I have to admit that I've seen people believe some pretty strange things in my life."

"That woman bugs me." Mary said angrily.

"Who?"

"Anastasia!" she said impatiently.

"Why does she bug you?"

"The way she looks at you all the time. She puts on that little-girl act of hers, puckers up her yummy red lips, and sighs deeply as she gazes longingly into your eyes."

"Mmm, I haven't noticed."

"Liar."

"Who? Me?"

"Yes. You know perfectly well what she does."

"Shucks, girl. She does it to every man in camp below the age of fifty."

"I know, but she really turns it on when she sees you. I'd sure like to know why."

Steven couldn't resist the feeling that Mary was preparing a trap for him. Maybe a test. "I have no idea."

"Maybe it's because you're so friendly to her," Mary probed.

"Of course. I try to be friendly to everybody."

"Well, maybe you're trying too hard when it concerns her."

"Wow! That sounds like jealousy."

Mary suddenly changed her tone. "Don't be silly. I'm not jealous at all. Jealousy is a weakness which is beneath a mature woman. A woman who truly loves and respects herself does not feel a trace of jealousy." It sounded like a line memorized from a self-help book.

"Yes, I've heard you say that before."

Mary went on. "All I'm trying to say is, when you're so friendly to Anastasia, she prefers to interpret that to mean you're interested in her personally."

"I am interested in her personally." Steven didn't intend to help Mary out.

"I mean, she interprets your friendliness as a sign that you're romantically attached to her."

"That's her problem then, not mine. What do you want me to do, grump and frown every time she comes near me?"

"Nooo. All you have to do is be a little less friendly."

"Okay, sweetheart, I'll try to follow your guidelines."

"Good. Remember, you're the spiritual and temporal head of Pioneer One, and your behavior must be above reproach."

"I'll try to remember."

After a minute of silence, Steven said, "Did we just have our first argument?"

"Of course not. We simply engaged in a mature discussion about relationships."

"Boy, that's a relief."

A little later, Mary said sullenly, "I certainly wish that hussy would get her own husband."

Steven chuckled. "Mary! Hussy?" He waited for her to take it back, but when she didn't, he said, "It seems that's what she's trying to do."

Mary was surprised. "What do you mean?"

"Paul tells me she's been spending a lot of time helping one of our single men pull a handcart. Apparently she's working herself half to death doing it."

"Which man?" Mary said hopefully.

"I'm not sure you know him. His name is Pierce Hudson. He's about thirty-three, tall, blond, good-looking, quiet, and has two children. His wife was killed last year by some thug. He has a wagon, which his twelve-year-old son usually drives, and a handcart."

"I believe I treated him for blisters. So is it serious?"

"Well, according to Paul, I may have to perform a marriage in the near future. Paul, as you might expect, pretends he's outraged that she would pick someone besides him."

Mary's voice revealed her delight. "Instant motherhood. I know what that's like. It'll be especially good for Anastasia."

"I'm glad you have her best interests at heart, dear." Steven gave her a very wet kiss on the mouth.

Several minutes later, when Steven was half asleep, Mary said, "Why was Brother Crowell so angry today?"

"Uh, well, one of his men gives him trouble once in a while, and it really upsets him. He's a colonel, you know. The details aren't important."

"It's probably good that he came to you and was able to express his anger."

"Perhaps you're right," Steven said. "Still, I suggested to Seth that he wasn't using his authority properly when he got so mad. The truth is, I'm coming to the conclusion that anger is always bad."

"I'm not sure it's always bad. There are schools of psychology which teach that venting your anger acts as a catharsis and dissipates the emotion."

"I've heard that before. However, some people believe that catharsis stuff is nothing but theoretical mumbo jumbo. Let me tell you my own theory on anger."

Mary rolled toward him and put her leg across his. "Okay. I usually like your ideas."

"I compare how people handle anger to the three degrees of glory. On the lowest level, the telestial, the angry person seeks revenge. He's so full of anger and hate that he seeks to hurt his enemy in some way. Eventually, he puts his desire into action. On the terrestrial level the angry person vents his feelings, but doesn't act upon them. Yet these explosions of emotion often become little more than practice, and so there is a danger that the anger may grow in intensity with the constant rehearsal of offenses. In the end it can consume a person's life and poison his relationships with others.

"Of course, if he expresses the anger directly to the people he's mad at, they end up returning the anger and hating him. On the highest level, the celestial, the person is so full of the Holy Ghost that he doesn't feel anger in the first place when provoked. He has the power to see the truth in the situation and usually reacts with love instead."

"I'm not sure I buy all that, Steven, but it's worth thinking about."

"Well, the scriptures say we should put away anger. They don't say we should express it, to relieve stress or for any other reason. Other scriptures say we should be slow to anger. If our final goal is to have the constant companionship of the Holy Ghost, what place will anger ever have in our hearts if we achieve that goal? The fruits of the Spirit are love, gentleness, kindness, patience, and so forth, not anger disguised as righteous indignation."

Mary said quietly, "But the goal of being so good that we never feel anger might be similar to the goal of perfection. It's an ideal we can strive for, but never fully achieve in this life."

"Yes, you're probably right . . . But to get back to Seth. I also suggested something else to him. Apparently it was a revolutionary concept he'd never heard of before . . ."

"What was it?"

"I counseled him to find out why people do what they do, instead of harping on nothing but performance."

"Hah! If you keep talking like that, you're going to make a lot of enemies."

Steven gazed at her curiously in the dim light, admiring both her beauty and her intelligence. "I suppose you're right on that one too." He felt a great fatigue come over him. "Well, we'd better get some sleep. We'll need to be rested and strong tomorrow." A few minutes later, he murmured, "Something tells me that the future holds hardships we can't even imagine today, and that we'll need all the strength we have to handle them."

Chapter 10

During the last few days the pioneers had been increasing their consumption of wild edible plants, and so far had experienced few problems doing so. But on Saturday many began to have gastrointestinal disturbances and sought help from Dr. Quentin Price. The beleaguered doctor soon found it extremely difficult to deal with the long line of sufferers who gathered at his wagon each time the caravan stopped. His advice was that they should back off on their intake of the new fare for a while and make sure the plants they consumed were not toxic. Since he knew nothing about natural pharmacology, that was the only advice he could give.

The thing which bothered him the most was the fact that many of the pioneers were beginning to complain of severe diarrhea, nausea, and vomiting. To some degree, he attributed these problems to the plants they were ingesting, but the intense and constant diarrhea seemed especially puzzling. Unfortunately, not only did he lack antibiotics, but he also had no lab facilities and could only guess as to the cause of the ailment. He figured that maybe the pioneers had drunk polluted water from one of the streams, but he couldn't be sure. Hoping that the problem would resolve itself naturally in a week or so, he encouraged the victims to avoid dehydration by drinking plenty of water, which they should purify by boiling.

The pioneers faced another serious problem when it came to taking care of their natural needs. Their meager supply of toilet paper had run out a few days after the trek had begun, and they had been forced to use the leaves of plants to clean themselves. This presented certain unique difficulties, because the supply of plants which bore leaves long enough and broad enough and soft enough to do the job were hard to come by. Often the pioneers chose the wrong plants and ended up with stinging rashes in very inconvenient places.

The herbalists in the company encouraged them to be patient and look forward to May, the month when nature's toilet paper—mullein—would begin to push forth its broad downy leaves.

In any case, after they finished their business, they had to dig a hole and bury the fruits of their labors with the soiled leaves. Before long, they learned to use a special board, which they carried with them whenever they wanted to commune with nature. It was eighteen inches wide and thirty inches long, and the round hole in the center had a diameter of seven inches. As soon as they reached an appropriate secluded spot, they dug a deep, narrow hole, placed the board across it, and used it as a portable toilet seat.

Some of the sisters insisted on raising the board a few inches above the ground so they could be more comfortable and not soil their clothes. It didn't seem to matter that their outfits were already covered with layers of grime and smelled horribly of sweat. They elevated the boards by propping logs or stones under both ends, or by having their husbands build board supports, so that these contraptions ended up resembling lap boards that people use when they wish to eat or read in bed. The great thing was that a dozen people could use the same board over the same hole and come away perfectly clean.

Some husbands made solid boards with sturdy supports at each end, but it took two women to carry one. Other husbands, motivated by love and respect, were particularly diligent and created boards which were light and elegant so that their wives might have less trouble carrying them to the relief site. In the second case, however, some of these favored sisters, demonstrating unusual confidence in their husbands' skill, plopped too vigorously on the boards and immediately plunged to the bottom of the holes as the boards snapped in half.

In spite of the convenience of the boards, it was often embarrassing for the sisters to deal with the natural need. In order for them to go to the rest room when the wagon train stopped, they had to gather into small groups of four or five women and, accompanied by their daughters, search for a spot out of sight of camp, but not so far away that they were in danger. At least one of the women carried a weapon to protect the group. Unfortunately, it was not always certain that those bearing the arms actually knew how to use them. Every time Steven saw a troop of women heading away from camp equipped with a shovel, a special board, and a rifle, he had no doubt as to what was going on.

The problem became even more grave when the pioneers learned that violent outlaws, who did not hesitate to rape and murder women, lurked in the nearby wilderness. Then it became more difficult to go to the toilet, because many women refused to leave camp without a man or two in escort. After they procured the assistance of some reluctant male, the sisters set out to brave the rocky wasteland, carrying the necessary equipment. When they found a suitable location, and the armed escort disappeared from view, the women and girls did what they came to do, fully assured that they had secured both their privacy and their protection.

But when other sisters heard what some were doing, they knitted their brows in disgust and marched off alone, declaring that they didn't need any man to take care of them. Steven let them go, figuring that if any savage was foolhardy enough to mess with those sisters, he deserved what he got.

The greatest problem came, however, when the saints had to go to the toilet while the wagons were moving. Most of the males handled the problem quickly and easily, but the females had a more difficult time of it—at least at first. At the beginning of the trek, the women and girls had secreted themselves in their wagons and had solved the problem with the aid of special plastic containers they had brought for that very purpose. But soon they had discovered that they ended up with the disgusting job of emptying and cleaning the containers when the wagon train stopped.

The situation became especially disagreeable for the sisters who had squeamish husbands, because they declined to relieve themselves in the open. Following the example of their wives, they also hopped into the wagons to do their duty. Unfortunately, however, by some strange quirk of the male mind, many of the finicky brothers had inadvertently used a family utensil instead of the designated containers. When this happened, the discord erupted so violently in some families that news of the event spread rapidly through the entire caravan. In spite of everything the sisters could do, the smell stuck to the container like flies on flypaper, and most grumbled and glared as they worked to scour and purify the indispensable vessel.

So as time progressed, most sisters resigned themselves to following the example of the shameless males. As soon as nature's urgent call struck, they made a beeline to the nearest bush, squatted until the work was done, then hurried to overtake the moving caravan. They soon learned that this simple technique had a double advantage: they could always claim, when questioned by some insensitive observer, that they had only gone to pick a lovely flower or a rare edible plant. However, a few determined sisters insisted on fighting nature's call until they thought they would die, or until the caravan finally stopped.

The wagon train stopped for the night just south of the town of Wanship, Utah, on the Weber River. Steven sent a group of armed men to investigate the town, and they found nothing to indicate violence—only a hasty departure. It was a mystery as to what had become of the town's citizens. Later, as Steven walked through the camp to check on the pioneers, he was shocked to see that the dysentery which had struck earlier in the day was becoming widespread. In nearly every wagon there was at least one person who was down with severe fever, vomiting, weakness, and diarrhea. The disease seemed to attack people of all ages and conditions. Steven consulted with Dr. Price and Mary, but they were at a loss to explain the cause of the malady or suggest an effective remedy. Dr. Price assured Steven that the sickness was probably not fatal and would soon run its course.

On Sunday Ruther rode out of camp again, declaring he wouldn't return until he located the gangs. The pioneers used the day to rest and renew their spirits. In spite of the fact that nearly one-fourth of the saints were sick with the new disease, the members insisted on having church services. The colonels organized and directed four separate meetings so that the people would not be gathered into one place. In the initial session everyone received the sacrament, heard a short speech, and sang several hymns. Afterwards, they divided into small classes to hear a lesson on the Lord's dealings with Lehi and his family in the deserts of Arabia. The entire service took no more than an hour and fifteen minutes. Most of the people sat on the ground during the meetings.

That night Steven insisted on taking a watch, in spite of the protests of John, who felt that the leader of the caravan should not put himself in peril. John also admitted his fear: if Steven were injured or killed, the task of leading the wagon train would fall upon him. As he stood guard, Steven tried to remember the lessons Ruther had taught him two nights ago . . . Oh yes. Keep your eyes open but, above all, penetrate the dark with your ears. Learn to recognize the normal sounds of the wilderness. Then, when he listened acutely, he would recognize the sounds that shouldn't be there, and he would know that danger might be near. Steven had to admit that simply having the old Baptist around gave him surprising reassurance. Where was he now and what had he discovered?

The pioneers set out early in the morning on Monday, continuing on the highway in double file. Soon the highway turned directly north and opened onto a wide, flat valley surrounded by low hills. The valley was full of farms, pastures, and long sheds. Once again, search parties explored the area and found that everything was where it should be, except the people. Even the animals were in their cages or grazing contentedly in the fields. As Steven double-checked one small community close to the road, the ridiculous idea came to him that the people had been raptured, just like the old Baptist had said would happen to the true believers.

News of the missing inhabitants spread like wildfire in the wagon train, creating consternation in the hearts of the pioneers. Steven saw terror in every eye, and some could not control their sobbing. The leaders did their best to assure the people that the Lord would not forsake them, and that Pioneer One had the strength to deal with any threat that might arise. Steven secretly asked himself many times if that were really true.

The pioneers reached the southern tip of Echo Reservoir in the late afternoon. In spite of their fear, many of the sisters could no longer bear the smell of their bodies nor the filth of their clothes. Nearly every female in the company gathered into one group and agreed to go together to the water for a bath. After explaining their plan to the men and warning them to stay in camp until they returned, they hiked down to the reservoir three hundred yards away. They spread out along its banks, threw off their clothes, and washed their bodies.

As soon as they had finished that task, they washed the clothes they had been wearing. Afterwards, they put them on wet, unless they were fortunate enough to have a fresh change of clothes. Then they washed the bundles of dirty clothes they had brought. A number of sisters brought rifles to protect the bathers. When they returned an hour and a half later, they were smiling and looking much happier. Some of the men were so impressed by what the bath did for the females that they decided to do the same thing. When they reentered camp after an hour, it was beginning to grow dark.

Even though the pioneers were now able to smile and talk pleasantly, a feeling of impending doom still lay heavy upon the camp. As they went about their chores, the travelers stopped frequently to search the growing shadows for any sign of danger. After asking John to increase the guard even more, Steven walked through the entire encampment to encourage the people, smiling and showing a confidence he didn't feel.

The next day the wagon train traveled alongside Echo Reservoir, which stretched for three miles beside the highway. The two parts of the freeway divided and continued on separate levels. A high ridge on the left shadowed the lanes they followed. Steven was constantly concerned that it would be easy for an enemy to wipe out the entire company from that vantage point with little danger to itself. Soon, he could bear it no longer and sent a contingent of men to climb the rise and follow the caravan along the top. He looked up the road ahead and was relieved to see the scouts, who were checking the road a mile in front of the main body. Suddenly, he noticed the road itself and was troubled to see that the number of fissures and gaps was increasing, making travel more difficult. The saints boiled under the hot sun, and many trudged along blindly and awkwardly. And yet the fear of what lay ahead seemed to make them forget their present pain for a time.

By mid-afternoon Pioneer One had reached the junction of I-80 and I-84, where the road turned sharply northeast and led to Evanston, Wyoming. Shortly after they made the turn, John, Paul, Jarrad, and Leonard came riding up to Steven as he walked beside the lead wagon.

"Steven," John called. "Aren't we getting close to the area Ruther warned us about? If the headquarters of the gang is near Windy Knoll Mountain, I figure it's only six miles from here."

"That's what I was thinking," Steven replied. "What do you suggest?"

"I'm not sure. Where could Ruther be? We certainly could use his advice right now."

"I suggest we bring the wagons up three abreast," Jarrad said. "Also, we could instruct the drivers to stay as close together as possible. Look at them. They're kind of strung out right now."

"Good suggestions, Jarrad," Steven said. "John, would you tell Murray Hutchinson to sound the danger signal?" Steven glanced at his wagon and saw the worried look on Mary's face.

"You got it!" John shouted as he trotted his Morgan down the line of wagons.

Steven turned to Paul. "Who's driving your wagon?"

"A teenage kid we bribe when we need to take off together."

As they continued to move with the wagons, Leonard declared, "This highway is a problem at times like this. It's so high above the surrounding terrain that it makes us sitting ducks."

Paul examined the sides of the road. "Steve, there's another problem. A big one. The terrain is so rough in this area that we couldn't get them off the freeway and into circles."

Steven looked around. "You're right. Trees and ravines everywhere . . . Think, brethren! We need to decide what to do if we're attacked."

They heard a bugle sound two short blasts, followed quickly by two additional blasts. After a short pause, the same warning was repeated again. A minute later they heard an identical signal repeated more faintly farther down the wagon train. Steven knew that the alarm would be repeated by several buglers the entire length of the caravan until every pioneer heard it. Quickly the drivers moved into triple file and drew their wagons closer together. John did not return, but Steven knew he was taking charge of the caravan's rear guard.

Steven smiled at Mary and called, "That makes me feel better." She waved him a kiss.

Steven said to the bachelors, "Okay, guys, what else can we do?"

Paul said, "What choices do we have? If the bandits attack, we have to stop the wagons and return fire."

Jarrad scowled. "What if they attack from both sides of the road?"

"Yes, of course," Paul replied. "I must be off my nut. Somehow I got it into my head that they would attack from the cliffs on this side." Paul gestured toward the Canyonland-type bluffs several hundred yards away on the north side of the highway. "If they hit us from both sides, we're dead."

The bachelors tied their horses to their own wagon, the third wagon in the caravan, and spread out in a line on the left margin of the road not far from the lead wagons. Before long, they were joined by other men armed with hunting rifles.

They plodded along like this for hours. When the time came—late in the afternoon—for the wagon train to pull in for the night, Steven urged them on because there was no place to stop in safety. Even though the travelers were consumed by exhaustion under the hot sun, and the grade was steeper, they sensed the urgency of the situation and increased their pace. In the next hour they covered almost two miles.

Steven was anxiously studying the land south of the road for an open spot, when he heard a resounding whack not far away. He whirled around, searching for the source of the sound. He heard the shouts of men and the cries of women and children, but he couldn't see what was happening.

Just then Paul and Jarrad appeared. Paul seized Steven by the arm and shouted, "It came from the cliffs on the left."

"The bullet smashed into the side of a wagon, but no one was hurt," Jarrad added.

At first Steven wondered why no one had returned fire, but then the thought flashed through his mind that his men probably couldn't see the enemy rifleman any better than he. Followed by Paul and Jarrad, he moved to the left margin of the road. As he scrutinized the bluffs, he heard another shot and thought he saw a movement half way up the hill. At the same instant, one of the young men on his left, Murray Hutchinson the bugler, dropped abruptly to the ground, his head blown half off. He heard a woman scream. Steven angrily raised his .30-06 to shoot back, but saw no one to punish.

Paul screamed in Steven's ear, "We've got to stop the wagons and take cover!"

For a moment Steven panicked, knowing that so many lives depended on him. Then all at once he knew what he had to do. "Double time! Now!" he shouted.

The men around him obeyed without question, and urged the people to pick up the pace, following the action of their leader. They continued at this stride for two minutes.

"Faster," Steven yelled.

They began a slow jog. During the next five minutes, they heard additional shots ring out from the bluffs, and bullets slammed into wagons and ricocheted off the pavement. Several saints were injured by flying debris, but no one was knocked to the ground. The saints were struggling so hard to maintain the pace that none bothered to return the fire. It was even more difficult now, since there were so many, including grown men, who had been attacked by the new illness and were too weak to do anything except lie in the wagons. During the desperate run to safety, a chubby brother, who had been gasping for breath, suddenly crumpled dead to the pavement. Steven guessed the pioneers had jogged at least a half mile and knew they couldn't continue much longer. The terrible thought struck him that perhaps his inspiration had been nothing but his own imagination.

Then he saw it. "Over there," he shouted, pointing to the south.

It was a wide open area on the right which was reasonably smooth and accessible. He ran across the road in front of the caravan and began to direct the wagons into the field. The men who had been trotting beside him followed his example.

Steven called to his helpers, "Tell them to put the wagons into two circles, one inside the other."

Steven and Paul watched by the edge of the road as the line of wagons rolled off the freeway and into the field. A man who was prodding his oxen into the gully at the side of the road crumpled abruptly. Steven saw a bloody spot spread across his back. Because of the rumble of the vehicles, he hadn't even heard the report of the enemy weapon. His heart ached as he wondered how many others along the line had been injured or murdered by the devils in the hills. Realizing then that their present position made them easy targets, he grabbed his brother's arm and pushed him into the ditch.

As the line of wagons went by him heading for the turnoff, Steven looked under them, trying to see the far side. Through the dust he saw other brethren spread along the opposite gully, facing the enemy. He recognized the face of Byron Mills, the "scriptorian" from the Grandview Second Ward. Most were firing their weapons. Steven and Paul trained their rifles on the cliffs above and shot at the slightest sign of movement. After a few minutes, they fired repeatedly into the ravines worn into the sides of the cliffs. They had little hope of hitting what they couldn't see, but knew that their fire would force their attackers to stay down. Steven asked himself why the enemy gunfire wasn't much heavier if the bandits numbered several hundred.

The fifteen minutes required to form the caravan into two circles seemed like an eternity to Steven. Suddenly John appeared as the last wagon exited the freeway. He joined his brothers. As soon as the drivers moved their wagons into position, they unharnessed their animals and drove them into the nearby countryside. Next they pulled the wagons close together until the wheels interlocked. The inner circle was formed perfectly, with two small gaps on opposite sides.

But the outer circle was too large for the number of wagons composing it, and there were eight large openings. The men filled the gaps with boulders, brush, and tree limbs. The women and children took cover inside the inner circle, while the men, older boys, and the women who could shoot found defensive positions in the space between the two circles. They waited for the enemy to attack in force, but the charge didn't come and the shots from the cliffs ceased while they were filling the breaks in the outer circle.

"Where are they?" Paul asked.

"You've got me, Paul," Steven replied.

"Do you think they took off?" Leonard said.

Jarrad answered, "I doubt it. They're probably trying to decide on how to take us."

"I wish Ruther were here," Paul said.

"I'm not sure he could tell us what to do in this situation," John replied. "Still, I'd feel safer with Ruther here wielding that Sharps Buffalo rifle. He told me he's used it to hit targets the size of a man as far away as a mile."

After a few moments of impatient waiting, Paul said, "If there are so many bandits, why wasn't there more shooting from the cliffs?"

"That's what I've been trying to figure that out," Steven said. "It's possible that only a few members of the gang were up there. The advance guard of the main group."

"That may be," Jarrad observed. "In any case, I bet they'll come in force when they finally hit us."

The bandits attacked an hour before sunset. A hundred heads suddenly popped up from the ravines and depressions on the east, and a heavy fusillade of gunfire fell upon the pioneers. Steven was astonished at the intensity of the assault. The defenders were forced to drop flat on the ground, as bullets whizzed over their heads and pounded into their wagons, showering them with painful splinters. The barrage was so great and constant that few of the defenders dared rise to fire back. And those who did were wounded or killed instantly. The initial attack lasted four minutes, and then there was silence.

"We're dead," John declared, his right cheek buried in the dirt. "There's no way we can stand up to that. They must have automatic weapons."

Jarrad agreed, "If they storm us, we won't have a chance of resisting."

Steven had the same thoughts, but was afraid to discourage the others by expressing his fear. He prayed to God with all his heart but heard no comforting voice to reassure him. From time to time, John peeked out to check on the enemy. After a while Steven moved to a sitting position and looked around. He saw three men lying in pools of blood, and a half dozen wounded. He remembered the grotesque condition of the corpses at Summit, and an overwhelming fear struck him. If these evil men overcame them, what would save the pioneers from torture and death? He sat there trembling, when he heard someone call his name.

"Steve! Steve!"

Steven glanced up. "Yes?"

"It's Leonard. Over here."

Steven spotted Leonard crawling toward him. When the young man was ten feet away, he said, "Some guy around the circle told me that the gang is gathering on the other side of the highway. About two hundred of them."

"Thanks, Leonard," Steven replied. He turned to the man next to him. It was Frank Hamilton, the young man Seth Crowell had complained about. Because of the intensity of the assault, Steven hadn't even noticed that Frank was close by. "Go south around the ring and tell every third person to move to the north side."

Frank nodded and hurried away. Steven and Paul arose and, crouching as low as they could, slipped past their comrades until they reached the northern section of the defensive line. The freeway was a hundred yards away, and Steven could see a multitude of heads just over the crest of the road. There was little movement except that the heads increased in number as he watched. He yelled for the defenders to hold their weapons ready and fire on his command. He was pleased when he saw other brothers and sisters arrive to take positions next to the protective wagons.

A short time later, he heard a fiendish scream from hundreds of throats, and the heads began to bob and grow larger as they advanced. At the same time, he heard the thunder of guns from the east side of the circle, and he knew that the bandits in that sector were firing again, no doubt to provide cover for the charge of the main body. He guessed that the same thing was occurring on the west side of his company. Steven waited patiently until he saw the enemy swarm to the top of the freeway, and then he yelled "fire."

The defenders fired as rapidly as they could, and the bandits began to take casualties. But as they drew near, voicing that same awful scream, dozens of them fired assault weapons from the hip, and the barrage became so intense that the defenders had no choice except to retreat behind the second row of wagons to avoid being slaughtered. Some didn't make it.

As soon as they swarmed into the inner circle, the beleaguered pioneers turned frantically and fired upon their enemies, killing many. Steven repeatedly pulled his trigger, feeling helpless in the tumult, the blinding smoke, and the violent movement of hundreds of people in conflict. The pioneers fought as gallantly as they could, but the bandits, even the females, were experienced warriors. They came from every direction and fell upon their prey, forcing them to the ground. Steven was surprised to see that the bandits didn't kill their captives outright, but disarmed them and intimidated them with their weapons.

Then two men came from behind and attacked Steven. In the struggle he managed to kill one with a shot to the head. But the second bandit, a hulk of a man, hit him in the chest with the butt of his weapon, slamming him to the earth and knocking his rifle away. Steven watched helplessly as his enemy, who seemed infuriated by the death of his buddy, snatched a short sword from a scabbard lashed to his back. His eyes red with hate, the man raised the sword and moved to strike. As Steven stared at the instrument of death, which began to arc toward him, an awesome force suddenly struck the brute and hurled him backwards into the air. Nine feet away he dropped to the earth, lifeless. A second after the bandit fell, Steven heard a loud boom above the din of the struggle around him. It came from the wilderness south of the circles.

The struggle was over in less than ten minutes. The attackers pushed the saints at gun point to the center of the inner circle, where they commanded them to huddle together on the ground. Steven searched for his family, fearing they might be injured or even dead, but saw them nowhere. Many of the pioneers around him were sobbing, and a few looked at him with accusing eyes.

Minutes later the bandits brought Ruther in. He wasn't carrying his Sharps. The old man sat next to Steven and said, "You okay?"

"Yes. That was you?"

"Yep. Couldn't let that runt kill a friend of mine, could I?"

Steven guessed that the old man had sacrificed his freedom to save him, but he didn't ask. "Thanks, Ruther."

"No problemo, as they say. You'd do the same fer me."

In a low voice they continued to talk for a while about the attack. Steven was particularly frantic concerning his family, and Ruther did his best to reassure him. Finally, several bandits stepped past the guards who were watching the captives. They pushed John Christopher ahead of them.

One of the thugs walked up to Steven, carrying an automatic pistol in his right hand. He nodded toward John. "This guy tells me you're the leader of this outfit. Get up."

Steven got to his feet. "That's right."

"My name's Good. Isaac Good. I'm the leader of this pack of wolves." Steven didn't answer. The leader went on. "What are you carrying in these wagons?"

"Clothes, bedding, provisions, tools, personal possessions. Things like that. Nothing more."

"We can use it all. Got any gasoline?"

"Very little."

"We're always looking for gas." Isaac showed a mouth full of rotten teeth. "You forgot to mention your weapons and ammunition. And all those fine animals."

"Take it all, but let us go. We don't mean you any harm."

The gang leader sneered. "Oh, we'll take it all, all right."

"Are you the ones who killed those people at Summit?"

"I don't answer questions—I ask them. Look, man, it's getting late and I'm tired. You've cost me a lot of time and some good people. So you're going to pay. I'll spell it out for you. We're taking your females with us. That kind of commodity is hard to come by these days. And the rest of you, we're going to kill. We spared your lives so far because we want to have a little fun with you tomorrow. It's one of the few enjoyments we get out of life these days. A few exciting games, a bit of torture. You know, that kind of stuff."

"You'd better git while the gittin's good, my friend," Ruther said matter-of-factly.

Isaac turned toward the mountain man. His eyes were cold and his face expressionless. "What did you say, old man?"

"I said you'd better git while the gittin's good. It may be too late already."

One of the leader's lieutenants advanced with his hunting knife drawn. "Why you—"

The leader stopped him. "Get back, stupid, and keep your yap shut." He faced Ruther again, licking his lips. "Why do you say that, old man?"

Ruther looked as calm and peaceful as if he were basking on a sunny beach at the French Riviera. He pulled a twig from the corner of his mouth. "Well, have yuh ever heard of the plague?"

Isaac froze, paralyzed by the word which had struck terror in the hearts of men for hundreds of years. "Sure," he said uncertainly. "Everybody's heard of it. So what?"

"Well, this here company's got the plague—the black death, the bubonic plague—and yuh kin get it faster'n a skunk kin lift its tail, if you're close to the afflicted. And them which does get it suffers the worst death yuh can possibly imagine. And there ain't no escape. Not for us or you or the animals. It kills everyone it infects. So if yuh all want ta meet your Maker right quick, I'd advise yuh ta stick around—just a bit longer. Personally, I'm a hopin' yuh do, so's I kin explain to the Almighty face to face what you fellers done today."

At first Steven couldn't understand what Ruther was doing, but suddenly it dawned on him.

The lieutenant who had threatened Ruther snarled, "If that's so, you old coot, why ain't you worried?"

Ruther looked at him with calm resignation. "Well, yuh see, I'm already a dead man. I accidently like ran into these folks and stuck around a mite too long without realizin' it, and now I'm infected somethin' awful. It takes a few days ta show up, but it's there all right, eatin' me up." He glanced at Steven. "Ain't that right, Captain?"

"Yes, it's only a matter of time." Steven tried hard to mimic Ruther's tormented resignation, but he fully expected the outlaw leader to burst out laughing at any moment. But to his surprise, the man didn't laugh.

John quickly joined in on the act. He wiped his nose with his sleeve and his eyes filled with tears. "My wife died three days ago."

Isaac trembled, but couldn't suppress his natural cynicism. "I don't believe you dirtbags for one minute, and I'm going to slice you up right now for trying to con me." He took out a twelve-inch knife from its sheath.

Ruther chuckled loudly. "Go right ahead there, boy. That kinda death would be down right pleasin' compared ta what I'm a facin'. Look, pardner, if yuh don't believe me, look in them wagons over yonder. Yuh'll see the black death starin' right back at yuh."

The thug eyed the closest wagon, hesitated, then said to Steven, "Show me."

They walked to the wagon, followed by Ruther, John, and two of the outlaw's lieutenants. Steven opened the rear flap, and Isaac peered in cautiously, trying to see in the dim light. He pulled back instantly and swore viciously.

"The smell!" he exclaimed. "The guy's puking like mad, and there's blood all over his blankets."

Steven had no idea who was in the wagon. "Yeah, those are the first symptoms of the black death. The poor guy came down with it yesterday."

The outlaw chief was terrified, but still wasn't convinced. He stopped at another wagon, but heard nothing. At the third wagon, he heard retching and pulled back the flap. Almost immediately he reeled backward, holding his hand over his mouth. He quickly checked three more wagons and found sick people in two of them.

Steven said grimly, "It's like that everywhere in the camp. All you need to do to catch it is get a little too close. Even I'm starting to feel sick."

"Let's get out of here, boss!" one of the lieutenants wailed.

The three bandit leaders paused for a brief moment. Then they bolted for the safety of the wilderness. Fifty other gangsters, who had watched Isaac check the wagons, followed their example. They rushed from the camp screaming "plague." They didn't even think about shooting their captives, but ran as if they were being chased by grizzly bears. News of the sudden evacuation spread quickly through the army of outlaws, and in seconds they fled from the Mormon camp. Many were so desperate to escape that they dropped their weapons and ammunition as they fought their way through the lines of wagons.

Ruther chuckled and turned to Steven, "Kinda shows what ignorance can do fer yuh, don't it?"

Steven gave him a bear hug. "Thank God you came, Ruther."

"Well, us Baptists ain't all bad, yuh know." John grabbed his hand and shook it vigorously. Ruther grinned and said to John, "As fer you, youngster, yuh done a right smart job of actin'. Yuh almost made me bawl when yuh talked about yer wife dyin' of the plague."

"Yeah, brother, I didn't know you had it in you," Steven said. John grinned.

Ruther became serious. "Listen, boys, yuh'd better go and locate yer families. They'll be a worryin'."

Steven and John hurried away to search for their families. The noise and confusion were unbelievable as the mob of pioneers jostled one another and staggered around looking for loved ones. Most had no idea why the band of criminals had fled in terror, but many released their pent-up anxiety by weeping. Some of the men recovered the weapons left by the frenzied outlaws and took defensive positions at the outer ring of wagons.

Steven ran to where his wagon had been rolled and found his family waiting for him. With joy they kissed and embraced each other. They asked him excitedly what had happened, and he related the ruse that Ruther had used to get rid of their enemies. The children clapped their hands in delight while their father acted out the entire scene, taking the role of each participant in turn as if he were a child. Soon Paul and the bachelors appeared unharmed, except for minor scratches and wounds. Steven told them the same story again. But soon their joy turned to grief when the colonels appeared and reported that they had found fourteen pioneers dead and dozens with serious wounds.

That night the saints built a few fires to warm their bodies and their hearts. But they didn't feel like eating and they couldn't sleep. Instead, they spent the night comforting those who had lost loved ones or nursing the sick. Now more pioneers showed signs of the intestinal illness. Steven feared that before daylight, he would have to place their bodies next to the slain, now covered with blankets near the center of the camp. He spent the night on the outer camp perimeter with Paul, Ruther, Douglas, and the bachelors. He said a silent prayer to God, thanking him for blinding the minds of their enemies.

Chapter 11

Steven vomited for the third time. His head was burning and hurt terribly. He had to go to the toilet so bad that he could hardly stand it. He looked at his watch: five in the morning. Maybe he should follow the example of the other brothers who had hurried to the ravine fifty yards out to vomit or relieve themselves, and had returned looking somewhat better.

Paul said, "Steve, you look awful. Why don't you go back to your wagon? Maybe Mary can help you."

"I doubt it. She's been working on people all night, but can't do much more than hold their hands. Besides, you guys are sick too."

Jarrad pushed his fist into his stomach and said, "Naw. Just a little gut pain."

"From the looks of you boys," Ruther said, "maybe I was right about that black plague stuff."

Steven smiled in spite of his discomfort. "It might be an infection of some kind, but you know perfectly well it isn't the bubonic plague."

"No, but my story sure 'nough fooled them bad guys. We ain't seen hide nor hair of 'em since."

Everyone laughed. They had rehearsed Ruther's deception several times during the night and still couldn't believe the stupidity of their enemies.

Paul said, "I bet they're still running for their lives."

"I hope they do die of some plague," Leonard said sourly. "They're nothing but cold-blooded killers."

"What is this sickness we have?" Jarrad asked.

Paul replied, "Doc Price told me he believes we may have picked up some common bacterial infection or perhaps a parasite from polluted water."

"Yeah, no big deal," Jarrad observed.

"What I can't figure out is why Paul and Ruther aren't sick." Steven said.

"I don't know about Paul," Ruther said, "but I'm too durn ornery ta get sick. Just let those little bacterias or parasites get up enough nerve ta wiggle down inta my gut, and they'll get burnt to a crisp by my powerful stomach juices."

After everyone stopped laughing, Paul patted Ruther on the shoulder and said, "I believe it, old fellow." He turned to his brother. "But seriously, Steve, you really look sick. Go rest awhile. We can handle it."

The others backed Paul up, insisting that Steven do as he was told. Reluctantly, Steven agreed, but first visited the ravine. Then he wobbled to his wagon, feeling weak and nauseated. He crawled into the wagon and saw with relief that his children were sleeping peacefully. A half hour later, Mary returned.

"I see you're a lot sicker than the last time I talked to you." Mary had visited her husband at 1:00 a.m. to see if he wanted a sandwich. He had refused, feeling too queasy to think about food.

"Don't worry," he said. It's nothing serious. Probably a little infection."

"Steve, three people died from that 'little infection' last night."

He was thunderstruck. "Three?"

"Yes, and there'll be a lot more if we don't find a cure."

Steven threw up and almost fainted. Mary held his head in her lap while she tried to clean up the vomit. Within a minute he felt better and crawled to the entrance.

"Where are you going?" Mary cried.

"I'll be back in a few minutes. I'm going to get the answer."

Mary didn't try to stop him.

He walked slowly to the south side of the camp, climbed through the outer ring of wagons, and headed for some huge boulders two hundred yards away. Curious eyes followed him as he staggered across the rough terrain. When he reached the boulders, he walked around them and fell to his knees. Tearfully, he pleaded with the Lord to help him know what to do to save Pioneer One. After repeating his simple prayer five times, he lay on his back and waited for the answer. A few minutes later, he heard a voice. It was almost imperceptible at first, but grew progressively louder.

"Ask your brother," a mild voice said.

"What?"

"Ask your brother." Now the peaceful voice was clear and penetrating.

"I don't understand."

"Ask your brother," the voice repeated.

Steven asked for clarification again and again, but got no further response. For a long time he lay there, too weak to rise and too confused to reflect on the message.

Mary walked around the boulders. "Steve," she called. Seeing him on his back, she cried in alarm and ran to him. "Are you all right?"

Steven lifted his head. "Yeah. Just weak and dizzy."

She sat next to him and put his head in her lap. "Isn't it dangerous to be out here?" she asked.

"No. I'm . . . sure they're gone . . . I got an . . . answer."

"I knew it," she said excitedly. "What is it?"

"A voice told me to ask my brother."

Mary frowned, perplexed. "But why? What does it mean?"

"I'm not sure. I have two brothers. Which one do I ask? And what do I ask?"

"The answer can't be complicated," Mary said. "The Lord doesn't play games."

"I know. Simple answers. No secret codes. But I . . . always . . . think things to death."

"What is there about your brothers which is different from the other pioneers?"

"I don't know. I guess it's an enigma."

Mary stared into the distance. "Yes, it is . . . Maybe the Lord wants us to do at least a tiny amount of work on this too. To solve the problem of the sickness, I mean."

"Great," Steven moaned. "I have to . . . think at a time like this." His head swam and he felt like fainting.

"So how are your brothers different?"

They discussed the matter another five minutes. That is, Mary discussed it. Steven vomited several times while she continued to probe.

Then Steven's face brightened in spite of his nausea. "I've got it. They don't have the sickness like the other pioneers do."

"John came down with it early this morning," Mary said.

"Oh . . . I guess that's not the answer."

"No, silly, that is the answer. Paul's the one you must talk to."

Steven was just too exhausted and dizzy to think. "What do I . . . ask?"

"You ask him why he isn't sick. He must be doing something to prevent it. Come. Let's get back to camp."

Mary helped him back to the wagon and went to find Paul. Steven sat against a wagon wheel and waited. After vomiting again, he felt better and his head was clearer. A few minutes later Mary returned with Paul.

Paul said to Steven, "Mary tells me you want to know why I'm not sick. Believe me, I have no idea why I haven't caught the disease like everyone else."

With Mary's help, Steven questioned Paul concerning everything he did during the day, and everything he ate.

"That's it," Steven said when Paul mentioned some pills he was taking.

Mary was skeptical. "You mean those two pills he takes every day have prevented him from getting this terrible disease?"

"I'm sure of it." Steven said. "Now I remember what Mom said before we left Provo. Take two or three of these tablets every day to protect yourself from a lot of problems."

"Yeah, Mom swears by grapefruit seed extract," Paul said. "Usually she's right, so I pop those babies every day, just to make sure."

Steven said, "She gave each of us several bottles of the stuff, but I forgot to take it."

"Not only bottles of the pills." Paul said. "She also stashed a gallon of extract liquid in all three of our wagons. The morning before we left."

"I wondered what was in that pill bottle," Steven said. "But I've been so busy that I didn't even check it out."

Mary said hopefully, "Where are the pills, Steve?"

"I don't know."

Mary climbed into the wagon. She searched ten minutes before she returned with a bottle of tablets and a canteen of water. The bottle was labeled GSE. Among other ingredients, the label read 250 milligrams of grapefruit seed extract.

"Paul, how many should I give him?" Paul had worked from time to time in his mother's herb shop, and Mary knew he had some knowledge of her products.

Paul examined the container. "Well, it doesn't say what to do if you get a deadly case of some unknown infection, but I figure Mom would say to take two tablets at the start, and one every four or five hours until the patient gets better. That's for serious cases. For those who aren't sick yet, I'd guess one or two tablets every day. The stuff isn't toxic, so we have a lot of leeway in the dosage."

Mary was in a hurry. After giving Steven two tablets, she said, "Paul, go get your bottles of tablets and some water." Paul dashed to his wagon a short distance away and returned within four minutes with a sack full of bottles. "Now we'll start around the caravan. You take the outer circle, and I'll take the inner. Treat everyone you find. Two tablets for those who are sick. One for everybody else. Insist they take the tablets while you're watching. Leave enough pills at each wagon for the rest of the day. If you run out of pills, find John and get his bottles. I'll catch up with you if I finish first."

As Mary worked, she was surprised to find that Sarah, Steven's mother, had also talked several other families into taking bottles of grapefruit seed extract tablets with them on the trip. When she and Paul met at Mary's wagon at the end of their work two hours later, they discovered that they had gathered a total of forty bottles of pills and several gallons of liquid.

Mary shook her head in amazement at the ingenuity and foresight of her feisty little mother-in-law. She hoped that the remedy would work for the others as well as it seemed to have worked for Paul. Though they had a great deal of the natural medicine, Paul estimated that they would be lucky to have enough of it to last the entire company until they reached Missouri if they ran into serious infections regularly.

The company remained in the same spot for the rest of the day. They buried the dead, both pioneers and outlaws, not far from the encampment and performed a short service over the graves. They spent the rest of the day nursing the sick and wounded and trying to recover physically and spiritually from the battle with the bandits. By the end of the day, most of the sick were already showing signs of recovery, and there were no additional deaths. Steven felt well enough to visit a number of wagons and to consult with company leaders.

Since John was recuperating, Steven asked him to get on his ham radio to report to the General Authorities. Elder Jason Widtsoe, a young apostle, received the transmission. John told him about their battle with the wild bandits and warned that Pioneer Two might face the same peril. He also described the disease which had attacked the saints and the remedy which had saved them. Jason was delighted to hear that the pioneers were safe and promised to inform the prophet.

Jason also made a report to John. First, he informed him that Robert and Sarah, his parents, were well and happy in Provo. Next, he told John everything he knew about the rumored threat of an attack against Utah from a huge army of Mexican renegades. He instructed John to inform the pioneers of the danger, but to encourage them not to worry, because the Utah saints were preparing for their defense. Also, the leaders knew the Lord would protect them. He added that the church might have to postpone the departure of Pioneer Two.

Within an hour every pioneer in the caravan learned of the trouble in Utah. Most took the news well, but others began to talk about returning to Salt Lake. At six in the afternoon Ruther sauntered out of camp on his big mule to search the surrounding wilderness for the location of the bandits.

It was late afternoon when Elder Jason Widtsoe visited the prophet's office.

He waved at the president's secretary and said, "Is he still in?" When she nodded, he continued past her desk and knocked gently on the door. He heard a muffled voice inside telling him to come in. He opened the door and saw Josiah at his desk examining maps and papers.

The prophet looked up and smiled. "Jason! Come in and sit down. I haven't seen you for days."

The apostle sat in a big armchair in front the prophet's desk. "I've been pretty busy, President Smith. Still working on the Mexican problem?" The General Authorities had come to speak of the reported threat from the south as the Mexican problem.

"Yes. I'll tell you where it's at in a minute. But first, have you heard from Pioneer One?"

"I just received a message from NB7EU." This was John Christopher's radio call sign, and many of the church leaders knew it by heart.

"All right, what is it?" the prophet said eagerly.

Jason summarized what had happened to the pioneers in the previous week. The prophet listened intently, asking questions now and then for clarification.

When the apostle had finished, Josiah said solemnly, "The Lord has truly blessed and protected them. And the leader he chose was the right man for the job . . . Jason, we need to see if we can procure a supply of grapefruit seed extract for the other wagon trains who'll travel to Missouri. Would you be so kind as to look into that for me?"

"Yes, of course. But what about the mountain gangs? They may still be in that area and present a grave threat to future caravans."

"I realize that. Also, they may be the reason we haven't heard from our Mormon communities along I-80 for so long." Both men were silent for a few moments. But Josiah couldn't bear to dwell on the scenes which suddenly came to his imagination. He went on quickly, "What do you suggest we do?"

"It seems we have only two choices. We postpone the departure of Pioneer Two, or we send an army into the mountains to handle the gangs."

"I'm afraid you're right . . . Are you coming to the emergency meeting tomorrow morning?"

Jason nodded. The president had called a meeting with the First Presidency and the Twelve for eight o'clock.

"We'll discuss this matter and the Mexican problem then. After the meeting, I want you to arrange for a party of men—about twenty of them—to go into the mountains to see if the gangs are still a threat. The men you choose must know the region thoroughly and be trained in wilderness operations. Of course, they should carry weapons to protect themselves."

"I'll make sure it's done."

"Thank you. Now, let me update you on the Mexican problem. The scouts we sent south to investigate the threat haven't returned yet. Haven't had time. But we've intercepted radio transmissions from Mexico which make it fairly certain that they're gathering a sizeable army and do intend to move northward in the near future."

After discussing the Mexican problem another half hour, the two church leaders went home to their families. The following morning the prophet discussed the two basic problems with the other church leaders. They decided that the departure of Pioneer Two should be postponed temporarily, until they had better information on the mountain gangs. They also concluded that they needed to continue gathering facts concerning the size and the intentions of the so-called Mexican Army of Liberation.

The exiles stood on a rise and gazed at the flames which consumed their hopes and their dreams. The inferno seemed to lust after the very sky itself as it devoured Kansas City. And in the darkness around them the refugees heard the constant sound of gunfire, and the screams of exquisite torment. They shivered and wept and held on to one another for comfort. Then they turned as one and headed back to their camp near the peaceful lake.

After Anthony and Noel Luce had found a comfortable spot near the family campfire, Noel said, "Dad, they want me to do the midnight watch tonight."

"No. It's too dangerous," said Rachel Luce, Noel's mother. Rachel looked to her daughter Kimberley for support, but the thirteen-year-old girl stared silently into the fire, her face besmirched with dirt and tears.

Anthony replied, "Don't worry. Noel can handle himself. And we really need every man we can get." Anthony had been chosen as one of the leaders of the Wyandotte Colony. He knew that what he had said about his son was true. Noel had saved their lives six days ago as they escaped from the city. Anthony was proud of his son who had suddenly become a man.

The refugees now numbered in the hundreds at Wyandotte County Lake Park, but the danger was so great that they had to stand guard twenty-four hours a day. Anthony and the other fathers who had fled from the city with him would be on watch during the early hours of the morning. One fourth of the men and boys in the encampment were needed around the periphery of the park at all times because they were under ceaseless attack. The assaults came from small gangs and individual rogues who sought frantically to satisfy their evil desires and needs.

After seeing the indescribable terrors of the last few months, Anthony was grateful that he and so many others had rejected the ignorant clamor of the gun control crusaders and the self-seeking arguments of politicians who had used every subterfuge in their efforts to convince America to surrender its weapons.

Things became especially hard to bear when other exiles tried to enter the park. Sometimes they made it, but often they were ambushed—just before they reached safety—by the creatures who lurked on the outer edges of the park. Through his binoculars Anthony watched what they did to their captives until he could bear it no longer. His greatest worry was that the anarchists would someday join forces and attack the park in a body. He avoided mentioning this fear to his family and friends, but he prayed in secret that God would somehow prevent their enemies from combining.

Another serious problem which the exiles faced was how to obtain food and supplies for 264 people. By Wednesday Anthony and the other park leaders had decided that their provisions would be exhausted in less than a week. Then the problem of survival would become critical. After consulting for several hours, the refugee leaders decided to send out regular armed detachments late at night to find supplies. Using information from the citizens of the new little community, Anthony and Noel made up a list of the most likely places to find the provisions.

The small French farmhouse was dark and still. The fugitives—Pierre, Diane, André, and Mireille—had watched it an hour from the protection of a small grove of trees. They had seen no movement in the shadows and no suspicious vehicles. Afraid that the green coats might track them down, or even be waiting for them at the farmhouse, they had spent the last five days hiding in the French countryside and sleeping in the minivan. But finally, hungry and desperate, they had driven to the farm of Pierre's friends and, with their lights out, had slowly driven the van toward the main building. Leaving their sleeping children in the vehicle, they had walked to within a hundred yards of the farmhouse.

"I think it's safe," Pierre Laborde said in a low voice. "Let's go on."

Mireille Renan whispered, "I'm afraid! The authorities know we were heading east on the highway. Maybe they even know where we were going."

"But how could they know?" Diane Laborde asked.

The friends had debated this over and over the last few days and couldn't agree. Pierre argued that someone might have seen them leave Paris and informed on them, but there was no way anyone could know their ultimate destination. They had not told anyone, except the people who owned the farm. André and Mireille had to admit that Pierre was right, but still something told them that they were in grave danger.

"It's impossible, I tell you," Pierre insisted a little too loudly.

Diane frowned and shushed him. "Pierre. If they're out there, they'll hear you," she whispered.

In lower tones, Pierre said, "Listen, I have an idea. You guys wait here, and I'll check it out."

They agreed, and Pierre moved toward the farmhouse. He kept to the shadows and made as little noise as possible. After watching her husband for a while, Diane said, "I can't let him go alone." She left the trees and hurried to Pierre. Together they approached the house.

Mireille and André watched them fearfully. As they strained to see their friends, who had disappeared against the darkness of the building, their eyes were struck all at once by blinding lights. Green uniforms sprang from hiding places everywhere and surrounded Pierre and Diane. Gasping from shock, Mireille and André pulled back into the obscurity of the grove and dashed to the minivan. The enemy knew that Diane and Pierre had been traveling with another family and might pursue them at any moment. The fugitives slipped into the vehicle and backed down the road carefully—their lights out—until they came to a spot wide enough to turn around. Then they drove away slowly.

The green coats pushed Pierre and Diane into the house, now blazing with light. Pierre's middle-aged friends stood huddling together in their night clothes on the far side of the room.

"I'm sorry, Pierre," the man said. "They said they'd confiscate our farm and throw us into prison if we didn't tell them you were coming. We had no choice."

Pierre and Diane were stunned and could not respond. The captain of the green coats ordered them to sit on a couch. When Pierre hesitated, the officer slugged him across the side of the head with the butt of his rifle. After he came to a few minutes later, the officer questioned him and Diane for forty minutes. At the end of the interrogation, he angrily accused them of being mortal enemies of the state. Then the soldiers forced the captives from the house and into a prison van hidden behind the building. The middle-aged couple clung to each other and sobbed bitterly.

⤜✥⤏

Ramón Sánchez, Chief Advisor to the president of Venezuela, looked to the north and saw the arrival of the Venezuelan National Guard. The guardsmen bivouacked between Maracay Lake and the Mormon settlement fifteen miles south of the lake. Ramón counted forty-one armored personnel carriers, or APCs, which carried twelve guardsmen each, and about five hundred foot soldiers. A total of a thousand troops. Behind the troops he could also distinguish two Abrams tanks, purchased from the United States, and ten pieces of artillery. Several miles behind the Guard, the Mormon Militia was hidden in the hills directly south of the great lake.

Ramón turned to Elder Gutierrez, and said, "Looks like they mean business. You'd think we were a foreign army instead of their fellow citizens." Carlos Gutierrez was a regional representative who had charge of the military operations of the Mormon settlement.

"They're driven by the green coats against their will," Carlos replied, lowering his binoculars.

Ramón raised his eyebrows in surprise. "There are green coats out there?"

"Most definitely. Use your binoculars. Study the men in the personnel carriers more closely."

Ramón followed his friend's suggestion and, after examining several APCs, caught sight of green uniforms. "So they're beginning to come out of the woodwork."

Carlos said, "They won't have it as easy here as they do in many foreign countries."

"What do you mean?"

"Well, in Europe, Africa, Asia, Japan, Malaysia, and many other countries our fellow saints have been thrown into concentration camps or have gone into hiding. But here we number a half million members and have far more power and influence. They won't find it so easy to intimidate us. And it's not only Venezuela. We're very strong throughout South and Central America. A mighty army, if you will."

Ramón said, "Well, I knew the church was strong in Latin America, but I had no idea we were so prepared militarily."

Years earlier the prophet had warned church members in foreign countries to prepare for a worldwide attack against the saints, and without hesitation church leaders in Venezuela had quickly organized their people and had made preparations. The saints had stored provisions of every type, including weapons and ammunition, and had created special communities in rural areas as places of refuge. There were seven of them in Venezuela alone, and the community south of Maracay Lake was the largest.

This settlement had nineteen thousand permanent residents, and space for another thirty thousand. After accumulating supplies enough to last two years, the citizens had built a concrete irrigation trench completely around their town. The reason given for the trench was to supply the community with water from the mountains, but the builders had made it ten feet deep and forty feet wide, much larger than was actually needed. Of course, the citizens of the community knew that the ditch, and the fifteen feet high chain-link fences which bordered it, actually served as protection against those who hated Mormons.

But the Venezuelan saints knew that their special refuges could only give them limited protection. If the government became their enemy and brought its armies against them in earnest, they would be in great peril. So they depended mostly on God and the hundreds of thousands of saints and friends who held positions in every institution in the country, including the government and the military.

After hearing his friend's review of the world situation, Ramón's face became tight with frustration. "How do you know all this, Carlos? I'm top advisor to the president, and I have heard nothing more than rumors regarding it."

"You've had much work to do with internal problems, especially since UGOT's cur, Diego Ortiz, arrived. And these things are of recent development. Within the last two months. Fortunately, we have several ham transceivers and have been able to monitor world events."

Ramón looked at the troops again. "Do you think they'll really attack?"

"Not with so few soldiers. The Mormon Militia includes three thousand well-trained soldiers, and we have another thousand guerillas hidden around the lake behind the government army."

Ramón grinned. "And that's not all. At least one in six of the Guard out there is a Mormon too. They're Mormon infiltrators, so to speak."

"Hah. You forgot the officers."

"Oh yes. One in four perhaps."

In spite of the danger, Carlos teased, "Yes, Ramón, there are so many infiltrators. For example, the president's chief advisor."

"Mmm, that gives me an idea. Maybe I should go over there and tell them who I am, and that I'm visiting this community. Would they avoid attacking if they knew those things?"

Carlos laughed. "I'm sure the green coats know you're a Mormon and the president's advisor. And they may know you're with us today. In any case, your presence here wouldn't stop them from attacking. In fact, it might encourage them even more."

"You may be right. I hope most of the saints in this country can hide better than me."

"It's much harder for them to track us down now. Church officials in Venezuela have deleted computer records of church membership in this country. If UGOT confiscates our computers and discs, it will find nothing. Only a few carefully hidden hard copies remain."

Ramón was pleased. "I have good news for you too. I had some of our best computer specialists—LDS specialists, of course—check government records to see if UGOT could identify church members through computer files. They deleted everything which might even begin to help our enemies to detect us."

Carlos patted Ramón on the back, and the two men raised their binoculars once again to observe the movement of the National Guard.

Chapter 12

The European media was in a frenzy of activity because today the great rally of MOM, or Mothers Opposing Madness, was to take place. For weeks television broadcasts had reported that half a million mothers from every part of Switzerland would march on the House of Parliament in Berne to demand that national leaders outlaw guns of any kind in this peace-loving country.

Two months before the great march, four people had met in a large room at the Bellevue Palace to plan the event. Three of them, two women and a man, were political activists from Paris and Berlin. The fourth person, who directed the meeting, was Martin Gannt, UGOT's Director of Media Relations.

When everyone had arrived, Martin invited them to sit around a table in the spacious dining room. Near the table was a long counter with several bottles of wine and a divided serving platter full of snacks and veggies. On the table in front of them he placed a bottle of red wine and four wine glasses.

"Well, people, thank you for coming," Martin said in English. "I know you by reputation and I've seen you on television. And, of course, I had a hand in choosing you for this assignment. But it's a pleasure to finally meet you in person." The three guests smiled and nodded. Martin knew that these people had been among the most dedicated gun-control advocates in Europe for many years and had been highly effective. "Do you know each other?"

"Not really," one of the women said.

"All right, let me make introductions." He pointed to the woman who had just spoken. "This is Marie Fayard. She comes from Tours, France, and is relatively new to our cause. I assure you that she's totally dedicated, shrewd, and full of boundless energy." Marie flushed at this praise. She was short and stout, and the gray streaks in her hair suggested she was in her late forties.

Martin nodded toward the second woman. "This is Ann Latimer. She's from Kingston, not far from London. I don't know if you realize it, but she played a major role in achieving universal gun confiscation in New Zealand several years ago." The others looked at Ann enviously. She was a tall, slim blond of forty-three. In spite of her square jaw and thin lips, she was very attractive. Her forceful personality seemed to hold a strange attraction for most men. Martin admired her most for her confidence and skill in handling the media.

"And this is Friedrich Bauer, from Berlin. He has been an important force in getting much gun legislation passed in Europe." With a quick movement of his head, Friedrich threw his long blond hair out of his eyes and gave them a quick nod. It was obvious he was proud of his handsome face, tall, muscular body, and all-round machismo. Martin considered him to be one of the most ruthless and skillful planners in the gun-control movement.

Martin went on, "As I told you on the phone, Ann will lead our campaign here in Switzerland. I ask you, Marie and Friedrich, to help with planning and to assist Ann in any way you can." Marie and Friedrich indicated their acceptance. "Are you all parents?"

Friedrich and Marie shook their heads, but Ann beamed and proudly announced that she had a five-year-old boy. Martin laughed inside, knowing that, like many film queens and other professional women, Ann had taken a break in her career as a lobbyist to "experience" motherhood, as if it were just another life event that a woman should go through at least once to feel what it was like. He couldn't resist thinking that this attitude was not too different from what some people have when they order a strange new dish for the first time in an exotic restaurant.

"Wonderful, Ann," Martin said. "Be sure to mention that fact if the media questions you."

"Yes, I will," Ann said. "My son is the real reason I go through this labor and pain. I do it for him and all the other innocent children."

"I knew your motives were noble," Martin said. He looked at Marie and Friedrich. "And how do you feel about our cause?"

With passionate conviction Marie said, "Guns cause crime and violence. I believe that if they were illegal everywhere, the world would be a safer and happier place in which to live."

"I completely agree. And you, Friedrich?" Martin said.

"Well, I have to admit that I enjoy a good fight. I love to prove wrong the arguments of the pro-gun addicts. It was even more fun when the NRA existed. Sometimes you have to juggle the statistics a bit, but it's for a good cause."

"Yes," Martin said, "the means justifies the end."

"That's not to say I don't believe in our cause completely, you understand," Friedrich added.

"Of course you do. I'm pleased to see that each of you is so dedicated to our great cause." Martin took a sip of red wine. "Drink everyone. As much as you want. It's on the house." From the nearby counter Martin brought another bottle of wine and the large serving platter. They poured glasses of wine and put snacks on the small plates in front of them.

Martin reached into his briefcase and removed materials. "Now, I should like to hear your ideas on how to handle the rally on April 27." The others also removed notebooks and papers from their briefcases. "Ann, would you like to begin?"

"Yes, thank you. First of all, I think we should stick to the basic theme that MOM has always stressed, and avoid any other. We mothers are marching to save the lives of our children from gun violence and gun accidents."

"But there have been very few such accidents in Switzerland," Marie pointed out.

Ann replied, "True, but the public doesn't know that. If we declare openly that it has occurred, even frequently occurred, and repeat it over and over, the people will believe it sooner or later."

"Yes," Martin said. "People seldom take the time or have the time to investigate the facts. Usually they don't have access to them. So if they hear something on television frequently enough, they'll believe it, even if it sounds ridiculous to begin with."

Friedrich laughed. "How true. Because of our skillful promotions and propaganda on TV, the public now accepts homosexuality and same-sex marriages as legitimate lifestyles."

Struggling to maintain his composure, Martin seethed inside. He was an avowed homosexual and was furious that this ignorant fool didn't know it. But he went on as if Friedrich had said nothing, "Even if some try to check the facts, they'll have to get their information from the authorities. And I can assure you that UGOT has consulted with the Swiss Government to make sure that the statistics any investigators find will verify that gun accidents have killed many Swiss children. It's a technique we learned from the defunct American bureaucracy.

"In any event, you are right to place the primary emphasis on the issue of saving children from the dangers of guns. Too many issues will confuse the public and weaken our position. Above all, the messages you convey must be full of emotional, heart-rending stories of personal tragedies. Choose fathers and mothers to appear on TV who have really lost children to gun violence or accidents. You don't have to get them from Switzerland, but from anywhere you can. Encourage them to weep bitterly into the screen over the horrible loss of their precious children. Their sincerity will deeply impress the viewing audiences.

"Make sure that such heartrending stories are depicted incessantly on TV. If you have trouble finding real tragedies, hire good actors to cry over made-up stories. You must convince the viewers that they're against mothers and children, and innocent life itself, if they don't demand that the government outlaw guns or regulate them into nonexistence. If you can, avoid statistics, logical arguments, or factual evidence. They can only get us into trouble."

"We've had a problem in the past which has given us a lot of trouble," Ann noted, "and it might occur again. Those who oppose gun control stress over and over that most violent crimes, such as murder, are committed by criminals, and that guns in the hands of decent citizens deter criminals. They conclude that guns save the lives of people, including children."

Martin smiled. "Well, if you can't avoid getting into such a debate, try to persuade people that the evidence proves most victims are murdered by individuals they know, such as relatives and acquaintances."

Marie countered, "But that doesn't square with the facts."

"It will if you get creative with language. If you define the word 'acquaintance' very broadly to include gang members killed by other gang members, drug pushers killed by junkies and other drug pushers, cabdrivers murdered by customers, prostitutes slain by clients, and so on, then it instantly becomes true that most victims are murdered by acquaintances or relatives."

"Tricky!" Friedrich exclaimed.

"Yes, you can do so much with vocabulary," Martin observed.

"I see," Marie said. "So if the government doesn't outlaw guns, those violent relatives and acquaintances—their 'friends'—will kill our children too?"

Martin enthused, "Exactly! In that way we can work the argument around to support our primary theme of protecting children . . . All right, let's move on. Who did you choose to symbolize the MOM march?"

Ann replied, "We found a wonderful woman. She's a tall, lovely brunette about forty-eight years old. The ideal mother. Two of her six children were playing with her husband's handguns and killed each other in a western-style gun battle. It really touches your heart when she tells her story."

"Wonderful. I want you to present her as the organizer and the soul of this march on Parliament. She's Swiss?"

"No, German."

Martin pondered a moment. "Um . . . well, that probably won't matter.

Her German will be quite different from that used by the Swiss, but if you get her a linguistic coach and have her memorize a prepared script, it should be fine."

Friedrich said, "We have also procured the services of two other women—Swiss this time—who will also relate their tragic stories in German."

"Good. What about stories for the French and Italian populations of Switzerland?"

Marie replied, "One of my friends and I will tell our sad tales in French."

Martin laughed. "About the terrible loss of your children? I thought you said you were childless."

"That doesn't matter," Marie said glibly. "Like you said, the end justifies the means. So ridding Switzerland of guns justifies inventing a story."

"I'm more pleased with that than if your story were actually true." Martin replied. Then he couldn't resist returning to his favorite compulsion—influencing the masses by manipulating television programing. "Don't worry. If people hear that on television, they'll believe it. They usually believe almost anything they hear on TV, and they never check the stories out. It used to be that most television programing was controlled by major corporations and special interest groups, especially in the late great United States, but now UGOT controls 90% of the programming on the major networks here in Europe. As a result, we can get the public to believe whatever we desire."

Friedrich said, "But there are many skeptical people out there. Don't they get suspicious if the news programs and documentaries consistently promote our politics and moral values?"

Martin looked at Friedrich in surprise. "Obviously, Friedrich, you haven't made a study of the propaganda uses of television. We do it the same way the old business moguls used to do it. We seldom present our ideas directly in newscasts and documentaries. We don't tell people what is true and good. We show them.

"I'm not sure I understand," Friedrich replied.

"Well, first of all we use sitcoms, movies, and soap operas. In that case, all we need to do is make sure the actors and the stories illustrate our values and ideas by means of the dialogue and the action. For example, in all these plays and skits the characters are involved—as a matter of course—in some type of extramarital or homosexual relationship. To be a virgin, or to have what old-fashioned people see as a healthy, normal family relationship, is presented as abnormal and is openly ridiculed by the attitudes, language, and behavior of the actors.

"In addition, we use talk shows to our advantage by choosing appropriate hosts and guests and by orchestrating the discussions toward acceptance of our politics and morals. All these techniques are vastly more effective than presenting direct analytical statements. The only time a newscaster is useful is when he or she reveals what they think and feel by their attitudes and their responses. A frown, a smile, the shake of the head, or even a word of surprise at the right time can all be quite effective."

Anxious to get back to her report, Ann Latimer wondered if Martin would ever stop. The second he halted for a breath, she broke in. "Thank you, Martin. That's incredibly valuable information on the media . . . But to continue, I found two Italian women who lost children. One child was shot by a robber, and another by her father."

"Seven testimonials. That's a good beginning. Now, tell me about the people you're bringing in to support you."

Ann said, "We're advertising this march throughout Europe, encouraging people to sign a pledge that they'll come to Berne to participate. The response from both women and men has been excellent so far!"

"How many pledges?"

Ann checked her notes. "After five weeks, uh, we've received 90,000 pledges. We hope to get at least 130,000 people by the time we're done."

"Tell the media that half a million mothers will be in the march."

"Half a million? I doubt we'll ever—"

"I understand that. But neither the media nor the public will know the difference. No one is going to walk around and count heads. Besides, 130,000 people gathered in one place can easily pass for half a million. We care about the effect, not the truth."

"I love it," Ann gushed. "I wish we had thought of that technique when we fought against guns in New Zealand." Marie and Friedrich looked impressed also.

Martin said proudly, "That's what I'm here for. To suggest the latest techniques . . . Okay now. Tell me about the opposition."

"Oh yes. Our loyal fanatical opposition. Well, let's see. With the generous budget UGOT provided, we were able to hire about six hundred people. We're already using them to gather the pledges, but at the rally they'll function in the normal way."

"I know how I would use them," Martin said, "but how do you intend to do it?"

Ann extracted a sheet from her briefcase and began to summarize. "Okay, we'll make sure they're in Berne two days before the march. We'll plant them in key places. We'll have them dress and act in ways which suggest to the public that they're fanatics. They'll carry provocative posters. They'll purposely shout insults at the marchers or try to provoke violent confrontations. Some will even throw fruit at the marchers."

"Please explain what you mean about planting them in key places," Martin said.

"I mean we'll put them in bunches of a hundred near the posts set up by the media. In this way, when the television crews pan, viewers will see either our scary fanatics, the peaceful citizens of Berne, or our well-behaved marchers."

"Excellent. That's exactly what I would have done. I suppose you'll also place several thousand gun-control advocates along the route to cheer the marchers."

"Standard procedure."

Martin was delighted. "I'm happy with the way you three are handling this. I'm sure UGOT will reward you appropriately if this march is a media success. Now one last word. Remember forever these two vital ideas: to rule the world as we desire, we must first control the media and then disarm the people. If we do not accomplish those two essential goals, we will fail miserably."

Next Martin pulled out a list of questions which covered the details of the operation. They spent the rest of the day, and the following day, going over their plans. When it was over, Martin flew back to London, pleased with the report he would give to Gerald Galloway. UGOT was very concerned about Switzerland. In a population of nearly thirteen million people there were an estimated twenty million guns. Since the country had no standing army, every male from twenty through forty-two was required to serve in the citizens' militia and to keep his ammunition and weapons, normally semiautomatic assault rifles, at home. And when the men retired, the law allowed them to keep those weapons.

Also, the Swiss had numerous gun clubs, even for children. They felt that target practice was more healthy and enjoyable than sports like golf. Indeed, UGOT would find it impossible to control the Swiss unless it became illegal to possess firearms in their country. Even that was no guarantee that a large segment of the population would not simply ignore the new laws and thus remain a constant threat to the power of UGOT.

In any case, the coming rally in Switzerland was important because it might be the first major step in outlawing guns in Switzerland, or at least in regulating gun ownership to death. Martin shivered to think of UGOT's armies trying to control a huge populace armed with millions of small weapons. Five million crack-shot guerillas in a country full of mountains. The lessons of

Afghanistan and Somalia had proven that the world's greatest nations were powerless to defeat such determined citizens. No wonder Hitler had left the Swiss alone.

The MOM march on the capitol on April 27 was a stunning success. The media reported that a half million demonstrators, most of them mothers, had gathered in the vicinity of Helvettaplatz in Berne by eight in the morning. The actual number was 120,000. The crusaders were very polite and well-behaved. At eight thirty, these champions of the family marched proudly northward on Kirchenfeldbrüke Street in a line a mile long, tears streaming down their faces. Soon they turned west on Kochergasse Street and headed for the House of Parliament. Their posters and banners proclaimed their profound concerns to the world: "Save Our Children," "My Child's Life Ended with a Bang," "Guns Kill People," "Stop the Slaughter of the Innocents," "We Love Kids More Than Guns," "Cease Arming Criminals," "Gun Laws Work," "Loopholes Lead to Bullet Holes," "Mothers Outgun Morons." Ann Latimer didn't see that last one until too late.

And the "opposition," organized by the three UGOT planners, was also combined. From the sidelines they hooted and stamped their feet. They strove to provoke shouting matches, or yelled insults at the marchers. They had their banners too: "Guns Don't Kill—Criminals Do," "Gun Laws Disarm the Good Guys," "Guns Deter Crime," "Only Governments Commit Genocide," and "More Guns Less Crime."

At first, the marchers ignored these fanatics and remained serene in the conviction that they were doing the work of God himself. But then, as they followed the predetermined route, some marchers, seeing the disgusting slogans of their opponents and hearing the insults, could bear it no longer. They raced to the side of the road and ripped enemy signs to shreds. Others got their message across with furtive obscene gestures.

When the marchers finally reached the House of Parliament at noon, the seven mothers told their touching stories and moved the hearts of millions. As a result, a number of fearless, crusading politicians stepped forward boldly and announced that they would do everything in their power to stop the mass slaughter of the nation's innocents.

Even the president appeared before the cameras and did everything he could to appeal to the emotions of the TV audience. The Swiss people came by tens of thousands to see the festivities and to hear the speeches. Millions of others saw it on television. But in reality, few had any idea that the entire show was orchestrated and they wondered, after all was said and done, what the fuss was all about. It was the first time they had ever heard that any children had been killed by gun violence in Switzerland.

Ralph Taylor was a good man. He didn't consider himself an ideal Mormon, but he went to church regularly and fulfilled most of the assignments he was asked to do. But when the prophet had called on the saints to leave Babylon and come to Zion last July, he had found better things to do. After all, if he had abandoned his growing business in Pasadena, California, how would he support his family? Besides, if times were really going to get tough, a business selling food storage and survival gear should really become lucrative. Before long, he'd have enough money to buy his wife, Lynette, a new minivan, pay for those piano lessons, help his fellow man, and save for the future.

So when Lynette and the four children had pleaded with him to drop it all and move to the Rocky Mountains, he simply didn't hear them. Lynette had done everything possible to convince him, but when he continued to refuse, she had packed up early one morning when he was still asleep, piled the kids into her old jalopy, and set out for Utah. She figured that was the only way to save her children and wake her husband up.

The trouble is, Ralph never did see the light. Even though he had lost the food storage to wandering thieves, he had managed to save most of the survival equipment. The things which were selling the best were the seventy-two-hour kits and the water purification devices. He had made a fortune, but to make sure the business was safe, he had found it necessary to sleep in his shop on South Raymond Street in Pasadena with a high-powered rifle close to hand. It was a lonely life. Several times he had succeeded in contacting his wife with the help of a ham radio friend, and had tried to convince her to return to Pasadena. She had always refused and tearfully begged him to join her.

Ralph awoke early on April 27. He figured it was just another day like any other. He ate a can of chicken noddle soup for breakfast and stepped outside his shop to get some early morning air. He was surprised to see so many people and such heavy traffic at that hour. As he turned to go back in, he felt a violent lurch which knocked him against the door jamb and then threw him to the concrete. He tried to rise, but the shaking was so vigorous that he could do nothing except sit on the concrete and hold on to the frame of the doorway.

But terror filled him when the wood of the frame splintered suddenly and the entire building began to collapse, threatening to crush him.

Lying almost flat on his stomach, he crawled frantically toward the street. Pieces of concrete and sections of roofing pounded his body and disintegrated on the sidewalk around him like bombs falling from the sky. He felt excruciating pain as the debris tore a bloody gash on the right side of his head. He had the strange sensation that his ear had been ripped away. Afraid of being buried alive, he ignored his pain and continued to crawl.

At that moment he heard a deafening roar which seemed to bear down on him from the north like some colossal freight train. He glanced up the street and saw the sidewalk and the entire street rise and fall like waves on a stormy sea. The lamp posts and trees shot into the air as if they had been fired from a great cannon. Every person on the street had been knocked to the ground, and vehicles of all sizes had been hurled against the crumbling buildings on the far side of what used to be a street. Above the roar of nature, he heard the screams and the wailing of the people around him. But he knew that there were many others who had been silenced under the crushing weight of collapsing buildings. He wondered if the shaking would ever stop. Suddenly he realized his stubborn foolishness and what his life meant, and he wished he had listened to his beloved wife.

After crawling halfway across the street, he heard a great ripping sound, and his heart was filled with horror when he saw in the distance a fissure traveling down the center of the road and growing deeper and wider as it approached at high speed. There were a number of people lying on the road directly in the path of the moving cleft. When the street opened next to him, Ralph was sure he would fall into the crevice, and he pushed away from it with all his might. He succeeded in avoiding the peril, but he knew that others had not. Fascinated, he glanced into the chasm, whose bottom was lost in the shadows. Seconds later, the sides of the fissure screamed as they clamped shut like the jaws of hell devouring its prey.

And then it was over. Ralph's heart raced wildly, and he struggled for breath. He was astonished to see that his world could be annihilated in less than a minute. Yet he was still alive! Near him and in the distance he heard the sound of crying, explosions, raging infernos, and ruptured water mains. He sat up painfully, but could not get to his feet.

"Help me, please!" a plaintive voice called not far away. He looked down the street and saw a woman on her knees. She was staring at a three-story apartment building which had been demolished. "Help me, please," she cried again and again.

Fifty people staggered up and down the street like zombies, trying to go somewhere, but having nowhere to go. Those who stumbled past the crying woman completely ignored her. As Ralph forced himself to his feet, searing pains shot up his back and his right leg. He must have several broken bones. He checked the right side of his head and was relieved to feel his ear still there, though it hurt terribly and was covered with blood. Hearing the woman again, he dragged himself toward her.

When she caught sight of him fifteen feet away, she cried out, "Help me, please. My baby. In that building."

Ralph looked at the lower part of her legs and realized that both were broken. "Don't worry. I'll find him. Or is it a girl?"

"A little boy, five years old," the woman moaned.

Ralph climbed onto the rubble and searched a half hour, digging with his hands until they were raw and bloody. It seemed hopeless. He could move some chunks of rubble, but others were impossible to budge without heavy equipment. Then he noticed the woman pointing to the south side of the building where a twenty-foot section of the outer wall remained standing. He stumbled over to that area and began to dig. As he worked, he felt that the wall might fall inward and crush him at any minute. The woman watched him anxiously but soon crumpled to the ground unconscious. Ralph knew he had to continue in spite of his pain. A few minutes later, two men with shovels and a wrecking bar joined him, and they attacked the debris together.

After digging almost an hour under a huge slab of concrete, they finally managed to break into a dark narrow passage. Ralph thought he heard a faint cry. He strained to listen and heard it again.

"He's in there," he said to the other men. "Alive, I think." He turned toward the street to tell the mother the good news, but saw two paramedics carrying her away. Ralph guessed that they were taking her to Central Park, not far away.

"Let's get him out," said one of Ralph's helpers as he began to enlarge the hole.

When the opening was large enough, Ralph slid under the slab and began to crawl through a long tight passageway. After he had crawled fifteen feet and made a partial turn, the tunnel became as black as an unlit cavern. He began to panic as his heart and chest tightened from fear. At that moment a terrible childhood memory suddenly returned to him.

It was the memory of the panic he had felt that night when, at ten years of age, he had disobeyed his parents and the warning signs and had foolishly crawled into a long, narrow tunnel beneath Tweedy Boulevard in Los Angeles when the city was enlarging the street. That tunnel too was pitch-black.

Halfway through, the tunnel had become so tight that he couldn't move forward or backward.

At that instant, he had thought one terrible thought after another. Would he be stuck there until he starved to death or the workers filled in the tunnel? Would the tunnel collapse and crush him or bury him alive? Would he ever see his parents again? The panic had been so dreadful that he had scarcely been able to breathe. But at last he had forced himself to calm down and to think. Then for a half hour he had wormed his way forward a fraction of an inch with every movement, until at last the tunnel began to widen. Five minutes later he had climbed out of the black hole, filthy but joyously free. As he had walked home, he had thought that it really wasn't such a big deal after all—but he'd never do that again!

Then his mind returned to the present. Realizing that the five-year-old child buried in the ruins must be experiencing the same fear that he had felt so many years ago, Ralph fought his way forward. Again and again he felt as though the walls around him were crushing his chest and he gasped for breath. After he had struggled along the tunnel for what seemed forever, guided only by the tiny voice ahead, he finally saw the child's head. The rest of his body was completely buried in rubble.

Upon seeing his rescuer, the boy smiled and said in a tiny voice, "I knew you'd come."

Ralph could tell by his tear-stained face that he had been crying. To the left he saw a vertical pillar which had caught some of the falling debris and had made a pocket of air the size of a small closet. He figured that was the only thing which had prevented the child from being crushed or smothered.

It took an hour to remove the boy from his prison, and as he worked, he partially uncovered the arm of a corpse entombed to the right of the child. He checked the boy for injuries and was amazed that he found none. He told the child to follow him as he crawled backwards up the passageway. During this struggle up the tunnel, both of them coughed and choked constantly from the dust and lack of air. Often he had to pull the boy toward him. To keep the child from thinking about the danger, he questioned him about his family and what he enjoyed doing. In this way, he discovered that the child and his mother had been living alone in an apartment.

A half hour later they emerged from the hole. Ralph breathed the air with joy and, limping badly, led the chattering boy slowly toward the park. Now he understood that his business and prosperity were nothing in comparison to a human life. Nothing compared to his family and his beliefs. Feeling gratitude to God for this understanding, he began to think of ways to travel to Utah.

Only later did Ralph learn the full extent of the damage. The immense pressures that had accumulated for more than a century and a half had finally reached the critical point, and the eastern boundary of the gigantic Pacific Plate suddenly lurched to the northwest in relation to the North American Plate. The results were unbelievably catastrophic along the entire San Andreas Fault, which extended eight hundred miles in western California. The offset in the southern section of the fault reached a maximum of forty-two feet, by far the greatest ever recorded. This was followed seconds later by similar slippage along the northern section of the fault. There had been no foreshocks to warn the people that the Big One was coming. Within one day tsunamis created by the earthquake caused great destruction throughout the entire Pacific Basin.

Seismic monitoring stations around the world measured the magnitude of the earthquake at 9.6 on the Richter scale. The great cities of Los Angeles, San Diego, San Francisco, San Jose, Long Beach, Oakland, Sacramento, and Fresno were completely flattened during the forty seconds that the quake lasted. Almost a fourth of the state's population died in the catastrophe. Two million people perished outright, and another three million were killed soon after by fires, disease, and starvation.

When the powerful shocks of the earthquake struck downtown Los Angeles, hundreds of tall buildings swayed a few seconds as if they were giant trees in a gale, and then collapsed in great heaps of rubble, like old vacant buildings toppled purposely by well-placed charges of dynamite. Instantly thousands of tiny human beings disappeared under mountains of stone, brick, glass, and concrete.

If the quake had occurred a year earlier, when the total population of California exceeded forty million, the death toll would have been much higher. But beginning in April of the preceding year, California, like the rest of the world, had been assaulted by one disaster after another. Plagues, famine, drought, civil wars, and disease had already decimated the population. On September 19, Los Angeles had been hit by a nuclear bomb and a million citizens had been killed and three million seriously injured. Because of these disasters millions of people, including a quarter million saints, had evacuated the state and sought refuge in safer lands to the east.

Chapter 13

Steven and Mary were grateful that most of the sick were recovering from their disease by Wednesday evening. Steven consulted with the leaders of Pioneer One to see if the caravan should rest on Thursday. They declared as one that they wanted to continue the journey without delay. They felt confident their people would support them in this decision. So they set out as usual at eight in the morning and continued east on I-80. Steven had organized a troop of thirty armed men on horseback to search the countryside near the freeway ahead of Pioneer One, and he felt safer knowing they were out there.

As they rode their horses up and down the line of wagons, Steven and Paul noticed that the pioneers seemed to be in good spirits in spite of the ordeals of the last few days. Some were weak and tired from the illness and from lack of sleep, but they smiled at the brothers and manifested new self-confidence. Steven knew, however, that many were still so weak that they were lying on beds in the wagons. Only those who had lost loved ones showed signs of despair and sadness. Steven's heart went out to them.

By eleven thirty the sun and heat had become almost unbearable. It was not unusual to see people faint suddenly and collapse to the ground. A few suffered from hallucinations and hysteria. On the advice of several leaders, Steven ordered an early halt for lunch. The travelers sprawled out in any shady spot they could find, mostly in or under their wagons. Following the instructions of the leaders, they boiled the water they took from Heirner's Creek, which flowed north of the highway, before they consumed it. In the early afternoon, Ruther Johnston emerged from the northern mountains and rode up to Steven's wagon.

Steven heard the approaching mule, but before he could crawl from under his wagon, his three children slid past and attacked Ruther as he descended from his animal.

"I'm right glad ta see yuh, Ruther," Andrew said, hugging the old man.

Jennifer grabbed his arm. "I love you, Ruther."

"We sure feel safer when you're around," William declared.

Ruther looked pleased as he hugged each of them in turn.

Suppressing a twinge of jealousy, Steven peeked out and said, "Ruther! It's you."

"Those pills of yourn sure does the trick," he said to Steven. "Glad yuh made me take a few along. Stomach up and started hurtin' 'bout ten last night. Popped a few of those little fellers and felt better by sunrise."

Steven scrambled from beneath the wagon and stood up. He was still weak, but getting stronger. Mary looked out from the wagon and, seeing who it was, climbed to the pavement.

"Glad to hear it," Steven said. "What did you do out there?"

"Hah! Checked their main camp. Seems like them boys done took off as if their backsides were afire and hightailed it north. Must be near Bear Lake by this time. Don't figure you'll ever see 'em again. They done beat it out of that camp so fast, they left lotsa valuables laying around. Have ta admit that I scooped up a few trinkets fer my trouble."

Steven smiled. "Come and set—sit—for a while. Would you like some lunch? We still have food left."

"Don't mind if I do."

They watched him devour Mary's soup with great relish, smacking his lips noisily. When he had finished, he sighed deeply and looked at Steven. "Had time ta do some thinkin' up thar in the mountains."

"About what?"

"Religion . . . Got lots of things ta put ta yuh, but now's not the time. I'm plain tuckered out. Yuh got room under that wagon of yourn for one more?"

Steven laughed and invited him to share their space. William hurried away to spread Ruther's good news. When Steven awoke at around two thirty, he walked a few hundred yards down the highway and saw the exhaustion of the pioneers. He had just decided to let them remain there for the rest of the day, when two colonels rode up.

"Why aren't we moving?" Jasper Potter asked. "It's past time."

"The people are beat. They need more time to recover from their sickness and fatigue."

Jasper snorted. "I don't think you're giving them enough credit, Steve. Have you asked them? I bet that if you give the command, they'll meet the challenge."

Steven studied their faces, wondering if he was paying too much attention to his own fatigue. "All right. Tell them to move out."

The colonels laughed, turned their horses, and trotted away. Within ten minutes the caravan was on the move. It continued up the road laboriously, but steadily, until Steven stopped it at half past five. When he saw the sign for Exit 180, he estimated with pride that the people had traveled seven to eight miles that day in spite of everything.

Shortly before dark, heavy black clouds began to swirl in from the northwestern sky, and soon a light rain descend upon them. The rain felt good and lessened the heat. During the night, thunder boomed and lightning flashed in the mountains around them, and the children clung in fear to their parents. Since the rain fell continuously the following day, the saints received hoped-for relief from the heat and made good time. Their temporary travel schedule was over, and they traveled ten hours. By the end of the day, Steven calculated that they had covered fifteen miles. He was surprised at this because they had lost a great deal of time crossing a number of gaping fissures in the road. Twice the wagon train had found it necessary to drive into the gully-strewn fields to go around chasms in the road that were too steep to handle.

The blizzard hit at ten in the morning while the caravan was on its way. Mary was driving the lead wagon when she saw the storm coming from the north and wondered how bad it would be. Even though Steven had ridden away with Ruther, Douglas, and the bachelors to check on the wagon train, she was grateful that the three children were in the wagon with her. Within fifteen minutes, the wind-driven snow was so dense that she couldn't see the highway in front of her. She feared that at any moment the furious gale would blow her wagon over, or that she would drive the mules off the highway by accident and be lost in the whiteout. Now she realized one of the great disadvantages of being the lead wagon. She asked herself how such a storm could occur as late as the end of April. Then she remembered when a blizzard had struck Provo years earlier on June 6. It had come with a vengeance, but had completely disappeared by one in the afternoon, without leaving a trace of snow on the ground. Something told her, however, that this blizzard wasn't going to end quite so quickly.

On and on she drove in the blinding wind, determined not to stop. After all, what would Steve and the other pioneers think of her if she didn't have the strength to face this little trial? But where were the scouts who had preceded the wagon train to assure the safety of the pioneers? Had they gotten lost in the storm? At first she could determine where the road was by the posts and rails along the side, but soon they disappeared from view under piles of snow. She had to depend on the instinct of the mules and on the slight curvature of the road which was barely perceptible ahead. Their wagon was buffeted incessantly by snow-laden winds.

William insisted on sitting next to her on the wagon seat, taking the reins from her regularly when her frozen hands could hold them no longer. She admired the courage of this boy of thirteen who reminded her so much of Steven. Jennifer and Andrew, wrapped in blankets, stayed directly behind her, close to the opening, and stared in awe at the stark whiteness.

Mary turned and shouted to Andrew, "Look out the back and see if the Cartwrights are following." As the boy went to check, she added, "And fasten the flap!"

A minute later Andrew returned. "They're not there. I don't see anyone."

Now Mary was really starting to panic. Where were the others? Did they stop as soon as the storm began? What would happen if she drove the mules into a gigantic hole in the highway? No, that's not possible. Ruther had told her that the mules were very intelligent and could sense danger ahead, even when they couldn't see it. According to him, mules were much smarter than horses. At that point, Mary began to worry about the mules. Were they suffering in that cold? And what about the cow tied to the back of the wagon?

"Andrew, is Stockings still tied to the wagon?"

"Yes."

Thank you, Father in Heaven, she thought. Then her mind turned to Steven. Where was he? She had no wristwatch and the blizzard prevented her from estimating the time from the position of the sun. But he must have been gone for hours. Had he ridden off the highway without realizing it and wandered into the wilderness alone? Maybe she would never see her husband again! Finally, Mary stopped the mules, figuring it had to be close to lunchtime. They would eat and remain where they were, waiting for the others.

Yelling above the howl of the blizzard, she told the children to move to the center of the wagon and climb under their blankets. The wagon shook violently, battered by the gale, and she feared that at any moment it might be blown over or torn to pieces. She was grateful that it was heavily loaded. She waited fifteen minutes, watching through the rear canvass flap, but no other wagons appeared. Then, thinking of the animals again, she grabbed as many blankets as she could carry and climbed from the front of the wagon. Struggling against the wind, she moved up to the closest mule on the left and tried to cover it with a blanket. But the wind struck the blanket and hurled it twenty feet away. Carrying all the blankets in her arms, she staggered over to the lost blanket and added it to her pile.

After struggling back to the mules and barely able to maintain her footing against the freezing wind, but determined to help the animals, she threw her load of blankets on the ground, close to the rear mules. Then she picked up one blanket and stepped on top of the others. She wrapped the nearest mule's head with the blanket, tying its corners securely. In this way, by hefting and dropping the pile of blankets again and again, she succeeded in attaching four blankets to the heads of four mules. She was astonished at how strong, patient, and immovable they seemed. When the task was done, she worked her way to the back of the wagon, leaning against the wagon for support.

By the time she reached Stockings she couldn't feel her hands or feet. She tried to cover the cow's head with the last blanket, but the animal swung her great head back and forth, mooing excitedly, and the blanket was suddenly torn away by the wind and landed some distance away. Mary mumbled some words of anger she wasn't proud of. Then, too tired to retrieve the blanket, she stuck her head into the wagon and asked Andrew to hand her another. At last, ten minutes later, her hands completely numb, she finished the job and climbed back into the wagon. When she reached the children, she was so exhausted and cold that she had to lie next to them for twenty minutes before her body would permit her to find them something to eat.

After they had eaten, Mary insisted they lie back under the covers to sleep. She told the children that by the time they awoke, there was a good chance the other wagons would have overtaken them, or that Steven would have found them. The children fell asleep quickly, but it wasn't so easy for Mary. The howling of the wind, the shaking of the wagon, which slid sideways at times when it was struck by extra heavy gusts of wind, and the mooing of the cow, kept her awake. But eventually her fatigue took over, and she drifted into sleep.

Hours later she awoke abruptly and was struck by the complete silence outside. Peeking through the rear flap, she saw nothing but dim whiteness. And the cow. She realized at once that night was approaching, and the cold was biting. She glanced at the children and saw that they were still sound asleep. She gathered five blankets and clambered out of the wagon. Running as fast as she could through the foot of snow which covered the road, or what she believed was the road, she hurried to the animals and covered the backs of each with a blanket. Back in the wagon, she nestled against the children and waited.

The six riders watched the northern sky for several minutes. At last Ruther glanced at Steven and said, "Looks like a storm. Headin' this way."

"More rain?"

"Nope. Blizzard."

"Blizzard! In April?"

"Sure. I don't know why you're so shocked. We're livin' in the last days, yuh know. It's blisterin' one day and freezin' the next."

Steven knew the old-timer was right. For months he had been amazed at the wild extremes in the weather. Still, this storm caught him by surprise, and he didn't know what to do. "What do you suggest, Ruther?"

"Find shelter quick or yer people will be in trouble, especially them pullin' the little carts. Yuh know, if my old memory serves me right there's an open spot somewheres near-by. Oh, I'd say it's about a mile or two ahead. Lotsa cliffs and trees. All of yuh ride ta the front with me, and I'll show yuh the place.

Steven shouted, "Okay, let's do it."

They took off at a trot, heading for the front of the company. But soon the storm hit with all its fury and began to blanket the region in snow. Steven was so blinded by the driving snow that he was forced to cover most of his face with his hat and a scarf. He could barely see Ruther ahead or the others nearby. It was astonishing that the old man could even stay on the road. By the time they reached the front of the wagon train, the caravan had already stopped. Ruther shouted to Steven that the open spot was only about three hundred yards ahead. Steven looked around but couldn't locate his family wagon.

Fearing the worst, he immediately called out, "Ruther, I can't see my wagon anywhere. Lead the caravan to the sheltered area. I'm going on ahead to find my wagon."

"Okay," Ruther shouted back, "but be careful yuh don't go far from the road and git yerself lost. If yuh do, we may never see yuh again."

As Steven trotted the mustang up the freeway, he strained to see between the brim of his hat and his scarf, trying hard to stay on the road. He went on for what seemed forever, and his fear steadily grew. Before long he pushed the horse into a canter, and almost immediately the animal lost its footing on the slick surface. Both horse and man tumbled to the ground. Ignoring the pain of the fall, Steven struggled to his feet and looked for his horse, afraid that the mustang had broken a leg. But the horse was already standing not far away, waiting for him. He checked the animal for injuries and, finding none, he remounted rapidly and continued his journey in the blinding snow. He felt a pang of guilt for leaving the wagon train, but what could he do that Ruther and the others couldn't? He knew that his primary responsibility was to his family.

He moved up the freeway at a walk for about two hours, searching hard but finding nothing. He was frantic. He couldn't understand how they could have come this far. Is it possible he had missed his own wagon? Had Mary left the freeway without realizing it? Were they lost somewhere in the wilderness, at the mercy of the storm or some unknown enemy? Before long, the wind died, and the sky began to darken. Nighttime was not far away. At last Steven decided to go back and search the sides of the highway as he returned to the wagon train.

As he walked the mustang back down the road, staying near the center, he scrutinized the snowy fields on each side until his eyes burned. He closed them frequently and briefly to stop the burning, and then returned to the exasperating search. After about one hour, he caught sight of a black dot on the right some distance from the road. At first he dismissed it as nothing but a bush or small tree standing above the white earth. But then he had the feeling he should check it out. He turned off the road, crossed the gully, and headed for the dark object. When he reached the spot, he dismounted and picked the thing up. It was one of his blankets.

Steven mounted his horse and directed him to proceed along the same angle as the blanket had been from the road. Soon he got the impression that beneath the snow there was a narrow trail. He dismounted again and quickly dug into the snow with his hands until he hit dirt and gravel. After widening the area of his search, he finally found the ruts made by a very heavy wagon. He grabbed the horse's reins and led him along in the direction of the ruts. Fifteen minutes later, he rounded a knoll and saw his wagon two hundred yards ahead. Jumping on his horse, he spurred him forward. As soon as he reached the wagon, he tied his horse to the rear and climbed in. He crawled over to Mary. "Wake up, sleepy head," he said softly, a wide grin transforming his face.

Mary's tired eyes opened slowly, but when she finally realized whose bleary face it was, she popped up and threw her arms around her husband. "I knew you'd come," she said, her eyes wet with tears. "What took you so long?"

After hugging his excited children, who awoke with shouts of glee, he explained the whole thing, especially the part about finding the blanket. Next he removed the coverings from the animals and turned the wagon back toward the freeway. The storm was over but the cold was biting. After they had traveled west on the highway for some time, it became so dark that Steven had great difficulty telling where the road was. He was afraid they would miss the place where Ruther and the others had left the freeway to find the sheltered area. But soon the figure of the mountain man appeared suddenly in the dark, only fifty yards away. High atop his big mule, he was waiting for them beside the road. Steven pointed his flashlight in Ruther's direction and saw the old man grin and wave for them to follow.

Ruther guided them to the pioneer camp, less than a quarter of a mile from the highway. The location was excellent. On the north there was a long ridge, and on the south, extensive groves of trees. The pioneers had rolled their wagons six abreast into the space between the trees and the bluffs. They had unhitched their animals and sheltered them at the base of the ridge in undercuts dug by erosion. The handcart people had pitched their tents between the wagons and the animals.

Steven brought his wagon into the line and, with the help of Ruther and the bachelors, unhitched the mules and took them to shelter. Afterwards, they pulled Steven's wagon up close against the others. Steven checked with them to see if any of the pioneers had run into trouble, and was pleased to hear that the move to shelter had been a complete success. Before long there were dozens of campfires burning bright in the blackness of the night, and the pioneers, wearing many layers of warm clothing, enjoyed a hot meal. Around nine o'clock Ruther and the bachelors left for their wagon, and Steven and his family gladly headed for their own. As soon as everyone had climbed under a small mountain of blankets, Steven read to his family by the light of a lamp until he noticed that they had fallen asleep.

Steven's family and friends ate breakfast around a blazing campfire, dressed in warm clothes. The night had been very cold, with temperatures not far from zero, and their buckets of water had frozen solid. Steven was grateful that Ruther had spotted this sheltered area from the highway. The old man had told him several times that as the leader of a company he should learn to read the trail. If he could do that, he would know how to spot places which offered food and water, good campsites, and natural protection against attack. Years ago, he had read in many Louis L'Amour novels the same lessons which Ruther taught, but he still couldn't really see what he was looking at. While they ate, Mary told everyone what had happened, and how Steven had found them.

"That was right fortunate, yuh tryin' ta put that blanket around yer cow's head," Ruther commented, chuckling a bit now that the danger was over.

"Because if she hadn't throwed a fit and shaken it off, Steve here might never've found yuh . . . I'm not sayin' we wouldn't have found yuh eventually, but it might have taken days . . . And I hate ta think of what yuh all would have looked like when we did." Nobody there could suppress muted laughter.

Mary laughed too, but her face turned red in spite of the cold. "It's really not funny. We were scared to death. Of course, if I hadn't covered the heads and eyes of the mules, they probably wouldn't have walked off the highway onto that turnoff in the first place."

Steven didn't think it was really a turnoff. The main road had turned slightly to the right, and there just happened to be a gravel road which went straight ahead. The dip into the narrow road ahead was hardly noticeable. He tried to soothe his wife's feelings. "Mary, I'm not sure that covering their eyes made them lose their way. Besides, you protected them from the storm."

"Yes, if it hadn't been for you, your mules and cow might be dead now," Elizabeth Cartwright said. "I think what you did was not only kind but also courageous." Douglas and the bachelors bobbed their heads in agreement.

"Yes siree!" Ruther joined in. "Dead, or with a bad case of the flu in their eyes and nose. And I agree with Steve that the mules probably wouldn't walk off the road jist because their eyes was covered. A mule's an uncanny smart beast, and he always seems ta know where he's a goin'."

"You're all trying to make me feel better," Mary insisted. "I know I was stupid."

Steven was proud of his wife. "Mary, you did what had to be done. A good person never goes wrong by following her heart."

That made Mary smile. "By the way, I'd sure like to know what happened to the advance scouts. I never did see them."

"I talked to a couple of them," Steven said. "It appears they went right past you sometime during the storm. But everybody is safe. That's the most important thing . . . Listen, today is Sunday and I think we should try to have a short Sunday service in spite of the bitter cold."

On Monday the pioneers awoke early, fixed a quick breakfast, and were on the road by eight o'clock. Two hours later the sun was bright, and the heat began to return. Most of the snow had melted away. After another hour one of the forward scouts spotted a small wrecking yard on the left side of the freeway, seventeen miles from Evanston, Wyoming.

The Moderns went wild.

Even some of the Ancients were happy too, because they hoped to replace their rickety wagons with better vehicles. Both groups swarmed the yard looking for the right thing.

Before long, they found ten conveyances which they could use: four vans, three family trailers, a U-haul trailer, a camper trailer, and something else hard to describe. The lower half of this last vehicle appeared to be the undercarriage of a large trailer, with modern axles and wheels. The semicircular top of corrugated metal looked like a small Quonset hut. The vehicle sat high above the road and had a stovepipe protruding through the roof. While forty-four pioneers gutted the vehicles of heavy, unnecessary parts, the Ancients argued for an hour over who should possess the weird, Quonset-type contraption. By three o'clock the Ancients and Moderns, working together diligently, had fixed up the ten "new" conveyances well enough that teams of draft animals could pull them. They planned to finish their work when the company stopped for the day. The other pioneers impatiently learned patience as they endured the long wait watching their fellow travelers do this important work.

By late afternoon on the following day the caravan reached Evanston, Wyoming. From his driver's seat Steven saw a throng of people heading west toward them on the eastbound portion of the freeway. They were about a mile away. Hundreds of them, running, shouting, and waving their arms wildly. Some carried guns. He stopped the wagon abruptly, grabbed his rifle, and watched them intently as they approached. Five LDS advance scouts came galloping back to the caravan as fast as their horses could run. Ruther, Douglas, the bachelors, and fifteen others came up from behind. One held an Uzi from the stash John Christopher had secured in a special trailer.

"Yuh want I should dust their thunder a bit, Steve?" Ruther said nonchalantly, holding his Sharps ready. All that thar arm wavin' looks a mite hostile."

"No, we don't know what their intentions are yet." Steven descended from the wagon.

Everyone watched the strangers carefully, growing more nervous by the minute. When the mob was three hundred yards away, they stopped abruptly. Steven guessed that one of the leaders had given them a command. Maybe his next command would be for the townspeople to take cover and attack Pioneer One. Strung out along the highway, the travelers were in a vulnerable position. Fifty additional brothers and sisters came forward to see what was going on. Steven was shocked by what the crowd of strangers did next. They laid their weapons on the highway and came on slowly and cautiously.

"Hold your fire," Steven shouted. "I think it's okay."

When the throng was fifty feet away, they stopped again. A tall man stepped forward and walked up to the waiting pioneers. "Welcome!" he said grinning broadly. "We knew you were coming. One of the men here has a radio and heard you talking to Salt Lake . . . But what took you so long?"

"It's a long story," Steven replied, relieved.

As soon as the greetings were completed, the mob rushed forward and embraced the pioneers with joy. Within fifteen minutes nearly two thousand people were milling around on the freeway and the adjacent margins, hugging one another, laughing, and chattering happily. Then the multitude began to walk slowly toward the town. While the men exchanged information and jokes, the women walked arm in arm, sharing experiences.

Even the townspeople who were not Mormons welcomed the pioneers eagerly. Because the countryside had been ravaged by famine and disease, and roving bands of lawless barbarians, nearly every inhabitant of this corner of Wyoming had perished. Only the people of Evanston had joined their hearts, minds, and resources and had survived. In spite of that, the population had been reduced from ten thousand to slightly more than a thousand, due to lack of food and diseases for which they had no medicines. Since there were so few decent people left in Uinta County, they were overjoyed to see the bedraggled pioneers.

The pioneer company drove their vehicles east until they came to the off-ramp that ended at Front Street. They followed this street to the center of town, where they parked their wagons. Then they joined the people of Evanston in a celebration. Both the townspeople and the pioneers contributed watchmen to stand guard around the town. The town brass band played, and the people had a square dance. The citizens contributed flour and sugar from their meager supplies, and the women made thousands of small cupcakes. The pioneers added root beer and herbal drinks.

Later in the evening, they sat around dozens of campfires and swapped tales and experiences. Some of the town leaders invited Steven, Mary, and their friends to join them at their fire. Steven was astonished at seeing so many jubilant people.

"They're really whooping it up, aren't they?" the city mayor said to Steven. "I haven't seen my people have this much fun in a long time."

Steven replied, "I can't believe it under the circumstances. They act as if they don't have a care in the world."

"You know, it's hard to walk around being miserable all the time," Doug Cartwright observed.

Elizabeth said, "Yes, even when things are the worst, people grasp often desperately for any chance to express happiness."

"Reminds me of a friend I had a few years ago," Ruther said. "Got mauled so bad by a b'ar that thar was no way ta save him. Happened in the Uintas." He pointed to the southeast. "The ole boy was in agony fer days, but all he could do was tell one joke after another. Right up ta the time he died."

"I believe that shows great courage," Mary said.

"That's what I'm a figurin'. He knowed I was doin' my best fer 'im and he didn't want ta git me worked up."

After the conversation went on for another hour, the mayor said, "I'm wondering if you folks can stay in town a few days. Maybe we could help each other solve some problems."

"I wish we could," Steven answered, "but we're already behind schedule. We have many things to do in Missouri before winter comes."

The mayor was LDS and understood Steven completely. "Yes, of course. But do you have medical people with you? The marauders killed or kidnapped our health care people, and we don't know how to deal with a lot of the problems we have."

"We'll do our best to help."

Steven sent the bachelors to round up the doctor and the nurses. The mayor led them to the high school where the sickest people were cared for. They spent the rest of the evening and part of the night doing their best to help, but there was little they could do because of the lack of medical supplies. Grapefruit seed extract helped some of the patients, but it did little to heal badly infected wounds. While Mary doctored the patients, Steven took care of the children. During the night he awoke several times because of nightmares. He kept dreaming of evil armies attacking the saints in Utah—especially his parents.

Chapter 14

❦

The pioneers arose early and pulled out of Evanston at eight o'clock. The townspeople, waving sadly, watched them go. Many citizens gave the travelers small gifts.

Two days later, an hour before the caravan halted for the day, one of the sisters screamed with joy as she passed over a small creek below the freeway. Within fifteen minutes, half the females in the caravan had run off the freeway to the south, packing homemade soap, towels, and bundles of soiled clothes. After stopping his wagon when he first heard the shrieks, Steven checked his map and saw that the stream was called Smith's Fork Creek, forty-one miles east of Evanston. As the women and girls poured off the highway in a mad dash for the water, the men either stayed in place or walked to the north side of the freeway and waited—sometimes patiently.

Since they had gone through this routine many times, the men knew better than to look off the south side of the road to make sure the bathers were okay. They especially had to keep their eyes on their young sons. It was very painful, but the men knew it was worth it, since the females would be much more pleasant to live with later. At times like this, some of the more civilized men also tried to take advantage of the nearby water as soon as the women had finished. But the other brethren, who didn't seem to notice all the disgusting sweat and grime on their persons, were so impatient to move on that those who were anxious to clean up had to forego the pleasure.

The pioneers saw no human life on the trail during the next few days of travel since leaving Evanston. The trek was becoming more difficult. In many places the highway looked as though it had been hit with bombs, and some sections were completely washed away by immense floods. The pioneers had to endure great heat during the day and freezing cold at night. A maddening hot wind buffeted them unremittingly. It dried their skin and parched their lips, covered their clothes with dust, and forced dirt and debris into every body orifice, especially their eyes. There seemed to be no way to escape it.

In spite of the difficulties, the pioneers made fairly good time, averaging more than fifteen miles a day. And in spite of their misery, Steven had the impression that the saints were grateful to face enemies they could understand. He was delighted to see that many who had been chubby at the beginning were now trimmer. Even those who still carried extra weight looked stronger and more fit.

As they approached Rock Springs, Wyoming, on May 9, they saw a dozen people watching them from a rise south of the highway. Steven and Mary studied them through binoculars. Jennifer peeked around the canvas cover and, shielding her eyes against the blowing wind, strained to see.

"They look like homeless derelicts," Mary said sadly. "Their clothes are filthy rags, and some are holding out their hands . . . They probably need food and water. They're not even armed. Steven, can we—"

"Too dangerous. Might be a trap."

Mary continued to watch through the binoculars. "Oh no! I see a mother and a small child. Please, Steven."

Steven's voice took on an edge. "There's probably an army hiding behind them."

"Dad," Jennifer retorted, "didn't the prophet say that if we show kindness to others on this trip, Father in Heaven will reward us the same way?"

Steven sighed, knowing he was outvoted and outargued by his two kind-hearted females. He stopped the wagon and called for William, who was riding the mustang not far away. After pointing out the beggars to the boy, he instructed him to tell Paul to take supplies to them, but to be careful. A few minutes later, Paul and several men left the wagon train and rode up to the derelicts. They talked for a short time. Steven was shocked when he saw that, instead of taking the supplies and leaving, the beggars followed Paul back to the caravan.

When the group reached Steven's wagon, Paul called out, "Steve, these people are Mormons. They want to go to Missouri with us."

Steven noticed that none of the vagabonds were armed. He was somewhat upset that Paul had told the wanderers that they were traveling to Missouri, but he jumped from his wagon and went to greet the newcomers. The group was comprised of two middle-aged men, two women of the same age, a young woman with a baby, a girl about eighteen, two boys around thirteen, and two younger girls. Eleven people in all.

"Welcome!" Steven called. "So you're LDS?"

"Some of us," said one of the older men. He was tall and skeletal, and his clothes were filthy and torn to shreds. The other derelicts were in the same condition. It was clear they were starving. The teenage girl's left arm was partly covered with a bloody bandage. "My name is Elmer Gleason." He nodded toward the people standing close to him. "This is my wife Luella, my daughter Erika, and my sons Jerry and Tommy." He pointed to the other man and his family. "That's my friend Luke Small, his wife Camille, and his two little girls Sophie and Clara. I don't know the young woman or her baby. We just ran into them a few minutes ago."

Her eyes glistening with tears, the young woman said, "I'm Kinsey Ritter. My baby's name is Emily. We live in Rock Springs. My husband was murdered three days ago by roving hoodlums."

Steven replied sadly, "I'm terribly sorry." Then he spoke more loudly to all the newcomers. "We offer you assistance and protection. You're more than welcome to travel east with us."

"For that we are grateful," Elmer Gleason declared with hope in his eyes. "Luke and I came from Chicago with our families. We've been wandering nearly seven months now, struggling to reach Utah. But I doubt we'd ever make it alone. Half the time we've had to lay low to avoid dangerous marauders. Since my family and I are Mormons, we'd be thrilled to join you no matter where you're going. I know Luke and his family feel the same way." Both Luke and Camille nodded.

Steven was dumbfounded. Chicago seven months ago. "That's about the time— Were you in Chicago when the hydrogen bomb hit?"

"Fifteen miles east of Chicago. We survived the attack because we had the protection of our homemade bomb shelter. A month later, we left for Utah. Luke and his family too. We've been traveling ever since."

"You're lucky to be alive," Steven declared. When he saw the expression on the faces of Elmer and Luella, he guessed that they knew why the wagon train was heading east. But this was not the time to discuss it. "Please go with my brother Paul and these other men. They'll make sure you have food, water, and accommodations. Unfortunately, we may have to separate some of you for a few days until we can make arrangements for you to have your own vehicles."

As the new travelers left with Paul, Steven climbed into his wagon and sat next to Mary.

Mary leaned over and kissed him. "Thank you, sweetheart. You're a good man."

"You're the one who's good. Look, the girl is hurt. Do you want to treat her?"

"Yes." Mary found her medical kit, climbed from the wagon, and started walking down the caravan.

The company did not stop at Rock Springs but continued on. When they finally stopped for the day, John gravely informed Steven that he was no longer able to contact Salt Lake City on the radio, because his transmissions were being jammed from some unknown source. For days afterward, Steven had difficulty shaking the feeling that they were completely isolated and abandoned.

Traveling during the following week was even more difficult than before. After leaving Rock Springs, they began the long trek across the Red Deseret, which extended a hundred and six miles. The terrain was monotonous, the sun blazing, and the hot dry wind battered them endlessly. Their only diversion was the hundreds of wild horses which still roamed the countryside. Every day Steven and the bachelors led parties of men on horse hunts, because the caravan needed mounts and meat. The rugged animals led the inexperienced brethren on one merry chase after another, in spite of Ruther's help, and it was only on their sixth attempt that they finally captured a few horses.

Twenty-five miles east of Rock Springs, the sisters abruptly insisted that the caravan stop. A couple of them had sighted Bitter Creek two hundred yards to the south, and in minutes hundreds of sisters headed for the body of water. Since the stream was not next to the freeway, Steven, Paul, and Douglas hurried to check things out before it was too late. As Steven approached the stream, he saw that its banks were twenty feet high and were littered with appliances, car parts, and every kind of trash. Fearing the water might be dangerous, he asked the sisters to wait until they found cleaner water. But several women informed him that the creek couldn't be as polluted as he said, because it had fish swimming in it. Steven turned and headed back to the caravan, knowing that their argument was better than his.

On May 16 they reached Creston Junction, about a hundred and eighty miles from Evanston. Since it was almost seven o'clock, Steven called a halt. Seeing no threat, he didn't pull the wagons into circles. The pioneers followed the usual schedule: feed the animals, supper, chores, and talk around the campfire. They were too exhausted to dance or sing. After a meeting with the leaders, which lasted only fifteen minutes, Steven joined his family and friends around their campfire. Steven asked Paul about the vagabonds they had rescued and was pleased to learn that several pioneer families had "adopted" them.

There was a short period of embarrassing silence, and then Ruther declared with great emotion, "Well, folks, ain't it great out here in God's country? Plenty of room ta breathe. No pollution. No noise. No city lights. No walls ta close yuh in. Delightful grub. And a beautiful, star-filled sky ta sleep under."

Mary fired back, "I've always hated camping. My father and my ex-husband always insisted on doing it the old-fashioned way. But even with modern equipment it's a pain. I'll never forget the miserable times I've had. The dirt and grime. Fires that won't start, or gas stoves which threaten to blow up in your face. Smoky, burned food. Irritating cleanups. Mosquitos, yellow jackets, and ticks. Flies which relish your flesh and follow you around camp. The smelly bug repellent you have to use, or forget to bring. Stupid tents which take Einstein to erect. Tight sleeping bags and the hard, lumpy ground. Interminable, sleepless nights. The wild animals that make weird noises at night."

Elizabeth piped up, "You forgot a few things. Abominable outhouses with their ghastly stench—you always wonder what's down there in that black pit under your exposed bottom. The frightening darkness. Supplies you forget or lose. Kids who insist on sleeping with you, and then crowd you or pee on you during the night. Snakes, lizards, and other crawly things. The times you sit in your tent all day while it rains. Tents that cave in the moment you finally doze off. Freezing lakes full of long slimy things . . . "

"Whew!" Ruther said. "Guess I opened a can of worms. Can I take back my words?"

Steven laughed. "Yes, it looks like you pushed the wrong button, Ruther." Steven didn't admit that he agreed with the women.

"I reckon I did."

"The women have a point," Douglas said. "I can think of a few delightful things myself. Chapped lips. Poison ivy and poison oak—got a rash myself once. Then there's the campfire smoke which follows you around no matter which way the wind is blowing. And the people who talk all night or play loud music . . . Yes, you really have to love the outdoors to appreciate camping."

Steven thought they had pretty much covered it all, but Mary wasn't done. "The thing that amazes me is how bad my memory was. I used to dream about traveling to Missouri to help establish New Zion, the most wonderful civilization on earth, where everyone would be righteous and perfectly happy. It would be the most marvelous experience of my life. But I completely forgot about camping. I didn't realize or even imagine that traveling to Zion would be like going on the worst camping trip ever! One which would last for months, and seem like forever. And we don't even have the benefit of modern equipment."

Elizabeth backed her up, "Well, I'm not LDS, so I never dreamed about going to Zion, but for some crazy reason I imagined that this trip would really be fun. Now I understand how foolish I was. Still, in spite of the many trials, pains, and discomfort, I'm honestly glad I came. I have learned to love you people so much. And I'm also learning to depend on the Lord and trust him more than I ever did before."

Tears welled in Mary's eyes and she hugged Elizabeth, who immediately started to cry. Then with difficulty Mary said, "Yes. I guess it's been worth all the tribulations, regardless of my whining."

Although Steven was touched by their display of affection, he couldn't resist making a joke. "When you think of it, this trip is a piece of cake in comparison to what the Israelites went through."

"What do you mean?" Mary asked.

"Well, the Lord made the Israelites wander in the wilderness for forty years. And they didn't have modern equipment either. Apparently, God wanted to delay their entry into the Land of Promise until the rebellious died off and the others were chastened and sanctified, worthy to receive their inheritance."

"That's certainly encouraging," Mary exclaimed.

With a glint in his eye, Ruther added, "Yep, and I unnerstand the wilderness they was in would make this here place look like the Garden of Eden. Much more bleak and deserty."

"I'm not so sure their wilderness was quite that barren, Ruther," Mary said, with teasing in her voice. "Besides, the Israelites got a lot more help than we're getting. After all, they had Moses and tons of free manna and springs flowing from rocks."

Ruther's eyes opened wide, but his mouth stayed shut.

Douglas decided to join in on the humor. "Well, I think you and Elizabeth are much better than manna and flowing springs. And Steven is sort of like Moses, isn't he? Only he's a lot younger and better looking." Everyone laughed, especially Jennifer and the two women.

After they chatted for a while about various things, Ruther said with a gleam in his eyes, "Yuh know, I like you folks so much, I really wish yuh had a better understandin' of the Holy Word. If yuh did, yuh'd probably be raptured someday like all us true believers."

Steven was amused at the way Ruther loved to bait them into religious conversations. "What do you mean, Ruther?"

"Well, in the first place it seems ta me yuh have the wrong idea of who Jesus is. And I figure yuh don't understand what the holy book says about how people get saved."

Steven said, "That's two different subjects, and we probably don't have enough time tonight to cover them both. So which would you like to discuss?"

"Shucks! Don't matter ta me. I suppose we could talk about how we get saved."

"How do we?" Paul asked.

"First, why don't yuh tell me what yuh Mormons believe?"

Steven noticed that Douglas and Elizabeth seemed very interested in hearing the answer. After looking at Steven, who signaled the go-ahead, Paul said, "We believe that through the atonement of Christ, people are saved if they believe in Christ and obey his commandments."

Ruther replied, "Well, thar yuh go. A mistake right from the git-go. Doesn't the holy book say that man is saved by faith alone?" Once again Ruther pulled out his old Bible. He thumbed through the book, obviously enjoying himself. He had marked the passages with pieces of paper so he could find them quickly. "Here we is. In the Book of John it says, 'He that believeth on the Son hath everlasting life.' It don't say nary a word regardin' good works." He flipped to the next passage. "And Paul in Romans says, 'Man is justified by faith without the deeds of the law.' And over here in Ephesians, Paul says we're saved by grace through faith, and not by works, lest any man should boast. Because of them scripts, and lotsa others, I don't see how you Mormons are justified in sayin' yer goin' ta be saved when yuh depend so much on yer own good works."

Elizabeth was visibly upset. As a Methodist, she believed in the importance of Christian charity. "But, Ruther, Christians must do good works or they aren't followers of Christ."

Ruther replied, "Of course, we does good works, but they doesn't save us. Only faith in Jesus saves. The works come automatically. Actually, it's Jesus doin' the works through us, not us doin' 'em."

Steven looked at Paul and his companions, knowing it was only a matter of time before they let poor Ruther have it.

Jarrad spoke first. "Ruther, tell me what you think about Mark 16:16."

Ruther turned to the passage and read, "He that believeth and is baptized shall be saved; but he that believeth not shall be damned."

"Doesn't that say you must believe and be baptized to be saved?"

"Yep."

"Isn't being baptized an action, a work?"

Ruther paused. "Uh, well, yes, but it sorta comes automatically. What about the times Paul the apostle says works aren't important?"

"If you read the passages in Romans and Ephesians in context," Paul answered, "you can see that Paul the apostle is saying that the deeds or the works of the Law of Moses will not save people. Jewish converts to Christianity in ancient times still had the habit of practicing the rituals and performances of the Law of Moses, and Paul is correcting them. When he speaks of faith, he's talking about the gospel preached by Christ, which includes works greater than those of the Law."

Ruther paused, his mind apparently working on the problem. "All right. Tonight I'll read all the scriptures around the ones I quoted ta see if what you're sayin' is right."

"Ruther," Jarrad said, "I suggest you examine the writings of the other apostles on this subject too. For example, let's look at the second chapter of James." Ruther turned to the place. "Here the apostle is instructing true believers in Christ to do good works. In verse fourteen James asks if faith can save a man if he does not have works. Look especially at verses seventeen and eighteen. In verse seventeen James declares, 'Even so faith, if it hath not works, is dead, being alone.' So if faith doesn't include the works of Christ, it's dead, or in other words, it's not true faith."

"But young Paul here just said that the word 'work' refers to the Law of Moses," Ruther observed.

"The term has two meanings in these scriptures," Jarrad replied. "In this context, it refers to the works of the gospel, not the works of the Law."

Ruther looked perplexed. "I have ta admit that you boys make a good argument. Still, it seems ta me that you're saying Paul and James teach two different gospels."

"Why do you think that?" Paul said. "The faith Paul talks about includes works. Do you remember what he says about faith and charity in chapter thirteen of First Corinthians?"

Ruther recited grandly, "'Though I speak with the tongues of men and of angels, and have not charity, I am become as sounding brass, or a tinkling cymbal.'"

"That's it. But in verse thirteen, which is the greatest between faith, hope, and charity?"

"Charity is the greatest."

"And charity is simply another word for good works."

Ruther wasn't about to give up easily. "Of course, yuh have ta be charitable. But since yuh believe in Christ, he takes yer life over, and he's the one who does the works, not you."

Steven had heard this strange argument many times before. "Are you saying that Christ controls your behavior, that you lose your free will? Does he move your mouth when you say kind things? Does he move your hands and legs when you help someone?"

"In a way, yes," Ruther replied.

"But then how can you merit the reward for good deeds when you don't even do them yourself?"

Ruther answered triumphantly, "Because yuh done accepted Jesus and yuh has faith in him."

Douglas said, "But Ruther, if that's true, why do the prophets and apostles, including Paul, constantly encourage their people—the true believers—to develop and display the Christian virtues if they don't have the power in themselves to do it?"

Suddenly Ruther was stymied, but he didn't want to admit he had no answer. "You folks are pretty good at ganging up on a poor, ignorant old man. If I had a couple of Southern Baptist ministers with me, we'd give yuh a run fer yer money."

Everyone smiled, but no one replied. It was obvious that Ruther had run out of arguments.

But Ruther continued, "So it's right what I heard."

"What did you hear?" Steven asked.

"You Mormons believe yuh can earn salvation by yer own good works."

"Not really," Steven replied. "We believe that it's a partnership between God and man. Christ does his part, and we try—or should try—to do our part. However, I have to add that without Christ's atonement, no man could go to heaven no matter how righteous he was or how many good deeds he did. We can save ourselves, but only through the Lord."

Ruther replied, "That's purdy nifty. But why in tarnation do yuh have ta complicate things by havin' two kinds of salvation?"

Steven was puzzled. "Two kinds of salvation?"

"Yep. That's what young Paul told me the other night while we was shootin' the bull in the bachelor wagon. We believe in two types of salvation, he said."

Now Elizabeth looked confused. "Two kinds of salvation?"

"Let me explain what I think Paul means, Liz," Mary said. "We believe that man fell because Adam transgressed God's law. The result was that all mankind would die and never be resurrected—unless God provided a remedy. We would remain spirit beings forever. As spirits we could never live with God, but would have to live with Satan in perdition forever. Obviously, if that happened, God would be unjust because people would receive a terrible punishment for a transgression they didn't commit."

"Yes, it would be unfair," Elizabeth observed.

"So God sent his Son to die for us, to pay the penalty. Because of that, we can be resurrected and saved from Satan. That's our first salvation."

"What's the second one?" Douglas asked.

"Well, just because people can be resurrected, it doesn't mean they're righteous. It doesn't mean they're worthy to live in heaven with God."

"No, I suppose not," Elizabeth agreed.

"So to receive the second salvation, to live with God, they must obey the Gospel of Jesus Christ. But as Steven said, even if people are righteous, they could not inherit heaven without the atonement of Christ. So the atonement has a double effect: it permits all mankind to be resurrected, and it allows the obedient to go to heaven."

Steven was pleased with Mary's simple summary of a doctrine which had many complexities to it.

"That's wonderful!" Elizabeth said. "It shows that God is both just and kind."

Even Ruther seemed impressed, but he wasn't about to admit it.

Elizabeth added teasingly, "Mary, I'm glad you placed the blame for the world's problems on a man."

Douglas looked at her in surprise. "What do you mean by that?"

"Mary said mankind fell because of a man—Adam."

"But Eve started it all," Douglas objected. "She talked Adam into eating the fruit."

Elizabeth poked her husband in the ribs playfully. "Well, he didn't have to listen, did he? What was he, some kind of robot?" Everyone laughed at Elizabeth's joke.

Steven realized that all of them were tired and that their conversation was over. Still he wanted to add one more thing. "Ruther, I know it seems like we were ganging up on you, but it seems to take all of us to hold our ground with a man like you who knows the scriptures so well. You've made us think and explain ourselves, and I'm grateful. Most of all, you always discuss religion without trace of anger or impatience. That's a great virtue we can all emulate. Please remember that even if we may not agree with all your points, we love you very much."

"Well, that's right kind of yuh, Steve. You boys know yer religion too, and you're right talented at known' how ta stick a feller smack dab between a b'ar and a mountain lion."

Seeing the mischievous look in Ruther's eyes, Steven asked himself some perplexing questions. Did this remarkable old man argue simply for the joy of arguing and baiting them? Did he know that Steven was now trying to help him save face? And did he actually believe all his own arguments? Steven wasn't sure of the answers. But one thing he did know for sure: there wasn't a dumb bone in the old boy's body.

Later in their wagon, after the children had fallen asleep, Mary said, "I'm sorry I griped so much about camping. It was stupid for me to talk like that when I'm supposed to set a good example."

Steven rolled over and snuggled up to her. "I think you made some reasonable points. Ruther was enjoying it thoroughly. Besides, no one can be a good example all the time. It isn't human." Suddenly the fatigue of the day hit him hard.

"I know, but I still feel guilty."

After a moment of silence, Mary asked, "Why do there have to be so many trials?"

"What did you expect?" Steven replied sleepily. "The Lord to swoop down and carry us to Missouri in the twinkling of an eye?"

"I don't mean that. I was thinking about the pioneers. Why do they have to fight so much, and complain, and talk about you behind your back? They're supposed to be saints."

"They're talking about me again? What is it this time?"

Mary hesitated. "Not just you. They also gossip about me, Paul, John, and others."

"So what's the latest?"

"Paul told me that some are accusing you of abandoning the wagon train during the blizzard for personal reasons."

"Oh brother! Of course I left it for personal reasons. I felt my family was in danger so I went after them. I left the company in good hands."

"I know. It's stupid. But that's the way gossip works. Both John and Paul think you have some enemies in the company who are spreading these rumors because they're out to get you."

"Have they discovered who the gossipers are?"

"Not yet, but they're trying hard."

"Good." After a moment of silence, Steven said, "As for the trials we're going through, I believe they're God's way of sanctifying the people. He can't use the saints to establish New Zion until they're holy enough to do it. So he chastens them."

"We don't have to be perfect, I hope."

"No, not perfect, but a lot more righteous than we are now." He gave her a kiss. "Well, we need to get some sleep. It's another big day tomorrow."

They tossed and turned for a while, the heat making sleep difficult. Finally, Mary said, "I can't sleep."

"Me neither."

"It's probably the heat."

"Right."

"Also, I was thinking about Ruther."

"Oh?"

"Do you think we were mean to him tonight? We sort of ganged up on him."

"Heck no. Ruther loves it. He tries to shake us up on purpose."

"Do you really think so?"

"Yes."

"I'm glad. I really like him. I hope he stays with us all the way to Missouri. He risked his life for you, you know."

"I realize that."

Mary hesitated, and then said, "You've been sort of depressed since the fight with the bandits."

"Who me? I always act this way."

"No, you don't . . . and I think I know the reason."

"You do?"

"Yes. You killed a man, and it's bothering you. You just don't want to admit it."

Steven swallowed hard. Suddenly, he felt very unhappy. "I suppose you're right. I've relived that scene many times during the night."

"You'll get over it in time. You only did what you had to do."

"Maybe. But I'm afraid that someday soon I may have to do things which are even worse."

Chapter 15

The angelic being appeared to Colton Aldridge more frequently now. Whenever he needed the faith and the power to perform a great miracle, he secluded himself in a secret room and poured out his heart. So on Wednesday, May 17, he was in his dark room praying fervently. Before long, a dazzling burst of light penetrated the ceiling and filled the room with splendor. Then a god-like personage descended slowly in a pillar of white flame. The glory of the magnificent entity infused Colton's body with joy. The light was so bright that it forced him to shield his eyes with his hands, but soon the brilliance gradually contracted to the body of the visitor until Colton could bear his presence.

"Lord, thank you for answering my prayer," Colton declared fervently. He was grateful that God had found him worthy of transfiguration. Without that, he knew that he would have been consumed by the entity's blazing glory. Even his lust for women did not render him impure, for he always received his Master's permission before he took the women unto him.

"Behold, I am the Eternal Most High," the being said. "And thy reward shall be great, my son, for thou hast been faithful in the errand which I gave thee in the land of China."

"Thank you, Lord." Colton was burning to ask the Master the question which had been torturing him for so long, but he dared not do it just yet. "But, Master, what do you want me to do here in Japan?"

"Gain control of the government."

"But how?"

"By warning Japanese leaders of a great disaster."

"How will that give me control?"

"They will not believe thy prediction. But when the disaster occurs, they will be struck by fear and give thee and thy friends more influence in this 'land of the gods.'"

"What catastrophe shall I predict?"

The personage revealed to Colton exactly what he must say and do. "Now, I perceive that thou desirest to know thy standing in my future Kingdom."

Colton was delighted that his god had read his thoughts. It did not occur to him that he had openly expressed to many what he believed his role would be. "Yes, Lord, thank you."

"Verily I say unto thee, thou art the one mighty and strong who shall set my house in order and steady the ark of God. But before that day cometh, thou must continue thy work among the nations, as I have instructed thee before."

At these words, the personage ascended and the light disappeared with him, leaving the room dark. Colton was ecstatic. He already believed he was above the rules followed by ordinary men because he lived at the highest level of gospel law. His Master had taught him those laws himself. But now he knew he was the one. The chosen servant of God. After he had reflected on his vision another hour, sitting alone in the dark, he arose, turned on the lights, and ordered a late night snack. Later while he was eating, he heard an abrupt knock. He went to the door and was surprised to see Lucienne Delisle.

"Colton, it's good to see you. The desk told me your room number. May I come in?" She looked at the tray of food near the bed.

"Of course." Colton stood aside to let her pass.

Lucienne hurried to the tray and began eating his strawberry shortcake. "I hope you don't mind. I'm so hungry."

"That's fine. I'm getting a bit plump anyhow . . . So what brings you to Nagasaki?"

Lucienne sat on Colton's bed. "Gerald sent me to see how you were doing."

"Yes, of course," Colton said with irritation. "But where are your people? In this hotel?"

"We have four rooms on the next floor down," Lucienne said, licking her fingers. "And yours?"

"They're all on this floor. I prefer my privacy, however, so I don't share a room with any of them."

"Do you have an appointment with the prime minister?" Lucienne asked.

"Tomorrow at ten. Gerald's operatives in the Japanese government made the arrangements."

"Any trouble?"

"Not at all. Ever since UGOT threatened to raise tariffs on Japanese manufactured goods sold in the West, the government and the Diet —Japan's bicameral legislature —have been fairly cooperative."

Lucienne probed. "So what are you going to do tomorrow to make the government even more cooperative?"

Colton felt his irritation rise. Even though Lucienne was the director of UGOT's Ministry of Religion and Spiritual Welfare, he resented her interference. Why had Gerald chosen her to head the ministry instead of him? After all, he was the prophet. "Well, the prime minister and his leading cabinet members are either Shintoists or Buddhists. They adhere to the beliefs and rituals of those religions. But at the same time, they're pragmatic men of the world. My job will be to convince them that there is a power greater than that found in science or their religions."

Lucienne leaned forward, intrigued. "How are you going to do that?"

"You'll see tomorrow if you join us at the meeting."

"Tell me now."

Colton's voice hardened. "No. I've been instructed to tell no one."

"Your master again?" she said cynically.

"Yes."

Lucienne was disgusted. "You know, you're just like Gerald. He sees his bright angel often, but refuses to tell me what he learns. I don't know why it's such a big secret. It's my job to know. Besides, if you don't tell me what your mighty master said, I'll die of curiosity. What harm can it do?"

"I don't know the reasons, but I must obey."

Lucienne downed the last of the treat. "At least tell me what happened in China. I read your report, but it lacked the juicy details."

"There's really not much to tell. My appointment was with the chairman of the Military Commission of the Communist Party, the most powerful man in the country."

"You went to his office at the government building in Beijing?"

"Yes. As soon as I arrived, they brought me to him. He was surrounded by the six members of the standing committee of the Politburo. I had my interpreter with me."

"The chairman is the man with AIDS?"

"In its final stages. I put my hands on his head and told him he would be cured by the power of God within two hours. The entire blessing took thirty seconds. Then I told them I would go for lunch and be back at one in the afternoon. They looked at me like I was insane, but I also saw awe in those beady little eyes. When I returned, the old guy was gorging himself on some strange food, his energy had returned, and his cough had disappeared."

"So he was cured?"

"His doctor thought so. He checked the chairman, and the sores were gone."

"That's incredible. What happened next?" Lucienne knew that Colton had already visited China several times and had gained a reputation as a miracle worker. A miraculous healing like the latest would only confirm his powers in the minds of the Chinese and their leaders.

"I warned them that if they did not put a great army at UGOT's disposal someday, at the time the army was needed, I would curse all twenty members of the Politburo with a disease ten times more virulent and horrible than AIDS."

"Do you think they believed you?"

"Absolutely. You never saw such fear."

"You can actually do that?"

Colton stood taller, and his eyes were full of conviction. "Of course. I can do anything."

Lucienne was uneasy, but struggled not to show it. At that moment she realized that this man was too dangerous to have around without tighter controls. She and Gerald would have to eliminate him as soon as he had served his purpose.

The next day the guard ushered Colton and Lucienne into a temporary office used by Yoritomo Muratari, the prime minister of Japan. He and three cabinet ministers were touring the Nagasaki Prefecture to inspect the serious damage caused to the coast of the southern island of Kyushu by a series of tsunamis. The Japanese officials bowed deeply, and the visitors mimicked the bow. The translator provided by the Japanese government translated their words quickly at the end of each speech. After the preliminaries, the prime minister presented his point of view.

"We appreciate the advisors UGOT has sent us," Yoritomo said. "But we cannot give them more power in our government. We alone are in a position to make wise decisions for our country."

Colton replied, "You do not understand. We can supply you with valuable information you cannot get from your leaders or experts."

"What kind of information?"

"Successful products to manufacture. Where and how to build public works. How to solve the problems of inflation, unemployment, health care for families. Those are a few examples."

Yoritomo laughed. "But we have many sources of information to help us solve such problems. We've been doing it for decades."

"Do you know when earthquakes and tsunamis will hit your major cities? Do you know when your volcanoes will erupt? Do you know when the next famine will strike?"

In spite of their powerful cultural beliefs in the rituals of politeness, the four leaders grinned at each other and almost burst out laughing. Yoritomo said, "No one can predict those things. We have the most knowledgeable geophysicists in the world, and even they cannot do it with certainty."

Knowing the immense value of surprise and a display of authority, Colton declared, "Mount Unzen will erupt today at sixteen minutes past noon. It will be the worst eruption in the history of that volcano, and many people will die. It is unlikely that you have enough time to evacuate the city of Shimabara."

Yoritomo smiled sardonically. "That is only two hours from now. Besides, if Unzen were acting up, Kyushu University at Shimabara and the Committee for Prediction of Volcanic Eruptions in Tokyo would have informed me. I am sorry, but it is impossible."

"Fly to Shimabara then and see for yourself. Since it's close to Nagasaki, you've plenty of time. Stand at the foot of the volcano if you dare."

Yoritomo's face registered sudden anger. "I do not have time for this foolishness. We will listen to your advisors when it suits us, but we will not give them more authority in the Japanese government. Good day, sir."

"You won't even warn the people of Shimabara?"

"No."

"In that case, their blood will be on your head."

Colton took Lucienne by the arm, and they exited the office without another word. She said little on the way back to the hotel, but the moment she entered Colton's room, she turned on the television, made herself comfortable on a couch, and waited expectantly.

After Colton and Lucienne had left his office, Yoritomo promised the ministers that he would find any excuse possible to expel every UGOT representative from Japan as soon as possible. Then they returned to their maps of Kyushu to examine the flood zone, completely forgetting Colton's strange prediction.

At sixteen minutes past noon Mount Unzen erupted, throwing one cubic mile of material into the atmosphere. This was four times as much rock and dirt as had been ejected from Mount St. Helens in 1980. The deadly pyroclastic flow buried Shimabara and killed more than fifteen thousand people. The volcanic ash in the atmosphere spread a distance of 450 miles within hours.

Yoritomo and his friends were not injured in the blast, but they heard it from twenty miles away. After watching the news reports on the eruption for a half hour, he telephoned Colton's hotel and asked to speak to the visitor from Europe in room 613.

As soon as he had finished talking to the prime minister, Colton turned to Lucienne and said, "I think he'll listen to us from now on."

"Colton, that was the most astounding thing I have ever witnessed in my life."

"Wonderful, wasn't it? Well, what country do we visit next?"

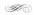

At noon André Renan left his perch overlooking the Rhine valley below and made his way down the rugged trail toward the camp where Mireille and the children were hidden. Once again, he had nothing exciting to report.

Three weeks earlier, they had driven the minivan up a tortuous road to an isolated spot in the Vosges Mountains in northeastern France, a few miles west of Colmar. After hiding the van, they had hiked a half mile farther into the forest and had built a makeshift shelter of branches, covering the floor with grass and leaves.

By one o'clock André reached the floor of the mountain valley and followed a deer trail to the shelter. Mireille and the four children were playing a game near the hideout when he arrived. The two younger children, a girl and a boy, belonged to their friends Pierre and Diane Laborde.

Mireille was always relieved to see her husband return. "See anything?" she asked.

"A few military trucks off to the west, but nothing coming our way."

"Did you eat your food?" André had left before breakfast to watch for signs of the enemy, and Mireille had insisted he take a small meal with him.

"Of course. It was delicious. Thank you. How are the kids?"

"Restless. They say they're sick of camping. It's understandable after three weeks." Mireille handed him a cup of water and a sandwich. "I made this for lunch."

"You're an angel. Thank you."

After watching André eat for a while, Mireille said, "How much longer do you think we'll have to hide in these mountains?"

"I don't know. A few more days perhaps, and then we'll head for Strasbourg."

"But there's no guarantee it will be any different with the people there!" They had sought refuge several times with Mormon friends in eastern France, but when they had arrived at the arranged time, they had discovered that their friends had already fled.

"I know, but we have to try."

"And what if the green coats or the police have imprisoned our friends in Strasbourg too?"

"We'll just have to keep moving."

Mireille sighed. "What do you think happened to Diane and Pierre?"

"Don't worry. I'm sure they're safe." He noticed that the two Laborde children were listening to every word they spoke.

Mireille put her face into her hands and cried. André moved to comfort her as best he could.

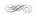

The largest concentration camp in France was a few miles from Arras in the north. On the day that Diane and Pierre Laborde were brought to the camp, there were 3,028 men in one compound, and 7,164 women and children in another. The puppet government of France transported two truckloads of people into the camp every day. The prisoners belonged to any religious or political group that UGOT saw as a threat. Among them were 986 Mormons.

As soon as the new prisoners arrived, they were lined up next to the trucks, issued drab gray uniforms, and cited the camp rules. And the list was long. It was made clear that anyone caught trying to escape, fraternizing with prisoners of the opposite sex or the guards, or breaking any other rule would be executed immediately. The camp commandant, Jules Pigalle, was proud of his sterling record. In the four months that the camp had been in operation, he had found it necessary to execute only four men for trying to escape. He knew that UGOT hoped to redeem these lost souls, and so he gave orders that any guard caught abusing the prisoners in violation of their strict guidelines would also be shot.

Pierre had listened to the prisoner indoctrination lessons every day from ten to noon in a barracks large enough to seat two hundred men. He understood that many other sessions were being held all over the camp at the same time. It was always the same thing. UGOT loved them and only wanted what was best for them and the world. Soon the planet would reap the benefits of having one mighty global government which would use the earth's resources for the benefit of all. No longer would the privileged exploit the masses. The new government would eliminate poverty, hunger, war, and disease. The only thing the people had to do in exchange was to cooperate and obey. Most of all, they must not allow their religious and political "biases" to interfere with future world happiness. Pierre was especially angry when the speakers made subtle references to the great Semitic Plague which was supposed to be the prime mover of all evil and corruption in the world.

While the teachers presented their lessons, Pierre sat there quietly, saying nothing. But his heart was full of fury. It was everything he could do to keep from standing and shouting that UGOT was nothing more than another Satan-inspired tyranny. Although he remained silent during the sessions, he openly attacked UGOT when the prisoners were alone in their barracks at night, using every argument at his command to expose the goals and promises of UGOT as a hoax. He was very careful in choosing his listeners because he knew the enemy had embedded informers throughout the camp. He believed that most of his fellow inmates agreed with him. He didn't realize that soon he would have to pay for his open opposition.

But Pierre's greatest suffering did not come from the lies of UGOT or the harsh conditions of the camp. He was in constant fear concerning the welfare his wife, Diane, imprisoned in the women's compound, and his two small children who were hiding somewhere in France with his friends, Andre and Mireille. Many times he considered taking the grave risk of trying to escape from the concentration camp just to rejoin them.

The prophet sat before his two counselors, nine members of the Quorum of the Twelve, and other church leaders in a small conference room not far from his office. It was seven in the morning. "Brethren, I called this second special meeting to report on the Mexican problem. First, I want to review the information we've gathered. Then I will relate a communication I had with the Lord . . . The party we sent to investigate the reports concerning the danger returned this morning and confirmed that an army is marching north. Our scouts risked their lives to bring us as much information as they could. Even at that, we don't have many details.

"Evidently, the army is called the Mexican Army of Liberation. They are nothing but renegades in government uniforms. This army has been forming for five months in the vicinity of the city of Morelia, west of Mexico City. Our latest report indicates that the main contingent of the army is now approaching the city of Chihuahua, 234 miles south of the U.S. border." The elderly prophet paused. He was obviously exhausted and having difficulty concentrating. "Perhaps you brethren could help me by asking questions."

The junior apostle said, "President, do we know how many soldiers are in this so-called army?"

The prophet turned to Elder Jason Widtsoe. "I'll ask Brother Widtsoe to answer that question. He's been working closely with me on the Mexican problem."

"Our scouts don't know for sure," Jason said. "The army seems to be approaching in several divisions by separate routes. The group the scouts believe to be the main one comprises between twenty to thirty thousand soldiers."

Samuel Law, the prophet's second counselor asked, "Do we know why they're traveling north? How do we even know they intend to attack us?"

Jason answered, "The radio transmissions which our people intercepted did not give us much information on that. As for our scouts, they only succeeded in obtaining indefinite indications that such might be the case."

"How long before we can expect them to reach our area?" Wilford Benson, the senior apostle, asked.

"No one knows for sure. It might be one month, maybe two."

The junior apostle observed, "But we have many church people living near the Mexican border."

"That's true," Jason said.

Another apostle said, "President, I understand that you sent out warnings to church leaders throughout the Rocky Mountains several weeks ago, after our last meeting. I was wondering if you were able to contact most of the stake presidents."

"Most, yes," Josiah said. "We contacted some by radio. To others we sent riders. However, because of difficult communications, it's not possible to update everyone continually. This is especially true now, because someone has been jamming our radio transmissions for the last eight days. We can't even reach Pioneer One."

The presiding bishop said, "Jamming on all frequencies?"

The prophet waved toward Jason. "Yes. Whoever is doing this has some sophisticated jamming devices."

The bishop said, "So in effect, it could take weeks for us to contact the entire church in the Rocky Mountains."

"We might be able to do it in one week," Jason answered. "But there's also the problem of how old our reports are when we get them, especially since we no longer have radio contact."

The prophet stood up and stretched. The joints of his back and knees cracked. "Sorry, brethren, I guess I'm getting old . . . But now I need to reveal what the Lord told me last night." The leaders sat forward in their chairs. "He said that a multitude of wicked men from the south lust after the blood of the saints, and that his people must take action to protect their lives. He commanded me to send word today to warn the saints."

There was a stunned silence. Finally, Bennion Hicks, the prophet's first counselor, said, "So the threat against us is certain, not simply a possibility. What do we tell the saints to do, President? Did the Lord provide details? Should we form an army and move south to intercept the enemy?"

"The Lord didn't say. I prayed all night, but he gave me no further directions. But I intend to continue praying in the hope that he will bless us with that information. At this point, we'll simply tell the saints what he has revealed. It should be sufficient." The prophet paused to collect his thoughts. "All right, brethren, let us turn to the problem of Pioneer Two. At our meeting on April 27, we decided to postpone the second wagon train because of the outlaws on I-80 and the threat of an attack from the south. Even though the mountain bandits seem to have withdrawn to the area of Bear Lake, there are other problems. At this time we cannot afford to send over a thousand people into the wilderness. First, we do not have the supplies. Second, we should keep our able-bodied men in Utah to meet the present crisis. As a result, I propose to cancel the second wagon train indefinitely. Do any of you disagree?"

The brethren accepted the prophet's recommendation without question. Most had already come to the same conclusion since their last meeting.

Samuel Law asked, "What about Pioneer One, President? Won't they be left completely without support?"

"Of course not. The Lord will provide for them."

Carlos Gutierrez, head of military operations for the LDS Maracay colony, and a number of other Venezuelan church leaders, had watched the troops of the National Guard arrive all morning. It was a frightening scene. Their fellow countrymen surrounding the settlement, preparing to use military might to destroy them because of their beliefs. But the saints knew the real culprits were the men sent by UGOT, the arrogant politicians and the green coats, to infiltrate and control the government and the military.

At noon another Mormon lookout arrived from his post in the hills behind the gathering troops of the National Guard. After speaking briefly to Carlos, he returned immediately to his post through one of the tunnels dug beneath the canal which surrounded the LDS community. Carlos motioned for the other leaders, who were standing nearby, to approach. Some were colony residents, but others were visiting from different parts of the country.

"The lookout brought me a report from Ángel Chávez, leader of the Mormon Militia, who estimates that government troops number about ten thousand now. One of our church members in the National Guard sent him a secret note saying that the Guard plans to begin shelling us at one o'clock, an hour from now." The Mormon Militia, which now comprised four thousand soldiers, was concealed in the hills behind the National Guard.

A stake president, Brother Gómez, said, "It looks like they now have from twelve to fourteen pieces of artillery." Gómez, who lived in the colony, had been watching the Guard through binoculars.

A bishop, Jaime Martínez, said, "What are you going to do, Carlos?" Jaime was one of the church leaders who visited the settlement from time to time. Like many Mormons in Venezuela, he helped support the colony, but did not live in this part of the country.

"Nothing . . . for the moment. We must be sure they strike first."

"Why haven't you given us more information about what the Guard is doing? How can we help if we don't know what is happening?" Jaime complained.

Carlos replied, "I'm sorry we haven't given you every detail. Even the church leaders here do not know exactly what my plans are. There have been many leaks—"

"Leaks?" exclaimed Pedro Cierva, another visiting bishop.

"Yes, perhaps from this settlement itself. There may be traitors among us. We couldn't take chances on the enemy learning how the compound is built or what our plans might be."

The leaders looked at each other with alarm. The very idea of traitors among the saints was inconceivable.

"Can you tell us now how you plan to defend the settlement?" Ricardo Lerma inquired. Ricardo was a bishop in one of the colony's wards.

"I will only tell you that we have a surprise for the government troops."

The stake president, Brother Gómez, said, "I know what's in your mind. You propose to shell them or drop bombs on them. But why wait? Let's do it now before they attack. By waiting you risk our lives."

Carlos frowned. "We can't do that, President Gómez. We've been on the radio with the General Authorities—"

"You succeeded in contacting Salt Lake City?" Bishop Martínez asked.

"Yes. In spite of the jamming, we finally made contact with Elder Jason Widtsoe. Just for a few minutes. We told him about our situation, and he made it clear that the prophet did not want us to attack first."

"The prophet is right," Bishop Cierva said ironically. "We must not take the offensive, even if they slaughter us before we can move to defend ourselves."

Carlos caught the negative tone of the bishop's words. "Apparently, bishop, you've forgotten why we built all those bunkers and why we placed most of our homes underground." Normally a kind, patient man, his voice was now severe. "I suggest we get everyone into the shelters as soon as possible."

An hour later the barrage began. It shook the reinforced concrete bunker where Carlos had secured his wife and grandchildren twenty feet underground. Even though the assault filled their eyes with dust and forced them to insert plugs into their ears, it caused no serious injuries. After fifteen minutes, the bombardment suddenly stopped.

Carlos heard distant explosions and what seemed to be the rat-a-tat of machine guns. He surmised that the Mormon Militia and their friends must be attacking the National Guard from the hills on the north. He knew also that hundreds of soldiers from the settlement were attacking the enemy from the south after crawling out of the compound through the hidden tunnels. This coordinated effort had been carefully planned by Carlos himself weeks earlier. He desperately wanted to leave the bunker and join the fray, but he felt that a man of seventy-five would be of little use in such fierce fighting. After five hours the noise of the battle ceased, and there was a strange silence. Carlos grieved, knowing that many brave young men had perished that day.

"How did it go?" Carlos asked his young general after leaving the bunker at six thirty.

The general smiled proudly. "I believe we accomplished the goals you gave us. Stop them from firing on the settlement, and box them in. We could have wiped them out, but resisted doing so, as you directed."

"I'm grateful you know how to follow orders. We have many brothers in that government army."

"Yes, of course."

"How many men did you lose?" Carlos asked.

"So far the reports say eight."

Carlos was amazed that the number of casualties had been so low. "I grieve to hear of those deaths, but at least we can be grateful it wasn't more." He looked at the chaos around him. "Of course, their artillery destroyed nearly every structure we built above ground."

"It's a price we had to pay," the general observed. "So what do we do now?"

"We move to the second part of our plan, as soon as it gets dark."

By ten at night all was quiet. An hour earlier, the Mormon Militia had withdrawn several miles into the hills so they would not be seen as an immediate threat by the government camp. In the distance Carlos heard the whine of gears growing steadily louder, as a heavy truck made its way up the winding roads, and then started downward into the federal camp. Standing close to the fence which enclosed the LDS settlement, he listened intently, fearing that at any moment he would hear the sound of guns. But he heard only the muffled shouts of soldiers, and the low growl of the motor as the truck continued to the center of the enemy camp. So far, so good, he thought. Now, if only the natural inclinations of the enemy soldiers would help him accomplish the next part of his plan.

A half hour later, unusual things began to happen in the distant enemy camp. Lights flashed in a dozen places, and one could hear the uproarious laughter of men and women and the joyous sounds of music and dancing. Carlos smiled to himself. Everything was going as he expected. The revelry continued until the early morning hours, when at last the enemy camp became still. Carlos ordered his men to open the main gate and lower the long ramp. Then he walked slowly to the National Guard camp. Four hundred armed men followed him, ready to fight at a moment's notice. As he approached the camp, Carlos saw soldiers lying everywhere, helter-skelter. It was clear they were sleeping off a heavy drunk. A guardsman suddenly rolled out of an APC and hurried toward him, his face transformed by a broad grin.

"Well, it worked, Brother Gutierrez. Just as you expected."

"So these boys couldn't resist the strong brew we shipped in last night?" Carlos said.

"Nope. They sucked it up until they dropped. Ten barrels of it, I think."

"What about their officers and the green coats? Did they hold back at all?"

"A few held back a little at first, but we convinced them it would be bad luck not to have at least one drink, and the stuff was strong enough to help them get over their worry."

Carlos was pleased over the success of his stratagem to overcome the government soldiers by getting them too drunk to resist. It had no doubt saved hundreds of lives. He hoped, however, that none of the drugged guardsmen turned out to be Mormons.

At that moment they were joined by other LDS guardsmen, soldiers of the Mormon Militia, and two dozen sisters in wild party dresses.

Carlos laughed. "You sisters sure don't dress like that in church. And what about the Word of Wisdom?"

The first soldier performed a fake drunken stagger, then smiled as he said, "I can assure you, brother, we only drank from the barrel marked with a red stripe, the one full of all that sweet Kool-Aid."

"Yuck. I despise the nasty stuff," a relief society president said, her mouth ringed by a bright red stain.

Carlos replied, "Come here, all of you. I want to smell your breath—no. I'm just kidding. And what about the morals problem?"

A primary president scowled. "Hah. Some of these boys got pretty frisky at times. But we handled it fine. A lot more whiskey and a purse with a rock inside."

"Beautiful!" Carlos exclaimed. "I wish I had thought of that myself. Did you disarm all of them?"

"Certainly," the Relief Society president said. "With the help of these wonderful Mormon soldiers. We're very wise to the ways of the world, you know."

"That's what I'm afraid of," Carlos teased.

The assassin's bullet almost killed David Omert as he was walking through a square in Jerusalem. An inch or two to the left and it would have exploded his head. Fortunately, a woman passed by, just before the gunman pulled the trigger, and spoiled his aim. The bullet struck the tip of David's left ear, and the attacker quickly disappeared in the milling crowd.

Menachem Hazony visited his nephew in the hospital room. "Do the police have any clues as to who the shooter was?" Menachem was the current Minister of Defense of the State of Israel. By his brilliant planning and bold operations, he had saved the country from destruction in the last war with the Arabs.

David held the towel against his ear to stop the flow of blood. "No, no one saw anything."

Chaim Yehoshua was sitting on his friend's hospital bed. "They suspect it was an Arab nationalist or a Jewish extremist."

"Yeah," David said scowling. "That really narrows it down."

A doctor entered the hospital room, removed the towel carefully, and examined David's ear. "It's not serious. You still have most of your ear left. He turned to the nurse standing nearby. "You can dress the wound now." The doctor hurried from the room, and the nurse began to clean and dress the wound.

Menachem said, "He could have belonged to a dozen different factions, all of them violent. There are too many groups in Israel today who think that violence is the only solution to their problems."

Chaim said, "The worst are the Palestinians. We all know how they raise the average Palestinian kid these days. They teach both boys and girls to attack physically anyone they see as their enemy. They praise them when they win a fight and ridicule them when they lose."

"Yes," David replied. "He's taught to hate and destroy his enemies from the time he's a baby. And his main enemies are the Jews."

Menachem added, "Yes, the hatred of the Palestinians and Arabs seems to know no bounds. I'm ashamed to admit that I've never known any Palestinian personally. I do my best to stay away from them. Since I've been Minister of Defense, they've threatened my life a hundred times and have opposed everything I've tried to do." He looked at David. "Well, have you decided how you're going to handle Israel's problems when you become prime minister in a few days?"

"I'm not certain the Likud party will capture the majority of seats in this election."

"I believe it's a done deal."

Chaim said, "I agree. It's certain that Likud will win and that it will choose you as prime minister. Then you can reinstate Menachem as minister of defense, name me as chief advisor, make permanent friends of the Arabs, solve the Palestinian problem, and create a united Israel for the first time in history."

"Chaim, you should be a stand-up comedian. As if it were that easy. The truth is, I don't have any cures—instant or otherwise. The leaders of Likud only informed me three weeks ago that they wanted me to consider taking the position."

"True, but you've been analyzing the problems for years. At any rate, I'm sure the extremists realize, by this time, that they made a mistake in assassinating Abraham Samet."

"Yes, indeed," Menachem said. "David's a much better choice for the Likud than Abraham Samet. Of course, Nephew, your greatest problem will be how to reconcile the Israelis with the Palestinians and the Arabs, and still maintain the freedom and security of the State of Israel. Knowing that you will be prime minister, I'm reassured that Israel will not surrender the Golan Heights to Syria simply because they make offers of peace. If you did, Syria would control our sources of water to the Sea of Galilee and the Jordan River."

David said, "I'm well aware of your feelings concerning the Golan Heights, Uncle. I assure you that I agree with you completely."

Menachem smiled and continued his questions. "But have you thought about what you'll do to draw Israel together? We have forty political parties who can't agree on anything, seven terrorist groups, regular suicide bombings and assassinations, thousands of teenagers toting guns in broad daylight, religious intolerance, a growing crime rate, open displays of hatred on the streets, and a ring of implacable enemies who seek every opportunity to annihilate us."

"You forgot that UGOT is promoting every kind of propaganda against us," Chaim said, "and the fact that we no longer have the support of the former United States. And what about the cultural differences among the Jews themselves? On the one hand, we have the westernized yuppies who spend their time in fancy restaurants and expensive resorts and don't believe in any God, and whose only concern is how much their investments will bring in. On the other hand, there are the religious Jews, who wear strange clothes and hair styles, and believe the slightest deviance from traditional ways is a direct offense against the God of Israel himself."

"Yes, the problems seem insurmountable." David heaved a sigh.

"It does look that way," Chaim said, "but if you're not voted out in the next election, which is usually the case, and if you're not assassinated—"

At that moment Chaim noticed Menachem glaring at him and his mouth snapped shut.

David laughed at his friend. He knew that Chaim often acted like a comedian, and many leaders did not take him seriously, but there was no one David trusted more to give him honest, insightful suggestions. "Listen, both of you, I've dreamed of ways to solve those problems, but as yet I have no definite answers."

Menachem softened, clearly sensitive to the position his nephew was in. He put his hand on David's shoulder and said, "It's a great burden to place on one so young."

Chaim could not resist one more comment. "No problem. With our help, David will solve every difficulty sooner or later."

Chapter 16

Pioneer One began its final travel schedule. It meant arising at five in the morning, hitting the road by six thirty, halting for lunch and a break from twelve thirty to one thirty, and stopping for the day at half past seven in the evening. Knowing they would travel twelve hours a day from then on, under normal circumstances, Steven hoped to make much better time. He figured that the caravan was at least a week behind schedule. Though there were endless up-and-down grades, the overall climb was fairly gradual. The people who had brought bicycles enjoyed themselves going down grade, but worked up a terrible sweat going up. From checking his maps, Steven saw that the elevation at Creston Junction was only about four hundred feet higher than it was at Rock Springs, eighty-four miles back.

By eight o'clock a cover of clouds filled the sky, blocking the hot sun. From time to time it drizzled, making travel cool and pleasant in comparison with the heat of past weeks. The greatest difficulty was that the caravan had to leave the highway every ten to fifteen miles to bypass sections that were demolished by floods or explosives.

After riding up and down the caravan to check on his people, Steven dismounted, tied the mustang to his wagon, and came forward to walk where he could see Mary. He looked at her often, puckered as much as possible, and threw her kiss after kiss. At first her eyes danced, then rolled, and finally refused to look his way. His three children and the five Cartwright kids alternated between trudging beside him, chattering incessantly, and running around the wagon playing games and screaming so loud that he heard their voices echo from the nearby bluffs. He was delighted that his legs no longer hurt and that he felt stronger and more fit. He guessed that many others in the wagon train had the same feelings.

At about ten thirty Ruther rode up to the wagon. After tying his mule next to the mustang, he caught up with Steven. "Makin' good time?"

"Yes. We just passed Junction 196. That means we traveled more than nine miles in four hours."

"Not bad. Think we'll make twenty-seven miles by day's end?"

"I doubt it. The people really get tired by mid-afternoon. I'd be pleased if we made twenty-two or twenty-three miles."

"Well, the weather's right fer it."

They walked a hundred yards without speaking. Then Ruther said, "Hope I didn't upset you folks arguing about religion and sech last night."

"Heavens no! I loved it. It wasn't an argument, but a friendly conversation."

"I see'd one or two people frownin' and I figured they was annoyed at me fer questionin' things. Maybe they was thinkin' I'm a troublemaker."

"I didn't see that reaction. Besides, who cares anyhow? Personally, I believe that whatever people think about me is none of my business, or at least it shouldn't be. It never fails that when some people hear others taking different positions on a gospel subject, or any subject for that matter, the first thing they say is 'contention is of the devil.' You can be talking in the kindest, calmest way possible, and still they cry 'argument!'"

"I wonder why that is," Ruther replied.

"There are dozens of reasons, no doubt. I suppose it depends on the person. Maybe they're afraid their comfortable world might be upset."

"Maybe so," Ruther mused. After a moment, he went on, "Yuh don't think much of us Baptists, do yuh?"

Steven dodged the Cartwrights' five-year-old boy, who came charging by, pretending to be Geronimo. "What? No, I love the Baptists. They're wonderful people."

"But yuh think we're lost on a trail headin' nowheres."

"Oh no. I just think some Baptists are intolerant of the beliefs of others."

"What does yuh mean?"

"Well, last January, I read Floyd McElveen's book called God's Word, Final, Infallible, and Forever. Floyd's a born-again Baptist."

"Yep, I've read it. He spends a lot of time attackin' you Mormons."

"That's right. At first he claims he loves the Mormons. He only wants to bring them to God. But in most of the book, he misrepresents what we believe—actually he doesn't understand what we believe. And he uses arguments invented by Mormon apostates. At the same time, he ignores all the evidence Mormon writers have given to show the falsehood of the apostate arguments."

"Yep. I admit that Floyd gets purdy ornery sometimes."

"He sure does. And he constantly shifts from one argument to another."

"What does yuh mean?"

"He constantly makes the point that God's word is perfect and true and unchanging."

"Yuh disagree with that?"

"No. Mormons agree on that point. But again and again, Floyd moves subtly from talking about the perfection of God's word, which is easy to accept, to the perfection of the Bible, which is impossible to prove. We agree that God's word is infallible and complete, but that's not the same as saying the Bible is infallible and complete."

Floyd looked perplexed. "Why not?"

"In the first place, Floyd takes a Bible reading and gives his own personal interpretation of what that reading means. As a result, it's his own interpretations which become perfect and infallible, not what the Bible actually says.

"In the second place, we believe the Bible is not the only word of God. We accept as the word of God many scriptures which are not in the Bible."

Ruther replied, "I heard about that. Yuh also have yer Mormon Bible."

"Yes, and other scriptures."

"So yuh think I do the same thing as Floyd?"

"No, you don't condemn like Floyd does. But you do seem to interpret the Bible like Floyd does. Many Baptists do the same."

"What does yuh mean?"

"Well, they maintain that the readings of the Bible are perfect and should be respected. But when they explain a doctrine, they choose the verses which support their claims and ignore those which disagree with their ideas."

"Yuh mean when we cite the passages on faith and ignore the ones on works."

"That's one example out of many. That's why we get so many different perfect interpretations from the Baptists we meet."

"I likes the way yuh think, Steve," Ruther said. "I'm not sayin' I goes along with yuh, but I likes the way yuh think. Do yuh have a copy of that thar Mormon Bible? I've read the reglar Bible ten times over, and it might be a mite relaxin' ta read somethin' a bit different. I'm not sayin' you're pursuadin' me ta become no Mormon, but I'd like ta see what yer Mormon book preaches."

"I'll get you one when we stop for lunch."

By the time they stopped at twelve thirty for lunch and rest, the pioneers had traveled twelve miles beyond Creston Junction. All the leaders expressed their happiness at the progress made. The light rain which had fallen during the morning had become little more than a pleasant mist carried on a gentle breeze. While Mary and Jennifer made lunch, Steven decided to explore the country north of the freeway. With his rifle slung across his back, he followed a gully for a quarter mile until he was out of sight of the wagon train.

A few minutes later, he came to the top of a ridge and saw a small valley two hundred yards ahead. There was a tiny stream flowing through the valley, and on this side of the stream was a stand of trees. He hiked down to the trees and sat on a boulder in the shade. He was impressed by how pleasant the place was and how completely isolated it was from the rest of the world. For a moment he forgot his filthy, sweaty clothes, which had not been washed or changed in a week.

After resting for a while, he rose to return, but was startled by a noise behind him. He whirled around and was shocked to see a man standing twenty feet away, smiling agreeably. He appeared to be about twenty-seven years old and six feet tall. He had light brown hair and piercing blue eyes. His strikingly handsome face showed no blemish and communicated candor and innocence. His body was average in build, but the ease of his movements suggested great physical strength. Steven was surprised at the man's clothes. He wore what looked like blue denim jeans, hiking boots, and a multicolored sport shirt. He had no hat to shade his eyes from the rays of the sun. But the thing that shocked Steven most was that his visitor seemed to have just stepped out of a fashionable spa in clean new clothes for a pleasant stroll in the hills.

"Good afternoon," the stranger said in a friendly voice.

"Good afternoon," Steven replied.

"Out for a walk?"

"Yes, and you?" Steven wanted to ask him why he was so clean.

"Yes, it's a good day for it. Rather isolated here, isn't it?"

"It sure is."

The man raised his hand to shade his eyes from the sun, which suddenly appeared from behind a cloud. "Do you belong to that wagon train on the highway?"

"I'm the leader," Steven said with a touch of pride. He saw the glimmer of a smile return to the stranger's face.

"I see. I should have guessed. You do have the appearance of a man of authority. But it seems strange to see such a large group of people traveling in this dangerous, forbidding land. May I ask where you're going?"

Steven hesitated, not wanting to reveal anything to a stranger. "We're heading east."

The man smiled more openly. "I see that."

Steven couldn't resist any longer. "May I ask you a question?"

"Of course."

"What are you doing out here? Where do you live? Why aren't you carrying a weapon? Why are your clothes so clean?"

The man continued to smile and did not look at his clothes. "That's four questions."

Steven was embarrassed by his overwhelming curiosity. "I'm sorry. It's just—"

"There's a small community about a mile from here." He pointed to the north. "On the other side of that ridge. It's a trading post, so to speak. We used to live in Rawlins, the town twelve miles east of here. However, when that town was occupied by bandits, we left to seek refuge at our cabin."

"Who is 'we'?"

"A few trusted friends and me."

Steven said, "Do you have any supplies to spare?"

"I'm afraid not. Only enough for our needs. So why are you going to Mis— east?" The stranger frowned. The man had slipped, and they both knew it.

Steven wondered how this man could possibly know they were traveling to Missouri. His instincts told him to disclose as little as possible. "We're seeking a land where we can be safe and happy."

"But you're moving away from the only safe place on the entire continent. Utah and the surrounding region are the only areas where you can find food, shelter, and safety."

"How do you know that?"

The maddening smile continued. "We hear radio reports. In my opinion you should turn around as quickly as possible and rejoin your people in Utah. Besides, they will need all the help they can get."

"What do you mean by that?"

"Well, we understand from monitoring the radio that there is a great army traveling from the south toward Utah. A cruel, bloodthirsty army of renegades. Apparently they intend to plunder and kill every human being living in the Mountain West. Your people in that region desperately need you. But if you insist on continuing eastward you will find that after you pass Laramie, this freeway no longer exists. The land all the way across eastern Wyoming and Nebraska has been scorched by armies struggling to destroy each other. There is not a tree or blade of grass left. The lakes and rivers have either dried up or been poisoned. The same is true in Iowa and Missouri. To travel east is certain death for you. Death from famine, drought, pollution, or roving gangs of maniacs who survive only by destroying the innocent. The very next city on your trail, Rawlins, has been completely taken over by bandits. I can't tell you what to do, but I say that if you love your wife, your children, and your people, you will turn around and go back."

Steven was seized by a terrible fear and he struggled hard to control himself. How on earth could this man know all those details concerning the Mexican army and the hundreds of miles of territory to the east?

Steven replied, "Thank you for your advice. I didn't realize how bad things were. The reports we have must be mistaken. I'll present your information and suggestions to the other leaders of the wagon train."

"You really have no choice," the stranger said. "You are the one who is responsible. Their lives are in your hands."

"I'm sure you're right."

"Yes, of course I am," the man said calmly. "Well, I have other things to do now. Good day and good luck." At that, he strolled eastward down the valley near the stream until he disappeared from sight.

Steven's heart was pounding wildly. He had never felt such fear. Somehow he knew that the stranger had sensed his terror and had relished it. Steven wasted no time. He climbed the next ridge, the one on the north. From the crest he searched the wide basin below for some time. He saw nothing but wilderness. No small community. Then he hiked back down the hill toward the wagon train.

Several hundred yards from the pioneer column, he thought he saw a movement on a ridge descending to his right. Could it be the same young man? Was he spying on Pioneer One for some reason? Steven decided to check. Turning right out of the gully, he labored up the slope. He surmounted the ridge and descended into another gully. There was no one in sight. He continued downward until the shallow draw emptied onto the flatter land not far from the highway. A minute later he saw a woman standing in the shade of a low cliff. It was Anastasia. As he drew near, she spun around, and he saw tears streaming from her eyes.

"Anastasia. What are you doing so far from the wagon train? Do you need help?"

She quickly wiped the tears from her eyes and said, "Steve. It's you . . . No, it's nothing."

"What's the matter? Can I help?"

At those words, she stepped forward quickly and threw her arms around him, sobbing. As he felt her face wet against his neck, his eyes darted around to see if anyone was watching.

After a minute of weeping, she couldn't keep her secret. "He doesn't want me!"

"Who doesn't want you?"

"Pierce Hudson."

"Oh." He carefully extracted himself from her embrace.

"He told me he loved another woman."

"Who?"

"Rachel Crell. He wants her because she's younger and more beautiful than me."

Steven remembered that Rachel was the third bachelorette traveling with Anastasia and Andrea Warren. It was difficult for him not to laugh. Anastasia was always so melodramatic. He couldn't imagine any woman in the caravan being more beautiful than her. If Pierce chose Rachel Crell over Anastasia, he certainly had better reasons than those Anastasia imagined.

"Anastasia, that's not possible. You're one of the most beautiful women in our caravan."

"Oh, do you really think so?" She embraced him again, harder this time.

He tried to free himself from her, but she held on stubbornly. "Anastasia, please let me go. Someone might see and get the wrong idea."

In a flash she stood on tiptoe, kissed him squarely on the mouth, and then released him abruptly. "You're so sweet. Too bad you're married."

In spite of the theatrics, Steven sensed that deep down she really was hurt that Pierce had picked someone else. He decided to console her as much as he dared. "There are at least six or seven young men in the wagon train who would give anything to have you love them. All you have to do is show some interest. Besides, if Pierce chose another woman, why should that upset you so much? It's good for you to know now how he really feels. I can't think of anything worse than ending up married to someone who doesn't truly love you." Steven felt stupid. Every consolation he could think of sounded clumsy. Some counselor he was.

"But, Steve, you simply don't understand how a woman feels in a situation like this. I'd rather die than think of another man. No, I'll never find anyone as wonderful as Pierce. But thank you for caring." After crying awhile longer, she dried her tears and said, "What young men?"

Steven rattled off the name of every single man he could think of, including Paul's. After listening to him intently, Anastasia declared with spite, "Well! I might have to marry all of them to end up with one decent man." At those words, she flounced away toward the caravan.

During the six hours of travel in the afternoon the caravan covered a record ten miles, for a total of twenty-two miles that day in spite of the upward grade. They pulled off the highway at seven thirty just past the continental divide and drew the wagons into three separate circles. They were only two miles from Rawlins. During the evening, as he went about his regular routine, Steven couldn't stop thinking about his unusual encounter with the stranger in the hills. Later, during the leaders' meeting, he considered mentioning it, but finally decided against it.

Besides, the leaders could talk about nothing except the dangers their families might be facing in Utah. They became even more anxious when John dropped the bombshell that the batteries he had saved for use in the radio were now depleted.

Steven decided to discuss the stranger with Mary later. He wondered if Rawlins was really inhabited by bandits as the unusual stranger had claimed. To be safe, he asked John to double the guards for the night watches.

That night, when their family was alone, Steven and Mary read to the children by the light of a lamp. Because of the increased hours of travel, the kids were extremely tired and fell asleep fifteen minutes later. After putting out the lamp and snugging up to Mary as usual, Steven related the story of the stranger.

"That's so weird!" Mary exclaimed. "Who do you think he was?"

"I'm not sure. At first I had no reason to doubt what he said. He seemed like a good man—actually a very special man. But after he said all those things I related to you, I got very suspicious. By the time he left, I was scared half to death."

"I know who he was."

Steven laughed. "How could you? You weren't even there."

"No, but from what you tell me he said and did, it's perfectly clear."

"It is?"

"Yes."

"Okay, Miss Smarty-pants, who was he?"

"Satan."

"You're kidding."

"No, I'm serious."

"What makes you think that?"

"A lot of things," Mary said firmly. "He appeared from nowhere, looking clean and fresh as a daisy, and carrying no weapon. He was young, good-looking, and had light brown hair. He knew we were heading to Missouri. He lied about there being a lodge on the other side of the ridge. He contradicted the revelations of the prophet by trying to get you to turn back after his frightful description of the dangers ahead. He appealed to your sympathies for the people in Utah. He inspired terrible fear in your heart. And finally, he strolled off into nowhere as if he were heading for the mall."

"Don't you think your imagination is getting the best of you? Do you think Satan would be dumb enough to make a verbal slip which showed he knew we were going to Missouri?"

"Well, when it gets down to it, do you really think Satan is all that smart? He's made plenty of slips in his career, beginning with rebelling against the all-powerful Father! Besides, how could a regular person, a genuine stranger, know where we were going?"

"Good question," Steven answered. "But why didn't I experience some cosmic evil force oppressing me like Joseph Smith felt in the Sacred Grove when Satan came there?"

"I don't know. Maybe he handles different people in different ways," Mary said simply.

"Okay, but why appear to me? Why would the number one Fallen Deity bother to try to trick me? I'm nobody."

Mary's exasperation made itself felt, even in the dark. "Don't be dumb, Steve. The prophet chose you to lead the first group of saints to Zion. That means you're very important. You know something? You have a bad habit of never giving yourself credit for anything."

Steven felt flattered and frightened at the same time. "Okay . . . but what do his looks and hair have to do with it?"

"That's an easy question to answer. In the first place, Joseph Smith said Satan has sandy-colored hair. Also, we know he's an ageless spirit and used to be the Son of the Morning and the Bearer of Light. Those things suggest to me that he'd look handsome and in the prime of youth."

"But, Mary, don't you think his great wickedness would make him look pretty darn ugly?"

"He's ugly inside, but not outside. That's one of the reasons why he can deceive people and appear as an angel of light. It's related to the idea that Satan often tells people many truths to get them to accept one lie."

"Where do you get that from? Satan appearing as an angel of light?"

"Steven! You've heard that before. Joseph Smith said it, and it's in Second Corinthians."

"But in the Book of Moses, when Satan appeared, Moses said he could distinguish Satan from God because Satan had no glory. That suggests to me that he didn't appear as an angel of light. How do you explain that?"

"As I said before, he appears to people in different ways. Sometimes he conjures up brightness and at other times he doesn't . . . Wait. I've got it. Maybe he can appear to an unrighteous person as an angel of light because he has more power to deceive him. But he can't do it when he faces a righteous man, like Moses, who can see through his deceptions."

"So where does that put me?"

"What do you mean?"

Steven gave a mischievous chuckle. "Well, my visitor, the man you think is Satan, appeared to me looking something between glorious and ordinary. So what does that say about me?"

Mary poked him playfully in the ribs. "You sure can be silly sometimes. I was only making a few personal observations, not reciting orthodox doctrine. Actually, you must be a real threat to Satan and his designs for him to try to influence you that way."

"You'd better believe it." Steven giggled and began to wrestle with Mary until she let out a loud squeal. She quickly controlled herself, afraid she might wake up the children. After they had squirmed around in silence for a while, Steven said, "Whew! That was fun. Now, to get back to something serious. Satan. The truth is—and I hate to admit it—I'm impressed by your idea that the good-looking stranger might have been old Lucifer himself. It never occurred to me."

"You need to pay better attention, young man. As the leader of this wagon train, you should develop the spirit of discernment."

"But why should I? I've got you."

Mary poked him a few more times, and he answered by tickling her until she couldn't stand it any longer. It's hard to giggle in silence. After they rested for a while, Steven said seriously, "You know, the problem of light and glory gets even more confusing when you think about deity appearing to mortals."

"What do you mean?"

"Well, sometimes God appears to people in glory and they must be transfigured by the Holy Ghost to avoid being consumed. That happened to Moses on the mountain. But when the resurrected Lord appeared to the two disciples on the road to Emmaus in the Book of Luke, they didn't recognize him or realize he was a Divine Being. All they said was that they felt a burning in their hearts. There's no evidence that they were transformed. And when God appeared to the murderer Cain and questioned him about Abel, there was no way such a wicked man could have been protected from God's glory by the Spirit."

"So how do you explain it?"

Steven laughed. "I explain it by saying there are a lot of things I don't know how to explain. Maybe God suppresses his glory when there's a good reason.

Or maybe he simply sends a messenger who represents him and therefore uses his name. In any case, it tells me how kind and loving he really is."

"Why do you say that?"

Steven sighed and put his arm around Mary's waist. "I used to ask myself why God didn't simply reveal himself. Then I could ask all the questions I wanted and get it over with."

"But we have to live by faith."

"That's essential, of course, but there's another reason too."

"Which is?" Mary replied sleepily.

"If he appeared when we wanted him to, we'd probably be consumed by the fiery heat of his celestial body. That's why we must first be holy enough to receive the Holy Ghost, who transforms us so we can endure the Lord's presence. On the other hand, God may also use the technique of restraining his glory for the benefit of those of us who are less spiritual."

"It's funny to hear you describe it as a technique. And why do you say 'us'? What makes you think the Lord will ever appear to us in this life?"

"Mary, you know the answer to that."

"I do . . . Yes, of course . . . but I'm so . . . too sleepy to think. Remind me."

"The prophecies say he'll visit the saints at New Jerusalem and Adam-ondi-Ahman. There's a chance we'll be there."

Mary's eyes popped open in the dark. "Oh great. Now I know what I'll dream about all night."

The next day Pioneer One reached Rawlins, Wyoming by noon. At the head of a group of twenty men, Steven rode into town. They found a small community of five hundred survivors, who were very friendly and grateful to see them. The townspeople had a small amount of extra flour, salt, and sugar, and asked the brethren if they wanted to trade. When Steven offered them some of the guns and ammunition recovered from the bandits, many of them wept. They had been attacked several times by roving outlaws and would soon be without the means to protect themselves and their families. They threw their meager supplies into two wagons, and the entire community followed the Mormon party to the wagon train.

As soon as they reached Pioneer One, the townspeople expressed amazement that so many people would dare to travel such a great distance from their homes, especially under extremely perilous circumstances. After unloading the supplies, John and the bachelors put fifteen semiautomatic rifles, several handguns, and two thousand rounds of ammunition into the wagons. Then the citizens and the pioneers fellowshipped one another during the lunch break. Seeing the kindness of these people, Steven realized that the mysterious stranger in the hills had lied when he had claimed that Rawlins was infested with bandits. Maybe Mary was right about him being Satan.

Two hours later, the saints hugged and kissed their new friends and said farewell. They exchanged mementos they really didn't need, and the pioneers gave the citizens copies of the Book of Mormon and a dozen other books. The townspeople accepted all the gifts with tears, especially the books, for their enemies had burned their reading material in a huge bonfire several months before while the people were running for their lives in the wilderness. Two non-Mormon families joined the wagon train in vehicles the Moderns had found for them in the local wrecking yard.

That night the pioneers halted at Exit 221, after covering twenty-two miles under the protection of a cloudy sky. The next two days they trekked another forty miles. On the second day they stopped for the night at Exit 260, not far from Elk Mountain. After such strenuous travel, the pioneers were grateful that the following day was Sunday, for Steven had promised them a full day of rest.

He had heard that sometimes the wind could gust to more than eighty miles an hour on I-80 near Elk Mountain, but for the last two days the breeze—thankfully—had been just gentle enough to cool the travelers down.

Early Sunday morning, one of the sisters awoke to find her fifty-year-old husband lying dead next to her. Dr. Price examined the body, but could discover no specific cause for the death. During the quick burial ceremony, several members gave short talks memorializing the deceased. Many spoke to the widow, trying to comfort her and offering their future assistance. Afterwards the saints held their meetings as usual. Though there was sadness in the camp, they were becoming accustomed to death, and so in the afternoon the adults spent their time reading, singing, and talking, while the children played games. The leaders had some difficulty controlling the children, who wanted to run off into the fascinating countryside to explore. As always, a ring of guards kept watch over the encampment. By late afternoon, Steven began to notice that Mary seemed sullen and avoided looking at him.

When he finally saw her alone, preparing the evening meal, he sat beside her and said, "What's the matter? Are you mad at me?"

"What do you care?" She arose abruptly and stormed away.

He looked after her, having no idea what the problem was. Selena, his ex-wife, had often run away exactly like that when she was upset with him. It was usually something he should have done or said but hadn't. Once, Selena had styled her hair in a new fashion, and he hadn't noticed—after all, hair is hair! But he should have noticed. Another time he had bought her a fancy electric can opener for her birthday when they were very poor. But he shouldn't have—for some reason—because she was very upset. To this day he still didn't know why Selena had been so mad.

And that business about repairs. All Selena had to do was mention—just once in an offhand way—that something needed to be fixed, and before long he was in deep trouble. Usually it was some small thing she wanted done, which he genuinely planned to do someday—just to make her happy of course, not because he thought the silly thing really needed fixing. Why did she ask him in the first place when she knew he was a complete klutz who had difficulty screwing in a light bulb? The result was, well, he simply forgot. Then the typical thing happened: for weeks afterwards he paid a heavy price for his little oversight.

Women could be so emotional and unpredictable. One minute you thought they hated you and regretted marrying such a jerk, and the next minute they were bawling their heads off because you didn't kiss them good night. Steven sincerely doubted there was any man on earth who could truly understand a woman.

Steven was lost in these "profound" thoughts when Andrea and Paul appeared. After they had spent several minutes talking about very little, Paul said, "What's up, Steve? Why so sad?"

"Oh, Mary's mad at me. And I have no idea why."

"I can tell you why," Paul replied quickly.

Steven looked at his brother hopefully. "Why?"

Paul grinned and his eyes flicked to Andrea. "She's a woman. They don't need a reason."

Andrea punched him. "You little baboon. You'd give anything if one of the single women around here would take you seriously." She looked at Steven. "I can tell you the real reason Mary's upset. That's why I'm here. Can I reveal the secret in front of this character?"

"Paul? Certainly. I trust him."

"Well, the grapevine has it that you were seen hugging and kissing Anastasia out in the boonies."

"What!"

"Not that I believe a word of it, mind you. But that's the gossip. It seems that someone started telling the juicy little story around camp a few days ago, and it got to Mary this morning."

"Have you heard this gossip too, Paul?"

"Yeah, I heard a few things, but I laughed it off."

Steven said, "Tell me everything people are saying." The thought popped into his mind that he had told Ruther several days ago that whatever people think of him was none of his business. Oh, well.

Andrea began, "Okay. It seems that someone saw you and Anastasia leave camp together several days ago around noon. You spent some time holding hands and talking intimately, and ended up hugging and kissing passionately. The conclusion is that you've been having an affair with Anastasia."

Steven was outraged. "Not one word is true! How can Mary believe it? Actually, I don't remember ever being alone with Anastasia, except five minutes last Wednesday." Steven told them the story of his encounter with Anastasia a few hundred yards from the caravan after his encounter with the enigmatic stranger.

"Have you told this to Mary?" Andrea asked.

"No. I didn't know there was a problem. But now, I doubt she'd listen to anything I had to say after the way she acted a few minutes ago."

"I'm going to solve this problem right now," Andrea said firmly. "Which way did she go?" Steven indicated the direction. "Stay here. I'll be back in a little while."

Paul said, "I'll help you find her."

"No. Stay here with Steve. This is a job for Wonder Woman. You'll only get in the way." Andrea hurried away, a determined look in her eye.

"Whew!" Paul said. "You don't want to mess with Andrea when she gets like that."

"Yes, she's quite a woman. Too bad some guy hasn't recognized it yet. What do you think she's going to do?"

Paul sat next to Steven. "I have no idea, but I intend to wait here and find out."

They spent the next forty minutes discussing the inscrutable nature of women. After deciding they probably wouldn't uncover any profound truths, they saw Mary and Andrea approaching. Steven was shocked to see that both were smiling.

As soon as she reached Steven, Mary kissed him on the cheek and said, "I'm sorry. I love you."

Steven's eyes went to Andrea. "So what did you do?"

"I made Mary come with me to find Anastasia. It didn't take long. All I had to do was locate the nearest batch of available males, and there she was doing her thing. It's a good thing polyandry isn't legal or doctrinal. I told Anastasia that we needed to talk. She said she was busy. I said that if she didn't come with us, I'd tell every eligible bachelor in the caravan what she said about each of them late at night in our wagon. Without a word she followed us immediately to a spot a little way from camp."

Paul said, "This is great. I can't wait to tell Jarrad and Leonard."

"This you will keep a secret," Andrea said imperiously. Paul's mouth snapped shut. Andrea continued, "I related every bit of the gossip to Anastasia. She denied everything. I gave her the worst evil eye I could muster and asked her if she didn't have something she wanted to get off her conscience. She hemmed and hawed a minute, but finally admitted that she was the one who had hugged and kissed Steven that day, in spite of the fact that he had done everything possible to escape. I told her that if she even so much as batted an eye at him in the future, I'd personally make her life a living you know what during the rest of this trip. After that, Mary and I left her standing there looking like she'd just lost her last bag of makeup."

Mary said sadly, "Steven, I'm sorry I didn't trust you. I should have known you wouldn't cheat on me."

Steven hugged her and said, "It's probably my fault. I know Anastasia is a flirt, and I shouldn't have tried to console her when nobody else was around. Hopefully, I've learned my lesson."

"I guess we have to be extra careful during this trip," Paul said. The gossip seems unusually bad and it spreads like wildfire. Jarrad and Leonard believe there are people traveling with us who are doing their best to discredit all the leaders."

"I agree with you," Andrea said. "I've heard rumors that John is making up the story that a foreign army is threatening Utah. He's supposedly doing it so the pioneers will depend more on the Christopher brothers. Also, I've heard that Paul is a wild, unstable womanizer."

"Womanizer!" Paul exclaimed. "But I don't even have one woman."

"You do now, buddy, more than one," Andrea quipped. "It appears that everyone knows who they are except you. I'm surprised people aren't saying I'm one of your girlfriends."

Paul replied, "Yeah, well, why aren't they? Is that so impossible?"

"Definitely. I don't believe in robbing cradles."

"Okay, you two," Steven said. "That's enough. We have a serious problem here. Paul, have you uncovered any further evidence as to who is circulating the rumors?"

"We're following some very good clues. It's only a matter of time before we find the guilty party or parties."

"Okay, let me know when you get something substantial."

Chapter 17

During the following week the weather remained mild along I-80, and the sun was partially blocked by cloud cover. The temperature never rose above seventy-nine degrees, even during the hottest part of the day. The combination of a fairly decent road, good weather, beautiful scenery, and relatively few problems infused the pioneers with energy and enthusiasm. One could often hear them laughing and singing as they marched along. In the evening they square-danced, performed miniconcerts, and played group games. In six days Pioneer One covered a hundred twenty-one miles, moving between two great mountain ranges of the Medicine Bow National Forest, past the cities of Laramie and Cheyenne, and down onto the western edge of the semiarid high plains of eastern Wyoming.

The pioneers were surprised when they saw no inhabitants whatsoever during the entire week. Along the freeway they spied bears, elks, deer, prong-horns, moose, squirrels, hawks, and other animals, but no people. It was as if the pioneers were the only human beings left on the face of the earth. While they were traveling over the Laramie Plains heading for Laramie, Steven decided to dispatch scouts to investigate every town and city on the highway, before the caravan reached them. His men usually came back with terrible reports.

Every community was a scene of horror. It appeared as though some great army had swept through the region, killing every person and burning every structure. After examining the evidence, Ruther and the leaders of the caravan surmised that the citizens of the area had fought bloody civil wars in order to survive, either between local factions or with government forces.

In the following days, the light rains and the cloud cover disappeared, and the temperature soared. In spite of the fact that the highway was in good condition and was descending rapidly through eastern Wyoming and western Nebraska, the pioneers suffered greatly from the hot winds and the blazing sun. It was everything they could do to place one foot in front of the other as they trudged along slowly, bodies aching and bathed in sweat, clothes heavy with dirt. It was easier for the cyclists. They could frequently move at a fairly good pace, expending little energy, with a soft breeze in their faces.

Steven asked the pioneers if they wanted to shorten the travel time, for a few days, to make things easier, but they smiled and refused. Steven suspected that some didn't want to be seen as weak, but he knew that many wanted to please God and were searching within themselves to discover what they were made of. Steven had to admire them. Like their leader, the pioneers still had many weaknesses, but they were growing in strength, courage, and faith.

Because of this doggedness, Pioneer One averaged more than nineteen miles a day for two weeks, excluding Sundays. They covered a total of two hundred and twenty-nine miles. As they passed some communities, including Kimball, Sidney, Ogallala, and North Platte, the travelers found friendly remnants of people doing their best to survive the difficult times. They lived in primitive conditions, without public services, television, medical facilities, or modern industries.

In spite of that, they gave the saints as much food as they could spare, helped them repair wagons, and added to their stock. They also contributed several worn-out vehicles for the travelers to convert into "covered wagons." The pioneers paid for some of those things, but they had to accept most as gifts of kindness. At times the local residents allowed them to work for what they received. In contrast to the situation in Utah and Wyoming, the pioneers found an abundance of safe water, for now their route paralleled the north bank of the Platte River.

After resting Sunday, they started off the next day at the usual time. By ten o'clock a mass of dark clouds formed in the northwestern sky and the atmosphere became more turbulent. By the time they stopped to rest and eat lunch, after covering eleven miles, the storm hit them. Thunder rumbled in the distance, and lightning cracked all around, illuminating the black sky with jagged streaks of light. As the pioneers ran for cover, the children screamed and clung to their parents.

The most violent part of the thunderstorm was over in forty-five minutes. All that remained was a moderate breeze and a continual downpour of drenching rain. At one thirty the caravan started again. Steven, Ruther, and the bachelors walked a hundred yards ahead of the lead wagon, searching for barriers or breaks in the highway. After traveling another half mile, Steven could scarcely see his scouts. They were on both sides of the road, about three hundred yards out, watching for possible enemies. As they passed various landmarks, Steven tried to keep track of where they were on his map in spite of the wind and rain. He was pleased to see that they were still making reasonably good time. They would travel twenty miles by the end of the day.

Then all at once Paul stopped short and said, "Look! The highway!"

Steven looked up from the map and checked the road. Two hundred yards ahead he saw that the highway ended abruptly. He stared into the distance as far as he could see, almost a mile, and saw no trace of the road. "What happened, Ruther?" Steven asked with despair.

"Don't rightly know. But it appears ta me that a flood or somethin' just swept this entire road south. Probably inta the Platte River. It ain't more than a half mile from here."

They walked to the end of the highway and looked down. Not only the surface, but the entire roadbed, had disappeared to a depth of seven feet. They saw nothing but a gigantic pit of mud which resembled the surrounding prairie. The wind began to howl and swept the rain in biting sheets against their bodies. A minute later Mary pulled up behind them and stopped.

"What do you suggest, Ruther?" Steven called.

"Well, it's up ta you. We can stay here on the highway and wait the storm out, or we can roll down the side and plod through the mud."

"How much time do you think we'll lose if we wait it out?"

Ruther grabbed his hat as a gust of wind nearly carried it away. Then he peered at Steven from beneath the brim dripping with water. "Cain't rightly tell," he yelled. "This here storm could go on fer another day or it could last a whole lot longer. After that, yuh might want ta wait until the mud dries a bit."

"How long?" Steven replied, more and more frustrated.

"Three or four days longer if the sun's nice and hot. It's hard ta tell."

"But what would you do?"

"Well, let's see now. If I was alone, I'd set here a month before I'd wallow in that muck. But, on the other hand, if I was you, I'd dive right in, considerin' all your responsibilities."

"Thanks, Ruther." Steven turned to his brother and said in a loud voice, "Paul, would you climb down there and see how deep that mud is?"

"No problemo, chief," Paul shouted as he hurried to the side of the highway. Leonard and Jarrad followed him. Without hesitating, all three scrambled down the side of the road and waded into the mire, sinking immediately a foot deep. Tugging his feet out of the mud so he could turn toward Steven, Paul called up the bank, "Not deep at all. I walked on side streets worse than this every day when I was in Atikokan." Paul had served part of his mission in Atikokan, Ontario, Canada, and loved to brag that it took a real man to preach the gospel in the Canadian bush country.

Steven knew he had to make a quick decision. If they waited, it would put them even further behind schedule and increase the danger that they would run short of provisions. But if they went into the mud, they might get bogged down and not be able to move at all. They might even lose wagons or endanger the lives of people and animals. He was still pondering the problem when the bachelors returned.

"I think we should keep going," Paul said. "It'll be slow, but at least we'll make some progress."

Steven wished John and the colonels were there. He glanced at Mary and saw her confident smile. The children were there beside her in the wagon. "All right! We'll do it. I have a feeling the highway begins again in a mile or two."

He waved Mary forward and pointed to the place where Paul had left the road to test the terrain. Mary's eyes opened wide, revealing her surprise and fear, but she followed his directions. While Ruther and the bachelors remained on the side of the road to encourage the other wagons, Steven sloshed into the mud, showing Mary where to go. He was stunned when his legs slid into the sticky guck half way to the knee. After dragging himself along a hundred feet, he turned and watched as the big mules entered the mud.

At first they seemed to have trouble with their footing, but soon plodded after him without too much slipping or sliding. When the great wheels bit into the slush, the wagon sank downward a foot and a half, lurched somewhat, and then began to roll slowly forward. After exchanging smiles, Mary and Steven looked ahead and continued the struggle eastward. Ten minutes later Ruther arrived on his huge mule and helped Steven maintain a straight course.

Steven was wrong. After six hours of fighting their way through the mud, and traversing only two miles, there was still no freeway in sight. The rain was coming down harder than ever, and the vehicles with modern tires had a particularly difficult time of it. In order to keep those "wagons" rolling, the pioneers used any means possible: men on horseback with ropes, extra teams, and any individual who could stay on his feet and push.

At seven thirty the caravan simply halted in its tracks. The exhausted pioneers did their best to feed the animals, fix a makeshift meal, and comfort one another in their wagons. Many were so tired they crawled into bed immediately to sleep away the forbidding night. The clothes and bodies of those who had pushed wagons were covered with a thick layer of partly dried mud. Only their eyes peeked through the muck, looking like ghouls in a horror movie.

Even those who had driven vehicles or ridden on horseback were soaked with splotches of mud.

"Mary, can you light the lamp?" Steven said. "I have to find the pail. The animals need grain and fresh water. William, please milk Stockings." The boy groaned, but did as he was asked.

It took Steven an hour to feed and water the animals. When he climbed back into the wagon, Mary had completed the job of straining the milk William had brought in. The cow had given two gallons at the evening milking. They took very good care of their thousand-pound Holstein, and she still gave them three to four gallons of warm milk a day in spite of the constant walking. Douglas Cartwright appeared with sandwiches and took a gallon and a half of the milk, enough for the eight people in his family, Ruther, the bachelors, and another large family. Mary kept a half gallon, which was plenty for their family.

"William says Stockings is fine," Mary noted.

"Must be," Steven replied. "She ate half a bucket of oats and sucked up two pails of water."

"Do you think the mud and rain will injure her?" Mary said.

"Heck no. That cow is like the Rock of Gibraltar. She acts as if she loves this weather."

"And Jimbow?" Jimbow was the name Jennifer had chosen for Steven's mustang when they'd first acquired him.

"He's fine."

"And the mules?"

"Tired and filthy but still perfectly fit."

Mary always went through this routine of questioning at night whenever there was a touch of cold, wind, or rain. "Won't they get sick standing all night in that mud?"

"Stop worrying. They'll be fine."

Steven spent the next half hour trying to answer a dozen questions concerning the storm and the dangers they might be in.

Andrew was the most concerned. "Dad, how do we know that we didn't walk right into that Platte River in the dark without knowing it?"

"Because the deep water and powerful current would have swept us away a long time ago."

"That doesn't prove we're safe," William observed. "We could still drown. This rain might make the river overflow its banks and flood this whole area. It could hit us any minute. We might be sitting ducks."

"That's highly unlikely," Steven replied. He didn't like the sudden fear William's words aroused in his mind.

"How do you know for sure, Steven?" Mary said.

"Mary! You too? You'll frighten the kids."

Jennifer said, "We're already scared to death, Dad."

"Okay. I'll get out of the wagon and explore the whole area to see what's going on."

"You will not," Mary cried.

"All right, we'll say a prayer and ask Father in Heaven to protect us."

"To protect the whole wagon train," Andrew corrected.

"Of course."

Steven offered a sincere prayer, and soon his mind was filled with peace and confidence. From the looks on their faces, he could tell his family felt better. "We'll be okay. Now let's get some sleep."

By Tuesday morning the rain had ceased, but the mud was as thick and wet as ever. And to make things worse, the highway was still nowhere in sight. They sloshed through the muck all day and succeeded in covering no more than four miles. Steven had just taken the reins from Mary and had resigned himself to spending a second night parked in the mud when he heard a shout. He looked ahead and saw Ruther a quarter of a mile away on his mule. The old man waved him forward and pointed southeast. Steven became excited. Ruther must have found the highway. They covered the distance as fast as they could, and soon they saw the highway about a half mile ahead. Never had they seen such a welcome sight!

After finally reaching the freeway, the column moved slowly up onto the road and soon stopped for the night, strung out more than a half mile. Even though they were exhausted and covered with mud, they danced, sang, and expressed their happiness. Then they joined together in small groups and gave thanks to God for his kindness. Steven was more convinced than ever that the Lord was guiding and protecting them.

During the early hours of the morning on Wednesday the sixth baby of the expedition was born, but died two hours later. Instead of burying the infant in the mud, they decided to wait until they could find a dry hill somewhere up the trail. The next day they found a beautiful spot on a bluff topped by a single lone tree. Steven himself performed the burial ceremony, while the young couple gazed sadly at the grave of their first child.

The Mexican Liberation Army of 101,000 soldiers reached the outskirts of El Paso, Texas at eleven fifteen in the morning on June 15. Their leader was the mighty warrior Fidel García. Although some El Pasoans had warned the city that a fierce, relentless invader was approaching, most of the citizens scoffed at such foolishness. They had mocked even more when 2,000 "radicals" had left the city on May 24, loaded with survival equipment, and had fled into the Potrillo Mountains forty miles to the northwest of El Paso.

But on that fateful morning when 216,000 citizens finally realized that a great army was upon them, they ran for their lives. The enemy quickly tracked them down and slaughtered them without mercy. After plundering the city, the invaders moved northward, butchering everyone they found in their path.

To the west, a greater army of 355,000 renegades would soon attack Tucson, Arizona. The ultimate goal of both invading forces was to ravage the great Mormon Kingdom to the north.

Stake President George Chester stood at the speaker's stand waiting for the 2,168 saints in the auditorium to quiet down. He prayed that this meeting, which he had announced just yesterday, would give stake leaders ideas on how they might deal with the threat of a Mexican invasion force. President Chester had also invited representatives from four other stakes to attend this meeting in Kanab.

Church leaders in this southern Utah community had not heard from the General Authorities for two weeks and were frantic. And since the towns in this part of the state were isolated, and without modern communications, George could only guess that other Mormon communities faced the same problems as his. He hoped that similar meetings were taking place all over southern Utah.

In this meeting George especially desired to discuss the prophet's recent communication with members of the stake. The message declared that a great wicked army from the south desired to destroy the saints, and that they must act to protect themselves. The situation was especially frightening since the community had just received unconfirmed reports that a second foreign army was attacking southern Arizona with unbelievable ferocity. In normal circumstances the priesthood leaders in Salt Lake City or the local leaders would make the decisions, but this was a very unusual and perilous emergency, and President Chester needed input from those who lives might be at stake.

According to the reports they had received, the only resistance which the invaders had met came from a few isolated tribes of Navaho and Hopi Indians, who had boldly fired on the renegades from hiding places in the remote wilderness. In one attack, five thousand Indians had succeeded in destroying a small Mexican detachment. The Indians had captured some heavy weapons, including thirty-one infantry mortars and two wagonloads of mortar shells.

The president raised his right hand to hush the noisy audience. After reviewing the information he had for them, he asked the members to raise their hands if they desired to ask questions or make comments. The recreation hall was hot and stifling. Since there was no electric power, the air-conditioning did not work. Yet the matter at hand was so urgent that no one seemed to notice the heat.

Some of the people in the meeting suggested they set up a fact-finding committee to ascertain if there really was a threat. Others said they should wait to get directions from the prophet in Salt Lake as to what they should do. Some of the people felt that the members should escape to the wilderness with their families to avoid being wiped out by the invaders. A few individuals indicated that they should follow their local leaders after those leaders had taken the matter to God in prayer. And still others believed they should immediately organize an army to defend themselves before it was too late. Since no one knew what to do for sure, there was a great deal of debate and even a bit of contention. The stake president showed great patience with the outbursts of some members because he knew that nearly everyone was very frightened.

After they discussed the issues for an hour, President Chester concluded the meeting. Later that day he and the heads of several other stakes met in prayer. After this short meeting they all agreed that they should increase the size of their forces to be ready in the event of an attack. They felt this decision was in harmony with the prophet's previous direction that they act now to protect themselves. Within seven days nine stakes assembled a total of seven thousand troops. George Chester had heard rumors that stakes throughout southern Utah were doing the same thing, but he couldn't confirm them.

In the eight days following the death of the baby, Pioneer One traveled a hundred and forty-two miles, averaging slightly more than twenty miles a day. Steven knew that the country should be more populated now, but the saints met only a few forlorn stragglers, who were delighted to see them and anxious to trade.

Since there was very little firewood available in their trek across Nebraska, the pioneers often had to do without a campfire in the evening. At every halt they searched the surrounding lands for small branches or dried dung chips left by passing animals. Once in a while they got lucky but usually they found scarcely enough to cook their evening meal. Before, they had found an abundance of edible wild plants, but now the plants were becoming rarer as they continued east.

On Thursday morning, June 22, they had covered almost three miles when Steven stopped his wagon abruptly and pushed the brake forward. Not far ahead, at Exit 366, a large group of armed men blocked the eastbound lanes of the freeway. There were about a hundred of them. At least those they could see.

"Who are they, Steve?" Mary said.

"That's what I'd like to know."

"What do you think they want?"

"I don't know that either."

As Steven climbed from his wagon, ten pioneers, including Ruther, Douglas, Jarrad, and Paul, arrived. Ruther began to study the sinister band through his binoculars.

"What do you think, Ruther?" Steven asked.

"Seen this type before. Motorcycle gangs. Leather jackets, jeans, Harleys. Pretty wild bunch. Spend most of their time carousin' and gettin' in as much trouble as possible. I'd guess they been havin' a big powwow of all the gangs in these here parts. Probably in Blue River Park southeast of here. Probably tryin' ta figure out how ta get oil and gas fer all those big bikes."

"What bikes?" Jarrad asked.

"The ones yuh don't see 'cause they cain't ride 'em."

Steven was fascinated. "How do you know so much, Ruther?"

"Heck, I ain't always lived in the mountains. Fact is, I was borned in a little town 'bout fifteen miles north of this spot. But I couldn't stand all these flat prairies, so I left for the Rockies when I was nineteen."

"I'm certainly glad you did. But what do you think they want?"

"Anything they can get."

"What do you suggest we do?"

"Don't give 'em nothin'. Stand up to 'em boldly and tell 'em yuh don't kowtow to no riffraff of the likes of them. Tell 'em yuh got five hundred sharpshooters ta back yuh up."

Steven was flabbergasted. "But won't that infuriate them and provoke them to violence?"

"Hah! I love the genteel way yuh say things, Steve. Heck no. Them boys is cowards deep down, and they'll be afraid of yuh, sure as shootin'."

Paul said, "Look. One is heading this way."

"Their leader, I'd say. Go out ta meet him, Steve, and remember what I done said. He ain't nothin' but a coward. We'll stay back here a ways ta keep yuh covered. I'll make sure he sees me with this here big Sharps. Paul, you head down the caravan real quick like and round us up a bunch of boys with rifles."

Steven walked slowly toward the approaching man. But soon the guy no longer looked like a regular man but some great hairy monster from a child's nightmare. Steven wanted to pull his rifle from his shoulder and hold it ready in front of him but was concerned how the gorilla might respond. By the time Sasquatch was fifty feet away, Steven was positive he was at least seven feet tall and weighed three hundred pounds. He looked like a cross between a giant cave man and a seventeenth century pirate.

Remember that this guy's nothing but a coward, he thought. When he was ten feet away from the creature, Steven stopped, looked up at him, and said firmly, "Good morning. Nice day, isn't it?" He regretted the words the instant they tumbled from his mouth. What a ridiculous way to show the monster he wouldn't put up with any of his guff!

"Hey, little fella, do you want ta live awhile longer?" the giant said matter-of-factly.

"Of course. What kind of question is that?"

"We own this road, and no one uses it and lives. Unless they pay."

"Pay what?"

"Whatever we want. In your case, we'll take twenty young females, forty horses, a ton of food, and all the gas and oil in your camp."

Steven had the insane urge to jump Bigfoot and tear him to pieces, even if he was killed in the process. But he controlled his anger and, remembering Ruther's words, quickly pointed his rifle at the man before he could react. "Look, Charlie Brown, I'm goin' ta give you and your boys ten minutes to hightail it away from these here parts. I've got five hundred sharpshooters back there, and there's a thousand more comin' fast two miles back." Steven figured that a bit of Ruther's bad English couldn't hurt in this dangerous situation and a little trash talk might not hurt either.

"You're bluffin', little man." The thug looked toward the wagon train and saw Ruther pointing his Sharps in their direction.

"Yuh think so? We came clear from Utah over the worst country you can believe. We've met bigger and tougher gangs than yours, and we're still alive and fit as a fiddle. We chased those suckers forty miles across the wilderness and wiped every one out. Haven't yuh heard how violent Mormons can be? We're headin' east and we don't intend to let a few punks like you stop us. Remember what I said: yuh got ten minutes."

With those words, Steven whirled around and started walking back to the wagons without looking back. It took all his nerve not to turn around and it seemed to take forever to cover the distance. Any second he expected to feel a bullet crash through his back and smash him to the pavement. The hair stood up on his neck, and he trembled with fear. Then, at long last, he reached his men and turned to look back. The giant had already returned to his buddies, and they were gazing at the wagon train. Steven supposed they were discussing whether to attack or leave.

Ruther said with a smile, "Seems ta me yuh done a good job because he didn't plug yuh in the back." He had watched the whole thing through his binoculars and had given the others a play by play description of facial expressions and body gestures. "What did yuh say?"

Steven looked at his watch, making the movement as obvious as possible in the hope that the enemy would think he was timing them. "I said exactly what you told me to. Of course, I embellished a little here and there."

Ruther guffawed. "Somehow I knowed yuh would. You're a master at high-falutin and persnickety talk."

"Actually, I used as much of your mountain man jargon as I could think of," Steven said. Ruther guffawed even louder.

Five minutes later the motorcycle gangs packed up abruptly and left the freeway. Ruther sat on the seat of Steven's wagon and watched them for ten minutes. Then he scrambled down and shouted with glee, "They is hightailin' it out of here as fast as their bowed legs can go! I never see'd sech speed."

"Which way is they a goin', pardner?" Paul asked.

"Back ta that recreation area, it appears." He walked up to Steven and gave him a great bear hug. "I'm right proud of yuh, son. Yuh done real good—for a little Mormon boy. I expect we can mosey on down the trail now as happy as a pig in a poke."

At that moment Steven realized fully that Ruther was one of the best gifts that God had given to Pioneer One.

Four days after President Chester had called a special meeting of his stake, Elder Jason Widtsoe knocked on the door of Chester's home at seven in the morning.

"Good morning. Do you know me?"

George was aghast. "You're Elder Widtsoe! Of the Quorum of the Twelve. Please come in." He showed the apostle into his living room and invited him to take a seat.

Jason got right to the point. "Please excuse my abruptness, but we need to conduct our business quickly. The prophet placed me and Elder Keith Bartlett in charge of all Mormon forces. I'm sure you know that our people may be invaded by renegade armies from Mexico. How many men have you gathered to support our defense?"

"About seven thousand."

"Great. Are they ready to fight?"

"Definitely."

"The prophet said you'd be ready. Apparently, many saints in this region consulted with the Lord, and he gave them all the same answer—organize their forces. And it's a good thing too. We've been doing our best to contact the stakes in southern Utah to organize them in time, but we've had great difficulty doing so. And when we finally did, they had already prepared. Just like your stake. If they had waited, we might be at the enemy's mercy. From the figures coming in now, I estimate we have several hundred thousand armed citizens in southern Utah at this time. I expect them to reach their assigned posts in two or three days. Also, we have approximately 200,000 troops gathering in northern Utah, but we're not sure when they can reach this area." Jason smiled with pride. "I call our forces the Mormon Legion . . ."

"I'm grateful we have so many men."

"Not only men. We also have about 40,000 female volunteers, and we're grateful to get them."

"Isn't that dangerous? The invaders are vile men."

"It might be, but we have no choice."

"You mentioned that our southern armies have been assigned posts. Where are they being stationed?"

Elder Widtsoe replied, "At five major roads into Utah, and near a few large cities. One of our big problems is, we don't have good information on precisely where the enemy is . . . Now let me give you your instructions and assignments quickly. Then I ask you to send men to the stakes I will indicate to give them the facts they need."

After the two men discussed the details, Elder Widtsoe cautioned President Chester to tell his legionnaires to bring as much food and supplies as they could comfortably carry. He also explained how his stake would participate in maintaining supply lines for the Mormon Legion.

"When do you want us to leave for our posts?"

"Today, if possible."

Chapter 18

After the guards brought Pierre Laborde into the room without windows, they tied him to one of the ceiling beams by two thick ropes. He stood in the center of the room with his arms pulled above his head, the ropes biting into his wrists. The glaring lights from several incandescent bulbs without shades stabbed his eyes. As soon as they had strung Pierre up, the guards sat on five chairs placed on one side of the room and waited. Two men and a woman, dressed in prison garb, occupied chairs on the other side. Pierre recognized the men as inmates in his barracks. Lousy spies, Pierre thought.

A half hour later, the French commandant of the Arras encampment, Jules Pigalle, and another man entered the room. Jules faced his prisoner, while the second man, who looked like Charles Manson, pulled several items from a briefcase and put them on a table seven feet away. Pierre looked at the instruments and knew what his captors had in mind. He was grateful that Diane and his children were not there to see.

The commandant spoke to Pierre in French. "Monsieur Laborde, my people tell me that you openly attack our lessons on responsible citizenship. In other words, they say that you corrupt other guests in your barracks by your refusal to be reasonable."

Pierre cursed his foolishness. Two weeks earlier he had realized that the enemy must have spies among the prisoners, and that he had been exposing himself and others to danger by openly opposing the indoctrination of UGOT. At that moment, he had changed his methods and had pretended he was being converted. But now he feared that he had acted too late. "No, I agree with the lessons your instructors give."

"That's not what I understand. Listen, I'm a busy man. I have no time to waste on you. You'll renounce your religion now or you'll be tortured." He nodded toward the man who had accompanied him. "My friend here is a master at getting people to do what he wants. He knows how to tear, dig, and cut just enough to make you scream and still keep you alive for days or even weeks."

"Please believe me. I'm not your enemy."

Jules slapped him viciously. "All right then, prove what you say. Renounce Jesus Christ and your Mormon church before these witnesses, or I'll let my friend start his work."

"I renounce Jesus Christ and the Mormon church before these witnesses."

"You will say that Jesus Christ was a fake and that your church is a false religion."

Again Pierre repeated his words exactly.

Jules turned to his friend and said, "How do we know this man is sincere?"

The torturer held up a long sharp knife. "Let me cut him up a little to verify his sincerity."

The commandant laughed. "What do you expect him to say? That he was lying to us?"

One of the prisoners sitting against the wall said fearfully, "Sir, may I speak?"

"Yes. What is it?"

"This man tells the truth. I saw him change . . ."

"Go on!"

"Well, he did show signs that he was beginning to accept our political and spiritual lessons. And I know these Mormons. They're complete fanatics. They would never renounce their beliefs, even if tortured. Because of that, I believe this man is sincere."

Jules looked at the second prisoner. "Do you verify this?"

"Yes, sir, he did change."

The commandant turned to Pierre. "So you've had a change of heart?"

"Yes, sir."

Jules scowled. "Remember your wife. She's in my power. If I find you're lying, my surgeon here will slice her into thirty pieces—and you also."

Pierre fought to control his overwhelming panic. "I understand."

"Good. You're a lucky man. I accept what you and these men say—at least for now. When you return to your barracks, I expect you to encourage the other residents to support UGOT. If you do this diligently, you'll save yourself and your wife." He motioned to one of the guards. "Cut him down and take him back to his barracks."

An hour later Pierre's prison buddy, Claude Morel, sat next to Pierre. "What happened? I was afraid—

"Not much." He related the entire story.

Claude was shocked. "You denied your religion? I never dreamed you'd do such a thing."

"What purpose would it serve if I had refused to do it? They would have tortured me to death. And who would benefit from my testimony and my courage? The animals in that room? They are so full of evil that they would have concluded I was nothing but a raving fanatic. It would not have converted any of them. Besides, it's easy for a person to think he'll be strong—no matter what—until he's faced with torture and death."

"What about the other prisoners in the room—the spies? They'll tell the whole camp what you did. It'll make all the Mormons here look like hypocrites."

"I don't know for sure they were spies. They actually spoke up for me. Maybe the commandant was using them as witnesses so they could tell the other prisoners what would happen to them if they ever tried to rebel. Listen. Don't worry. I know what I'm doing."

"Meaning?"

"I can't say."

There was a minute of silence as the two men stared into each other's eyes.

"Pierre, I'm not condemning you," Claude said at last. "I probably would have done the same thing. You don't owe honesty to tyrants who use brute force."

"I prefer you don't repeat what I've told you. Maybe the witnesses won't tell the other prisoners what I did."

"Okay. Mum's the word. But won't the guards spread the story?"

"It's a possibility. We can't do anything about that. But if they do, the prisoners may decide, hopefully, that the guards are lying."

Martin Gannt, UGOT's Director of Media Relations, was in a bind. Gerald Galloway had ordered him to do more to discredit established religions in the world media. The Supreme Leader wanted something big and he wanted it now. Martin cursed Gerald for forgetting so soon Martin's key role in the brilliant success of the MOM march in Switzerland.

That evening Martin ran into his friend Jules Pigalle at a party in Paris. After drinking half the night, the media man poured out his heart. Jules offered a reasonable solution.

"Get some people to renounce their religion on TV," Jules suggested. "Telecast it to the world. You'll touch a half billion people that way."

Martin laughed. "And you think people would believe that kind of stuff? It's pretty obvious that such disavowals are a fake. Everybody will simply wonder how much the government tortured them to get them to recant."

"Not everybody. It depends on how you handle it. I'm sure you can convince hundreds of millions of viewers that the repudiations are genuine. Especially if you make it a regular feature. When the viewers see all those people denying their beliefs, one after the other, they'll buy it eventually. Repeat anything bold enough and long enough on international TV, and the people will believe it eventually."

"You don't think much of the intelligence of the general public, do you?" It felt strange to Martin to have his friend repeat to him the same things he had taught others many times.

"No, the masses are, for the most part, stupid robots . . . You should at least try the abjuration technique. At our concentration camp near Arras we've used the normal lessons of indoctrination to control troublesome people for about a half year. But last month we received instructions from UGOT's Ministry of Dissident Control to experiment with as many techniques as we can to persuade dissenters to conform to the goals of the government. They want us to become more creative and effective. So recently we've tried using repudiations, both real and faked, to undermine the religious and political ideals of our residents. It's too early to ascertain the final results, but it seems to be working."

Martin said, "I don't know. Maybe it would work on international TV."

"It couldn't hurt to try. Even if it's only a partial success, at least the Twelve would get the impression you're trying hard to satisfy them."

"Yes, but it might backfire, in which case I might as well jump off the Eiffel Tower."

Jules finished his whiskey and began searching for a cigarette. "At any rate, you'll have to do something soon. Our masters aren't very patient. You know, I do what UGOT tells me but I'm still not clear as to its final goals. What's Gerald Galloway's purpose in controlling and discrediting established religions? Is he simply against religion in general or is it part of his general plan to make UGOT the only world government?"

Martin offered Jules a cigarette. Jules took one, which Martin lit with his Bic.

Martin said, "In the final analysis, I suppose Galloway wants to promote UGOT. But no one knows for sure what Galloway really thinks. He's a man of mystery. I've heard he despises all traditional religions. On the other hand, there are rumors that he wants to establish his own world religion. That's why he has those crazy prophets of his running all over the world, visiting both the great and the small."

Jules laughed sarcastically. "Yes, I've heard of them. Especially one—a mystic named Colton Aldridge. What a freak." Suddenly, Jules grabbed Martin's forearm. "Listen, I may have the perfect man for you to start your TV series with. He's a Mormon, I think. A few days ago we had him in our little torture room, but before my specialist got started, he disavowed everything he's believed all his life. I've had secret informants watching him carefully, before and since, and he appears to be sincere."

"Hah! Why take a chance? I could use one of our own people. Someone who's a good actor."

Jules went on with enthusiasm. "Why use an actor when you can have the real thing? At this time my man still has the public reputation of being a dedicated Mormon and an opponent of UGOT. His face has been on TV a number of times. His recantation would really mean something. Also, the guy oozes candor and sincerity. He'd be very convincing on a special TV segment."

"What's his name?" Martin asked.

"Pierre something. I don't know for sure. But I do remember what my spies say."

"Spies?"

Jules nodded. "Yes, they live in his barracks."

Martin was now more interested. "What do they say?"

"He's always praying for his wife and children. He's always preaching Mormonism—or at least he used to. The wife lives in my camp too. His family is another reason why we can depend on his cooperation."

"Well, my friend, let me think about it a day or two. You're returning to Arras tomorrow?"

"Today. The clock on that wall says five in the morning. I must leave by eight. If the booze doesn't knock me out cold before then." They both laughed.

Martin said, "Can you send this man to me here, if I decide to use him? Very quickly, I mean."

"From the time you give me the word, you'll have him within six hours. I'll transport him myself."

Pioneer One made good progress on Thursday. By the end of the day Steven was overjoyed. In spite of the delay caused by the motorcycle gang and a few gaps in the highway, the pioneers had covered a record twenty-five and a half miles. He gave credit to the gradual descent of the road, the cloud cover, and the pleasant breeze, which made traveling easier. Mary teased him about being all smiles because of his triumph over the hoodlums. After supper Pierce Hudson and Rachel Crell appeared and asked him to marry them. They wanted him to perform the ceremony as soon as they reached Independence, Missouri.

Since they were only five miles from the great city of Lincoln, Steven was concerned about what the pioneers would find there. After supper he told Mary he wanted to ask God what they should expect. He walked to a secluded spot several hundred yards from the encampment. When he returned, he called a special meeting of the wagon train leaders. He also invited Ruther.

"Brethren, we need to change our route. I want to remain on I-80 and head northeast, instead of traveling southeast on Nebraska Highway 2, as we planned."

Seth Crowell, one of the colonels, cried, "But that's out of the way! We'll lose time."

"What's the reason, Steve?" John Christopher asked. "That route has to be forty miles farther."

"And we'll have to go through Omaha," Seth growled. "That could be very dangerous."

Paul spoke up, "Calm down. I'm sure Steve has a good reason."

"I'm sure," Seth replied. "I've heard he has good reasons for a lot of things."

John looked at Seth coldly. "What do you mean by that?"

Seth hesitated, wondering whether he dared to speak his mind. Then after a full half minute, he said, "I mean he probably wants to lead us to another place instead of Missouri."

"That's ridiculous," Paul said. "You shouldn't listen to idle gossip, Seth."

Seeing John's growing anger, Steven said quickly, "I prayed about what we should do, and the Lord told me to take the new route."

Kent Booth, another colonel, seemed upset also. "But why? It doesn't make sense."

"The Lord said we'd be in great danger if we followed Highway 2."

"I see no reason to argue," said Jim Burnham, a third colonel. "Steve's our leader, and if he says the Lord directed him to take another route, that's good enough for me." Jim was a small, compact man of forty who always supported Steven without question.

Seth Crowell said, "Well, look now. I think we should discuss this for a while. Maybe vote on it."

"Listen, boys," Ruther said, "I ain't got no say in this group, but it seems ta me that yuh'd better follow your leader. Don't yuh believe God called him ta lead yuh?"

The fourth colonel, Jasper Potter, nodded but said nothing.

Jim nodded. "Ruther's right. Besides, we don't make decisions by voting, unless Steven requests it."

"All right," Seth said. "I have no choice except to go along. Still, I don't see why the Lord couldn't tell us what the danger might be."

After discussing the new route for an hour, the meeting broke up, and the men returned to their families. That night Steven told Mary about the answer the Lord had given, and about how the leaders received it. After she probed him for every possible detail, he explained that he had heard the same voice as before and knew it was from God. Even though the Lord had not given him details, he was determined to obey anyhow.

The next day they arose at the usual time, watered their animals once again in the creek which flowed near the highway, and allowed them to graze on its banks. Steven had not noticed the evening before, but today he saw that the stream had very little water in it. By six thirty-five they were on their way. As they traveled, the surrounding countryside became gradually drier. When they had trekked an hour, Paul hurried up to Steven, who was walking in front of his wagon.

"I have something important to tell you," Paul said, dismounting from his horse.

"What?"

"I've heard talk that there's a mutiny in the works." Paul led his horse by the reins as he walked beside Steven.

Steven had expected something like this and wasn't worried. "What do you mean?"

"It seems that a lot of people refuse to continue on I-80. They plan to follow Nebraska Highway 2, according to the original plan."

"I was afraid of that," Steven said sadly. "How many people?"

"I'm not sure. Most of the pioneers, I think."

"Where did you get this information?"

"Seth Crowell. He said the colonels consulted with their people and learned that most of them reject your idea of staying on I-80."

"When did this happen?" Steven said.

"Last night and this morning."

Maintaining his stride, Steven said with conviction, "Paul, I want you to go to Seth and tell him that if the pioneers take Highway 2, they will endanger their property and the lives of their families."

"You know this for a fact?"

"Yes."

"Okay. I'll make sure they get the message." Paul jumped on his horse and sped back down the line of wagons.

Steven glanced up at Mary sitting on the wagon seat. She had overheard most of his conversation with Paul and looked worried. At about nine o'clock they approached the suburbs of Lincoln. The scene which gradually unfolded before him was beyond anything he could have imagined. Desolation was everywhere. He stared in disbelief, trudging along slowly as if in a nightmare. Some great conflagration had consumed every structure and every living thing. Instead of moving closer to investigate, he continued on, dread oppressing his heart.

Steven was still walking when they reached Exit 397. He guided the wagon train northeast and continued on I-77, which would soon become I-80 again. He couldn't bring himself to look back, afraid of what he might see. Then he heard a shout from behind. He walked slower until Douglas Cartwright pulled up next to him.

Douglas leaned out from his wagon and said, "Some of the wagons aren't following us." Elizabeth, who was sitting next to her husband, was peeking back around the right side of their wagon.

Steven called, "I know, I know. Follow me." He picked up his pace until he reached the front of his own wagon. After fifteen minutes he turned and saw a line of wagons following him on I-77. Gratitude filled his heart to see that many saints were not abandoning him. After another mile they had almost passed Capitol Beach Lake. He couldn't bear it any longer. He motioned to Mary to keep going, walked to the right side of the road, and looked back through his binoculars. He had expected that most of the company, except his friends and family, would forsake him. But he received a pleasant surprise when he saw that about one-third of the caravan was proceeding with them up I-77. At the same time it was heart-wrenching to witness so many others going the other way, heading for Highway 2.

A quarter mile later, Steven decided to call a halt. Since Oak Creek was not far away, he felt it was a good place to water and graze the animals. He waited for the others to pull up. Within fifteen minutes a noisy swarm of people surrounded him. Mary and Steven's children were at the front of the crowd. Near them he saw familiar faces: Paul and John and Tania; Douglas and Elizabeth Cartwright; the two bachelors, Leonard and Jarrad; Ruther, holding his Sharps rifle; Pierce Hudson and Rachel Crell; the "rebellious" captain, Frank Hamilton; Elmer Gleason and Luke Small, the vagabonds from Chicago;

Wesley Duke, supporting his injured ankle on crutches; Wesley's friend Judd Hawk; Byron Mills, the scriptorian; Jasper Potter and Jim Burnham, two of his colonels. The families of these people stood with them.

Big Jim Burnham raised his hand high, and the horde grew quiet. "Steve, I assume you know about the others."

"Yes, Jim, thanks."

"Well, we want you to know that we are with you."

The crowd cheered. Mary beamed, her eyes full of tears. Steven was deeply moved and couldn't speak. Soon the throng quieted down and waited for him to respond.

"Is there anything we can do?" Jim went on.

Steven said, "No, we can't force them to do anything. They have their agency, you know. Do you know who's leading them?"

"Yes. Seth Crowell and Quentin Price," Jim replied.

Steven was taken back. "Dr. Price?"

"Yes," John said loudly. "It seems he's the ringleader."

"Why do you say that?" Steven asked.

"From what Paul told me last night."

Paul jumped in to explain. "Well, in the last few days Jarrad, Leonard, and I learned from solid sources that Dr. Price is the one who started and spread the gossip attacking us as leaders. He tried to circulate lying rumors to every person he treated."

"But why would he do it?" Mary asked.

"Beats me," Paul replied. No one else offered an answer either.

"I suppose we'll have to ask him," Steven said.

"But when?" Douglas Cartwright asked. "It could be weeks before we see him and the others again."

Steven smiled. "No, it won't be long before we see them."

Jarrad Babcock, the bachelor, seemed confused. "But how? I thought we were heading northeast."

Steven explained, "We'll rest here a few hours. I want our animals to get all the water and forage they can take, because those things will be more scarce later. Then we'll turn and follow the others."

Everyone looked stunned. Finally, Jim Burnham said, "Do you mind sharing the reasons with us, Steve?"

Steven answered, "Last night in our meeting I didn't tell you everything the Lord said. He commanded me not to. But now I can tell you more. He also told me that there would be a mutiny, that most of the company would take the wrong route, and that they would go through a great trial. He explained that the purpose of this tribulation was to try his saints and chasten them so that they might learn obedience by the things which they suffer. They must learn to become a Zion people."

John hesitated. "I'm not sure I understand why you want to follow them if it's the wrong route, and they're facing a disaster?"

"I don't know, John. The Lord told me to do it, but didn't say why. But we must obey his will."

They waited until two in the afternoon and headed out again. When they reached the junction of I-77 and I-80, they turned southeast and headed for Highway 2. By the time they halted for the evening, they had covered a total of fifteen and a half miles for the day and were still in the southern suburbs of Lincoln. Since they were anxious to leave this scene of devastation, they found it difficult to camp so close to the city. All day they had searched the road ahead, but did not catch sight of the brothers and sisters who had left them behind.

Two days after talking to Jules Pigalle in the Parisian nightclub, Martin Gannt telephoned Jules and asked him to bring the man who had abjured his beliefs to Paris. Using the authority of his office as UGOT's Director of Media Relations, he convinced Planète and four other major networks to preempt all programming in order to televise the religious recantation of a man named Pierre Laborde during prime time on Sunday evening. The segment, which would last fifteen minutes, including renunciation and commentary, would be carried to more than a half billion people. And if things went well, it would be repeated a dozen times within a week.

Chapter 19

Steven started the company as usual early in the morning. But now they found the going much more difficult. The rolling hills surrounding them seemed more and more like a desert, and the vegetation which covered the loamy soil was sparse. They were alarmed to see that Beal Slough had only a trickle of water running in it. They stopped for the night at the usual time on the highway just north of the town of Unadilla. Fortunately, there was still some water in the Little Nemaha River, which ran close to the town, and its banks offered nourishment to their livestock.

Alone, Steven rode east for some distance to locate the group which had preceded them. Before long he saw wagons miles ahead near a turn in the highway. With a heavy heart he returned to his people. That night the pioneers who had followed Steven gathered and kneeled as one, offering a prayer for themselves and their fellow saints ahead. Many could not contain their tears, for a feeling of gloom and despair weighed heavy upon them. After supper the usual friends and family gathered around Steven's campfire to discuss the events of the day.

"Tomorrow is Sunday, Steve. What are we going to do?" Paul asked.

"We'll keep traveling. As I told you, the other wagons are about ten miles in front of us. I'm sure they'll continue on, and I don't want them to get too far ahead. Besides, we must get out of this region as quickly as possible. Do you agree, Ruther?"

With a twig protruding from the corner of his mouth, Ruther replied, "Well, I'm not sure why yuh want ta stay so close ta those who rebel against yuh, but I agree with that part about gettin' out of this country."

"Why are you so concerned with keeping up with them?" Douglas asked.

Steven coughed from the campfire smoke which seemed to track him around the circle. "I don't know for sure, to tell you the truth. But I don't feel complete without them, for some reason."

Ruther said, "Can I ask yuh all a question that's been buggin' me?"

"Of course," Steven said.

"Look, I don't want ta get yer dander up or nothin', but I cain't unnerstand why those people out there—the ones who left us—call theirselves saints when they don't act particularly saint-like a lot of the time. You know, spreadin' evil gossip about some nifty fellers like Steve here, complainin' all the time, criticizin' people who don't part their hair the way they does, and then rebellin' like they done. Ta tell yuh the truth, I don't get it. I always thought a saint was a pure, holy person, like Joan of Arc, who could do miracles and things like that there."

Steven replied, "We don't use the word 'saint' precisely that way, Ruther. To us a saint is a member of Christ's church. It refers more to what we hope to be, not necessarily what we are. As for why some of us act the way we do, all I can say is that we need to learn to be more patient and charitable. That's why God put every person on the earth. But I've never heard a Mormon claim to be perfect. If you think back on everything that has happened on this trip, you'll have to admit that most of the people in this company, in spite of their faults, have put up with a lot and done some very courageous things."

Ruther pondered a moment, then said, "Yeah, I have ta give yuh that."

It was very windy the next day, and once again Steven walked beside his wagon. As they traveled along, Steven's company began to overtake stray wagons, whose owners were purposely moving slower than normal. When he overtook them, they sheepishly apologized for their rebellion. They explained that after praying about the problem over and over, the Spirit told them they had made a mistake. Steven accepted their repentance with an open heart and invited them to rejoin his group. At eleven thirty Paul rode up, dismounted, and walked beside Steven, leading his horse behind him. After a few minutes he told Steven that it looked as though nearly half the company had rejoined them.

"Do you want me to take down the names of those who are with us?" Paul asked.

"Why?"

Paul blushed. "Well, to keep track of the people who aren't trustworthy."

"Forget it, Paul. We're not running an Inquisition here."

"Okay, okay. It was just a thought."

Steven hugged his brother. "Thanks for your diligence, but I think we'd better avoid that kind of stuff."

At noon the highway turned abruptly to the northeast. Steven noted from the map that after they continued in this direction about two miles, the highway headed directly east again. He estimated that the other company was only seven or eight miles ahead. It was difficult to read the map because the wind had picked up even more. Next to him rode Paul, Douglas, and Ruther. William drove the family wagon not far behind.

"Look!" Douglas said. "What is that?" He pointed to the northwest.

Steven turned his mustang and looked in that direction. He beheld a great storm moving toward them. But the dark front had a yellowish tinge and seemed to be surprisingly close to the ground. The wind was becoming stronger, and the gusts which whipped them pushed horses and men toward the right side of the highway. "Looks like a storm," he shouted. "Heading this way."

"It's a storm, all right," Ruther shouted, holding on to his wide hat. "A dust storm. We'd better take cover fast."

"How? Where?" Steven yelled.

"Roll yer wagons into the gully on the right side of the road and git down!"

The four riders waved the front wagons toward the ditch, and the caravan began to roll off the road immediately. Although the pioneers did not know exactly what the danger was, they reacted instinctively, dropping as low as possible in the depression and protecting themselves and their children behind or under anything they could find. Most of the animals turned their backs to the wind, while others dropped to the ground. Steven and Paul forced their horses to the ground at the bottom of the gully, and then rushed to Steven's wagon. After they had made sure Mary and the children were safe inside with their heads covered, they climbed the embankment to check the storm. Ruther stayed with Steven's family.

By this time the clouds of dust had filled the entire horizon and loomed thousands of feet above them, darkening the sky. The rotating waves were almost black near the earth, but as the border of the clouds turned upward in gigantic swirling lobes, they grew lighter and more yellowish brown. It looked like a tornado six thousand feet wide and fifty miles long, lying on its side against the earth and rolling toward them. Steven was so fascinated by the unusual sight that he stared at it without seeking cover.

Paul pulled him toward the gully just as the main bank of clouds hit them. The wind drove the fine particles of dust into their noses, ears, eyes, and down their throats. Coughing and choking, they stumbled down the embankment and climbed into the wagon. While Steven and Paul struggled to breathe, Steven's children peered at them fearfully from under their blankets.

The storm lasted about twenty minutes. As soon as it was over, everyone scrambled from the wagon coughing and shaking billows of sand and dust from their clothes. Steven couldn't resist laughing when he saw all those walking shadows of dust, with clear round eyes peeking out. He noticed that Stockings stood there as unconcerned and immovable as ever, mooing softly. But she was utterly filthy! When he saw the thick layer of fine brown powder and debris which covered every object in sight, he estimated that it would take weeks before things were back to normal.

"Well, it appears like we done lucked out," Ruther declared solemnly.

"Lucked out! You must be kidding." Steven replied.

"Nope. We only got the edge of that storm. I'm a fearin' for yer friends up yonder." He nodded eastward. "They got the brunt of it."

"Can dust storms kill people?" Paul asked.

"You betcha. The bad ones kin cause lung damage, loss of eyesight, and all kinds of other problems. And lots of property damage."

"Would that be considered a bad storm?" Steven inquired.

"Durn worst one I ever see'd."

The pioneers spent the next hour shoveling debris from their wagons, caring for the animals, and cleaning themselves and their possessions. They could have spent the rest of the day performing those tasks, but since Steven was anxious to overtake the forward company, they left as soon as possible. Because of what Ruther had said, he dreaded what they might find.

As the wagons traveled east, they had to maneuver constantly around heaping mounds of dust. In many places the storm had filled the gully north of the highway, and in other spots the dust had buried the highway's side rails and spilled partly across the road. Many signs were partially buried or their posts ripped from the ground. Finally, around four o'clock the travelers saw people and wagons. It soon became clear that the dust storm had struck the advance company with such fury that it had blown most of the people, livestock, carts, wagons, and converted vehicles completely off the highway into the fields south of the freeway.

The scene was unreal. There were hundreds of people in the field, spread out for a mile, as far away from the road as a quarter of a mile. Some were struggling to upright vehicles. Others walked up and down looking for family members or possessions, stopping frequently to cough. Many were occupied nursing injured people or animals. A few sat alone, too dazed to know what was going on. None seemed to notice that the other half of Pioneer One had arrived.

Steven stopped his caravan, and hundreds of people poured into the fields to help. Steven approached one of the brothers who had followed Seth Crowell and Quentin Price. With the help of his wife and children, the man was repairing a wagon wheel.

He looked up from his work and said, "Good to see you, Brother Christopher. I had no right to expect it, but somehow I knew you'd come."

Steven held back his tears. How grateful he was for those words. "When did the storm hit you?"

"About four hours ago. Around noon."

"From the look of things, it seems as though it just struck a few minutes ago."

The man put down his hammer and stood. "Well, most of us were knocked out, or buried in mounds of dust, or simply too beat up to do much of anything until a short time ago. Except to make sure our kids were okay."

"It doesn't look like you folks took cover."

"No, we didn't know what to do. No direction or guidance of any kind. I guess most of us thought it was nothing except another rain storm. We all waited for it to come, right in the middle of the highway. A few people took cover in their wagons."

Steven decided to ask the question which was bothering him most. "Any casualties?"

"I heard that at least six men, three women, and four children were killed. Quite a few animals too. Nearly everyone ended up with cuts, bruises, broken bones, or breathing problems. As you can see, there was a lot of damage to wagons . . . One thing for sure, we made a big mistake following Quentin Price."

Steven wondered if this man had the answer. "Do you know why Quentin did it?"

"I have a pretty good idea. Once, while he treated me for a cut, he complained about the leaders of Pioneer One, and said that the prophet should have chosen him to lead instead of you."

"You're sure that's what he said?"

"Absolutely certain."

Steven shook his head sadly, "Thanks, Clint. I didn't know . . . Well, I need to check things out. See you later."

"Steve, before you go. I want to tell you how sorry I am. You were right all along. What we did was wrong, and I suppose we got what we deserved. From now on my family and I are with you no matter what."

"I appreciate that."

A few minutes later Steven learned that Dr. Quentin Price and his wife Rose were two of the people killed by the storm. They left three young children. In spite of Quentin's betrayal, Steven regretted losing him, for he had given valuable medical service to the pioneers. To recover from the disaster, Pioneer One remained in that spot, nine miles west of the Iowa border, for the rest of Sunday and the next two days. Those who were strong and well helped the weak and injured to the best of their ability. They buried a total of thirteen people, repaired vehicles and equipment, and shared one another's burdens in every way they could.

Martin Gannt was worried Sunday evening. Because the renunciation segment had been put together so rapidly, the Program Director of Planète, Louis Lagrange, had not had time to order it videotaped beforehand. It was already six in the evening, and the piece was scheduled to air at seven thirty. Martin and Jules Pigalle were in Lagrange's spacious office discussing that very problem. In near-perfect French, Martin said to Louis, "What if this man tries to be a hero?"

Jules, commandant of the Arras concentration camp, spoke before Louis could respond, "It won't happen. Trust me. I assure you that Pierre Laborde will do what we say. He wants to live." Louis smiled with overweening self-confidence. "Yes, I'm sure we have nothing to fear in telecasting your piece live, Martin. I'll be in the control room myself. I've explained the problem to my technical director, Anatole Léger, a very good man. He and I will be watching the master monitor. If your abdicator makes one undesirable slip, Anatole will simply touch a button and cut instantly to commercial."

"If there's a mistake, Gerald Galloway will make us all pay dearly!" Martin warned.

Jules replied, "There won't be any slipups. I warned Monsieur Laborde that if he gets cute, we'll kill him on the spot and later his wife. Also his children if we can find them."

"So you'll have some of your men in the studio wings?" Martin asked.

"Four guards. I've instructed two of them to execute the prisoner at my command."

Martin felt better. "Sounds like you both have things under control . . . Now then, Louis, tell me what you think of my abjuration text?"

Louis picked up a paper from his desk. "Let me read it again . . . I, Pierre Laborde, have been a member of the Church of Jesus Christ of Latter-day Saints, or the Mormon church, all my life. I was taught in my youth that Jesus Christ is the Son of God, and that only through him and his gospel can a person reach heaven. However, as a mature adult, I have completely reevaluated the beliefs of my youth, and I can now say, in complete freedom of conscience, that everything I have believed for so long is an absolute lie . . . That's very good, Martin. And you had to write it so quickly. I have one question, however."

"Which is?"

"I thought this was supposed to be a casual conversation between my commentators and Monsieur Laborde. Don't you want to avoid the appearance of a rigid speech, given under constraint?"

"I do, I do. But since the piece will last fifteen minutes, your interviewers will have plenty of time—before the recantation—to ask friendly questions about Pierre's life and family. But near the end, I want Pierre to look at your Teleprompter and give this little speech word for word. It can be read slowly in about forty seconds. That way, there will be no mistake as to the message communicated to your viewers. After that, your commentators can follow up with a few more friendly remarks, and the thing will be done. Viewers will believe Pierre is just another guest, and won't have a clue that he's a prisoner."

"That'll work," Jules remarked. "I'm sure of it."

"Okay, it's your show." Louis said.

Fifty minutes later the special piece was only a few minutes from being telecast. Anatole Léger slumped in his seat before the row of television monitors in Control Room One. His shift had already started, but still his head was swimming. He cursed himself for drinking so much Vodka and getting so little sleep. But what a party it had been! He drank more coffee to clear his head. Hopefully, he'd feel better by the time Control Room Two turned direction of the following segments over to him. He tried to focus on his control board, which was directly in front of him. It was made up of a confusing number of lights, buttons, and levers. Sometimes it seemed as if the whole mess became one big blur.

Anatole looked to his left and saw that the audio engineer, Pascal, was back from his break, looking as fresh as ever. Zut! How he hated teetotalers like Pascal. It just wasn't natural. Then Louis Lagrange, the program director, entered the room and sat close by. Anatole drained his cup quickly and poured another, hoping the caffeine would straighten him up. If the director saw his condition, he'd be suspended again and he couldn't afford that. He looked at the line monitor and saw a man and a woman take seats on the stage—the interviewers. It was almost time.

Martin Gannt took a seat in the audience area next to Jules. He watched the television crew finish their preparations for the broadcast. Two men operated the broadcast cameras. A technician was adjusting the boom microphone. A woman stood ready next to the Teleprompter, which would show a line by line view of Pierre's statement. All he had to do was read what was printed on that roll of paper. A technical director with a head microphone in front of his mouth stood to the left on an extension of the stage. There were two dozen other people seated in the audience area. Martin guessed they were either employees of Planète or reporters.

Two interviewers appeared from the wings and sat in armchairs behind a low table which held three glasses and a pitcher of ice water. The entire background was a simulated view of the Ville-Lumière or City of Light at night. A minute later four green coats escorted Pierre Laborde onto the stage from the left. After Pierre took his seat, the guards separated, two in each of the wings. The sight of their semiautomatic pistols in a television studio was shocking to Martin. The technical director hurried forward from the left and placed a lavalier microphone around Pierre's neck. He rushed back to his post and called out a countdown for all to hear.

The first seven minutes of the interview went very well. The interviewers asked Pierre cordial questions about his work and family. He answered in an honest, straightforward manner. Martin was impressed by Pierre's sincerity and soon began to relax and enjoy the piece. He had heard that Gerald Galloway and other members of the Supreme Council were watching this landmark telecast, and he was elated at how pleased they would be. Pleased with him for thinking of the idea and pulling it off. Finally, the crucial moment arrived as Pierre announced that he wanted to make a statement. In spite of his efforts to relax, Martin's throat constricted involuntarily.

Louis Lagrange watched intently as the camera zoomed in to Pierre's face. He knew that if this character dared to show any signs of rebellion, he could cut him off the instant he made a move. A few moments later Pierre looked directly into the nearest camera and began to speak. His voice was strong and clear.

"Now I would like to make a personal statement. I have written it down so I could express exactly how I feel." He paused a few seconds and took a deep breath. Then he read from the Teleprompter. "I, Pierre Laborde, have been a member of the Church of Jesus Christ of Latter-day Saints, or the Mormon church, all my life. I was taught in my youth that Jesus Christ is the Son of God, and that only through him and his gospel can a person reach heaven. However, as a mature adult, I have completely reevaluated the beliefs of my youth, and I can now say, in complete freedom of conscience, that everything I have believed for so long is the absolute truth. I bear my—"

Louis screamed at Anatole Léger. "Cut to commercial!"

"—testimony that Jesus Christ—"

"Cut, you fool!"

Anatole shook his head trying to clear his brain. "Huh? We should—"

"—is the divine Son of God, and that—"

"Cut!" Louis bellowed.

Anatole reached for the cut button, but had trouble finding it. "Okay . . . I'll . . . I'll cut."

"—the Church of Jesus Christ of Latter-day Saints is the—"

"Cut!" Louis hollered, charging toward Anatole's console.

"Can't find it," Anatole muttered as he pushed the wrong button.

"—only true Church on the earth."

At last Anatole found the right button and cut to taped commercials. Through the intercom attached to his collar, Louis shouted, "We're in commercials."

Every person in the studio looked stunned, and for a moment no one said or did anything. But when the technical director heard Louis Lagrange's words on the intercom, he repeated, "We're in commercials."

Jules jumped to his feet and made a sign to the two green coats. They rushed forward instantly, raised their pistols, and shot four rounds into Pierre's body. Pierre fell to the floor like a broken puppet, his head and chest gushing blood. Spellbound, Martin gazed at the terrible scene, feeling that in Pierre's death he also beheld his own destruction. Suddenly, he felt someone tug on his arm.

"It was my drunken technician who allowed this to happen," Louis Lagrange declared frantically. "He didn't cut him off in time." Martin gazed at him numbly, unable to speak. "And that stupid statement you wrote. All the fanatic had to do was change the last word or two."

"We're dead men," Martin finally mumbled.

The next day a female prisoner entered one of the women's barracks in Arras and approached Diane Laborde grimly. After she whispered something in Diane's ear, she turned quickly and left the building. Diane dropped to her cot and looked around at the other prisoners, as if seeking help. Seeing nothing except pity and vacant stares, she put her head into her lap and sobbed bitterly.

Chapter 20

❧

The pioneers trudged along much slower now. The dryness, the heat, the mounds of dust, the mutilated road, the injuries, the supplies ruined by dirt, the scarcity of food and water, the depleted livestock, and the damaged vehicles all combined to make their lives almost unbearable. And yet they scarcely seemed to notice the pain, for every heart rejoiced and gave thanks to God. More than ever before they were one—made one through trial and suffering. Steven was delighted to see their obvious increase in kindness, friendliness, gentleness, patience, and love. He felt the same growth in himself and in his family.

The pioneers covered less than fifteen miles a day in the following days. Many became so weak from a lack of food that they fainted and were laid in their wagons. Shortly after they crossed the Iowa border, they turned south on I-29 and headed for Independence. There was devastation everywhere and no sign of life. When they reached St. Joseph, Missouri, fifty-four miles north of Kansas City, on July 4, they stopped for rest.

Eighty-one days had elapsed since they had left Provo, Utah. Because the saints complained of flu and other sicknesses, Steven decided to stay near St. Joseph for several days to let them regain their strength. No one seemed to be in the mood to celebrate Independence Day. Their leader figured that the gruesome scenes they were witnessing every day might be the real cause of their growing malaise. He asked the other leaders to encourage the pioneers to read prophecies about New Zion to restore their spirits.

Steven was surprised when many saints came to him two days later, pleading to continue the journey. He laughed because of their determination and ordered the company to march. Even the following Sunday, after early morning services, the pioneers insisted on traveling, at least part of the day.

Shortly after noon on that day, they stopped near Exit 6, a few miles northwest of Kansas City, Missouri. They had covered 143 miles from the place of the dust storm. In contrast to the bleakness of the rest of the country, this was a pleasant spot, for they could see Lake Waukomis a half mile to the east and three other lakes a little farther away to the west and southwest.

The Mexican Liberation Army finally crossed the southern border into Utah. Their general, Fidel García, boasted that he would invade Salt Lake City within four weeks and conquer the entire Mormon Kingdom in seven weeks.

The eastern division of Fidel's army, numbering about 100,000 soldiers, entered Utah on Highway 191. This was the division that had plundered El Paso, Texas.

The route of the second army, made up of about 355,000 troops, was more complicated. After attacking Tucson, this division had traveled north and pillaged Phoenix. At that point the division had separated into two contingents. The smaller detachment of 95,000 renegades had traveled north and entered Utah on Highway 89, heading for Kanab. The larger contingent of 260,000 men had traveled northwest on Highway 93, anxious to raid Las Vegas. After pillaging that great city, it had rushed toward St. George on I-15.

In this three-pronged attack, Fidel García hoped to catch his victims by surprise. His troops possessed automatic and semiautomatic rifles, .50 caliber machine guns, infantry mortars, hand grenades, and fifty light howitzers.

The leaders of the Mormon Legion were astounded when they learned the size of the enemy armies. They concluded that someone—possibly apostates or other enemies—had falsified the reports which had been sent north. The defenders were also surprised to hear that the Mexican army possessed seventy armored personnel carriers, sixty ten-ton trucks, and eighty-one jeeps. Later reports revealed that the enemy had been stockpiling war matériel, including gasoline and oil, for nearly a year, and had obtained many supplies from the cities and towns they had pillaged.

The three enemy divisions struck Utah with such savagery and suddenness that the defenders could not contain them. On the day the fighting began, the total force of the Mormon Legion near the southern borders of the state was about 302,000 dedicated men and women. Among these troops there were 20,000 Hispanics who lived in Utah and were decent, law-abiding citizens who completely opposed the actions of the renegades of the Mexican Liberation Army. At least 10,000 of the Utah troops were not LDS, but they too were determined to fight for their homes. The problem was, they were not all in the right place, at least not at the beginning of operations. Another 199,000 volunteers of mixed races and faiths were racing southward from northern Utah as rapidly as possible, but were still hundreds of miles from the battle fronts.

The Mormon fighters were well organized, had excellent leadership, and adequate lines of supply. But they did not possess the military training of the enemy and had only a small number of heavy weapons. Most of all, because of bad communications and inaccurate intelligence reports, they had little knowledge of enemy plans or movements. As a result, they had spread their forces too thin, trying to defend five roads along the southern border and a few of the larger cities.

After three days of fierce fighting, the enemy had reached Cedar City via I-15, Panguitch on Highway 89, and Blanding on Highway 191. In spite of the fact that the invaders had superior numbers and fire power, they lost 17,000 men in this push, while the defenders lost 8,000. In a very short time, the Utahns learned to organize a multitude of small patrols, whose job was to ambush the invaders from the hills, woods, and ditches adjacent to the main highways. This hit-and-run tactic resulted in many enemy casualties, but could do no more than slow their advance.

As the Mexican outlaws proceeded north, they hoped to ravage the entire countryside and kill every person they could find, including women and children. But when they found very few victims, they went insane with rage. The farms and towns which they attacked had already been abandoned. The women and children had escaped to the safety of the mountains, while their husbands and sons had hidden themselves in the woods and fields near the main roads, looking for every opportunity to ambush enemy patrols or individual combatants.

The prophet had personally chosen Elder Jason Widtsoe and Elder Keith Bartlett, another apostle, to lead the Mormon Legion in its defense against the foreign invader. They had military experience, youth, boldness, and a special connection to the Holy Ghost. In the town of Beaver, the two apostles sat at a table in a private home with ten other Utah generals.

"Do we have radio contact with any of our troops yet, brethren?" Jason asked.

Arthur Conway, one of the Utah generals said, "My radioman has been able to get a few reports late at night on certain frequencies from various locations in the southeast corner of the state." Conway commanded twenty thousand troops in the area of Hanksville in south central Utah.

"Well, that's an improvement." Keith exclaimed. Normally the various Utah command posts communicated by fast riders in a type of pony express. But they were always trying to do so by radio whenever possible because it was infinitely faster.

"It sure is," Jason agreed. "I wonder why the renegades seem less capable of jamming us now?"

Bruce Wilkins, the general stationed in Escalante, said, "Maybe it's because they're getting neglectful. Or overconfident."

"You may be right," Jason said. "In any event, what do the transmissions say?"

General Conway double-checked a report in front of him on the table. "All our people in the southeast part of the state have gotten the message that the enemy's eastern army is still pushing north on Highway 191."

"All of them?" Jason asked hopefully.

"Yes, almost 100,000 troops."

"And our men in that region are handling the tactical defense the way we directed?" Keith asked.

"Pretty much," General Conway said. "They're redeploying as fast as possible to head the Mexican army off from the north. Also, I sent my army east under the command of three colonels."

Jason looked thoughtful. "Apparently, some of our express riders got through to them, because they seem to understand that our goal is to stop the enemy before they reach Moab, if possible . . . But what do you mean, general, when you say 'pretty much'?"

"It seems that some of our people insist on attacking from the rear."

Jason saw Keith's consternation. "What do you think, Keith?"

"Well, I guess it's all right if they strike from the rear, as long as they don't get trapped. It's too bad they don't have more firepower than rifles and pistols. They'll sting and taunt the enemy, make his life more difficult, but they won't stop his advance. However, I prefer to position the bulk of our forces to the north of the invaders. That way, we can impede their advance by blocking the highway with large boulders and slabs of concrete, poisoning the water supplies, and burning the forage. Also, we'll have a better chance to prepare ambushes and traps for the enemy to fall into."

"I agree," Jason said. "We seem to be getting better results that way."

Keith jotted something on the notebook in front of him. "Okay, what about our other troops in southern Utah? Have they all received our messages about redeployment?"

"All the transmissions we've tried to send and receive have been jammed," said General Wilkins. "But several pony express riders have brought me reports that our troops in south central Utah are also moving west to intercept the enemy army moving north on Highway 89."

"We've gotten similar reports from our contingents in the southwestern part of the state," said Bert King, the general who had been stationed at Cedar City.

"That's good news, brethren," Jason said. "I've been very worried about this, because of our lack of good communications. If it wasn't for our express riders, I don't know what we'd do."

"They're sure as good as the old pony express," General Wilkins said. "Some of our boys travel seventy-five miles a day."

SATURDAY, APRIL 22–FRIDAY, JULY 7

The decent citizens of Kansas City and vicinity had lived in Wyandotte County Lake Park for fifty-four days, surviving as best they could, while small gangs of thugs tried their best to destroy them by guerilla tactics. Then toward the middle of June the gangs finally got the idea of joining forces. Early in the morning on June 15, more than twelve hundred hoodlums attacked the park in force. The defenders, now numbering nearly five hundred people, including women and children, were ready for them. But after two days of fierce fighting, the defenders saw they were losing. Since they had only about a hundred and fifty people capable of wielding a weapon, the odds against them were simply too great.

In the dark of night on Friday, June 16, the families made their escape during a lull in the fighting, carrying all the supplies they could. With as little noise as possible, they slipped around the north edge of Wyandotte Lake, turned north on I-435, and crossed the Missouri River. Many of the women had to quiet their little ones by holding their hands over their mouths.

Anthony Luce, one of the leaders of the refugees, heard nothing but eery silence from the enemy until they had traveled about five miles. Then, as they turned onto River Road heading east toward the town of Parkville, he heard a burst of angry shouting and gunfire south of the great river when the hoodlums finally realized their victims had fled. Anthony rejoiced because he believed it was too late for the enemy to stop them. He urged his people to hurry because they had another three miles to go before they reached Riss Lake.

Several days earlier, the leaders of the Wyandotte Community had heard that there was another well-established colony in the region of the three lakes, which were named Riss, Weatherby, and Waukomis. One of Anthony's scouts, while searching for supplies, had stumbled onto the other group and had returned with the report that the Riss Community was grateful to know they existed. The new colony already included more than a thousand people. If the Wyandotte people could reach them, their combined fighting force would total five hundred men. Also, Anthony figured that, if necessary, they could muster a supplementary force of women and teenagers.

The fugitives were overjoyed when they saw volunteers from the Riss Community coming to meet them at one thirty in the early morning. Apparently the Riss people had heard the gunfire and had decided to investigate. The two groups joined forces and hurried on together. Behind them from the west they heard the wild shouts of their pursuers. Fortunately, they reached the main settlement near the lake before the gangs overtook them and attacked.

For eighteen days, from June 17 through July 4, the battle continued, with neither side gaining a decisive advantage. Anthony Luce counted forty-seven of their people killed, including a few women and children. There were at least a hundred individuals who had received wounds. As for the enemy, Anthony estimated that they had lost from ninety to a hundred combatants.

The citizens of the new Riss Community spent part of their days burying the dead, including hoodlums whose bodies had been left to rot in the sun by their buddies. Noel Luce, Anthony's nineteen-year-old son, recognized one of the enemy dead as Silas Kitch, the gang leader who had nearly succeeded in murdering his family as they were escaping from Kansas City six weeks earlier.

On Wednesday morning, July 5, Anthony, Noel, and other refugee leaders climbed a low hill and saw a new army motor out of Tiffany Springs Park four miles to the northwest. As Anthony studied them through his binoculars, he was surprised to see that the ragtag army of about five hundred men had a small fleet of jeeps and pickup trucks. He saw no heavy weapons, but he did catch sight of what looked like submachine guns.

Noel reached for his father's binoculars. "Let me see, Dad." After studying the scene a moment, he hollered, "Saved by the cavalry! Now the gangs won't have a chance."

Anthony took the binoculars from his son and passed them to Lee Bates, one of the leaders of the Riss Community. "What do you think, Lee?"

Lee gazed at the newcomers with suspicion. "We'll see."

They continued to watch as the small army continued south on I-435. At the junction of I-435 and Highway 45 the army stopped, and a pickup truck turned east on a smaller road and rolled toward them. The citizen leaders descended the hill and walked toward the road. A mile farther along the road fifty Riss defenders also watched the approaching truck from hidden coverts. A few minutes later the truck stopped forty yards away. A uniformed colonel got out, followed by an aide. The colonel wore a goatee and a long moustache, looking like an officer in the French Foreign Legion. Neither he nor his aide carried a weapon.

The colonel walked up to them casually. "You are the leaders of this community?"

"Yes," Anthony replied.

"We've been watching you and your friends a couple of days now."

"Our friends?"

"Just an expression. I'm referring to that rabble spread out along the Missouri River south of your camp. Why are they attacking you?"

"They're savages who love to kill, that's all," Lee responded.

"I see. Well, we must put an end to it. I'm Colonel Norman O'Neill, commander of the Missouri Patriots Militia." Anthony recognized the organization as a paramilitary army. "We're the only force in western Missouri that holds the anarchists in check. They're nothing but filthy vermin." He continued his rant, enumerating in vulgar terms all the classes of people he despised. "People like them and the government itself, are the cause of the destruction of this great country. Do you want to be free of the slimeballs attacking you?"

Anthony shivered at hearing the litany of derogatory terms. "Certainly."

"Okay. Follow my plan, and we'll wipe them out today. Take all the men and boys you have, or anyone else who can carry a weapon, and go around Riss Lake until you reach a position on the enemy's east flank. In the meantime, we'll move in from the west. Then at noon we'll all hit them at the same time with everything we've got. Don't worry. We have some heavy firepower. I guarantee you that they won't last more than an hour or two."

Anthony's heart skipped a beat. "Uh, all right, let's do it!"

"Yes, it's a great plan," Lee Bates agreed, a bit too quickly.

"Good. I like men of decision." The colonel checked his watch. "You have three hours to deploy your men. This afternoon we'll celebrate the enemy's destruction with some good old Missouri whiskey." He wheeled around, strode confidently to his vehicle, pushed his aide inside, and drove away. Anthony and the others started back to their encampment.

"Wow! What a leader," Noel exclaimed. "That guy isn't afraid of anyone. With his plan, it'll be easy to defeat the anarchists."

"I don't trust him," Lee stated flatly.

"Me neither," Anthony concurred.

"The guy's dangerous," a third leader observed.

Noel eyed them in disbelief. "But his plan—"

"Stupidest thing I ever heard," Lee said.

"Great for him, disastrous for us," Anthony added.

Noel stamped a foot into the dust. "What? You're not going to follow it?"

"Of course not," the third leader said. "It's an obvious trick. He wants us to leave our families defenseless, and then move in to enslave or murder them."

"Kill the kids and capture the women," Lee declared.

"I trust him," Noel insisted.

Anthony put his arm around his son's shoulders. "Noel, that would be as dumb as trusting the thugs who tried to get us to drop our guns in Kansas City. These guys are the same type of creatures."

"But I thought the militias stood for everything decent and American."

"No. Some militias might be okay, but others are no better than renegades. Didn't you hear the vile words he used to show his hate for other races?"

"Yeah, it was disgusting," Noel said.

"Well, what do you think he'll do to those among us who happen to fit into his hate categories?" Noel's eyes dropped and he didn't answer.

Anthony, Noel, Lee, and four other leaders watched the militia all morning from a knoll not far from Riss Lake. Instead of moving to the anarchists' east flank near the Missouri River, one-fourth of the citizens' army moved in that direction, while the rest headed directly for the town of Weatherby, located at the southern tip of Weatherby Lake. From this place, four hundred militiamen could pose a deadly threat to an unprotected community. What the enemy didn't know, however, is that Anthony and Lee had posted hundreds of Riss fighters in front of the four hundred militiamen. At eleven o'clock they witnessed—through binoculars—their "ally" and three other men traipse into the camp of the anarchists.

"The colonel certainly must think we're stupid," Lee remarked. "In broad daylight he surrounds us with his army and then visits the anarchist camp in time for tea."

"Well, they're convinced that we're all on the eastern front patiently waiting for them to start the action," Anthony said.

"I can't believe I was stupid enough to believe that fake colonel," Noel said angrily.

"Don't sweat it," Lee said. "We all make mistakes."

Noel shot a high karate kick at an imaginary foe. "I'd like to get my feet on that guy. What do you think they're doing down there?"

"No doubt explaining their real plan to the terrorists," Anthony said.

"Yes, and deciding on how to divide the spoils," Lee added.

At noon the action began. The northern contingent of the militia attacked with naive confidence in their power to make short work of any defenders who might still be guarding the refugee camp. But as soon as they came within range of the defenders' rifles, they suffered a devastating shock when twenty-three militiamen perished in the first volley.

On the southern front a thousand anarchists and a hundred and twenty-six militiamen swept eastward in a huge wave, screaming like wild animals. They seemed to be mimicking an Apache war party attacking a hated enemy. It wasn't until they had pushed the "enemy" all the way to the freeway, three miles away, that they realized there was no enemy.

By early afternoon the thugs and militarists finally understood that Colonel Norman O'Neill's subterfuge had failed. So, more furious than before, they attacked the family encampment once again. Since the militia had joined forces with the anarchists, their army numbered about fifteen hundred men. However, even though they had superior forces and had surrounded the exiles, they could not gain a victory.

The battle raged on for days. Around noon on July 7, there was a break in the fighting. The community leaders gathered quickly for a council and had to accept the fact that their defeat was only hours away. Two leaders suggested they try to negotiate with the enemy, but most insisted that it would be better to fight to the last man. For the first time since they had begun their struggle with the outlaws, the leaders felt complete despair. Then near one o'clock they heard a sudden burst of rapid gunfire. It sounded as if another great engagement had begun south of the colony. Figuring that the lull was over, Anthony and Lee sent Noel up a tree to check things out.

"Indians!" Noel shouted down excitedly, pointing to the southeast.

"What did he say?" Lee asked.

"I think he said Indians," Anthony replied.

They waited as Noel climbed down. He hung from the lowest branch a moment, and then dropped to the ground.

"What did you say?" Lee inquired.

"I said Indians."

Lee was shocked. "Indians! I can't believe it. How many are there?"

"About five or six hundred."

"Are you sure? I didn't know there were that many left in the entire country."

"What are they doing?" Anthony asked anxiously.

"Attacking our enemies."

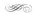

The Indian attack was so violent and such a shock to the anarchists and militarists that their army of fifteen hundred men in the south fled to the west and did not stop until they had reached I-435, four miles from their original position. Before long, the militarists in the north also gave up their offensive and joined their comrades to revise their strategy. Late in the afternoon, the leaders of the Riss Community, which now included the Wyandotte Colony, saw a small group of Indians walking up the trail toward their headquarters. Even though most of them were clothed in the traditional dress of their ancestors, there were a few cowboy shirts and jeans among them. The community heads hurried to meet their new allies.

"Welcome!" said Austin Meyer, one of the leaders.

The tribal chief stepped forward, his right hand raised. "Hey. Thank you. My name is Vernon Freeman. I am the commander of the Northern Cherokee Nation. Looks as if we arrived in the nick of time."

Anthony was surprised to hear the chief use colloquial American English without an accent. "Yes, you did. We're grateful to you."

"Why would you risk yourselves for us?" Lee Bates asked.

Vernon chuckled. "It's no risk really. People like these outlaws have been persecuting our people for years, even before the government fell. Just two months ago a band of these same anarchists killed sixty-two of our people in a night raid near Clinton, Missouri. We've been tracking them ever since."

The colony leaders invited the chiefs to eat with them, and they all gathered in a secure grove not far away. Although supplies were short, the settlers shared what they had. During the meal, the men discussed strategy. Not far away, Noel leaned against a tree, listening intently. Lee posed an important question to the chief. "So you don't think the bad guys will give it up?"

"Never. They can't afford to. Rape, murder, and pillage is the way they survive. It's all they have."

"Then we have a serious dilemma," Anthony said. "Since more of them arrive every day, their chances of cutting off our access to supplies and exterminating us are increasing."

Austin Meyer's lips were tight with anger. "The only solution I see is to attack them in force and destroy them all while we have the chance."

"A very dangerous proposition," Lee said.

The chief put down his plate, rubbed his belly, and sighed with great satisfaction. The other tribal leaders grinned at their leader's antics. None had eaten a decent meal in weeks. "You won't have to do that," Vernon said.

"Why?" Austin said.

"Well, we have five thousand warriors heading this way. They'll take care of those creeps in short order."

"Five thousand warriors!" Anthony cried.

Vernon began to pick his teeth with a pointed twig. "Yep. Maybe more. All Cherokee braves."

"Are you sure?" Austin said.

Vernon looked insulted. "Hey, man, you bet I'm sure."

"When will they arrive?" Lee asked.

"In about one week. They have to come from northeastern Oklahoma. All we need to do is hold out until then."

Chapter 21

❧

By Saturday, July 8, the three divisions of the Mexican Liberation Army had pushed nearly two hundred miles into Utah and continued their advance. The division following Highway 191 reached Price by eleven in the morning and immediately pillaged the city. The force on Highway 89, after sweeping through Sanpete County, reached Highway 6 and then proceeded down the canyon toward Spanish Fork. As for the largest army on I-15, it reached the area of Santaquin by noon.

The defenders had fought valiantly, but had only succeeded in delaying the progress of the enemy. Many times they had mounted attacks, but the superior numbers and firepower of the invaders had always prevailed. The relief army of the Mormon Legion, which had been recruited from the cities of northern Utah, and now comprising almost 200,000 fighters, hurried down I-15, but were just leaving Salt Lake City on the morning of July 9.

Jason Widtsoe and Keith Bartlett, leaders of the Mormon Legion, anxiously awaited their arrival, but they had serious doubts that the relief army would be any more effective against the enemy than their other troops. Also, Jason and Keith, now headquartered in Provo, had recently received reports on two strange mysteries.

After assembling his military leaders in a hotel in Provo, Jason took up the first mystery. "This report says the Mexican army on Highway 6 stopped, but it doesn't give the reason. Why would the enemy do that?"

"I'm not sure," Keith replied. "Maybe they're waiting for their eastern army, the one coming from Price, to join them."

"I hope so," General Wilkins said. "That would give us two or three extra days." Wilkins was commander of a division of the Mormon Legion near Escalante.

"But why would they do that?" Jason repeated. "Surely they know that by waiting, they give us more time to get our forces down from Salt Lake."

"Perhaps they don't know that," General Conway said. "Their communications aren't any better than ours. Also, it's possible they believe our northern army is already in Provo. As you know, we've been circulating false reports for days concerning the whereabouts of our troops."

"Well, whatever their reasons," Jason said, "I hope they don't decide to attack Provo and Orem before we're ready."

The other leaders expressed the same hope.

Keith was anxious to bring up the second mysterious report. "What about this communiqué regarding Indians?"

Jason had read the report also. "We don't know how accurate it is."

General Conway looked perplexed. "Maybe you should fill the rest of us in, brethren."

"Yes, of course," Jason replied. "Recently we received a report that bands of Indians are harassing the invading armies."

"What Indians?" General Wilkins asked, his eyebrows raised.

"No one knows," Jason said.

"How many Indians?" Conway asked.

"A great number, it seems."

Pioneer One arose early on Sunday and gathered quickly for church services. Then the caravan traveled several hours until the noon lunch break. After eating a quick meal, the members of the Christopher family crawled wearily into their beds under their wagon for a short nap. After what seemed like two minutes, Steven awoke with a start and struggled to see his watch through bleary eyes. It was already one forty and past time to start the wagons again! I'm getting to hate that schedule, Steven thought as he tried to force his body to move. Finally he found strength enough to glance around. Mary and the kids were still sound asleep. It would be cruel to disturb them, wouldn't it? His head plopped back onto the pillow. He had barely dozed another minute, when he felt William tug at his arm.

"What are those explosions, Dad?" William yelled.

Half asleep, Steven muttered, "Well, it's the Fourth of July, isn't it? Or close to it. Oh no . . . it's the ninth."

"Dad. I'm serious. Listen. In a second you'll hear it again."

Steven rolled up laboriously onto one elbow. "Yeah, yeah, I'm listening."

Just then he heard a volley of shots echoing over the rolling hills. He squirmed from beneath the wagon and stumbled to the west side of the highway. William and Andrew followed him. As he studied the area, he heard more shots. It sounded like a war. He was fully awake now. "William, run to Paul. Have him send word down the wagon train to all the leaders. We need to talk."

After William scooted away, Mary and Jennifer rushed up. "What is it, Steve?" Mary asked fearfully. "Are we in danger?"

"I don't know. There's a lot of gunfire over there, but I can't see anyone. Too many obstructions."

"It sounds as if a million people are trying to kill each other," Jennifer said.

Mary hugged Jennifer to her. "How far away are they, Steve?"

"About two or three miles, I'd say."

Within fifteen minutes Paul, John, Douglas, Ruther, two colonels, and a few captains had gathered not far from the lead wagon. After they had listened to the gunfire for a while, Steven said, "Any ideas, people?"

Colonel Jasper Potter spoke up, "It's too far away to tell what's going on, but it can't be good. I suggest we send scouts down there to check it out."

"I agree," Colonel Burnham said. The others nodded their approval.

"All right," Steven said. "John, choose a couple of good men for the job. Tell them to stay together and be careful. How long do you think they'll need?"

"Two hours at the most."

Steven checked his watch. "Okay, it's two o'clock now. That means we can expect them back by four or sooner. Tell them to hurry as fast as they can. In the meantime, we need to tell our people what's going on. They should remain as quiet as possible but be ready to defend themselves."

The men sped away on their various assignments. An hour later the leaders returned to await the report from the scouts. Shortly past three thirty they saw the two young men running toward them. After the men had climbed the embankment, they stopped and one of them, fighting for breath, blurted out, "A war . . . Looks like a war!"

Steven waited briefly for them to recover. "Who's fighting?"

The second runner said, "Bandits attacking families."

"And Indians," the first runner added.

"Indians? Helping the bandits?"

"No, they're . . . they're attacking the bandits."

After pumping the runners for all the information they had, the leaders discussed what course of action they should take.

"We can't go down there," Seth Crowell contended. "That would be fool-hardy. We have our families to think of. And the cause of Zion." Steven had considered relieving Seth of his leadership position because of his recent mutiny, but decided to wait until they reached Independence. Even though Seth's disastrous experience should have taught him humility, he still had a tendency to make what Steven saw as rash and cowardly decisions. Steven noticed, however, that most of the pioneers in Crowell's charge no longer took him seriously.

"We can't just abandon those innocent people to a mob of outlaws," Colonel Burnham said.

"What do you say, John?" Steven asked.

"I say we help them. When the bandits see our Uzis and semiautomatic rifles, they'll probably take off running."

"And you, Paul?"

"I agree with John. We have no choice."

"What do you think, Ruther?"

"Well, Steve, I would kinda like ta git a crack at those bounders with my little Sharps here."

"What about the rest of you?"

All of the leaders present, except Seth Crowell, indicated their desire to do their best to rescue the families, in spite of the danger.

Steven hesitated. "I think this is a decision all the pioneers should make. It's their lives that are at stake. Brethren, I want you go down the wagon train and take a quick poll. Explain the problem, and ask for volunteers. Meet me back here in half an hour."

Around four thirty the leaders began to return. With the exception of Seth they grinned as they approached, followed by more than a hundred armed men.

Jim Burnham said, "Most of my group say they know God wants them to come to the aid of their fellow man. The others ask for time to pray about it."

"I had the exact same reaction," Jasper Potter noted.

"All right," Steven shouted. "Let's move the wagons off the freeway and down that road." He pointed to a fairly decent semi-paved road heading west not far away. "The pioneers have had plenty of time to pray."

After beckoning to Mary, Steven turned and headed down the embankment, William tagging behind. Without hesitation, she released the brake, flicked the mules, and followed her husband. The two younger children were jammed in next to her, their eyes bright with excitement. Within twenty minutes every wagon and vehicle in the caravan turned off the freeway and followed their leader. Only one, the wagon of Seth Crowell, vacillated for a while near the edge of the road, but then rolled slowly downward after the last wagon.

When the anarchists and militarists finally caught sight of 252 primitive wagons, 45 handcarts, and 63 converted contraptions, rolling boldly into the war zone from the northeast, they lost heart. Especially when their scouts brought back frightening reports that every man, woman, and child in the caravan appeared to be armed with some type of high-caliber weapon, including several submachine guns. First, the two local colonies had joined forces. Then, the lousy Cherokees had to interfere. And now, a mob of strangers from heaven knows where! Within hours the anarchists and militarists had escaped to the safety of the wilderness fifteen miles to the west where they could decide in peace whether or not they wanted to tempt fate again.

After making sure their enemies had really left the area, the families of the Riss Community fell upon the saints with tears of joy. The pioneers responded in the same way, and someone even claimed that he actually spied moisture in the eyes of Seth Crowell and his wife. After posting a heavy guard, the new friends sat around a multitude of fires in small groups to compare notes and share experiences.

"How long can you stay with us, Mr. Christopher?" Anthony Luce asked.

"Call me Steve."

"Okay—Steve."

"We should move on right away to Independence."

Lee Bates said, "To build your New Zion?"

"Yes."

"What a marvelous dream," Anthony said with great feeling.

Mary said, "An impossible dream that we hope to turn into a reality, with God's help."

"Are you worried that the gangs will return?" John probed.

It was Noel Luce who responded. "There's no doubt. They'll never give up until they destroy us or we destroy them."

"Yes, that seems to be their nature," Anthony agreed.

"When does yuh expect 'em?" Ruther Johnston asked.

"It's difficult to say," Anthony replied. "Probably in a few days. I have to admit that Lee and I hoped you might stay until the Cherokees come."

"I don't understand," Steven said. "Aren't they already here?"

Vernon Freeman, the Cherokee chief, explained, "We only have about 500 braves here now, but we expect to be reinforced by 5,000 more braves in about five days. They're traveling to this area from Oklahoma."

"And we'd be grateful if you could remain with us until that time," Anthony said.

"If you continue on alone," Lee said, "you'll be more vulnerable than if you stay here. The anarchists might decide to follow and attack you. But together we're much safer."

Steven said, "Yes, but . . ."

"That's not all," Anthony said. "Right now Independence and the surrounding region are no more than ruins and ashes. In fact, the area you're in now is one of the few places where you'll find trees, grass, herbs, wild animals, and decent water in the entire Midwest."

Steven was overwhelmed by the weight of that argument.

"And we might be able to sweeten the deal even more," Anthony said slyly.

"In what way?" Doug Cartwright asked.

Lee answered for Anthony. "Well, some of our people have told us that if you stay here until the braves come, they might be interested in going with you to help build your ideal community. If you want them, of course. You may even decide it's worth your while to find living space for them. Believe me, we are sick of living in tents and makeshift shelters."

"How can we refuse that, Steve?" Paul said.

"I say we accept," Jarrad Babcock added.

"The truth is, I feel the same way," Steven said, smiling. He turned to the Riss leaders. "I promise you we'll stay in your camp a few days at least. In the meantime, I'll put it to the entire company to see if they want to stay until the Indian reinforcements arrive. My greatest concern is that it would delay us in growing late-season crops."

The pioneers chose to stay with the Riss Community. After learning that most of their leaders desired to accept the invitation of their new friends, they decided almost unanimously to follow their judgment. Both saints and colonists were grateful for the time to make new friends, repair equipment, replenish supplies, make preparations for the defense of the colony, and restore their spirits.

Four days later the gangs and militarists returned and surrounded the settlement. Since the enemy legions had increased to 2,500 soldiers, their camps pockmarked the entire region.

⚬

At about four in the morning a coalition of Indian nations savagely attacked the eastern division of the Mexican Liberation Army near Soldier Summit, Utah on Highway 6. A great army of 109,000 braves surged out of the mountains near the highway and fell upon 100,000 sleeping Mexican renegades. A few of these "braves" were really Hispanic immigrants.

When the Indians had first seen the depraved renegades pushing through Mexico, then Arizona, they had fled for the safety of the wilderness. But after the outlaws had passed, the tribal leaders had united their people with other tribes. In Mexico the descendants of the Aztecs, the Mayans, the Tarascans, and the Zapotecs had gathered as one. Then farther north the Navahos, Hopis, and Utes had joined their southern "brothers." This confederation of tribes had also accumulated supplies, arms, and numbers as they followed their enemies north.

During their journey to Utah, the renegade armies, whose goal was to conquer the "Mormon Kingdom," had murdered, raped, and pillaged whites, Indians, Latinos, and people of other nationalities. Because of this, the alliance of Indians had been desperate to stop the monsters and therefore had tracked them for months, at last finding a perfect spot to make their great assault.

On Highway 6 in Utah the initial slaughter was terrible. But because the Mexican renegades had good training and heavy weapons, thousands survived, regrouped, and held the Indians at bay. A half hour after the battle began, an express rider—an Indian brave—brought news of the struggle to the commander of a division of the Mormon Legion, stationed eight miles to the northwest. Immediately, he ordered 40,000 citizen soldiers to march to the gruesome battle scene. As soon as this division of the Utah army arrived, they fell upon the enemy. As a result of this second assault, the renegade army disintegrated and fled in all directions. By the end of the day, most of the Mexican outlaws had been captured and butchered by the braves tracking them.

On Wednesday, July 12, two other battles occurred almost simultaneously farther west. They were even more terrible than the one near Soldier Summit. The first offensive began on Interstate 15 three hours before dawn with a sudden barrage of hundreds of shells from cannons of the Mormon Legion, causing death and destruction in renegade ranks. At the same time 150,000 Indian braves—no more than shadows in the dark—sprang from their hiding places and fell upon the enemy, shouting their chilling war cries. The second major offensive took place at about the same time when an army of 123,000 warriors attacked the unwary bandits in Spanish Fork Canyon.

When the leaders of the Mormon Legion learned of the fighting, and the identity of the combatants, they ordered their armies to attack in force from several points in Utah County.

All the contingents of the two enemy armies were caught by surprise, and were routed after eight hours of fierce fighting.

News of these astonishing victories spread rapidly through the communities of Utah, and the LDS people and their fellow citizens wept tears of relief and offered humble prayers of thanksgiving to the Lord.

On Wednesday morning the anarchists and militarists made a concerted attack against the Riss Community. Governed by lust, they simply could not resist the juicy rewards dangling before them, just waiting to be picked and savored. But, after twelve hours of ferocious fighting, they were finally repulsed by the defenders of the community. The result was a stalemate which seemed to last forever. Because the main army of Cherokee braves did not arrive on the day expected, or on the day after, a great concern arose in the Riss camps that they were not coming at all. However, Chief Vernon Freeman insisted that his people would not let them down. To insure their safety at all times, especially at night, they surrounded the encampment with sentries.

During the following days fifty-six people in the settlement lost their lives, including eighteen saints. But Steven was sure that Mormon casualties would have been greater if they had continued on immediately to Independence. The leaders of the colony estimated that the defenders had killed at least ninety-eight outlaws.

They received many reports from their scouts, which at first puzzled them, but soon renewed their hope. The messages told of numerous fights and disagreements between the gang leaders and the heads of the militia. Also, small bands of thugs actually raided other anarchist campsites and murdered those with whom they had some quarrel. Steven, Lee, and Anthony surmised that the power struggles within enemy ranks may have prevented them from overwhelming the community with their superior forces.

On Sunday Steven awoke with a start at six in the morning. Several people stood outside his tent, calling him. Without combing his hair or straightening up, he pushed past Mary and the children and stepped through the entrance of the tent. Shaking the sleep from his brain, he mumbled, "Uh, yeah, what's up?"

"They're gone," Paul yelled.

"Gone?"

"Yes!" Lee Bates cried. "Every last one."

Steven was still half asleep. "The Gadianton robbers?"

John shook him vigorously. "Wake up, Steve. You must have been dreaming about secret combinations. We're saying that our enemies disappeared sometime during the night or early this morning."

Finally he could see them all clearly. "But . . . why?"

Anthony said, "We don't know yet. But our scouts report that nearly all of them are heading northwest on any road they can find. It looks like a herd of cattle in a wild stampede instead of an organized retreat."

Vernon Freemen mysteriously appeared from nowhere, and said casually, "I believe they may have discovered that our main army of braves are here and they took off while escape was still possible."

Everyone there began to celebrate noisily. But soon they ran off to spread the good news.

A half hour later Steven watched through his binoculars as thousands of Cherokee warriors moved past the settlement on the south. Vernon had told him that his relief army had picked up five hundred extra men on their way north, but had been delayed by a few skirmishes with several gangs of anarchists. The total number of warriors now pursuing their foes was 5,600 braves, including Vernon's advance party. During the day, several scouts returned to the community and reported that their enemies had disappeared into the Kansas wilderness.

Since the threat seemed to be over, the pioneers insisted on setting out for their ultimate destination. At seven in the morning they said good-bye to their non-Mormon friends and headed southeast on I-29. One hundred and forty-two members of the Riss Community accompanied them. A strange sight it was to see more than eleven hundred people prancing through lands of utter desolation, laughing, joking, hugging one another, and singing songs of happiness. By late afternoon they had covered the sixteen miles to the western border of Independence. They pulled their wagons into three separate circles near Independence Avenue and I-435. Then they walked in small groups into the eastern section of what used to be a city.

The saints began to return at the approach of dusk. As Steven and Mary entered the camp with their children, they noticed that many of the women were weeping, and the faces of many men disclosed frustration and disillusionment. The young couple understood how the saints felt because they also had been disheartened by the devastation they saw in their own explorations.

Since there was a grove of trees not far away, which had partly survived the fires, the saints gathered wood and began to build campfires. But not even this unforeseen blessing could lift their spirits. Leaving the children to prepare the evening meal, Steven and Mary left the camp again, climbed a low hill several hundred yards away, and watched the shadows gather in the east.

"Not much to see, is there?" Steven said as he found a seat on a log burned at one end.

Mary sat next to him and put her right arm around his broad shoulders. "That's an understatement. It's a terrible, ugly sight! I don't see how a small number of people with hand tools can transform this torn land into the greatest, most beautiful land on earth. It's impossible."

"I don't believe that. The prophet told me we would feel this way."

"He expected it?"

"Yes."

"And what did he say after that?"

"He said that with God's help we can do anything."

Mary began to cry. "I know, but it's so discouraging. How can we have a baby in these conditions?"

"Well, if we work together—" He stopped abruptly. He had focused on her tears, not her words. "What did you say?"

"How can we have a baby in such miserable conditions?"

"A baby! Are you serious? You're pregnant?"

"Yes. I have been for about five weeks."

Steven gazed at her in disbelief. "But how do you know? How can you be so sure?"

"Well, I missed my period, and besides, a woman knows these things."

"Why didn't you tell me before?"

"I wasn't sure myself until a couple of days ago."

Steven jumped to his feet. He kissed Mary on the mouth and lifted her from the log. Pulling her close, he swung her in circles in the air. Then, suddenly, he lowered her gently back to the log. "Sorry. Did I hurt you?"

"Whew!" she exclaimed, laughing. "Don't . . . worry. You can't . . . hurt me." She pushed her hair into place. "You took my breath away."

Steven was enchanted. Mary was going to have their first child! "I'd better tell everyone tonight."

"I'm not sure, but I think a few people already suspect."

"Oh? Who?"

"Andrea and Ruther."

"Ruther?"

Mary looked embarrassed. "Yes, he saw how nauseated I was while preparing breakfast yesterday morning, and guessed the truth. I had only come to the same conclusion the day before that."

"Good old Ruther. He's very perceptive," Steven was rather ashamed of himself. Ruther had noticed his wife's pregnancy before he had. He kissed Mary again. "Why didn't you tell me two days ago?"

"You've been so busy with all the problems, all the fighting. Besides, I wasn't completely sure."

"I see." As his eyes feasted on her beauty, another idea occurred to him. "But there's something I don't understand."

"What?"

"I really don't see how you could be pregnant. You know, with the trials we've had, the kids around all the time, the cramped quarters."

"Steve, all I can say is, you're a very resourceful man." They both laughed at that.

They spent the next half hour discussing her pregnancy, the baby's gender, and all the names they might choose. Finally, Mary said, "I'm sorry I was such a baby just now."

"No, I felt like crying too, but it's not something men do easily. Instead, we usually get mad." There was another period of silence. "I was going to tell you what else the prophet said."

"Yes?"

"He told me how to establish New Zion."

"He did? How?"

"He said we should first make a general plan, which we divide into its basic steps. Then we start with the first step and work only on that, not allowing ourselves to think of any other steps. If we focus only on that first small phase, it will seem surprisingly easy to accomplish. As we proceed we do the same with all the other phases. And when we have completed all the stages, we shall have accomplished a miracle—a very big one. But if we insist on looking at the entire project as a whole, without putting it into a logical, step-by-step order, the job will seem impossible to do. In short then, we'll build New Zion one small part at a time."

Mary kissed him on the mouth. "You make it sound so easy."

"Not easy, but possible."

Mary was smiling now. "Okay, my husband, where do we start?"

"First we set up a semi-permanent camp, preferably not far from Independence. Next we plant late-growing crops, gather all the edible and medicinal plants we can, hunt for meat, and build solid dwellings."

"Is that all?"

"No. In our spare time we try to clear Independence of its debris."

"Seems to me as if that would take a lifetime."

"I think we'll all be surprised at what over eleven hundred determined people can do."

Mary sighed and got to her feet. "Steve, I'd better check on supper. The kids have a tendency to burn everything. Are you coming?"

"I'll stay a few minutes longer."

He continued to watch the darkness spread gradually over the bleak scene before him, making it even more oppressive. He didn't really feel as courageous and enthusiastic as he had pretended for Mary's sake. She was right. It was an impossible task! How could a man with no experience at construction or organization achieve it? After all, he had spent most of his adult life training to be a translator in French and Japanese. And as far as he knew, there were no builders in the pioneer company. With a heavy heart, he continued to stare fixedly into the gloom ahead.

After some time he perceived small particles of light emerging in the vastness of the black night. It was as if a star-filled night was beginning to materialize magically before him. Soon both earth and sky glowed, and the brightness gradually intensified until—at first—it hurt his eyes. He continued to watch, fascinated, as the brilliance formed into shapes and patterns. At the same time, the mysterious light penetrated his mind and body, filling him with exquisite joy. Then, suddenly, he realized what he was seeing. It was a great city of dazzling splendor.

As the outline of the city slowly filled in, he perceived details of buildings, trees, animals, and people walking on golden streets! Before long, the radiance began to take on the hues of a dozen vivid colors. In the center of it all, he saw a spectacular building with many parts, and he knew it was the temple of the Most High. Then the resplendent scene slowly faded until it disappeared, and nothing remained except blackness.

But the exhilaration of the marvelous panorama he had just beheld lingered in his soul. No longer did he feel so helpless and ignorant. Now he understood what could be, because the Lord in his kindness had given him a vision of the future City of God, which he would help to build.

After waiting in the darkness until the quickening subsided, Steven walked down the hill and headed for camp. From a distance he saw his family and friends sitting around a campfire close to his wagon. When he approached, they looked up and grinned. Steven guessed that Mary had already told them about the baby.

As he sat next to his wife, Douglas said, "Congratulations, Steve." Paul, John, Andrea, and Ruther added their compliments. Mary stared at his face in the light of the fire.

"So Mary told you. Thanks. I'm very excited about it."

After they had discussed the baby for a while, Mary said, "What happened, Steve? You look so different."

Paul agreed, "Yeah, you've got this strange glow."

"He hasn't looked this happy in a long time," Andrea said seriously.

"What's up, Steve?" John said.

"We will build New Zion. And it will be a land more glorious than you can possibly imagine. The Lord just showed me his holy city in a vision." As he described the vision in detail, Mary held his hand tightly, and his children sat at his feet, captivated. The Spirit of God filled every heart with a witness of the truth of his words.

Ruther acted as if he had been struck by lightning, and tears filled his eyes. "Listen, I ain't got no say here, but I suggest yuh tell that thar vision ta your people tomorrow. They're mighty discouraged right now."

"I intend to, Ruther. I intend to."

Steven and his family got little sleep that night. They had passed the time talking about the gleaming city that Steven had seen and how they hoped to live there when it was built. Above all, they wondered what they would say and do and be when the Lord came to the city and filled it with his all-penetrating light.

The next morning at nine o'clock, Steven sent the caravan leaders to gather the pioneers for a short meeting. He had slept no more than four hours, but his joy exceeded his fatigue. As soon as the multitude stood around him, Steven stepped up on a charred stump and looked around slowly, gazing into many familiar eyes. He saw many emotions: disappointment, pain, and fear, but also curiosity and hope.

He simply smiled and said in a loud voice, "Last night the Lord showed me a vision of the New Jerusalem, and I desire at this time to describe exactly what I beheld. He spent the next thirty minutes depicting the scene in detail. As he told his story, he saw a great change come over his listeners, and many of the sisters began to weep.

When he had finished, one of the brothers called out, "But what does it all mean, Brother Christopher?" Steven recognized him as Clint, the man he had found repairing a wagon wheel after the great dust storm.

"It means many things," Steven said, his voice slightly lower now. The saints strained anxiously to hear, but he wasn't concerned. He knew that those who heard him now would spread the word to the others in good time. "It means that the Lord is with us. He will strengthen and guide us in building a mighty city, the center place of Zion. From this spot, the land of Zion will grow and spread throughout the American continent. It may seem impossible to us now.

But since God wills it, it shall be. No power in heaven or earth can prevent it. Let me reveal to you a truth: you are the only people on earth that the Lord has prepared—that is, made worthy—as a group, to begin the difficult task."

Steven paused a minute to let his words take effect. Then he said, "Now I want you to know that you can see the same vision as I beheld, if you desire it strongly enough. All you have to do is ask God, and he will reveal it to each of you individually. His Spirit has given me that promise. In this way, you can know as I do that, with God's help, you do have the power to establish New Zion."

As Steven delivered his message, a transformation came over the people. Instead of pain and disappointment, there was peace and confidence. Instead of sadness and doubt, joy and faith. And when he descended from the stump, the people of Pioneer One returned to their wagons with new determination. That same day, they began to build their Promised Land.

THE END

We hope you enjoyed Pioneer One. The first chapter of Promised Land, the next novel The Last Days series begins on the next page. Or you can read more about the after the sample chapter.

THE LAST DAYS
VOLUME 3

Promised Land

Kenneth R. Tarr

Chapter 1

❦

It began to rain around ten in the morning on Tuesday, August 8, and the settlers left the fields and hurried home to their cabins. When Steven and Mary Christopher reached their cabin, they sat on chairs on the small sheltered porch to watch the rain while their three children went inside to play a board game. Half an hour later the rain stopped.

Mary looked at her husband and said, "Look, it stopped raining."

Yeah, but check out the clouds to the southwest. A really big storm is heading this way.""Oh, it's got to be fifty or sixty miles away. We have plenty of time to take a little walk."

"Take a walk! Now?"

"Yes, right now."

"But our feet will get muddy and our clothes wet from the water on the ground and bushes."

"Well, we'll just put on our rubber overshoes and stick to the trail. Listen, dear husband, you're usually so busy solving the problems of our people that we hardly ever spend time alone together. We haven't taken one walk in the three weeks we've been here."

"But you're pregnant. What if you slip and fall?"

"Silly man. I'm not going to slip and fall. Besides, I'm only eight weeks along."

Steven let out a big sigh, knowing she was right. "Okay. Where do you want to go?"

"To my favorite spot north of the camp. It's only about a quarter mile away. There's a small trail most of the way."

After telling the children where they were going, they slipped on rubber overshoes, light jackets, and backpacks and set off on their walk. Unfortunately, by the time they had gone almost a quarter mile in the wilderness, the storm was nearly upon them, much sooner than they had expected. Vast ominous clouds began to streak toward them as if seeking terrified victims. The bolts of lightning, which brightened the heavens with growing frequency, were followed by distant rumbling, and they felt a light rain touch their faces.

"Now we're in for it," Steven said. Leaning his rifle against a fallen tree, he struggled to pull a raincoat from his backpack.

Mary stared with amusement at his frantic efforts. "Don't be such a baby, Steven. You've told me many times how you never let a little bad weather bother you when you want to do something. I remember with crystal clarity your constant bragging about all the trips you used to take from Provo to Salt Lake in dangerous snowstorms, while everyone else was cowering—as you put it—in their safe, snug homes."

"This wasn't *my* idea."

"What wasn't?"

"To leave our warm cabin and take a merry promenade when we were obviously in danger of being drowned or struck by lightning." Steven looked to the southwest and saw a swirling mass of black clouds. "Look at those clouds! That's a tornado formation. Let's get back to camp."

Mary gazed at him in disbelief and laughed. "A tornado! This is Missouri, not Kansas or Oklahoma."

Steven scowled. "Tornadoes occur frequently in Missouri, and in some of the surrounding states. Let's get going. It doesn't pay to take chances." Ignoring Mary's skeptic look, he drew the raincoat over their heads, took her by the arm, and marched with determination toward the encampment. "When we get back to camp, you can ask Ruther if you don't believe me, and I'm sure—"

He stopped abruptly. In the growing darkness he saw shadowy forms materializing from the bushes fifty yards away. At first he thought they were small trees or clumps of shrubbery, but quickly realized he was wrong when the forms moved toward them with surprising speed. It happened so fast that he was momentarily paralyzed by fear. The apparitions transformed into six men—if that is what they could be called—who grunted and snarled like fiends as they rushed forward, surrounded the young couple, and reached out to take hold of them.

"Lookee here, boys," one of the creatures cackled. "We won't go hungry after all."

From several decent people who had joined their community recently, all of them non- Mormons, Steven had heard frightening stories of widespread cannibalism in Missouri and Kansas. Were these men cannibals? He guessed that the man who had spoken was their leader. The fellow was covered with rags and his depraved countenance betrayed an individual of brutish nature, who indulged in every degenerate vice.

The other animals snorted with glee, and one of them snarled, "Hold it, boss. The little one's a woman. Let's do her first before we dine. It's been so long." The speaker was a hunchback about five feet tall with a huge beak for a nose and eyes that bulged as if they might pop from their sockets.

The incredible stench of their filthy bodies assaulted Steven's nostrils. "Stay back, you devils," he yelled as he aimed his rifle at them in the semidarkness. Unfortunately, he fired too quickly and the bullet went over their heads.

The creatures were too close for him to shoot again. Four of them jumped him while the other two seized Mary. Wrenching the weapon from Steven's grasp and throwing it to the side, the attackers began beating him with fists and clubs. In seconds he was barely conscious and only dimly perceived the dull thuds against his body and head and the strange wetness that spread across his face.

Mary struggled with the men who held her fast, but she couldn't break away. She stared in horror as the other fiends beat Steven. *Oh no! They're killing him! What should I do?* she thought with desperation.

After the thugs had smashed Steven to the ground, the leader threw a short rope to one of them and ordered him to tie their victim's hands and feet. Next he rushed toward Mary, followed by his toadies. The man with the rope dropped next to Steven and began to tie him. Anxious to get his turn with Mary, he did the job in great haste. Then he sprang to his feet, kicked Steven in the ribs, and hurried away to join the fun.

Steven shook his head, trying to clear his mind. He fought to get up but couldn't. Distant shouts and the frantic screams of his wife came to him as if in a dream, and he agonized over his complete helplessness to do anything to help her. Next, he heard hooting and the sounds of struggle. What were those savages doing to Mary? He tried again to rise, but his body refused to respond to his will.

All the brutes had surrounded Mary, grabbing at her clothes in an effort to tear them off. Apparently they had decided to make a game of it, for each man took his turn moving toward her, mocking his victim as he dodged from side to side, and finally reaching out for her. At first Mary was so terrified that she flailed her arms wildly and scratched at each attacker as he drew near, but she forced herself to calm down and to think about the lessons she had learned a year earlier in karate class.

After all, she had earned a brown belt in wado-ryu karate and had also taken a good class in self-defense. At that moment she decided to attack her enemies instead of just trying to ward them off. She realized she had no chance of overcoming the six creatures by herself, but she had heard her husband's rifle shot and knew help would soon arrive from the nearby Mormon camp.

As the next brute moved forward to take his turn, she stepped toward him, swung her right leg upward with bent knee, and snapped her foot forward, striking the man in the belly with the ball of her foot. The man dropped to the ground like a rock, stunned and groaning from pain. The others derided him boisterously for letting a mere woman get the best of him, but soon they returned to their sport.

Another attacker moved in, and this time Mary stood facing him with both fists up in front of her body, with elbows slightly bent. When the man drew close, she stepped forward quickly with her right leg and, at the same instant, pulled her left fist back against her left side as she snapped her right fist forward into the man's chest. This blow, called the *junzuki*, used leverage and opposing body movement to deliver a punishing blow to an opponent. Her enemy toppled over backward, stunned into silence and clutching his chest desperately.

At this shocking sight, the prostrate man's confederates laughed with glee, obviously relishing this unusual contest. Never before had they seen a woman defend herself so effectively and they delighted in the discomfiture of their "rivals." They were full of merriment because they knew that in the end each of them would have his way with her.

Forty feet away, Steven continued to shake his head to clear his mind as he tried to sit up. Soon, in spite of the noise of the approaching storm, he could distinguish some words from the voices shouting nearby. He asked for God's help, praying he'd be in time to save his helpless wife. Frantically he pulled at his bonds and finally felt them begin to loosen.

By this time, Mary's attackers had apparently decided she was no ordinary woman. They rushed her as a group, held her arms, and slugged her until she was unconscious. She slumped to the ground, and they returned to the work of removing her clothes. She was almost naked when she regained consciousness. Suddenly, she felt them stop and move away. But her hope of a reprieve was shattered when she realized they were struggling to remove their own clothing.

Two of the men succeeded in taking off their trousers at the same time and rushed in to throw themselves upon their victim, but they stopped short when they heard a fierce scream from the leader. "Back off! Touch her and you die. First me. After you can do what you want."

He stared at Mary with his eyes full of lust as he finished removing his clothes and began to approach. Mary saw him coming and prepared to use a simple maneuver she had learned for self-protection. In fact, during some special sessions on self-defense, and many times afterwards, she and Andrea Warren had jokingly practiced these moves on each other until they had become automatic, but they had never dreamed they would ever really have to use them.

The terrible thought struck her that these monsters might actually succeed in raping and killing her, but she was determined to give them all the pain she could. The most important thing was to stall them as long as possible, because she believed that Ruther or Steven's brothers or someone else from the settlement would arrive in time.

As the drooling leader dropped to his knees and leaned toward her, Mary punched him with all her might in the Adam's apple using the first two knuckles of her right fist. Bellowing like a bull struck by a sledgehammer in a slaughter house, he rolled over onto the ground, clutching his throat.

While Steven was freeing his hands, he located the loud voices and soon was able to see the enemy. They were almost naked and stood in a semicircle looking down. He searched for Mary and finally caught a glimpse of her lying partly naked on the ground. In a frenzy, he groped for his rifle in the gloom. Was it close by or had the men thrown it some distance away?

The brutes roared with laughter when they saw their leader choking and gasping for breath and suddenly falling unconscious. One of his underlings kicked him spitefully in the head. But quickly their attention returned to the prostrate woman. They fought with each other like mad dogs for several minutes until one of them came off victorious, making the others cower by brandishing two long knives.

After making a few final threatening gestures, the victor turned to throw himself on Mary. With surprising calm and determination, Mary met him by slamming the heel of her hand against the bridge of his nose. The man screamed in pain and ran away from the group, his nose broken and bleeding. The other four watched him in surprise for a moment before advancing on Mary as a group, waving knives and clubs and snarling with anger and hate.

At that moment, Steven found his .30-06 a short distance away in the grass. To keep his head clear, he lay close to the ground, supporting the front of his body on his elbows. He trained the weapon on the men threatening his wife. He couldn't tell exactly what they were doing, but he had no intention of waiting to find out. The powerful gun boomed and one of the men, who was about to club Mary, dropped to the ground as if he had been struck with an axe. His confederates froze at once, apparently stunned by the new threat. One of them shouted something, pointed at Steven, and turned to escape.

Without hesitating, the others fled after him toward the woods not far away. What a ludicrous sight it was to see three nearly naked men running desperately for their lives!

The leader of the group, after regaining consciousness, struggled to his feet and, still coughing and choking, began to stumble toward the black line of bushes from which the savages had originally emerged. His soul full of fury, Steven aimed carefully and shot the fellow. When the man's back exploded into a bloody mass and he fell headlong into the mud, Steven rejoiced at his success, at the same time feeling ashamed of doing such a violent act. But he told himself it would have been only a matter of time before that evil creature would have raped or killed someone else.

He hobbled over to Mary and took her in his arms. "Thank God you're here!" Mary sobbed, clinging to him.

"Are you all right? What did they do?"

"Beat me and tore off my clothes. The truth is, I think I gave them as much as they gave me."

Mary had not told him what he really wanted to know, and he hesitated over how to ask her. "Did that beast hurt you?"

Mary's face twisted in disgust. "His filthy naked body. Coming toward me . . . No, I stopped him with a punch to the throat. I was so glad when I heard the rifle shots. I knew it was you. How many did you shoot?"

"Two, I believe."

"But I thought those men beat you senseless and tied you up. How did you . . . ?"

Steven could scarcely hear her because of the drenching rain and the deafening roar of the turbulence falling upon them. "I'll explain later," he yelled. "Hurry. We've got to find shelter." As he wrapped his thin jacket around her, he looked at the western sky and was astonished to see a great black funnel spiral down to earth. He guessed it was less than half a mile away. Remembering the gully they had crossed just before seeing the six demons, he grasped Mary's arm and pulled her toward the depression.

When they reached the gully, they descended to its bed and flattened themselves face down against the wet earth. To protect his wife, Steven tried to cover her as much as possible with his own body. The thundering of the tornado was so loud now that they couldn't understand the words they yelled to each other.

The wind whipped around them with terrifying violence, hurling small pieces of rock and wood into their flesh. Steven felt that at any moment both of them would be sucked upward into the black maw of the swirling monster.

He flattened himself tightly against the ground and clung to Mary with all his might, praying they would survive the onslaught. It seemed as though it would never end, but then—suddenly—the worst was over.

"Stay down," Steven said. He climbed the embankment and saw the tornado turning abruptly southward and moving away.

"The pioneers are in for it," he said when he returned to Mary.

"You mean—?"

"Yes, it's heading south toward the camp and may hit them face on, unless it turns again."

Mary burst into tears. "The children! Our friends! What can we do?"

Steven realized that his words had expressed more alarm than he had intended. He took Mary into his arms and spoke with as much assurance as he could muster. "Don't worry. I know God is with us. He didn't bring this people clear to Missouri to allow them to be wiped out by a tornado. Just think of all the ways he guided and protected Pioneer One on the trip here."

Mary tried to smile through her tears. "You're right, of course."

"We have to return to camp as fast as possible, but first let's see if we can find some of your clothes."

Since the wind and rain had let up, they returned to the scene of the attack. After searching a few minutes, they found Steven's raincoat and pieces of Mary's clothes. They created a temporary outfit for her from the torn clothes and the raincoat and then started off toward the pioneer settlement. Steven guided her carefully over the soaked ground, troubled as to what he might find when they reached their destination. Their progress was particularly difficult, for the muddy earth was strewn with trees, torn earth, and every type of debris. They had plodded along for about ten minutes when they heard a shout from the direction of the camp.

"I think it's Ruther and Paul," Steven said, straining to see the distant figures.

Hurrying even faster, they stumbled and fell in the mud several times as they strove to reach their would-be rescuers. Steven soon recognized the faces of Paul and Ruther, and he hoped they could tell him news of the encampment.

Their rescuers finally reached them. "Thank God, you're all right," Paul cried, embracing first Mary, then Steven. "Wow! That was some tornado. Felt like an F4 or F5. Did it come close to you?"

Steven explained how they had found shelter in the gully. "What about you?" Steven asked. "Didn't the tornado head right for you? How did you guys avoid it?"

"We crawled inside a tunnel under a road not far from here. Got knocked around by some pretty bad winds but we escaped the full brunt of the twister."

Paul noticed their wounds and the strange way Mary was dressed. "Tell us what happened. How did you get those cuts and bruises? Was it the tornado? And why are you dressed like that, Mary?"

"I'll explain everything later."

"You ornery cuss, Steve," Ruther said with bluster, apparently trying to hide the fact that he'd been worried about them. "I told yuh not ta go traipsin' off like that in this here weather. That's the trouble with this durn world. Nobody never listens to us old folks, even when we is the ones which knows the most."

"But when did you tell me—?" Steven had a terrible headache and was dizzy from the blows he'd received on his shoulders and head. He certainly didn't feel like arguing.

"Don't give me no buts, young feller. I knows it was your wife that drugged yuh away, but a real man knows how ta stand up ta them females."

Steven shrugged. "You're right. I should have been more firm. But the camp. Do you know what happened?"

"You're the prophet of this here company, ain't yuh? How d'yuh 'spect we're supposed ta know? We heard shots and figured we'd better hightail it out your way in case you was in trouble."

Mary gave the old mountain man a big hug. "Thank you so much, Ruther. We love you." Ruther blushed and Paul grinned.

The four of them set out immediately to return to the encampment. As he made his way through the debris, Steven found himself dreading what he might find when they arrived.

Kenneth R. Tarr taught French language and literature at Brigham Young University for fourteen years, and French and Spanish for three years at Snow College. He received a master's degree in French and Spanish at Brigham Young in 1965, and a doctorate in French at Kansas University in 1973, with a minor in Medieval history.

Kenneth was born and raised in southern California and has been a member of the LDS church all his life, serving in many capacities. He and his wife, Kathy, have been married fifty-one years and have eight children and twenty-seven grandchildren. Currently they live in Utah where they operate an herb store. Kenneth enjoys writing, reading, exercising, doing repairs, and listening to good music.

Pioneer One is Kenneth's second published novel and the second in his *The Last Days* series. He has also written a third novel, *Promised Land,* that will be released soon. A fourth and final novel for the series is in the works. The author welcomes questions and comments. You can contact him at tarrk@yahoo.com.

BASEMENT

FEB 2 1 2017

MAR 07 2017

P7/172

40562088R00146

Made in the USA
Middletown, DE
16 February 2017